SHA

NAGNATH S. INAMDAR (1923–2002) is one of Maharashtra's foremost novelists, with a writing career spanning over five decades. He wrote sixteen historical novels some of the most popular ones being *Jhep, Shahenshah, Zunj, Mantravegala* and *Rau*, the love story of Bajirao and Mastani which was recently made into a Sanjay Leela Bhansali film. Inamdar wrote his autobiography in three volumes, *Tya Swapnanchya Athwani, Chandrati Ranglya* and *Vallya Phulat*. His novels are born of a detailed historical research and crafted from his vivid imagination.

VIKRANT PANDE is passionate about making Marathi classics available to a wider audience. He has published Ranjit Desai's *Raja Ravi Varma* and Milind Bokil's *Shala*, both of which have been made into award-winning films. Currently, he is working on the English translations of V.P. Kale's *Karmachari*, Ranjit Desai's *Shriman Yogi*, V.S. Khandekar's *Kraunch Vadh*, amongst others, all to be published by Harper Perennial. He is also translating N.S. Inamdar's *Rau*. A graduate of the Indian Institute of Management, Bangalore, Vikrant has worked for over twenty-five years with various multinational companies and is currently heading TeamLease Skills University at Vadodara.

PRAISE FOR *SHAHENSHAH*

'*Shahenshah* has a wealth of exquisite and well-researched detail on the inner workings of the Mughal courts and the zenana. And, Inamdar's Aurangzeb is not just the uncompromising king of our history books, but a father, a husband and a lover with real fears, passions and frailties. Here is Aurangzeb, the sixth Mughal Emperor of India, as you've never seen him before.'

     – **Indu Sundaresan**, author of the *Taj Trilogy* and *The Mountain of Light*

SHAHENSHAH

The Life of Aurangzeb

N.S. INAMDAR

Translated from the Marathi by

VIKRANT PANDE

HARPER PERENNIAL

NEW YORK • LONDON • TORONTO • SYDNEY • NEW DELHI

HARPER PERENNIAL

First published in India in 2016 by Harper Perennial
An imprint of HarperCollins *Publishers*

P-ISBN: 978-93-5177-771-7
E-ISBN: 978-93-5177-773-1

2 4 6 8 10 9 7 5 3 1

N.S. Inamdar asserts the moral right
to be identified as the author of this work.

HarperCollins *Publishers*
A-75, Sector 57, Noida, Uttar Pradesh 201301, India
1 London Bridge Street, London, SE1 9GF, United Kingdom
Hazelton Lanes, 55 Avenue Road, Suite 2900, Toronto, Ontario M5R 3L2
and 1995 Markham Road, Scarborough, Ontario M1B 5M8, Canada
25 Ryde Road, Pymble, Sydney, NSW 2073, Australia
195 Broadway, New York, NY 10007, USA

Typeset in 11/14 Adobe Jenson Pro by
Jojy Philip, New Delhi 110 015

Printed and bound at
Thomson Press (India) Ltd

Dedicated to my father 'Nana' who instilled in me
Marathi pride and love for history.
– Vikrant Pande

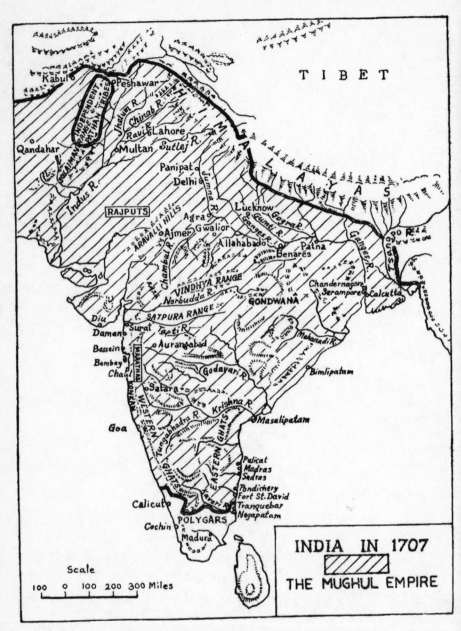

THE MUGHUL EMPIRE

INDIA IN 1707

Scale

100   0   100 200 300 Miles

Source: http://orbat.com/site/maps/india/map_list.html

Cast of Main Characters

Adil Shah: Ruler of Bijapur

Afzal Khan: General under Adil Shah of Bijapur; was killed by Shivaji

Anwar Khoja: Aurangzeb's personal assistant and an enuch

Aurangabadi Mahal: One of Aurangzeb's wives, she was so named as she entered the harem of the Shahzada in Aurangabad but died in the bubonic plague of 1688. She had one daughter, Mihr-un-nisa.

Danishmand Khan: Senior official and a confidante of Aurangzeb

Dara Shikoh: Aurangzeb's brother

Dilras Banu Begum: One of Aurangzeb's wives, she was the daughter of Shah Nawaz Khan, whose great-grandfather was the younger son of Persian King Shah Ismail. She had two sons, Muhammad Akbar and Muhammad Azam and three daughters Zebunissa, Zeenat and Zubdat-un-nisa.

Diwan Murshid Quli Khan: Diwan in Deccan and later Diwan of Bengal

Durgadas Rathore: Commander with Jaswant Singh and his confidante

Hira Bai: Also known as Zainabadi, she was not a wife but the only romantic connection in Aurangzeb's life. He was infatuated the moment he saw her in his Aunt's Zainabad gardens at Burhanpur. Death cut the romance short and Aurangzeb grieved her loss for a long time.

Jaffar Khan: Senior official with Aurangzeb

Jahanara: One of Aurangzeb's two sisters, who preferred to stay with her father, Shah Jahan in the Agra Fort

Kazi Abdul Wahab: One of the most influential clerics in Aurangzeb's court; later chief kazi

Malika Banu: Aurangzeb's aunt and sister of Mumtaz Mahal. She was married to Saif Khan, the Thanedar of Burhanpur and a senior official.

Mir Hasham: Aurangzeb's teacher

Nawab Bai or **Rahmat-un-nisa:** One of Aurangzeb's wives, she was the daughter of the Raja of Kashmir. She had two sons, Muhammad Sultan and Muazzam and a daughter Badr-un-nisa.

Raja Jai Singh: General under Aurangzeb and was titled Mirza Raja later

Raja Jaswant Singh: Ruler of Marwar and later senior official with Aurangzeb

Ram Singh: Elder son of Mirza Raja Jai Singh

Roshanara: Aurangzeb's sister and confidante who stayed with him

Sambhaji: Shivaji's son

Shahu: Sambhaji's son

Shaista Khan: Aurangzeb's uncle

Shamim: Managing the affairs of Aurangzeb's harem

Sheikh Sadulah: Aurangzeb's personal advisor

Shivaji: Founder and ruler of Maratha kingdom

Udaipuri Mahal: One of Aurangzeb's wives, she was a slave girl of Georgian descent and was originally part of Dara Shikoh's harem. She had one son Kambaksh.

BOOK ONE

The sand on the banks of the Tapi glistened in the heat. Unheedful of the greenery around, hot winds blowing from the riverbank reached Burhanpur, heating the stone walls of the haveli. The Jama Masjid's tall minarets shimmered in the shrunken river as the call of the muezzin travelled across from the mosque to Mumtaz Mahal's grave in the Zainabad gardens. The area around the grave, surrounded by dense foliage, had been temporarily cordoned off by white tents.

Malika Banu knelt at Mumtaz's marble grave, her black veil pulled off her face, her delicate hands pointed skywards, as she prayed for the peace of her sister's soul. Then she touched her head to the ground and stood up with a deep sigh. Her maid waited a few feet away holding her sandals. She laid them before her as soon as Banu stepped out.

Banu walked lost in thought towards her palanquin where her bearers waited with their heads bowed.

'With your permission, Begum Sahiba, may I say something?' She heard a voice as she was about to step in.

Her foot hanging in mid-air she said, 'Speak.'

'Aurangzeb is expected …'

Malika Banu frowned at her beautiful attendant: 'Hira, haven't I told you before? Aurangzeb is my nephew and while I have the right to call him by his first name, it only shows your impertinence when you do.'

'I apologize, Begum Sahiba. I have erred,' Hira said. Looking down, the young girl continued: 'Begum Sahiba may recall the jewellers and textile merchants who have been commanded to deliver the best of gems and clothes for her favourite nephew?'

'I do remember; and I am sure that by now they would have been delivered to the haveli.'

3

'Nothing has been delivered yet, Begum Sahiba.'

Malika Banu raised a delicate eyebrow. 'Why so?'

'I am told Khan Sahab issued urgent orders to cancel the delivery after reading a message that was delivered from Agra this morning.'

'Where is Khan Sahab at the moment?'

'He is supervising the preparations for the arrival of Shahzada.'

Malika Banu clapped once and a khoja, one of the eunuchs meant to guard the ladies, stepped forward and saluted. Malika Banu commanded, 'Please send a message to Khan Sahab that I wish to see him.'

Malika Banu was surprised to find the khoja still standing there after receiving her orders. He said, a little hesitantly, 'Please pardon me. I would have acted on your command right away, but I was asked to deliver a message to you.'

'What is it?'

'Danishmand Khan has arrived from Agra and has requested an urgent audience with you.'

'He wants to meet me?'

'Yes, Begum Sahiba. He is waiting in the daroga's tent outside the zenankhana.'

৩৫ ৩৯৵

A silk curtain hung outside the zenankhana. Inside, a few large cushions were laid out in the sitting room. Danishmand Khan, in his early thirties, was escorted to the other side of the screen the moment Malika Banu seated herself, resting her back against a thick pillow.

'*Kahiye*, Khan Sahab. What is the message?' Malika Banu asked from behind the curtain.

'It is a delicate matter and I wanted to convey it to you personally.'

'When is my nephew Aurangzeb reaching here?'

'I escorted him till the banks of Chambal when he went out for shikar along with a few select men. I was to escort his zenankhana from Agra.'

'So I suppose you came along with his zenankhana?'

'I could not. In fact, I was not given the permission to do so.'

'Permission? Who needs to permit you? Are you not worried of Shahzada's anger when he realizes that his orders have not been followed?'

'I was stopped by the mace-bearing gurzbardars.'

'I cannot believe it! On whose orders were you not allowed?'

'It was a direct order from the Badshah not to allow the Shahzada to take his zenankhana when he moves to the Deccan. I sought an audience with the Badshah but was denied. I was told that the orders have been issued by Shahzada Dara, under the authority given by the Badshah himself.'

'I wonder how Aurangzeb will react when he hears of this? *Ya Allah!* I am unable to fathom the reason for the enmity between the two brothers.'

'Begum Sahiba,' Danishmand Khan interrupted, 'the brothers may not get along, but the Badshah should not have favoured one of them.'

'I fear to imagine the outcome of all this enmity. Dara, Aurangzeb, Shuja and Murad are my sister's sons. What an irony that I pray for her soul to rest in peace while her sons are fighting amongst each other. It is good that she died young. Her innocent soul would not have had the strength to see all this infighting.'

There was a sudden flurry of activity outside and Danishmand Khan turned as Malika Banu's husband Saif Khan entered the tent. He was a fair heavyset man who walked with the authority bestowed upon him as Burhanpur's thanedar. Watching him twirl his moustache Danishmand Khan said, 'Khan Sahab is coming this way. You will get to hear more from him.'

Saif Khan said, 'I am sure you have apprised Begum Sahiba of the strange events we have had to face.'

'I have heard a lot more than what I was told here,' his wife commented from the other side of the screen as a khoja served a platter of freshly prepared paans to Saif Khan. He picked up one and offered the tray to Danishmand Khan who bowed slightly in acknowledgement before picking one up.

'Tell me, Begum. What have you heard?' Saif Khan asked, chewing on the paan.

'I am told we have been barred from getting any jewellery or clothes for Aurangzeb.'

'As you know Shahzada is en route to the Deccan to take charge as its subedar. The orders are not to spend any money from the royal treasury for his welcome.'

'But as a subedar of the Deccan, does he not have a right over the royal treasury? How can we refuse if he asks?'

'We could not have, in normal circumstances. But I have no choice having received the *shahi firman*. I am bound by it.'

'I wonder at the reason behind such strict measures.'

'I too am confused. It is true Aurangzeb and his troops had to face defeat in the Kandahar campaign. But in war there are defeats as well as wins. Not allowing his zenankhana to accompany him is quite surprising.'

'It beats me,' Malika Banu said, her voice rising with anger. 'After all the Badshah had camped in Lahore himself for many years without any success.'

Saif Khan got up and sighed deeply, 'Danishmand Khan, we are Badshah's servants as well as the Shahzada's. You need to tell me a way out of this dilemma.'

Danishmand Khan preferred not to respond, lost in his own thoughts.

༺ঌৎ ঙৎ༻

It was late afternoon when rising dust clouds, a couple of miles from Burhanpur, announced the arrival of two messengers on horseback. They soon reached the Zainabad gardens and saluted Saif Khan.

Handing over the message from Aurangzeb, they added that he was due to arrive in Zainabad within the hour.

Saif Khan ran his eyes over the message and nodded to Danishmand Khan. Immediately they both jumped on to their horses and galloped down to personally receive the Shahzada. Within a few minutes, they were in sighting distance of his caravan. The procession stopped seeing the two senior officials galloping in its direction. The two men dismounted and walked the remaining few hundred yards. Shahzada Aurangzeb sat atop an elephant in a silver howdah decorated in regal splendour. The royal insignia, hoisted on two elephants that flanked the Shahzada's, fluttered in the wind.

Saif Khan glanced up at the Shahzada and bowed in salute the moment he met his eyes. The mahout instructed the elephant to sit. Bells, hanging on silver chains on the side of the elephant, tinkled as the huge beast bent its forelegs. A servant came running forward to place a velvet-covered foot ladder.

Saif Khan observed the Shahzada as he stepped down. He was a tall man in his mid-thirties. A loud voice announced, 'Muhi-ud-Din Muhammad Aurangzeb; Shahzada-e-Badshah Hindustan; Farzand-e-Shah Jahan Sahib-e-Kiran saani!'

A faint smile played on Aurangzeb's face. The jewel in the aigrette of his Mughal-style turban twinkled when it caught the sun. He wore a flowing kaba with gold border, and the pearl-edged tips of his trousers partly covered his Turkish shoes.

Saif Khan quickly knelt to kiss the edge of Aurangzeb's robe. The Shahzada put his hands on Saif Khan's shoulders and asked him to get up. His penetrating gaze was difficult for Saif Khan to meet and, gathering himself, he saluted elaborately and addressed him in formal tones, 'It is a great honour for this humble servant to welcome Shahzada Muhi-ud-Din Muhammad Aurangzeb.'

Aurangzeb kept his gaze on Saif Khan's face. 'Are you really pleased by my visit?'

'Beshak! Beshak! We have been eagerly awaiting Shahzada's arrival.'

'I hope it is not a bother,' Aurangzeb said.

A shiver ran down Saif Khan's spine. The taunt was evident. 'How can it be a bother? Rather it is our honour and pride to be able to welcome Shahzada.'

'Good to know that. Let us move then,' Aurangzeb said, as he mounted the horse kept ready for him. Saif Khan and Danishmand

Khan followed suit and they proceeded towards Burhanpur with a few select soldiers in tow. Aurangzeb, seeing Saif Khan keep a respectable distance behind him, indicated to him to come forward. Keeping his eyes on the road ahead he asked: *'Chachaji, sab khairiyat toh hai na?'*

'Haan, haan, Shahzada. Sab khairiyat.'

'Then why do I sense some hesitation?' Aurangzeb continued to look ahead, guiding his horse through the dense vegetation on both sides of the path. After a while he added, 'I am aware of the situation, Chachaji, but I assure you that my stay will not cause you any trouble.'

'I am obliged,' Saif Khan muttered under his breath.

༺⊙ ⊙༻

As they reached the outskirts of Zainabad, the cantonment set up for Aurangzeb's caravan, came into view. The royal insignia fluttered atop the large shamiana erected for the Shahzada.

The officials, assembled there to welcome Aurangzeb, saluted as soon as he entered. A raised seating arrangement had been erected in one corner. Aurangzeb sat on it resting his back against a large cushion, but Saif Khan, Danishmand Khan and the other officials continued to stand. Aurangzeb's eyes scanned the people in attendance, but no one dared to meet his gaze. On cue from Saif Khan a quartet of dancing girls entered, their anklets tinkling as they gently trod the carpets. The lead dancer stepped forward and bowed in salutation before turning back to begin her dance with a flourish. The beats of the tabla and other musical instruments matched her energetic movements. The officials in attendance enjoyed the performance but kept an alert eye on Shahzada and Saif Khan. Aurangzeb, after a casual glance at the dancers, bent forward to pick up a paan from the silver tray in front of him. He asked Danishmand Khan, 'Danishmand, I hope the task allotted to you has been done to satisfaction.'

Danishmand Khan did not reply but continued to look down at the carpet.

'Danishmand, you didn't answer.'

'I request Shahzada not to push for an answer here. I will present the entire case to you at a suitable time.'

Aurangzeb was surprised but did not say anything. He put the paan back on to the tray and continued to look at the dancers with an expressionless face. The dancers, having ended their performance, stood expectantly with their heads bowed. Saif Khan asked, 'Did Shahzada enjoy the performance?'

Aurangzeb replied, his face showing the hint of smile, 'Yes, Chachaji. After all, if you like it, I too must.'

'I am not able to follow you.'

'Chachaji, it may be inappropriate to say it at this juncture, but I assumed you would know.'

'What, Shahzada?'

'That Islam does not approve of dance and music. You know I am a devout follower.'

'I know ... but I thought today's occasion being special ...'

'What special occasion are you talking of? Or are you referring to our defeat in battle?'

'No!' Saif Khan hurried to explain. 'The thought never crossed my mind. I believe Islam's diktat on music and dance is applicable to people who are older in age. Shahzada's age is meant for royal pursuits and enjoyment; if you do not, who else will?'

Aurangzeb smiled. 'I am happy at the dance performance you presented in my honour.' Sheikh Sadullah, who managed Aurangzeb's personal affairs, stood nearby holding a tray. Aurangzeb briefly touched the tray as a gesture of his approval and Sadullah removed the cloth to expose a pearl necklace lying on it. It was a gift to the lead dancer who, after accepting it, walked backwards a few steps repeating her salutes and stepped out of the shamiana.

'Chachaji, you are elder to me. I hope you don't mind if I pull your leg.'

'I am after all Shahzada's servant.'

'You would be my servant when I take charge as subedar of the

Deccan. At this moment I am merely your guest. I must say I am pleased with your choice.'

'What choice?'

'The dancer; she seems to be your choice.'

Saif Khan blushed and said, lowering his eyes, 'To tell you the truth, I do indulge in a bit of such luxuries. I am happy that Shahzada liked my choice. Shahzada is, after all, at an age where he should be enjoying such pleasures.'

'But I have been engaged for the past eight or nine years in campaigns and other battles.'

'I suggest Shahzada should keep such campaigns on hold after assuming charge of the Deccan.'

'Why do you say so?'

'Shahzada should spend time on shikar, but of a different kind!' Saif Khan said, pointing to the egress where the dancer had exited a few minutes back. 'Such a shikar too befits a man!'

'That reminds me, Chachaji, of a shikar we enjoyed a few days back.'

'Is that so? I am not privy to the details.'

'We entered the dense jungles on the banks of the Chambal while returning from the Lahore campaign. It was a great shikar.'

'Oh yes! I remember now Danishmand Khan talking about it.'

'What do you think I managed to capture?'

'Nothing is impossible for Shahzada; I am curious, though.'

Aurangzeb glanced at Sadullah and he in turn indicated two servants to exit the shamiana silently.

'Chachaji, you showed me your delicate shikar. Now let me show you mine. Look!'

Those present turned their heads to see a ferocious tiger tied in chains and being pulled by two slaves. The tiger let out a loud roar, shaking the shamiana to the core, while a terror erupted amongst the birds and other animals kept in cages outside. The slaves dragged the tiger to the entrance of the shamiana and managed to hold it steady.

'Do you see, Chachaji? I hunted a lot of tigers, but we managed to catch this fellow alive.'

'I see!'

'It was a pair. I saw the female and fired a shot at her. She died instantly, but the male caught me unawares when he pounced on me from behind the bushes.'

A female voice erupted from behind the laced gossamer curtains which separated the female audience, *Ya Allah! Ya Parwar Digaar!*'

Seeing Aurangzeb's questioning look Saif Khan clarified, 'It's Begum Sahiba.'

'You mean my aunt?'

'Yes, Shahzada.'

Aurangzeb got up instantly from his seat and, turning in the direction of the curtains, bowed respectfully. For a moment he stood without saying a word and then, sitting down, said, 'Chachaji, I have got the tiger as a present for you. Luckily, the wounds on my body have healed thanks to regular medication, else you would have seen me as a battle-scarred hero.'

The talks continued for a few more hours till it was time for Aurangzeb to perform his evening prayers. The durbar was dismissed.

⟶ ⟵

Malika Banu prepared to meet Aurangzeb two days later. The meeting was to take place in the deer garden. The garden had been temporarily cordoned from all sides and, except for a select few women from the zenankhana, no one else was present. It was late afternoon and the sun's heat had considerably reduced. The shadows of the tall trees lengthened across the garden and the water fountains gurgled. The rose gardens spread as far as the eye could see with casuarina trees lining the horizon. A seating arrangement had been created in the shade of a huge mango tree with velvet pillows and carpets laid out for comfort.

Aurangzeb strolled leisurely in the garden, soaking in its beauty. Female laughter erupted from the tents while the womenfolk, hiding behind the trees, watched as the Shahzada walked along the flower beds. He was enjoying the attention he was getting. He sat down on the carpet resting his back against a pillow. A maid, her anklets tinkling as she walked swaying her hips seductively, came in and, touching her palm to her forehead in salaam, said in a mellifluous voice, 'Huzoor-e-Alam, Begum Sahiba will take some time to arrive. She has asked me to entertain you in the meanwhile. If you permit, this humble servant would like to show you around the garden.'

Aurangzeb arched his eyebrows appreciatively at her voluptuous figure and the way her eyebrows danced as she spoke. He said, 'It will be my pleasure.'

'I request the Shahzada to step into the garden. I am sure he will be pleased.'

She took a few steps back and waited for Aurangzeb to get up. Looking at her he asked, 'Were you not the one who danced that evening at my reception?'

She gently fingered the pearl necklace which adorned her neck. 'Yes. It is this *nacheez* who had the honour of dancing for you. I hope Huzoor liked it.'

Instead of answering her, Aurangzeb asked, 'Did you like the necklace?'

'This humble servant would have been happy with just a gift of your smile. There is no reason not to be happy when presented with such an exquisite pearl necklace.'

'Oh I see! Your words are as sweet and graceful as your dance.'

'I suppose that is the least you can expect from one under the tutelage of Begum Sahiba.'

'What is your name?'

'I am called Hira.'

'Hira! So the Persian pearl necklace has been handed to the right person, I suppose.'

Casting a sidelong glance at Aurangzeb she said, 'I request Huzoor to step into the garden.'

A group of ladies had assembled in the shade of a tree and were busy chatting away. They got up the moment they saw the Shahzada walking towards them.

'If Huzoor so desires he can enjoy a song. These maids have been specially trained and their voices are as sweet as the koel bird.'

'*Bahut khoob!* And what is that group on the other side doing?' Aurangzeb asked, pointing to an assembly of women sitting a little further away.

'They are Begum Sahiba's personal maids, each one of them trained in different musical instruments. Would Huzoor care to listen to the dilruba, pakhawaj or sitar?'

Aurangzeb caressed his pointed beard in contemplation when his attention was diverted by a loud laughter coming in from another direction. Hira clapped once and said, 'It seems Huzoor is curious. I am sure you will enjoy their entertainment. Please follow me.'

A few hundred steps away was a rectangular pond built out of stones from Rajasthan. An arched doorway led the visitors to broad marble steps guiding them down to a pool of clear blue water. Hira gently stepped on to the marble steps while Aurangzeb followed her. A group of eight or ten women were enjoying their swim with carefree indulgence.

'See,' she said, pointing to the group frolicking in the water. 'The maids and laundis are playing ball with each other. If Huzoor so wishes, he can relax on the carpet here for a while and watch them.'

The women played with gay abandon, their soaked blouses hugging their buxom figures. They stretched tantalizingly out of the water to catch the ball and then swam languidly to chase it. The ball got entangled in the long tresses of one of the maids and there was a general clamour to release it. Aurangzeb took one final look at them and walked up the steps, without saying a word.

'It seems Huzoor did not enjoy their game.'

'Of course I did! But I would rather watch some sport played by men.'

'*Afsos!*' Hira blinked her eyes coquettishly with a finger on her lips. 'There is no male except Huzoor in this entire garden. You cannot possibly watch men play.'

'That's right!' Aurangzeb said, laughing to himself. 'I did not realize that. I will then wait for the arrival of Begum Sahiba.'

Hira said, 'There is one game which can be called manly.'

'And that is?'

'Huzoor may look in that direction,' Hira said, pointing towards one corner of the garden. A herd of deer grazed, their bronze skins glinting off the rays of the evening sun. A huge antelope stood nearby watching them.

'If Huzoor permits, I would like to show him something.'

'Zaroor! Zaroor!'

'This laundi has learnt a bit of archery.'

'Achchha! Let me see.'

'Can you see the antelope there? Do you see something stuck in between his horns?'

'Yes, I can. What is it?'

'It is a blouse. On hearing a clap, the herd will move towards the rose garden and I will aim and pierce the blouse with my arrow as the antelope moves.'

'Oh! So it seems you enjoy a men's sport.'

'It will be my pleasure to show you my skill. Shall I hit the arrow on the right side or left?'

'I do not understand.'

Hira blushed and said in a low voice, 'Huzoor, the blouse has two parts. I will hit the one you say.'

'Oh! The right side, if you may.'

Hira picked up a bow placed near a tree. Placing an arrow on the bow, she asked Aurangzeb to clap. On hearing the sound, the herd moved towards the garden. Hira's arrow spliced through the air and cleanly pierced the target. Then she whistled with her fingers between her teeth and the antelope came ambling towards them.

'See, Huzoor!' She held up the blouse for Aurangzeb's inspection.

'Shabbash! I am pleased.' He then added mischievously, 'Galat. Ekdum galat!'

Hira was surprised at the remark.

'I do not follow you, Huzoor.'

'I had asked you to aim at the right side. The arrow has hit the left.'

Observing the blouse Hira exclaimed, 'Oh! I have never missed my mark. It must be the first time.' At that moment, two maids rushed in and saluted saying, 'Huzoor, Begum Sahiba has arrived and is waiting for you. She says she will be happy to meet you once you are done with your walk.'

'*Beshak! Beshak!* I too am eager to meet her. Let us go.' The maids walked ahead followed by Aurangzeb.

৯৫ ৯৯

The garden was lit with mashaals hanging here and there on trees. There were some lamps atop tall pillars and a few other liberally scattered across the sitting area. Malika Banu's ethereal Mughal beauty was further enhanced by the soft glow of the lamps. Fruits, sweets and other refreshments had been placed in silver trays on the carpet. Flowers were arranged around the trays, adding to the beauty of the ambience. Banu guided Aurangzeb holding his hand and settling him comfortably. A long-necked earthen pitcher decorated with minakari work, was placed near him, and a maid brought in two silver tumblers.

'Begum Sahiba, what is this?'

Banu looked affectionately at her favourite nephew saying, 'Shahzada! This has been especially ordered for you.'

'Is it *sharaab*?'

'Yes, but it is no ordinary wine. You may choose what you want: Shirazi, Abbasi, Irani or any other. We have wines from the Balkh and Badakshan regions too, if you so desire.'

'Mausi! I am sure you are aware I do not touch any of these things.'

'I had heard of it and I assumed you do not do so when on a campaign. You are in your aunt's house and there is nothing wrong in sharing it with her. After all, it is a Mughal tradition.'

'I beg your pardon, Begum Sahiba, but I am not in the habit.'

'But why, if I may?'

'It is not approved by Islam.'

'Islam may not approve it but humanity does. After all what is a man without his wine.'

'Begum Sahiba, I have never touched it and will request you not to force me.'

'Oh I see! I won't force you to do things against your wishes.'

A maid came in and quickly cleared the tray and tumblers. After some small talk Banu asked, 'I believe there is no need for me to tell you certain things. I am told you are already in the know.'

'Yes, Begum Sahiba. I have come to know of them.'

'And Shahzada still continues to keep his quiet?'

'Yes. It does not surprise me any more. The Badshah has not favoured me for the last few years. In fact, I would have been surprised had he not acted in this fashion. He has sent me here to take charge of the Deccan with all the liberties of a prisoner. And …' Aurangzeb did not complete his sentence. He turned his face away to hide his emotions.

'Shahzada! Don't stop. Say what comes to your mind.'

'The Badshah does not trust me. He fears I will revolt once I take charge of the Deccan and he feels he can keep me in check holding my family back in Agra as hostage. He has taken such a step under political pressure.'

'*Afsos!* Alas, I don't understand politics. But what I do know is that a father should trust his son.'

'It is not in the Mughal tradition to trust one's progeny.'

'What is the tradition then, Shahzada?'

'For a Badshah to look after his own interests rather than his son's.'

'What do you mean?' she asked, her voice rising.

Aurangzeb said, 'I am sure Begum Sahiba is aware of the happenings in Agra and Delhi. Please do not expect me to elaborate everything. You are like a mother to me and I don't want to speak my mind. But I know one thing for sure; Badshah fears his own shadow these days.'

'You are reading too much into it, Shahzada.'

'I wish I were wrong, Begum Sahiba. But before coming here, I learnt something that reaffirmed my fears.'

'Is it about the *firman* not allowing you to withdraw any money from the royal treasury?'

'No. Had it been just that, I would have been happy. Aurangzeb is not faint-hearted to mourn over such trivial issues.'

'What then are you talking about?'

'My elder brother Dara returned from his campaign in Kandahar losing lakhs of rupiyas and the lives of thousands of our men in the process.'

'I have heard of it.'

'And do you know, Begum Sahiba, the way he was felicitated by the Badshah on his return?'

'You mean he was honoured after being routed so badly?'

'That is the irony! I have won many a battle but never have I been felicitated. And here, my brother returns after an ignominious defeat and gets a warm welcome in court. Not only that, he was referred to as the future Badshah of Hindustan. Keeping Mughal tradition aside, he was made to sit on a throne near the Badshah. I am certain Badshah is looking for every opportunity to insult me.'

'I can understand the situation,' Banu said to herself. 'Shahzada, you are now the subedar of the Deccan and we are the governors of Burhanpur under you. We cannot write to the Badshah without your permission.'

'Can you elaborate?'

'I wish to request the Badshah to allow your zenankhana to proceed to Burhanpur. Would you mind?'

'Don't do that. His suspicion would be directed at you as he would believe you are advocating on my behalf.'

Banu decided not to pursue the topic further. Aurangzeb got up and said, 'It is time for my namaz. I will take your leave now.'

A maid got a pitcher of water for his wudu and poured it over his hands. Within moments, the silence in the gardens of Zainabad was broken with the words, '*Bismillah hir rahman nir raheem.*'

❧☙

The Deccan, fraught with troubles, was generally considered one of the most difficult territories to manage. Ten years ago, Aurangzeb had been nominated subedar of the Deccan and had worked very hard to improve the revenues and streamline the overall administration. But differences with the Badshah led to him being recalled to Agra. He had managed to gain some of the emperor's trust largely due to the efforts of his sister Jahanara Begum. He was entrusted with minor jobs for a while, but when the Badshah realized that the problems in the Deccan had surfaced again, he thought of Aurangzeb as the person to manage the affairs. Aurangzeb, busy in Kandahar, was ordered to move to the Deccan directly. Despite the *firman*, Aurangzeb decided to call upon his zenankhana and visited Agra for a month before leaving for Aurangabad via Burhanpur. He had now been camping in Burhanpur for over a month, but had not made any plans to move to Aurangabad despite a spate of reminders and messages from the Badshah enquiring about his move. Aurangzeb was busy arranging for funds to manage his huge army, which he had to provide for. The question of managing his finances loomed large and his primary concern was to sort them out before he took charge of the Deccan.

One day, Aurangzeb sat in his tent discussing matters of revenue with Sheikh Sadullah who had presented some accounts. Mir Hasham, Aurangzeb's senior-most religious tutor sat with his knees folded on the carpet. His eyes were half closed but his attention was complete. Aurangzeb looked at the papers handed over by Sadullah and said, 'Why have you allotted ten thousand rupiyas towards my personal expenses?'

'I did not give it in writing as I wanted to explain to you personally,' Mir Hasham explained. 'During the Kandahar campaign, Shahzada may recall having selected around a hundred small boys to be made into khojas. Tabib Wazir Khan, in charge of the harem, has asked for this amount for their welfare, their clothes, food and other such amenities.'

'I remember now! How many years has it been since we bought those children?'

'It has been two years now. We need to castrate them before they turn eight. Else there is a possibility of them dying of infection.'

'I am aware. How many do we need for my personal protection?'

'As the subedar of the Deccan, this is the first time you are creating your own group of khojas. Earlier you were able to borrow from the royal zenankhana at Agra. The *shahi firman* states that you need to take care of your personal needs on your own. That is why we need our own khojas. We need to plan for the future too,' Sadullah explained.

Danishmand Khan sat nearby. He too was a khoja of the royal household. The talk disturbed him. He said in a modest voice, 'Shahzada Sahab, if you permit, I would like to say something.'

'Khan Sahab, you don't need to ask for permission. Please speak.'

'Shahzada, is it necessary to castrate these young ones at such a tender age? Are we not destroying their future?'

Aurangzeb did not answer immediately. Instead he looked at Mir Hasham, who sat telling his rosary. He was in his seventies and had been Aurangzeb's teacher since his childhood. 'Ustadji, what is your view?'

Mir Hasham said, 'I am surprised hearing Danishmand Khan. The practice of buying young boys and turning them into khojas for the zenankhana is not new. This has been going on since Zille Subhani Akbar's time.'

'That is why I feel the time has come to change such practices.'

Ustadji continued, ignoring Danishmand Khan's comment, 'The prestige of a Badshah is measured by the strength of his zenankhana – not just in Agra but in Iran, Afghanistan, Turkistan and other countries. Not to forget the fact that we need khojas to guard the zenankhana. It is Islam's diktat.'

Aurangzeb continued to hear the conversation without allowing any emotions to cross his face. He asked, 'Ustadji, does the Quran Sharif say so?'

'Yes, Shahzada. It is mentioned in the Quran Sharif that a Badshah should have khojas in his zenankhana.'

'I think you are mistaken, Ustadji,' Khan interrupted. 'I think you mean the *Ain-i-Akbari* and not the Quran Sharif.'

'Maybe so. After all, what's the difference between the two?'

A smile broke onto Aurangzeb's face. He said, 'Ustadji, Quran Sharif is Allah's words while *Ain-i-Akbari* and *Deen-e-Elahi* were created during Badshah Akbar's reign. How can you equate them?'

Mir Hasham did not answer. He picked up the rosary placed on the carpet and continued to tell his beads. Danishmand Khan continued, 'There may be some guidelines laid out in *Ain-i-Akbari*. But I believe man has no right to take away the powers given by Allah to another human being.'

Aurangzeb stared at Danishmand Khan and asked, 'Danishmand Khan, these words sound strange coming from you. What do you mean by powers bestowed by Allah?'

'Shahzada, these are not my thoughts alone. I had met a firangi hakeem in Agra who showed me many books. All of them were against the right to take away what Nature has bestowed upon another man.'

Mir Hasham said, 'Unlike Khan Sahab, I am not in the habit of reading books written by kafirs. But he should keep in mind this old man has spent his lifetime studying the holy Quran.' He added with a sarcastic smile, 'I wonder, since when did Khan Sahab become the expert on Nature's rules?'

His snide remark brought tears to Danishmand Khan's eyes. He said, 'Sheikh Sadullah and Ustadji here are much older than me. I am a mere khoja. How can I know Nature's gift? But I am aware that a man is bestowed with the power of Nature when he turns fifteen or sixteen. I believed that one may not need these powers in the old age. But I am told Ustadji himself has married for the seventh or the eighth time a few months back. And that too a fourteen-year-old ...'

'*Khamosh!* Don't forget Mir Hasham's status as Shahzada's ustad. It is against propriety to speak of his personal matters openly,' Sadullah thundered.

Danishmand Khan was overwhelmed with emotions. He said in a low voice, 'I apologize for not following protocol. I have no right to break it though others may not follow. I should have known that. Please pardon my impertinence.'

Aurangzeb put his papers away and looked at both of them: 'You have not committed any mistake, Danishmand Khan. But I cannot ignore a Mughal custom that has been practised for hundreds of years now. I don't think there needs to be any relation between age and marriage. But you must learn to accept the situation Allah has put you in and be happy about it.'

'Precisely,' Mir Hasham added. 'Danishmand Khan has been influenced by the firangi hakeems in Agra. There are too many like the Frenchman Francois Bernier and other English ones. We need to burn their religious books. How else will we be able to spread the word of Allah all over the world? *Ya Allah! Ya Parwar Digaar!*' Mir Hasham looked at Danishmand Khan from the corner of his eyes as he caressed his long beard.

Sadullah, long experienced in matters of the court, knew how to diffuse an ugly situation and said, 'We cannot afford to waste Shahzada's valuable time discussing matters of religion right now. Shall I go ahead and hand over the money to Tabib?'

'Do we have this amount in our treasury?'

'You can always withdraw from the royal treasury, if need be.'

'Sadullah, the treasury is in Daulatabad and we are camped here in Burhanpur enjoying the hospitality of Saif Khan. If my mere acquiescence could shower wealth from the skies, I would not mind.'

'I have a way out of this problem,' Danishmand Khan said.

'Tell me.'

'Shahzada, it is well known that the subah of Deccan is considered a difficult territory to manage. The subah has wealthy neighbours like Bijapur and Golconda. The mines of Golconda are spewing diamonds by the dozens and international trade has added to the wealth of both the Badshahs immensely. Why should one be bothered of wealth, when one's neighbours are sitting on huge amounts?'

Aurangzeb was experienced enough to not allow his emotions to appear on his face. He said, 'I am unable to understand your logic of our problems being solved by the presence of two wealthy neighbours.'

Just then a guard came in and said, 'There is a request for an urgent meeting by Saif Khan Sahab, the thanedar of Burhanpur.'

Aurangzeb answered nonchalantly, 'Inform Saif Khan that I am not free at the moment. It is time for my afternoon prayers. I will see him after my namaz, if there is some spare time.'

The guard continued standing there and said beseechingly, 'Saif Khan Sahab is eager to meet and if he is unable to get an appointment he ...' his words trailed away.

'You probably want to say that we may have to cross swords, isn't it? Let it be. Send him the message that Shahzada Aurangzeb meets his servants when he wants to and not because the servant is eager to meet. Tell him the subedar does not have to find time to meet his thanedar.' Aurangzeb got up and walked out through the rear exit into his private tent.

❦❦

Eight days passed. Each day Aurangzeb would receive a request from Saif Khan for a meeting. Saif Khan would return to Burhanpur after waiting for hours without a meeting. Finally he was granted an audience. His ruddy Pathan face had turned sallow. Dark circles around his eyes suggested he had spent the past week in anxiety.

Aurangzeb ignored his salute and continued to look at the papers spread out before him. Saif Khan said, 'Shahzada, the thanedar of Burhanpur wishes to seek an audience with you.'

Without raising his eyes from the papers Aurangzeb replied, 'I am aware.' He continued to study the papers and asked, 'Chachaji, what brings you here?'

'I have come here in the capacity of thanedar of Burhanpur.'

'That is what I mean, Chachaji. You seem to have tanned a little.'

Aurangzeb's deliberate nonchalance was difficult for Saif Khan to tolerate, but he had no choice. He said, 'I am surprised my face is not completely black after all the insults I have had to bear.'

'Saif Khan, I prefer my employees to come to the point.'

'I will be frank, Shahzada. I want to know what made your men commit the dastardly act of looting the Burhanpur treasury, which is under my command.'

'Oh, so that is what the thanedar is angry about.'

'I am sure you are not bothered about me getting upset. I did not expect you to ignore the royal *firman*. Had I known, I would have been alert.'

'In other words, you would have repulsed the attack?'

'If need be. Pathan loyalty is not yet dead. We Pathans do not follow the Mughal tradition of trading their loyalties for personal gains,' Saif Khan's eyes were red and his fists curled as he stood there in defiance.

'Khan Sahab, I am the subedar appointed by the Badshah and you are the thanedar of Burhanpur, yet you speak as an equal. I am surprised you have the audacity to threaten me.'

'How surprised should I be to know you have ignored the royal *firman*?'

'What *shahi firman* are you talking of, Saif Khan?'

'We have received a *shahi firman* explicitly forbidding you to be given any money from the Burhanpur treasury. It was for that reason I had refused any money when you sent a request for your personal expenses. The Pathan in me is unable to understand how you respect the *shahi firman* when you send your men to forcibly take charge of my treasury.'

'Khan Sahab, you don't understand politics. The Pathan in you, whom you admire so much, does not understand practical aspects of life.'

'What practical aspects are you talking of?'

'That the *firman* is being sent to you instead of me.'

'What I do know is to honour the *firman* I received.'

'It is not a *shahi firman*, Thanedar.'

'That is strange! I have seen it with my own eyes. It has the royal seal. How does the Shahzada claim that it is not?'

'Thanedar, I understand the running of Delhi Durbar better than you. The *firman* may carry the royal insignia and the necessary seals, but I know Ala Hazrat has not sent it. These are my elder brother's deeds. There is hence no need to honour the same.'

Saif Khan could not believe his ears. He naively said, 'Shahzada, it is not my job to question the *firman*. As a loyal employee, my job is to honour the same and follow instructions. I am not aware of the politics behind it. Nevertheless, I am sure the Badshah would be upset knowing you have taken charge of the treasury.'

'Saif Khan, I am not in the habit of predicting the effects of all the actions I take.'

'I may have suggested a way out had you asked me before taking a decision to loot the treasury.'

'Would you have handed over the treasury had I asked?'

'Shahzada, had you asked me, I would have gladly handed over the keys to the treasury along with my resignation and walked away to Agra.'

'Saif Khan, I do believe you; but what is done cannot be undone. I am going to ask you for a favour. So think before replying.'

'Please! Pathans do not waste time thinking.'

'So, would you stand by your word?'

'Yes, Shahzada. We always do.'

Aurangzeb's eyes glinted. He had a habit of narrowing his eyes to pierce through a person's soul. No one had the courage to return his gaze then. 'Chachaji, I believe you. I would ask you when I need something. I would not force you. Are you in agreement?'

'But what about the treasury?'

'I have already taken care of it. The same night I despatched a messenger to Agra with the details of the events. If the Badshah is upset, he will be angry at me and not at the thanedar.'

⚬୧ଓ⚬

The month of Ramzan fell in the peak of summer. The daily fasts were being strictly followed in the cantonment, but the oppressive heat added to the suffering as the men had to go without food or water throughout the day. Drapes of vetiver grass were hung outside the private tents and were constantly kept wet, providing a natural cooler. The fragrance of the khus grass along with the cool air lessened the heat. Aurangzeb spent most of his day studying the Quran and reading namaz. Two days before the end of the fasting month, Aurangzeb sent word for Mir Hasham. Aurangzeb would hardly entertain a meeting or call for someone during this month. Mir Hasham was thus surprised at the urgent summons as he hurried as quickly as his obesity would allow towards Aurangzeb's tent.

Hearing footsteps outside the tent, Aurangzeb set his book aside and got up to receive his old teacher. He welcomed him warmly and holding his hand gently guided him to sit. Mir Hasham was thoroughly confused at the reception. He had not seen Aurangzeb with such a gentle face. It was impossible for Mir Hasham to look into Aurangzeb's eyes and not feel restless. The penetrating eyes seemed mellow.

'Mir Sahab,' Aurangzeb began, his voice sounding emotional. 'You have been my guide and teacher all my life and have helped me to read the namaz and follow other rites. I was under the mistaken assumption that I have understood everything, I find that even in this religious month of Ramzan my mind is not at peace. I have called you here to discuss some religious matters.'

'I am surprised to hear you say this,' Mir Hasham said. 'I am not sure if there is anything you do not know related to religion. Your knowledge can challenge even the most learned of the mullahs.'

'I find I am unable to concentrate on the reading of the Quran.'

'Shahzada, I was told you spend all your time reading the Quran. Why then are you not able to concentrate?'

'Mir Sahab, I have kept all the duties aside and have focused on my rites. I have not allowed any event, whether good or bad, to affect my duties.'

'Yes, I am aware of it. And I feel proud,' Mir Hasham said. 'I had been a little hesitant when the Badshah first nominated me as teacher, not knowing your inclination towards these things. But you surprised me time and again asking insightful questions from the Quran and the Hadis.'

'Those are things of the past, Mir Sahab. Ever since I have come to Burhanpur I am unable to concentrate. I fear I am losing control of my mind.'

It had been twenty years since Mir Hasham, on orders of Shah Jahan, had taken Aurangzeb under his tutelage. He had never seen Aurangzeb display a weak mind and heart. He used to boast that his favourite student could beat any mullah in a religious debate. He remembered an instance when, in the midst of gun shots and arrows flying all over in a war, Aurangzeb had knelt down on the ground and performed his namaz. The Badshah had gifted Mir Hasham a princely sum of a thousand rupiyas when he had come to know of this. Mir Hasham realized Aurangzeb wanted to pour his heart out and did not want any advice. He decided to give him a patient hearing. Making a façade of advising Aurangzeb he said, 'Shahzada, frankly speaking, you do not need any advice. You know the matters of the world. Nevertheless, as an elder I will say a few things. The human mind is by nature restless and it is precisely to control the same that our religion has prescribed reading the namaz five times a day. The entire country and the maulvis have high hopes on you. Do not do anything which will shatter their hopes.'

Aurangzeb said, sighing deeply, 'Mir Sahab, I am sorry to have bothered you. I will pray at the grave of Ammi Jaan at the Zainabad gardens. I will perform the namaz with the crowds at the Jama Masjid. Let me see if this helps in reducing my restlessness.'

Mir Hasham took leave muttering to himself as he walked towards his quarters. To his dismay, Aurangzeb had not opened up his heart and shared his anxiety with him.

The month of Ramzan ended and the cantonment wore a festive look on the day of Eid. Wearing special clothes befitting the festive occasion, Aurangzeb reached a tent specially decorated for him to receive his visitors. Trays were laid out for him to distribute gifts. He would touch each tray with his hand and it would be sent out for distribution amongst the poor. Mir Hasham sat in one corner observing Aurangzeb. It was clear to him that his mind was elsewhere.

Aurangzeb hurriedly dispensed with the distribution of alms and reached his private quarters. He asked the khoja in attendance to call for Saif Khan.

'Did the Shahzada ask for me?'

'Chachaji,' Aurangzeb said, without meeting Saif Khan's eyes. 'Do you remember that day?'

'What day are you talking of, Shahzada?'

'Chachaji, I am speaking to you as Aurangzeb and not as a prince.'

'It is the day of Eid and not one for formalities,' Saif Khan agreed, relaxing on the pillows nearby. 'We are fortunate to have you at Burhanpur on this day. I am unable to understand though the reason for your summons.'

'Chachaji, I admit I forcibly took over your treasury.'

'Let bygones be bygones. Why are you raking up the subject of the treasury now?'

'You had promised me something when I had taken over your treasury. You remember you had given me your word?'

Saif Khan's smiling face turned serious. He asked, sitting upright, 'What did I promise you that day?'

'You remember you had said if I liked something from your treasury, I would ask for it rather than try to take it forcibly?'

Saif Khan pondered for a moment and said, 'Yes, I remember that clearly. Today is the day of Eid. I have not forgotten my promise.'

'That is why this Aurangzeb is begging to you today.'

'Aurangzeb!'

'Yes, Chachaji. In our tradition one does not refuse a beggar on this day, isn't it?'

'I know that. I have promised you long back. Ask what you want and I shall present it to you right away.'

'Are you sure?'

'This Pathan can lose his life but not renege on the promises made.'

'Chachaji, I want you to present me Hira, the priceless gem of your zenankhana.'

'Aurangzeb, I cannot forget the fact that you are a Shahzada. I have not forgotten my word to you. But I am aghast that you have asked for my favourite concubine from the zenankhana. You know how much a Pathan values his zenankhana.'

'Do I need to remind you the stress you put on a Pathan's promise? If you intend not to keep your word, I have nothing further to say.'

'But Shahzada ...'

Aurangzeb interrupted him, 'I have begged for something I desperately want. I pine for her. I am restless without her. Chachaji, I can't put it across more bluntly. Eid Mubarak!'

It was late in the evening, but the Eid celebrations had not died down. One could hear the sound of dance and music from different quarters. A palanquin arrived from Burhanpur and stopped outside Aurangzeb's tent. One of the bearers handed over a letter to Sadullah who arched his eyebrows in surprise reading the note and stared at the palanquin for a few moments. He then instructed the palanquin to be taken to Aurangzeb's private quarters.

༄༅ ༄༅

The summer ended and clouds looming large heralded the onset of the monsoon. Aurangzeb's cantonment moved from Zainabad to Burhanpur and he took up temporary residence in the erstwhile haveli of the local thanedar, adjacent to the Jama Masjid on the banks of the Tapi. The monsoon drenched Burhanpur with torrential showers and very soon the brown swirling waters of the Tapi breached the banks. Aurangzeb watched the wild dance of the river as he sat in the haveli contemplating his next move.

It was evening. The candles and multicoloured lamps threw intriguing shadows on the thick carpet. Taking a seat in the lounge, Aurangzeb asked Anwar Khoja to fetch Shamim, the chief daroga responsible for general supervision of the zenankhana. She entered and, after saluting, presented a tray with some letters in it. Without looking at them Aurangzeb asked, 'It there anything important?'

'The usual, Huzoor,' Shamim replied. 'Huzoor may look at the papers related to zenankhana's accounts later, but there is an urgent request from Sheikh Sadullah to look at some papers from Agra.'

'What is there to look at? I am fed up of hearing the same stories regarding who taunted me behind my back and who is plotting against me in Agra.'

'Huzoor may look at them later then.' Shamim stretched her hand forward to pick up the tray. The bangles on her arm shone in the candlelight and reminded Aurangzeb of a pending task. He asked, 'Have the jewellers from Golconda sent the jewellery we ordered for the new begum.'

'Ji, Huzoor. I personally sent across the jewellery to Hira Bai's quarters. I have something to ask in that regard.'

'What is it?'

'Hira Bai has been here for two months now. I had made temporary accommodation for her assuming she would move out soon. But it seems she is likely to be here for a longer while. In which case, I need to make proper arrangements.'

'She is going to be here permanently.'

'What about the marriage then?'

'That need not be a daroga's concern. Let me worry about it. We have an Irani mahal and a Rajput mahal; now we will have a Burhanpuri mahal here.'

'Ji, Huzoor,' Shamim acquiesed. She was worried of the consequences, though. As a daroga, she was responsible for informing the Emperor at Agra of all the important happenings in the zenankhana and she was not sure of the news being received favourably in the Mughal court. She said, a little hesitantly, 'Shahzada, her background …'

'It is your responsibility to ensure no one reminds her that she was earlier a concubine in Saif Khan's harem.'

'As you command. But I would like to add that I can hardly influence the Irani Begum Dilras Banu.'

Aurangzeb was aware of the high-handed attitude of Dilras Banu who never lost a chance to boast of her Iranian roots and would insult Aurangzeb's family and the Mughal traditions calling them barbaric and ancient. He nodded his head saying, 'I know. Let me handle that.'

Aurangzeb dismissed Shamim and moved to Hira's quarters,

Anwar leading the way holding a burning mashaal in his hand. After announcing Aurangzeb's arrival at the door, he moved away silently.

Hira's quarters were brightly lit with burning lamps. Flower garlands draped the walls and an intoxicating smell of perfume pervaded all around. She stood in front of a full-length mirror, admiring her looks as she adjusted the jewellery around her neck. Sensing the presence of someone in the room, she turned around. She made a show of trying to adjust the dupatta on to her head while a subtle flick of her fingers ensured that it fell back promptly on to her shoulders. Her left hand continued to play with her dress while her right performed an elaborate salaam. She said, 'It seems Huzoor was very busy the whole day. This servant of yours was worried that she may have been forgotten.'

The seating arrangement was invitingly decorated with thick pillows. A tray laden with dried fruit was placed on a small table. Aurangzeb sat down resting against the pillows while Hira knelt in front of him. Lifting her delicate chin with his right hand, Aurangzeb looked into her kohl-lined eyes and said, 'Anyone stricken by these lovely eyes is your slave for life. How could I forget?'

Taking his hand into hers she said, 'I don't know about others, but everyone knows Huzoor well.'

'Are you saying I don't have a heart? Am I not human?'

'Ya Allah! Am I hearing right? Huzoor using words like heart?' Hira flirted with Aurangzeb as she snuggled close to him.

'I am aware of the games fairies like you play. First you overpower their hearts and then make them your slaves. We men do not fear the cannon balls in battle, but a single arrow shot from these doe eyes is enough to make us fall. Isn't that right, Hira Begum?'

'Begum? Since when did this lowly maid become a begum?'

'Since the day in the deer garden when, with your archery skills, you pierced this heart of mine.'

'But here in this mahal no one considers me so. Everyone feels I am a mere laundi, a concubine, meant to entertain you for a few months,' Hira said in mock anger.

'I have issued instructions today. They have been expressly asked to treat you as my third wife.'

'Huzoor, I am deeply obliged.'

Pulling her closer he said, 'Hira, I cannot think of anything but you. I am your slave. I don't feel like doing anything but sitting here and looking into these eyes of yours.'

Hira wriggled out of his embrace and made a face saying, 'Lies. All lies! I know I do not have the fortune to capture your heart. I am aware of the age-old tricks men use to trap gullible women like me.'

'If only I could take my heart out and show it to you.'

'The other maids have told me all about Huzoor's likes and dislikes. I am told the Irani Begum is far more beautiful than me. I also heard of how Huzoor was head over heels in love seeing the pink cheeks and lovely fair skin of the Kashmiri Begum. Now Shahzada talks of being in love with me. I am not such a fool to fall for it.'

Aurangzeb tried desperately to convince her. 'Hira, my dear! If only you could hear what my heart speaks. My ustad Mir Sahab, Sadullah, and all the other officials are all surprised at my behaviour. I know I am not at an age to get infatuated, but everyone knows that your arrival into the zenankhana has changed me. I have lost my heart and mind to these almond eyes and lustrous black hair.'

Aurangzeb had bared his heart and soul to her. He continued trying to convince her. At that time the call of the muezzin from the nearby Jama Masjid announced the time for the namaz. '*Allah o Akbar ...*' the voice rang clear in the middle of the night. Ten-year-old Anwar, standing outside in readiness, gently said, 'Huzoor, I have kept the water ready for your wudu.'

Anwar's voice broke the reverie. A glimmer of anger and sadness passed through Hira's eyes when she said, 'It is time for your namaz. You are known to be a devout follower. This slave of yours can wait, but you should not keep Allah waiting.'

Aurangzeb could sense that Hira was hurt. He looked at the door for a moment and said, 'I am famous as well as infamous for the same.

I shall go only if you permit me. I shall read my prayers and come back to this heaven as soon as I finish them.'

'If Huzoor finds his prayers more important than spending time with me, he is most free to do so. I have enough stars in the sky to count sitting at the window here.'

Aurangzeb was taken aback. 'What did you say? I don't understand.'

The imam's voice rang in the air, 'Allah o Akbar, Allah o Akbar ...'

'See! You are getting late. Huzoor talks of not being able to live without me and then promptly discards me to perform his duties. Why should he leave his prayers for a mere kafir like me?'

'Oh, so that's what it is! It is this reading of prayers that you are not happy about.'

'Do you care whether I am happy or sad?'

'Beshak! This devout namazi Aurangzeb does not have the courage to look into those tears filled eyes.'

'Really?'

Aurangzeb held her tightly in embrace. 'Shahzada Aurangzeb may be a devout follower. But Muhi-ud-Din Muhammad Aurangzeb cannot leave this heaven on earth here. I will go only if you push me away. Now, does that make you happy?'

'Yes! There is nothing else that can give me more happiness!'

'Listen to what the imam is saying.' The words rang out again, 'Allah o Akbar, Allah o Akbar ...'

'The words are not right.'

Hira, rubbing her cheeks against Aurangzeb's asked, 'What should they be?'

'He should be saying, Allah o Aurangzeb, Allah o Aurangzeb ...'

Aurangzeb tightened his embrace around Hira's waist. Anwar, after patiently waiting for his master for a few more minutes, retreated with silent steps. Through the window the stars could be seen shining in the sky. A crescent moon, emerging through a gap in the clouds, glanced stealthily at the amorous lovers.

The work in the subedari, the office of the governor, the subedar of the Deccan, had come to a near standstill. Daily messages and papers sent for Aurangzeb's perusal lay without being attended to. The swirling waters of the Tapi continued to lash against the walls of the haveli. The river outside was in full spate as was the romance inside the haveli. A sixteen-year-old in the peak of her youth and a thirty-five-year-old Mughal royal: both were lost in the world of love and physical pleasures. The daily prayers as well as the Friday visits to the mosque had long been forgotten. Anwar, after diligently waiting with the water for Aurangzeb's prayers each day, would return with a sigh. Days passed. The world outside had ceased to exist for Aurangzeb.

Sheikh Sadullah was worried while Mir Hasham was dumbstruck at Aurangzeb's changed behaviour. Shamim, the daroga at the zenankhana, had no clue how to confront the situation. One day a *shahi firman* arrived from Agra. Sadullah was worried that the *firman*, if not received with the protocol deserving of one arriving from the Mughal Emperor's court, would create further problems. He tried in vain sending messages through Shamim.

To add to Sadullah's worries, another piece of news arrived from Agra. Aurangzeb's uncle, Mirza Abutalib alias Shaista Khan, had left Agra with Aurangzeb's zenankhana and was expected to reach Burhanpur any day. But when Aurangzeb had not bothered to receive the *shahi firman* itself, who in his right mind would volunteer to convey this message to the Shahzada?

Finally, Sheikh Sadullah took recourse in Aurangzeb's aunt, Malika Banu, and sought her appointment. As soon as the khoja informed him of her presence behind the screen he beseeched, 'Begum Sahiba, please help! We are in deep trouble.'

Malika Banu replied, 'Mushrif, please gather yourself. I hope Shahzada's health is fine.'

'He is fine, Begum Sahiba, but please pardon my being direct. I would have to use words not suitable for the zenankhana though I am sure the gossip from the bazaars of Burhanpur would have reached you by now.'

'Are you talking of Hira Bai?'

'Yes, Begum Sahiba. I can understand falling in love, but Shahzada's behaviour beats all logic. The work of the subedari has been suffering for months now.'

'But why should the work suffer when he has appointed capable men like you to run the affairs?'

'Begum Sahiba, I am not a novice to come running to complain about a casual infatuation. Who does not fall for beauty? But should one forget one's duties towards the state? I do what I have to, but there are certain things which the Shahzada is supposed to look into.'

'Can you elaborate?'

'It has been eight days since a *shahi firman* arrived and is awaiting the Shahzada's attention. You know people are waiting to complain to the Badshah against him. The Badshah may, out of affection, pardon Shahzada for his carelessness, but I will be taken to task for not fulfilling my duties.'

'Are you saying the Shahzada has not read the *firman* yet?'

'Yes. This is despite me sending repeated messages and requests. Begum Sahiba! I implore you to intervene!'

'Sadullah, you need to manage the situation. You know he has been upset about the fact that his zenankhana was held back in Agra for no reason at all.'

'I have just received the news that Shahzada's uncle Shaista Khan Sahab is personally escorting the zenankhana to Burhanpur.'

'Is that so?'

'Yes. The Shahzada had sent Danishmand Khan to Agra. He used Shaista Khan's influence to convince the Badshah who finally relented to allow the zenankhana to shift to Burhanpur. Unfortunately, we have not been able to inform the Shahzada about this too.'

'I will meet him today and I am sure he would not neglect his duties. Don't worry. Allah is benevolent.'

৵৽৽ ৶৽

Dilras Banu's worries were resolved in an unexpected manner.

Hira's hands had been decorated with henna by one of the maids. She got up early to wash the henna off and asked Anwar to pour water from the silver container. Hira, washing her delicate fingers, looked up when she found Anwar's attention wavering. She asked, '*Anwar miyan, kya baat hai?*'

'Nothing, Baiji. I am fine.'

Hira noticed Anwar was trying to hide something in the pocket of his kurta. She confronted him saying, 'Anwar, what is it that you are hiding?'

'Nothing, Baiji. There is nothing.'

Hira insisted. 'Anwar, please show me what it is.'

Anwar reluctantly put his hand forward holding a letter.

'Baiji, I am scared. If found out, I will be thrown out of this place.'

'What is it?'

'I was given this by Sheikh Sadullah to be handed over to Huzoor the first thing in the morning.'

Hira took the letter from him. There was a message written in bold Persian characters. She did not know how to read the script. Folding the letter she said, 'Let it be with me.'

'But Sadullah Sahab ....'

'I will take care of it, don't worry. If he asks, tell him that you have handed over the letter to Huzoor.'

'Shamim!' Hira called out to the daroga.

Shamim came in hurriedly. 'Did you call for me, Begum Sahiba?'

'Begum Sahiba? Since when did this Hira become a begum, Shamim?'

She said, 'That is the custom of the zenankhana, Baiji. One enters as an ordinary bai and is then made a begum. I have been instructed to call you Begum Sahiba.'

'Shamim, can you read Persian?'

'Yes, of course. I wouldn't be made a daroga if I didn't know how to read and write.'

Hira held out the letter, 'Read this out to me. Remember! You should not mention this to anyone.'

Shamim's eyes scanned the letter and putting a finger on her lips exclaimed, '*Ya Allah!* This is a letter from the Mushrif. It is a request to the Shahzada to take time out of the zenankhana and look into the affairs of the state.'

'Are you saying he does not look into the matters?'

'Begum Sahiba, it has been months. It is my duty to present the letters to him. The pile of documents awaiting his attention has now grown to such a height that it may touch the ceiling soon. There is chaos outside.'

'Didn't you try to warn him?'

'All attempts have fallen on deaf ears. He is so engrossed in you that he does not bother to know the state of affairs outside. How do you expect him to look into the matters of the subedari?'

At that moment Anwar announced the arrival of the Shahzada, and Shamim made a hurried exit.

'I am told your hands have been decorated beautifully. Show me,' Aurangzeb said, entering the room.

Hira, hiding her face with her hands said, 'I will; but you have to agree to a condition of mine.'

'Do I ever refuse anything?'

'I want you to teach me to write the Persian script.'

'What do you want to learn Persian for?'

'Now don't go back on your words. You have made a promise. Don't you carry out all your official duties in Persian?'

'My subedari is standing right here. And she is very proficient in the language she should be proficient in. No one can beat her in that.'

'May I know what language Huzoor feels he does not know well enough?' Hira teased Aurangzeb, hiding her hands behind her back.

'It is the language of love. You have mastered the art and taught this thirty-five-year-old man a little bit of it. You are my ustad here. What would you do, learning the dry Persian script?'

'I know you are trying to dissuade me. But don't think that I will give up. I am determined to learn.'

Aurangzeb looked at Anwar, standing at the entrance. 'Anwar, get a bottle of ink, quill and paper.'

Aurangzeb was curious to know the reason behind Hira's new-found desire to learn the script. Anwar came in with the things ordered. Sitting next to Hira, Aurangzeb dipped the quill into the ink and wrote on the paper saying, 'Aleph'. He then drew the next alphabet, 'Be'.

'Uh, huh,' Hira said, making a face. 'I don't want these letters or this paper.'

'How will I teach you then?'

Hira showed the papers she had been holding in her hand. Aurangzeb scanned the paper quickly and with rising temper said, 'I wonder who has dared present these to you when I have left explicit instructions not to allow any official work here.' Turning towards the door he shouted, 'Shamim!'

Hira tried stopping Aurangzeb. 'There is no need to call her.' To divert his attention she said, thrusting forth her palms, 'Don't you want to see my henna?'

Aurangzeb caressed her palms. 'I wonder who has had the temerity to put such dry official papers in these lovely, soft hands. I need to ask Shamim.'

'There is no need to ask her. I will tell you. I am told Huzoor has not stepped out of this mahal for months now. The work of the entire subedari is at standstill in your absence.'

'I don't care.'

'Huzoor, you cannot say so. You have your duties as a Shahzada and as subedar of the Deccan.'

'I don't agree. My only duty is to be with you. That's all!'

'Huzoor, think about me.'

Pulling her towards him, he hugged her tightly and said, 'Whom else will I think of?'

Hira rested her head on Aurangzeb's shoulders. She whispered, 'I have no doubt about that. But do you know what the people in Burhanpur will say? That the Shahzada is under the influence of a mere laundi and has forgotten his duties.'

'I dare anyone to say that while I am alive.'

'I beg of you to think of what I said with a cool head.'

'Cool head?' Aurangzeb shouted. 'Hira, if I am not going to get peace in your arms where else will I get? It is in these arms that I wish to say my last prayers to Allah …'

Hira put her fingers on his lips stopping him in mid-sentence. 'What makes Huzoor say such things? If someone has to go then let that be Hira. Huzoor is needed to take care of the subedari. There are hundreds of officials waiting for your command.'

It was after a lot of persuasion from Hira that Aurangzeb finally relented. Getting up, he clapped twice and, when Shamim came in, said, 'Convey my message to Sheikh Sadullah that I will be ready to receive the *shahi firman* in the evening at my quarters. Ask him to get other important papers too. I will have a look at them.

Shamim could not believe her ears and stared at Aurangzeb for a few moments. Recovering quickly, she saluted and took a few steps back to exit.

৵৫ ৯৶

Shaista Khan arrived in Burhanpur escorting the zenankhana. The arrangements for their stay were being supervised by Shamim. It had been a fortnight since they had arrived, but Aurangzeb had not met or called upon them. Each day, after finishing his official work, he would go to Hira's quarters for meals and rest. The Irani Begum, tired of waiting for Aurangzeb to call, summoned Shamim. Dilras Banu, an Iranian beauty, thirty-two years of age, sat lost in thought resting her cheeks on her palms. She looked striking despite wearing a simple flowing kurta with a blue salwar. A satin dupatta completed the attire. A tray with exotic Persian perfumes and another with betel leaves was placed on either side of the sitting arrangement. A framed portrait stood in one corner.

Shamim entered adjusting her dupatta on her head. Looking at her with her kohl-lined eyes, Dilras Banu made a face, 'Shamim, it has been two weeks since our arrival here. The Shahzada has not had time to visit us. Is he so busy at work these days?'

Shamim bowed before answering, 'Begum Sahiba, I have ensured that your message is conveyed to him each day before he retires.'

'Then why is he ignoring us?'

'When I tried talking about you, he gave me such a cold stare that I dared not raise the topic again.'

Shamim looked at Dilras Banu. She knew her nature. The tears gathering in her eyes could not be held any more and flowed freely down her cheeks. She turned her face to avoid Shamim's gaze.

'Begum Sahiba, please don't take this to heart. I am sure he will visit you shortly,' Shamim said, a little embarrassed at the begum's show of emotions.

'Lies! All lies! This Banu has spent enough time in the Mughal zenankhana to know that is not true.'

'Begum Sahiba should be patient.'

Wiping her tears with the edge of her dupatta, Banu said, 'Shamim, I need to get used to it. After all, everyone knows how much the Shahzada loves me!'

'Begum Sahiba, I have spent enough time in the Mughal zenankhana to know that nothing is permanent. Even the mighty sun has to come down to touch the horizon. Please have patience.'

'Patience?' Banu screamed. 'You may have spent your lifetime here, but I know these uncouth Mughals far too well to get carried away …'

'Begum Sahiba!' Shamim interrupted her.

'Let me speak! I mean what I say. The Mughals are an uncultured and an uncouth race. They have no interest in the finer things of life. All they know is to fight wars. And for that they need their heirs. That is the only reason they spend time in their zenankhana.'

'Begum Sahiba, no one has insulted the Mughals so. As a daroga of the zenankhana, it is my duty to ensure protocol and I cannot allow such language in my presence.'

'Let me speak, Shamim. My father Shahnawaz Khan was an official in the Mughal court. It is through him we used to hear of the customs of Iran and how the menfolk there treat their women with respect. I have spent sixteen years in this zenankhana, but I am yet to hear the Shahzada speak a few words of love.' Two large teardrops flowed down Dilras Banu's cheeks.

Shamim said, 'Begum Sahiba, I agree the Irani customs may have
been different from those of the Mughals. But you make it a point to
rub it in each time you meet the Shahzada, thus distancing him further.'

Banu snapped: 'My fault is that I have given birth to two daughters
and not sons. That is all!' The tears were flowing unabashedly now.

'Begum Sahiba, don't be disappointed. You may have two daughters
but that does not stop you from having a male child.'

'It is not me but the Shahzada who is disappointed. Look at my
two daughters, Zebunissa and Zeenat! They are such beauties that
any father would have been proud of them. But all the Shahzada did
was to promptly go and marry that Kashmiri princess. She was lucky
to give birth to two boys thus isolating me further. Shamim, I have
tolerated enough. I won't do so any more.'

'Please don't do anything to undermine your position. Womenfolk
have to weave their way into men's hearts with sweet words. If you
insult him, he will further distance himself.'

'I don't care,' Banu said, her voice rising with temper. 'Why should
I tolerate such insults day after day?'

At that moment, two girls entered the room. The older girl was a
fifteen-year-old beauty, her fair skin glowing with the blush of youth,
the younger was just ten years old. They both touched their palms to
their foreheads in a quick salaam before hugging Banu. 'Ammi Jaan,
Ammi Jaan!'

Caressing their backs Banu asked, 'Zeb, Zeenat! Where were you
two since morning?'

The elder, Zebunissa, moved out of her mother's embrace and
knelt in front of her. Zeenat continued to sit on her mother's lap with
her arm around her neck as she rested her head on Banu's shoulder.
Zebunissa looked like a Persian goddess, a shade more beautiful than
her mother. She was a rose in bloom. Her long tresses flowed over her
shoulders and touched the carpet on the floor.

Seeing her sister sitting on her mother's lap, she said in mock
anger, 'Zeenat, don't trouble mother by sitting on her lap. It is not
good manners.'

Zeenat looked at her mother and said, 'Do you object?'

Kissing her cheeks Banu said, 'Dear, how can there be any troubles when you are around?'

'Ammi Jaan, don't encourage this behaviour. She is getting pampered by the day. Get up, Zeenat. Come and sit here,' Zebunissa said, patting the carpet.

Looking at her mother Zeenat said, 'I do know how to behave, but why can't I sit on your lap for a change?'

Dilras Banu smiled ironically. 'It is not for me to decide protocol, nor do I rule the zenankhana.' Looking at Shamim she said, 'It is for Shamim to decide all this. I follow whatever she says.'

Shamim replied in a low voice, 'If they are not taught etiquette at the right age, it will become very difficult for them later.'

Ignoring Shamim's comment, Zebunissa asked her mother, 'Ammi, can you guess where we were since morning?'

'Playing near the fountains, I suppose; or fighting with each other.'

'No. You can't guess.'

'Then why don't you tell me?'

Zebunissa showed a piece of paper which she had been clutching all the while. 'We were busy writing *shayari* since morning.'

'Poetry? *Ya Allah!* What will Shamim say hearing such words in the Mughal zenankhana?' She said throwing a snide glance at Shamim.

'Who am I to stop the Begum Sahiba from doing what she feels like?'

Turning to the girls Banu said, 'Show me what you have written.'

'We intend to show it to both you and Abba Jaan together.'

Banu's voice took on a serious tone hearing Aurangzeb's name, 'You may then have to wait for a lifetime.'

'Ammi Jaan, we have been here for weeks now. When are we going to meet Abba Jaan? We have so many things to tell him.'

Pointing towards Shamim, Dilras Banu said, 'Ask her. She is the one who will know.' Suddenly an idea struck her. She said, 'Shamim, why don't you tell the Shahzada to visit us at least for the sake of his daughters if not me?'

'As you wish, Begum Sahiba. I shall convey the message today itself.'

Zeenat spotted a portrait wrapped in a thin cloth. She opened it, and put her fingers to her lips in excitement, 'Waah! What a beautiful portrait? Whose is it?'

Shamim hurriedly covered the portrait and pushed Zeenat gently away. 'Zeenat beti, this is not for young ones to look at.'

Zebunissa had, in the meanwhile, caught a glimpse of the portrait. She asked, 'Ammi Jaan, is it not a picture of Abba Jaan's new wife?'

'Don't speak so casually,' Shamim scolded her.

'There is no point in reprimanding her, Shamim. After all it is common news known even to the maids and the laundis in the zenankhana. Zeb is not a kid any more. Anyway, I have seen the portrait. You may take it away now.'

Banu sat down with a deep sigh. Caressing the backs of her daughters, she said, 'Zeb, Zeenat! I am reconciled to my life in this zenankhana. I wonder if I would have the good fortune to see some happiness in your lives.'

୬୧ ୧ୠ

Nawab Bai, Aurangzeb's Rajput begum, carefully applied sindoor looking at her face in the mirror.

Her maid Nargis, watching from a distance, remarked, 'Baiji, you know the Shahzada does not like you putting sindoor in your hair as per the Hindu traditions. Yet you insist on doing so.'

The Kashmiri beauty turned to face her maid. Her pride was visible when she spoke. 'Nargis, my father had explicitly stated this at the time of marriage that I will be allowed to follow our traditions.'

'But you know it upsets Huzoor.'

'For that matter, he is upset with the Irani begum too.'

'But you know the reason.'

'Yes, he is upset because she has given him two daughters. I have given birth to two sons, yet he is upset. I am fed up.'

'I suggested what I felt was right. You know better,' Nargis said, as she stepped out of the room.

Nawab Bai spent the better part of the next hour in front of the mirror, admiring the diamonds adorning her ears, neck, hair and nose. She sat on her swing, the tinkle of the golden bells attached to the bars matching the sound of her anklets. She was humming a song when the khoja announced the arrival of her sons. Soon, fourteen-year-old Sultan and ten-year-old Muazzam walked in and bent in an elaborate salute with their hands almost touching the floor. Nawab Bai admired her sons; the older one was a spitting image of his father.

Pulling Sultan closer to her she asked, 'I hear you are already busy with the work of the subedari. Is that true?'

'Yes, Baiji. I had to be in the court at Agra for two hours a day. It has become a habit now.'

'What is the news from the Agra court?'

'Don't ask me. You will not be happy hearing it.'

'Sultan, I have not been happy ever since I have come into this Mughal zenankhana. You can tell me.'

'I am surprised to hear that, Baiji. I thought you were very happy here.'

'Sultan, you are grown up now. I can share my feelings openly. Anyway, forget about my problems. Tell me what the Badshah was saying.'

'Baiji, it is painful for you to hear that. I was insulted every day in the court in front of other officials. He would insult Abba Jaan in his absence.'

'Did you tell your Abba Jaan about this?'

'Yes, I did tell him when I met him.'

'And what did he say?'

Sultan smiled. 'Does he ever react? When I told him, I saw him curling his fists and pursing his lips for a brief moment. But he was otherwise his usual self. I could not gauge his feelings. He then changed the topic and asked me about some of the work related to the subedari.'

'Did your Abba Jaan not comment on the gossip which is being heard from the havelis of the amirs in Agra?'

Sultan looked around and then asked, 'How do you know of it?'

'Sultan, I was not sitting twiddling my thumbs in Agra. I am aware of the talk going around. I fear there is some conspiracy being hatched and it may happen sooner than later.'

Nawab Bai was worried. She asked her younger son to leave and then, sitting close to Sultan, said, 'Your Abba Jaan is surely aware of the goings-on and is not the one to sit idly. I fear we are going to witness some usurping soon.'

'The rumours in Agra were flying thick and fast, but on coming here, I was surprised that Abba Jaan is spending so much time in the new mahal ...'

'Sultan, you should not be saying these things.'

'Ammi Jaan, isn't there a limit to a person's carelessness?'

'You are still a child, Sultan. You don't know your father. He is most alert when he looks careless.'

The mother and son sat chatting for a long while.

༺ এ ৩৯ ༻

Aurangzeb's uncle Shaista Khan, after escorting the zenankhana to Burhanpur, stayed back for a month before returning to take charge of his subedari at Malwa. The uncle and nephew spent many a night in discussions that no one else was privy to.

The rains had abated. Just before the onset of winter, the trumpets announced the departure of the cantonment to Aurangabad. The caravan lumbered along with all the equipment and soldiers and reached its destination in two months. The city of Aurangabad, under the supervision of Diwan Murshid Quli Khan, had readied itself to welcome their subedar. Palaces had been built for the royals while havelis and other official residences had been erected for the amaldars and amirs, the high ranking administrators of the Mughal Empire. An artificial lake had been dug near Hursool to supply water. Another two months passed before the cantonment was finally in shape.

Winter had arrived and official work picked up pace. One day, as Aurangzeb sat in his office perusing some papers, Sheikh Sadullah came in with four maulvis. Aurangzeb gave them a sidelong glance.

They wore Mughal-style turbans and full beards and carried their rosaries. Aurangzeb raised an eyebrow at Diwan Murshid Quli Khan. The diwan waited for Sheikh Sadullah to introduce them.

'These poor souls reside at the border of our subah spending their lives in the study of the Quran. Of late, they are being troubled by some rebellious mansabdars from Adil Shah's territory. Our thanedar had complained to Adil Shah at Bijapur but to no avail.'

'Maulviji, tell me your problems.'

'Subhan Allah! What can we say! We are not able to perform our religious duties or read the Quran in peace.'

'But why so? You were not troubled earlier? What is our thanedar doing?'

'What can the poor fellow do when he has no support from the local ryots? The rebellious amaldars attack us and they have managed to convince the ryots to act against us too.'

Aurangzeb narrowed his eyes and asked, 'I am sure there must be a reason for them to revolt against the establishment. You must have done something to irk them.'

'Huzoor, we have done nothing of the kind.'

'Think about it. Maybe you usurped the property of the ryots by force. Or insulted their womenfolk ...' Aurangzeb stopped mid-sentence and waited for their reaction.

Sheikh Sadullah came in support of the maulvis. 'Huzoor, the ryots are all kafirs. It is possible that a minor transgression may have been committed. But that does not give the amaldars the right to trouble the maulvis.'

Aurangzeb's face was inscrutable. He said, 'I agree. We will not tolerate any such acts from the kafirs. But I am not in favour of troubling them without rhyme or reason.'

Murshid Quli Khan interrupted, 'Huzoor, the ryots are refusing to pay their taxes under the influence of the amaldars. We cannot allow that. These Marathas are inciting these ryots.'

'Marathas? Who are these people?'

'They are the landlords in the Deccan.'

'But are they not under Adil Shah's rule?'

Sadullah said, 'Yes, Huzoor. We need to warn Adil Shah. If he cannot keep the Marathas in check it will be difficult for us to sit quiet and tolerate these acts.'

Aurangzeb closed his eyes in contemplation. He remembered Danishmand Khan's words: 'We need not worry about money when we have Golconda and Bijapur as our neighbours.' Aurangzeb realized an opportunity had presented itself. He said, keeping his voice calm as before, 'Send a strongly worded letter to Adil Shah.'

Sadullah cleared his throat and said, 'If Huzoor may permit me ...'

'Please speak your mind freely, Sadullah.'

'Huzoor, such warnings have been issued from the Mughal court at Agra, but Adil Shah pleads his helplessness in controlling the errant Marathas. He has expressed this many times.'

'Oh, I see! Then inform him that if he cannot keep the Marathas in check, he may soon lose control over his territory.' Turning to Diwan Murshid Quli Khan he said, 'Diwan, I cannot allow the revenue targets falling short. We need to collect the rents without any laxity. Send a strong word to the amaldars – they are to collect the taxes at any cost. If the ryots refuse, they should not hesitate to behead the offenders. Let the maulvis know that while the Deccan is being ruled by Muhi-ud-Din Muhammad Aurangzeb they have nothing to fear. The followers of Islam are safe.'

⁌ ⁍

Tartar warrior women, with unsheathed swords, had been specially brought in for the personal safety of Aurangzeb and his begums in the zenankhana. Shamim's instructions were to not allow even the khojas near the quarters when the Shahzada was visiting one of his begums.

It was an hour before dawn. The candles in the chandeliers had long burnt out. A lone lamp burning on a tall pillar lit the room with faint light. Hira Bai and Aurangzeb were in deep slumber.

It was time for the morning prayers. Aurangzeb gently removed Hira's hand from his chest as he heard the call of the muezzin from the nearby mosque, but did not get up. He looked at the sleeping beauty lying next to him in her crumpled satin kurta and salwar. Her red lips trembled as she murmured in her sleep, lost in her dream. For a moment Aurangzeb dismissed the idea of his namaz, tempted by the thought of kissing those luscious lips. At that moment he noticed her lips contort into a scream. Aurangzeb hugged her tight asking, 'Hira, my dear! Janeman, what happened?'

Hira opened her eyes. She blinked a few times trying to come back to reality. Beads of sweat had gathered at her brow. Putting her head on his shoulder she started sobbing uncontrollably.

Aurangzeb patted her back. 'Hira, what is the matter? What happened?'

Looking up at Aurangzeb, she said, 'Am I dreaming of being in Huzoor's arms or is the dream I saw real?'

'What did you dream? Hira, wake up! You have nothing to fear when I am around.'

Hira's chest was pounding loudly. Wiping her tears, she gently touched Aurangzeb all over, trying to reassure herself of his presence. 'Shahzada, are you really here?'

'Yes! I am here and will be. Now, tell me what you saw in your dream.'

Hira looked into his eyes and said, 'Would Huzoor laugh at me if I tell?'

'I won't. I promise.'

'I was sleeping alone in my room when two women entered all of a sudden. They had bloodshot eyes, their hair untied. They clutched my throat and started strangling me. I screamed in fear, only to wake up and find myself in your arms.'

Aurangzeb smiled and pulling her into his embrace said, 'Allah's ways are strange!'

'Why do you say that?'

'Alongwith an exquisite body and a face, he has given you a timid heart.'

'There is always some hidden message behind these dreams. They are often harbingers of things to come.'

When Aurangzeb came to Hira's quarters to have his meals at noon, he found her still preoccupied with the terrifying dream. 'I want Huzoor to agree to a request of mine,' she said, while preparing a paan for him,

Taking her hand into his he said, 'These eyes have the capacity to make anyone their slave. How can I resist anything they ask for?'

'Now don't try to find an excuse. I want your stamp of approval.'

Kissing her on her cheeks he said, 'Tell me where all you need me to put my stamp of approval.'

Hira made a fuss of pushing him away gently and said, 'I know Huzoor has a habit of trying to change the topic under discussion. I want Huzoor to listen to me with all attention.'

'I am all ears, dear!'

'I believe one should pray to the Lord when in danger.'

'I read my namaz five times a day. You too should pray to the Lord, if you feel so.'

'Yes, that is what I want to do,' Hira said excitedly. 'There is a Mahadev temple at Verul. I wish to perform an abhishek there.'

'What is an abhishek? Is it some form of idol worship?'

'It is a religious ceremony where the idol is washed with the waters from the sacred rivers.'

'Oh, I remember now! I have heard my brother Darabhai discuss this with the Hindu priests.'

'I suppose I have Huzoor's permission then?'

'Hira, you are my begum now. Should you not give up these practices followed by the kafirs?'

Hira was hurt at the suggestion. She turned her face away.

'Oh dear! Don't be upset!'

'So all the talk about your promises was just to please me?'

'I didn't say that. Hira, you know ...'

'You like Hira but not her religion.'

Aurangzeb let out a deep sigh. He said, trying to avoid her questioning eyes, 'Dear, all I can think of is you when I am here. There is no other thought.'

'Lies!'

'Tell me what will convince you that I mean it.'

'I don't want you to prove your love. Promise me one thing,' she said snuggling close to Aurangzeb. 'I want you to be there with me when I perform the abhishek.'

'*Uff!*' Aurangzeb erupted, letting out his frustration. He moved away a bit, but seeing her hurt face, he held her palm and caressed it.

Hira had tears in her eyes. 'If it is much of a trouble for Huzoor, he can forget the idea. I will not insist.'

Aurangzeb wanted to argue with her and convince her to drop her religious ideas, but his heart was not in a mood to entertain such thoughts. Her beauty was too difficult to resist. Each part of her body, from her fair forehead to her painted toes, mesmerized him. Holding her tight, he uttered, 'My dear!'

The tears, waiting to burst, now flowed freely down Hira's cheeks. Aurangzeb showered her with kisses saying, 'Dear, your eyes are enough to make one your slave. Don't make me drink these drops of poison. The arrows of passion have struck deep in my heart. I am beyond discerning what is right or wrong. Whatever you say, I agree. I agree; a hundred times!'

᪣᪣ ᪣᪣

Mahashivaratri day was a fortnight away. Shahzada's new begum Hira Bai, was to perfom the abhishek at the temple of Grishneshwar at Verul that day. The orders to the thanedar at Verul had been issued by Sheikh Sadullah. A large number of devotees were expected and all arrangements were made to ensure the safety of the royal couple. The news that Aurangzeb himself was attending the function spread like wildfire. *A zealot Musalman to enter a kafir temple!* The maulvis found it difficult to believe and dismissed it as mere gossip, but soon the news of the security measures being taken forced them to change their mind. It was discomfiting for the ulemas. They had never expected such behaviour from Aurangzeb. There was no scope for them to express their feelings openly for they knew that every word uttered would be promptly reported back to the Shahzada. His network of spies was well known! After all, the fakirs, dervishes and the maulvis lived on the largesse provided by the Shahzada and could not afford to speak against him. But such an act of blasphemy wherein their subedar was to enter a kafir's temple and participate in idol worship was not easy to digest. They suffered silently.

A different problem presented itself within a few days. Aurangzeb sat in his office scrutinizing some papers when Sheikh Sadullah came in with a request.

'Huzoor, some pandits from the Verul temple have been arrested. They are here to plead their case. If you permit, I will present them to you.'

Aurangzeb, hearing the name Verul, was instantly alert, but did not show any signs of concern. He casually waved his hand asking Sadullah to usher them in. 'I have some time before we take a break for the evening namaz. Let them in.'

Four Brahmins, tied in chains, were marched in. They wore simple dhotis with an angavastram draped around their shoulders. Their foreheads were smeared with three horizontal lines of ash depicting their Shaiva faith. Their hair, with a small knot at the top, flowed down to their shoulders. The middle-aged, slightly portly foursome had a streak of arrogance that Sadullah noticed as he presented them to Aurangzeb. 'These are the Brahmins from the temple at Verul.'

'What crime have they committed?' Aurangzeb asked, looking at them while he directed the question to Sadullah.

'They were planning to lock the temple and run away when they came to know of Shahzada's proposed visit.'

'What is their crime?'

Sadullah licked his lips nervously: 'We cannot allow such open revolt in Shahzada's territory.'

Aurangzeb nodded his head in the direction of the ulemas in attendance, ready for their views on any religious consultations. 'Please consult the Quran and the Hadis and tell me what crimes these kafirs have committed.'

The ulemas sat telling their rosary beads. One of the Brahmins said, 'Shahzada, our crimes cannot be found in these books. We will tell you what crimes we are being accused of.'

'*Khamosh!*' Sadullah shouted.

Aurangzeb lifted his forefinger indicating Sadullah to stop. 'Let the men speak.'

'The fact that we are alive in your reign is a crime in itself. What bigger crime can we think of?'

The amaldars in attendance were incensed. The ulemas continued to look at the Brahmins.

Aurangzeb betrayed no emotion, 'You have been brought here to seek justice. If you don't elaborate on your crimes, how can you expect any justice?'

'We have nothing to say,' the Brahmin continued. 'The temple is ours and we perform the rites as per religious protocol. If the temple is going to be desecrated by the visit of the Mughal subedar's begum we would rather shut the doors and go away. If that is the crime, so be it.'

'*Tauba, tauba!*' The ulemas uttered. 'These idiots do not understand that the subedar himself has condescended to visit the temple thus increasing its prestige.'

Aurangzeb raised his left hand indicating the ulemas to keep quiet. He continued, 'Panditji, do you mean to say the visit of our begum would desecrate your temple?'

'Yes, that is precisely what we mean.'

'You enjoy your freedom thanks to my rule and yet you hold your views?'

'Subedar, the only person who rules us is the Lord above. He is the one who takes care of everyone, whether the subedar or mere mortals like us.'

'But it is my kingdom here on this earth.'

'We have no comments.'

'Don't you respect the Badshah?'

'Yes! We consider the emperor an avatar of Lord Vishnu himself.'

A faint smile flickered across Aurangzeb's face. 'I am that emperor's son.'

'We agree. The best we can do is offer the prasad for you to partake. But we cannot allow you or your begum to enter the temple and desecrate it. We have been insulted for no fault of ours. We were handcuffed and dragged all the way. The only way the begum can enter the temple is over our dead bodies.'

'Panditji, are you planning to fight us?'

'If we had such strength, we would not have stood here with our heads bowed.'

Sadullah interrupted, 'I beg your pardon, Huzoor, but I have information that these people have support of some of the zamindars from Bijapur. They would not have had such courage otherwise.'

'Present those zamindars here,' Aurangzeb ordered.

'We got the information that they ran away a few days back towards Chakan.'

'Oh, I see! Sadullah, ask these Brahmins if they would be willing to change their stand if we give a large donation to the temple.'

'Subhan Allah!' The ulemas erupted in unison. 'Subedar, this is not possible. The holy books do not permit such things.'

'I will deal with that later. Sadullah, ask them.'

'I can hear you clearly. You need not ask him to ask us,' the Brahmin retorted. 'We cannot allow the temple to be desecrated. Any amount of money won't change our stand.'

Aurangzeb leaned back against a pillow and closed his eyes in contemplation. No one had dared insult the subedar in such a fashion before. The people in attendance waited with bated breath. Opening his eyes after a while Aurangzeb said, 'Panditji, I pardon your crimes. If you believe that our begum's visit to your temple would despoil it, I too will not come there. This Shahzada was planning to come with his head bowed. Now, it is the pillars of the temple that will have to bend.'

He mumbled, 'La ilahi illilah Muhammad rasool lillilah.'

༄ৎ ৎ঒

Dilras Banu had not accompanied Aurangzeb to Aurangabad as she was pregnant. She had stayed back at Burhanpur in the residence of Malika Banu. Other than Hira Bai, Nawab Bai was the only begum in Aurangzeb's zenankhana. Aurangzeb was on his way for his usual afternoon siesta to Hira Bai's quarters when Shamim came forward and bending low in salute said, 'I have a message from the Rajput begum. If the Huzoor can spare a little time, he is requested there.'

Aurangzeb ignored her request and was about to enter Hira Bai's quarters when Shamim repeated, 'What shall I tell Begum Sahiba then?'

Aurangzeb paused for a moment. He said, 'Fine. I will visit her right away.'

Aurangzeb entered Nawab Bai's quarters. She got up from the bed to bend in salute.

'It is my great privilege to have the Shahzada visit me today.'

Aurangzeb sat down on the bed and, sniffing a bunch of flowers kept in a tray nearby said, 'Begum, there is no need to be sarcastic.'

'Has the Shahzada bothered to look at me ever since the new begum came? Please pardon me if I may have blurted out something inadvertently.'

'You called for me. What is it about?'

'If Shahzada has a few moments, I would like to say something.'

Aurangzeb was restless to go. He was tempted to make a snide remark but checked himself. 'I have a lot of time. Tell me what you have in mind.'

'Your son Sultan is grown up now. I am worried.'

'What about?'

'He is going to turn fifteen. I am sure the Shahzada has thought of his marriage.'

'I have already fixed his marriage.'

'With whom, if I may?'

'What do you think of my elder brother Shuja's daughter Gulrukh Banu?'

'Banu is a nice girl. But is she agreeable to the marriage?'

'I have not asked yet. But the alliance was proposed by my sister Jahanara Begum in Agra.'

Aurangzeb could see traces of irritation on Nawab Bai's face on hearing his sister's name. He knew they did not get along. To gauge her reaction he asked, 'Did you have anyone else in mind?'

'I suggest we get one begum for him as per your choice and another as per mine,' Nawab Bai said, fiddling with her dupatta.

'Tell me your choice.'

'Huzoor's sister is married to Jaswant Singh of Jodhpur. I am told his daughter will be a suitable bride for Sultan.'

It was a tradition since Akbar's time to marry Rajput princesses. It was Shah Jahan who had started a reverse trend when he married his daughter from a Rajput begum to Raja Jaswant Singh of Marwar. It had been a great political alliance and had succeeded in getting the support of the entire Rajputana. Aurangzeb and many orthodox maulvis had not approved of such alliances. Nawab Bai's reference to the marriage did not go down well with Aurangzeb. He frowned saying, 'Begum, I am surprised you are suggesting something so ridiculous.'

'What is so ridiculous about it? Marriage to Jaswant Singh's daughter would get the Rajputs on your side. Is that not a great benefit?'

'I suggest Begum Sahiba keep her political views to herself. I am not going to get my older son married to these kafirs for such petty politics.'

'Kafirs?' Nawab Bai asked, raising her voice.

'What else do I call Jaswant Singh then? Begum, I suggest you maintain the protocol in the zenankhana and not raise your voice.'

'Please pardon me,' Nawab Bai said, lowering her voice. 'I too am a kafir, for that matter. Why did Huzoor marry me?'

'That was because the Badshah was insistent. That's all!' Aurangzeb stood up turning his face away. Nawab Bai did not have the courage to confront him further.

Pressing his forehead with his palm Aurangzeb said, 'I don't know what crimes I committed to be punished thus. The Irani begum, who should have given birth to my sons, has given me two daughters and the Rajput begum, who need not have had any children, is the mother of both my sons!'

He had hit her where it hurt the most. Clutching her dupatta in her palms she said, 'Huzoor, I don't know what punishment Allah will mete out, but I can surely tell you about the torture carried out by humans.'

'Begum!' Aurangzeb exclaimed.

'Huzoor, I wait from dusk to dawn to hear a few words of love. I sit at the window waiting to hear your footsteps, but all I can hear are words like *kafir* and *kambhakt*. I am pained to hear your wish that the Irani begum should have borne you sons. You support her despite having got nothing but insults from her when she puts the Mughals down against her Iranian superiority.'

'Enough! I don't want to hear any more. I want you to know that you are my begum thanks to the alliance made by Ala Hazrat. Unfortunately, you are the mother of my two sons. You have a place in this zenankhana and you have a right to stay here. Beyond this, don't expect any more favours from me.'

Tears flowed freely down Nawab Bai's cheeks. 'It would have been better for Huzoor to have poisoned me than making me hear such harsh words. If the Shahzada himself treats his begum in such fashion, what can I expect from others?'

'I have clearly told you that you have your right to stay in this zenankhana. Why are you worried?'

'You may not be aware of your relatives waiting to insult me. Your behaviour would encourage them further.'

Aurangzeb turned to face her. He said, 'Begum, I may not love you, but I will not allow anyone to insult my zenankhana. Whom are you referring to?'

'Your cousin Bahadur Khan!'

Aurangzeb raised his eyebrows in surprise. 'Begum, why have you not mentioned this to me earlier?'

'Has Huzoor ever given me time? Years go by before I get a chance to see you. With whom shall I share my insults and my grievances?'

Aurangzeb could not believe someone would dare transgress his zenankhana. He asked, 'When was this? And where?'

'It was in Agra when you were in Kandahar on a campaign. The Irani begum had accompanied you. Bahadur Khan took the liberty to enter the zenankhana one evening.'

'He came into your quarters? That is impossible! What about the servants and the guards?'

'The guards are for outsiders. What can they do when your own milk brother walks in? The daroga simply announced his presence from the other side of the screen.'

'Uff!' Aurangzeb slapped his forehead with his palms in disgust. 'What an insult! Begum, why did anyone not tell me earlier?'

'Who will tell you? Only Bahadur Khan and I know of it. I confronted him and asked him to leave immediately, but I had to bear the cross silently all this while.'

Aurangzeb was silent for a long time. Avoiding her gaze, he continued to look outside the window.

⋇⋇⋇

Aurangabad was witnessing unprecedented activity. After all, the Shahzada himself had now taken charge as the subedar. Havelis had come up as residences for the officials. The mosques, dargahs and serais were overflowing with fakirs and dervishes. The bazaars were stocked with all kinds of imported items. The nautch girls and the dancing bars were busy till the wee hours. Love was in the air and the havelis of the amirs were filled with fun and frolic each night. Aurangabad, with its newly found prosperity, glowed like royal princess.

Aurangzeb stepped out of the newly built Jama Masjid after his Friday evening prayers. He descended the steps distributing alms to the beggars gathered there. Sadullah, walking alongside him, suggested, 'Shahigunj's bazaar has been beautifully done up. If the Huzoor so wishes, we can take a detour through the bazaar. It will give you an opportunity to see the markets too.'

Aurangzeb nodded in acknowledgement. The royal elephant

moved in the direction of the bazaar while the slaves, khojas and foot soldiers cleared the crowds ahead. Senior officials, astride pure-bred Arabian steeds followed. They were accompanied by almost two hundred armed foot soldiers led by the city kotwal. When they reached Shahigunj, a group of fifty aulias and dervishes blocked the road despite the khojas trying to push them away. Seeing the commotion, the kotwal rushed towards them waving his unsheathed sword.

Aurangzeb raised a hand indicating the kotwal to stop. He asked Sadullah, who was astride a horse behind the royal elephant, 'Find out what the fakirs want. If they are expecting some alms, inform the treasury office to take care of it.'

The fakirs presented themselves bending down on their knees. Putting their hands together and pointing skyward they said, '*E Khuda ke bande*, protector of the poor! Are you aware of the atrocities being committed in your reign? We spend all our time reading the holy books, yet your amaldars harass us.'

There was commotion all over the street. The dervishes and fakirs, their heads covered with a coloured cloth and eyes lined with kohl, had gathered around shouting, '*Insaaf, Insaaf!*'

Aurangzeb indicated to the mahout. The elephant sat down. Pointing at the leader of the fakirs he asked, 'What is your problem? Who is troubling you?'

'Huzoor-e-Ala, it is your amaldars.'

'What exactly have they done?'

'Insulting Huzoor is akin to insulting the Muhammad Paigambar himself. We cannot tolerate that.'

'Please elaborate.'

'Huzoor, when we heard that the Brahmins at the temple at Verul refused to allow Begum Sahiba to enter the temple, we had planned to destroy ...'

Aurangzeb raised his hand to interrupt. 'What? That too without my permission?'

'Why do we need any permission for such a noble act? After all, the Quran Sharif states that Islam is the world religion. By destroying all such symbols of other religions we are following the Paigambar's diktat.'

'What happened then?'

'We were thrashed by the thanedar at Verul and ordered to leave. We have come here with the hope for justice. After all, if Muslims are not treated well under your rule where else will they get justice?'

'I am the subedar of the Deccan. And I cannot allow any such actions on your part without explicit permission from me.'

'But Huzoor, this is a religious matter.'

'That too needs my permission.'

'If we don't have Huzoor's permission we are willing to lay down and get crushed to death by your elephant. Let the world know that despite the Delhi Durbar being ruled by a Muslim Badshah and his Shahzada being the subedar of the Deccan, the fakirs and dervishes do not have the liberty to perform any religious acts.'

'Beshak! Beshak! I have told you what I thought. You are free to decide your course of action. And so am I.' Aurangzeb indicated to the mahout. The elephant stood up ready to proceed.

'Din! Din!' The fakirs and the dervishes shouted lying down on the road. Mir Hasham, astride a horse, watched the entire drama. He took one of the fakir leaders aside and whispered in his ears, after which, the fakirs quickly agreed to give way without any further resistance. Aurangzeb's elephant proceeded with its slow march.

The elephant had reached the royal palace, but Aurangzeb continued sitting there, lost in thought, his eyes closed in deep concentration. His left hand caressed his beard while the other hand told his rosary beads.

After waiting for a while the mahout hesitantly asked, 'Huzoor …?' Aurangzeb opened his eyes and, after glancing at the palace, put his rosary aside and said, 'Ijazat hai.'

৯০৹ ৹৯৹

Aurangzeb sat alone on the terrace of his haveli. The stars shone bright under a moonless sky. A lamp burning in one corner threw a dim light onto the terrace; further away a khoja stood guard at a respectable distance. He announced Sheikh Sadullah's arrival. Aurangzeb acknowledged Sadullah's salaam and then, indicating to him to sit, said, 'Sadullah, what do you make of the drama at the bazaar today?'

'I wanted to say something. I hope the Shahzada won't mind me being direct.'

'Please! I need to know what you think. Please speak your mind.'

'Huzoor, it may not be appropriate for me to comment on Huzoor's zenankhana,' Sadullah said, looking down at the carpet, 'but I believe the zenankhana, the maids, the concubines and others, should restrict themselves to providing pleasure to the Shahzada.'

'Sadullah, I have called you here for your advice. Please don't use this politically correct language and beat around the bush. Please state your point clearly.'

'Huzoor, I believe the ryots were not happy with the begum's behaviour.'

'What do you mean?'

'The news of her plans to visit the temple had spread like wildfire. People were afraid to voice their opinion, but today's events would embolden them.'

'I am aware of your faith in our religion and I saw the respect these fakirs and the dervishes have in Islam today. I was surprised to find that our religion has such diehard fanatics, ready to go to any extent to spread the word of Allah.'

Sadullah raised his head to look at Aurangzeb but was unable to see his face clearly in the dim light. Aurangzeb continued, 'I can understand if the common man is not happy hearing our begum's plans. But I don't believe the maulvis and the fakirs are upset for that reason alone.'

'Does Huzoor doubt these men of faith?'

'So you have not grasped the reality yet! I am surprised to see such revolt when the Zainabadi begum announced her intention to visit the temple at Verul. But no one in Agra and Delhi seems to be making any noise despite my older brother Dara's open support to the Hindus. The true Muslim would have hung his head in shame.'

'But Huzoor ...'

'Let me explain. Dara withdrew money from the royal treasury to build silver railings for the temple at Mathura. Regular donations are being made for the upkeep of the temple. I am aghast the so-called zealots are not disturbed seeing such acts. But they are willing to pick a fight when my begum says she wants to visit the temple. Isn't that strange?'

Sadullah fumbled to come up with an explanation. Aurangzeb continued, 'I am aware of the political alliances since Emperor Akbar's times to get the Hindus on to our side. My older brother Dara Shikoh too is following the same tradition. It has nothing to do with religion.'

'Beshak, Beshak!' Sadullah said, nodding his head.

'Sadullah, in the same manner these dervishes and fakirs, whom you respect a lot, have no religious reasons to attack the temple.'

'Why do you say so?'

Aurangzeb's eyes pierced Sadullah before he answered. 'I am surprised that at your age, you have not been able to find the real reason behind their revolt. The idols in the temple are decked with precious jewels, gold and silver jewellery. These fakirs are greedy and want to loot the temple and amass the riches. They are keen to find their heaven by becoming rich and not by following Allah's path. There is no paucity of temples in the Deccan, if their sole purpose was to destroy the symbols of Hindu religion. But they chose this particular temple. The other day, while visiting Satara, I razed the temple of Khanderaya there to ground. It had no riches to plunder. But these fakirs target the temple at Verul as they have a totally different motive.'

'I never expected the Shahzada to derive such convoluted motives to the fakirs' actions.'

'Please carry on Sadullah. I respect your opinion.'

Sadullah sensed sarcasm in Aurangzeb's tone but ignoring it said, 'Shahzada is the subedar of the Deccan. You have enemies in Agra and Delhi whose spies ensure that any word you utter here reaches the Badshah's ears the very next day. I suppose the Shahzada is not aware of this threat.'

Aurangzeb smiled condescendingly, 'Sadullah, I am surprised that you don't know me despite being with me for ages. Please remember, if today's news reaches the durbar at Agra tomorrow, you may rest assured that I come to know of what is going to be discussed tomorrow in the durbar today itself!'

Sadullah looked surprised. He muttered, 'Shahzada, I was not aware of this.'

'Sadullah, unfortunately you may not be aware of many things, but I have to be.'

'I suppose then the news that I came to deliver may already have reached you.'

'You are a close confidant. Please speak without hesitation.'

'The spies returned from Agra this morning and I perused the papers. One of the papers, I think, needs to be seen by you.'

'What is it about?'

'I request Huzoor to read it out himself. I don't have the courage to do so.'

Sadullah handed an ordinary cloth bag which contained the post. Aurangzeb poured the contents out on the floor. Amongst the papers was a small piece of satin cloth. He unfolded the cloth to inspect it, his eyes showing surprise, but in the flickering light of the lamps Sadullah was not able to clearly see Aurangzeb's expressions. It was evidently clear to Aurangzeb though. It was the blouse that Hira had pierced in the deer garden. He closed his eyes and recalled the moment. The deer, its large eyes filled with fear, had stood still as Hira loosened the knot which tied the blouse to its horns. Aurangzeb stood there clutching the cloth in his hand, his lips pursed. Someone had surely deceived him. He had to find out. 'Read the letter accompanying it. You may go near the lamps to read it out.'

'I don't need to. I remember the words.'

'Please tell me.'

'The spy, writing on behalf of Danishmand Khan, states that the incident that took place in the deer garden was reported to the Badshah. This was produced as a matter of proof to state that you have been spending all your time in the zenankhana and have been neglecting the affairs of the state.'

Aurangzeb was silent. The lamp flickered violently in a brief gust of wind and Sadullah was able to see Aurangzeb's face clearly for a fleeting moment. To his surprise he could not spot any sign of worry on his face. Folding the piece of cloth carefully Aurangzeb said, 'I am not worried if the Badshah comes to know of the *aish-o-aaram* I am enjoying here. It would create a storm right up to Iran though, if I were to make public the kind of acts the Badshah is indulging in at his age!'

Sadullah shuffled his feet embarrassed at Aurangzeb's comments. Though he worked under Aurangzeb, he had been appointed by the Badshah. He tried feebly to defend the Badshah, 'But Shahzada, Shah Jahan Badshah after all ...'

Aurangzeb did not notice Sadullah's interruption and continued, his voice filled with contempt: 'Sadullah, romance is meant for people my age. I, who swear by the holy book, have a right to fall in love and enjoy the company of the one I love. But it is unfortunate that the Badshah, who at his age should be reading the Quran and spending all his time in the praise of Allah, is indulging in such transgressions that would put you or any man to shame. What a pity that his body, withered with age, craves for lust even now. Anyway, let that be! We shall discuss them at some later date. Tell me Sadullah! Tell me the name of the traitor who has dared to talk about me and Zainabadi begum in the Agra court. Give me a name.'

'I beg your pardon, Shahzada. Please don't force me to reveal the name.'

'Oh, I see! Are you ashamed?'

'It is not out of shame. I dare not for fear of causing you a shock.'

'Sadullah, I am used to bigger shocks. I can bear one more. Tell me.'

'I request Huzoor not to force me to speak. I am sure you would come to know of it.'

Aurangzeb lost his patience. 'Why should I wait? Sadullah, I know the name of the person. Do you want to hear it?'

'Huzoor, I am but a mere servant of yours.'

'Let me tell you, Sadullah; it is the person nominated by the Badshah himself since my childhood. Mir Hasham, the man who was appointed as my ustad, is the traitor, isn't he? Correct me if I am wrong.'

Sadullah was silent and continued to look down at the floor. 'Your silence speaks for itself, Sadullah. But I am not going to let you go scot-free. Tell me; isn't that true? Isn't Mir Hasham the traitor?'

'I have no choice but to agree with you. If I may, how did Huzoor arrive at this conclusion?'

'Sadullah, I have spent my lifetime reading people's minds. The incident at the bazaar today must have given you a glimpse of who the actual ruler of the Deccan is. The fakirs and dervishes, who were willing to snub the subedar of the Deccan in person, meekly moved away when Mir Hasham whispered in their ears. It was then I knew who the traitor was. This is a classic example of keeping one's enemies at close quarters.'

It was late in the night and the lamps were on the verge of dying. Aurangzeb, with his hands clasped behind his back, walked down the steps lost in thought.

⚜

Unlike the dimly lit terrace, the chandeliers in Hira Bai's quarters burnt bright. The sitting arrangement was decorated with thick rugs and soft pillows. Embroidered curtains hung from the windows and the ventilators. A long-necked pitcher with silver engravings stood on a wooden tripod in one corner. A matching pair of silver glasses, embellished with precious stones, reflected the light of the lamps.

Hira Bai, preening in front of the mirror, did not notice when Aurangzeb walked in silently. He stood at the door admiring the decor. Hira's beautiful figure bought a smile to his face and putting his hands on her shoulders he muttered, 'Hira, my love! Are you so lost in your thoughts that you did not get up to salaam when I entered?'

Hira got up hurriedly. Noticing her blush with embarrassment, Aurangzeb hugged her tightly. 'Allah has done a great favour giving me something so beautiful. You are the light of my life. The darkness in my heart vanishes and I forget everything else the moment I see you.'

Hira carefully took off Aurangzeb's Mughal turban and placed it on the side table. Extracting his small dagger from the cummerbund she said, 'This slave of yours is happy to offer whatever help she can. But, of late, I am told I am creating more problems for you than giving you solace.'

Sitting on the bed with her Aurangzeb said, 'That may be true in the world outside. With you here, it is only jannat! That's all!'

'Really? It seems the request I made a few days back seems to have been forgotten quite soon. Isn't that so?'

'What request are you talking of?'

'See what I meant! You have forgotten. Tomorrow is Shivaratri. Did you not promise to visit the temple at Verul with me?'

'Oh!'

'Don't you remember?'

'I do.'

'Then do I have the permission to visit the temple tomorrow?'

'Beshak! Beshak!'

'I was given to understand you have cancelled all the arrangements.'

'Who told you so?'

'The servants and the khojas here.'

'Don't you believe me?'

'I am a mere kafir. Shahzada is a true devout Musalman. Thinking that he may have changed his mind, I decided to keep quiet.'

Aurangzeb kissed her passionately on her lips saying, 'That's it! I don't want to hear any more. I have given my word. That is final.'

'Huzoor, it is difficult to convince me that the Shahzada would love me so much. I am at a loss to understand why the Shahzada, who has access to all the riches and pleasures of the world, would shower his love on an ordinary slave like me.'

'Hira, my dear! There are so many things in the world which are beyond comprehension. The hand that feeds the young ones is capable of wringing their necks as well. Allah's world is strange. It is only the non-believer who feels Allah is not looking after him.'

Hira put her delicate fingers on Aurangzeb's lips and said, 'I would never say that. This slave of yours has been blessed by Allah beyond her wildest dreams.'

'Is that so?'

'Just look out and see. The stars shine like jewels in the sky and a soothing cool breeze blows. I have the Shahzada sitting next to me. What else can I ask for?'

She gently extricated herself from Aurangzeb's clasp and, offering a tray of fruits to Aurangzeb said, 'I would be grateful if Huzoor partakes something here.'

'I have no strength to deny anything offered with these loving hands. Anything which touches your lovely lips must be very sweet. How can I then refuse?' Aurangzeb was enjoying the flirtation. The lamps and the candles burning in the chandeliers died down on their own late in the night.

ഛ ഇ

It was an hour before dawn. Aurangzeb got up silently without disturbing Hira who slept like a child. The lamps outside threw a mild light. Aurangzeb stepped out of the room. The khojas outside were dozing, but the Tartar women guards, seeing him at that early hour, scrambled to attention. Ignoring their salutes, Aurangzeb went back to his quarters, lost in thoughts of the pleasant night spent with Hira.

The guards outside his quarters were relaxed as they knew he was spending the night elsewhere. The only one waiting for him in attendance was Anwar. He was ready, as usual, with the water for Aurangzeb's wudu before his morning prayers. Aurangzeb poured water on his hands and then washed his face. In the meanwhile, Anwar had readied his bath. By now, he knew the days when Aurangzeb would take a bath before his morning prayers. Aurangzeb spent a quarter of an hour in his bath and then came out wearing a simple cotton shirt which complimented his white pyjamas. He took the necklace of white pearls offered by Anwar and, putting it around his neck, sat down on his knees to read the namaz facing the western horizon.

It was dawn by the time he finished his prayers. He gave instructions before moving towards his office. 'Ask the stable hand to keep my horse ready. I will be leaving for Verul. Ask Shamim to help Hira get ready for the trip. Get the special white horse for her.'

Anwar saluted and left for the task at hand. Sadullah and some officials were in attendance waiting for Aurangzeb when he reached the office. Accepting their salaams he said, 'Sadullah, I am not in a mood to look into the official matters today.'

'Huzoor, you had agreed to inspect the risala today. The mounted troops have been waiting for your inspection.'

'Oh! The risala!'

'Huzoor, if you recall, you had taken special permission from the Badshah to add another ten thousand cavalry to your army. We have ordered horses from Arabia, Afghanistan, Iran and Kandahar and the traders have been waiting for your inspection for over a month now. These risaldars have selected ten thousand of the best steeds for you. We have recruited the soldiers while the weapons and the cannons are ready for your perusal. You were to inspect all of these this morning.'

'I remember now. But I have some urgent personal work today. Let us inspect these some other day. Ask the risaldars to train the cavalry in the meanwhile.'

Sadullah was nonplussed. He had worked hard for many months to raise the cavalry with the help of Diwan Murshid Quli Khan. Protocol required a formal inspection by the Shahzada to get them inducted into the army. The soldiers' salaries were due and the horse traders were getting impatient to receive their money.

Diwan Murshid Quli Khan stood nearby. His stature as a diwan was higher than Sadullah's and he was responsible for the treasury. He said in a low voice, 'Huzoor, what can be more important than inspecting the troops?'

'I am visiting the temple at Verul with Zainabadi begum. We will be marvelling the splendours of the caves there which I am told are no less than Allah's work.'

'Huzoor, for the past eight days, Mir Jumla's men from Golconda have been waiting to show you the jewels. It was decided that he would be showing the same in the zenankhana today.'

Aurangzeb thought for a moment. Mir Jumla was the diwan of the Badshah of Golconda. Aurangzeb had been in secret correspondence with him over the past few months. Mir Jumla had sent a few select jewels to Aurangzeb as gift under the pretext of showing some samples. He badly needed the jewels, but his heart was set on making the trip with Hira. His plan was to go alone, just the two of them, sans any servants or guards, and roam the hills freely. He visualized the two of them, walking hand in hand enjoying the beauty of the caves and the carvings inside, stopping at the banks of a stream for rest and then spending the night there. He wanted to divert her mind from performing the pooja at the temple.

Aurangzeb was in a dilemma. The prospect of spending a carefree day with Hira was too tempting. He thought of ways of postponing the tasks presented to him by Sadullah and his diwan.

A commotion attracted the attention of those present. Aurangzeb raised an enquiring eyebrow. The daroga hurriedly came in and, after a quick salaam said, 'Huzoor, Shamim Banu has requested an immediate audience. If you permit, I will arrange for her to be there behind the private screen right away.'

'Please go ahead.'

A vetiver screen was quickly pulled down in a balcony which was a part of the zenankhana. The moment the screen touched the ground, Aurangzeb heard Shamim Banu's voice, '*Tasleem, Huzoor!*'

'What is it Banu? Is Hira ready to leave?'

'*Huzoor, qayamat!* Allah did not want her to go, it seems.'

'What is it? Talk to me clearly.' Aurangzeb could detect Banu's voice trembling, but he maintained his composure.

'Huzoor, Zainabadi begum ... Zainabadi begum ...' All he could hear was a loud sob from behind the screen.

Aurangzeb asked, his voice rising impatiently, 'Please tell me clearly. Is Hira Begum waiting for me? Tell her to be ready to accompany me in another half an hour.'

'Huzoor, the situation is a little different. When I went in to wake her up she was lying on her bed and seemed to be sleeping.' Banu's voice quivered.

A faint smile crossed Aurangzeb's face. He remembered the night gone by. He said, glancing at Sadullah for a moment, 'What is so surprising? It is your duty to wake her up and get her ready.'

'Huzoor, words fail me. I don't know how to say this ... but she is beyond waking up.'

'What nonsense.'

'Huzoor, she was dead when I went in. Allah has beckoned her.'

Aurangzeb stood up immediately. Sadullah felt as if a bolt of lightning had struck the place. Without warning he walked up and pulled aside the curtain. The men in attendance were shocked and quickly turned their faces away lest they insult the modesty of Banu, who sat there with her face exposed, her veil pulled back.

Aurangzeb pulled Banu's palms covering her face and screamed, 'What are you saying? It is not true. It cannot be true!'

'Huzoor, it is,' Shamim said, wiping her tears with the edge of her dupatta. Aurangzeb did not wait any further. As he ran towards the door that led to the inner quarters, Shamim Banu ran ahead of him. The servants, taken by surprise on seeing him, saluted, but Aurangzeb was too perturbed to return their salutes and he rushed past them, his lips quivering. Pushing aside the Tartar woman guarding the door, he ran to the bed. Hira seemed to be lying in the same position as he had left her that morning: the hair dishevelled, her delicate fingers holding the edge of her dupatta. Nothing seemed amiss. She seemed to be in deep sleep. But then he noticed that the eyes, which had reminded him of a timid doe, had lost their fire. The lips, normally red as pomegranate seeds, had turned dark.

It was after a few moments that reality hit Aurangzeb. Screaming, 'Hira, my dear Hira!' he flung himself on her lifeless body and sobbed uncontrollably.

❦

Aurangzeb could not control himself seeing Hira's coffin being carried out and let out a cry of anguish. It was a sight the officials and the servants had never seen before. Aurangzeb thumped his chest with his hands as he sobbed loudly. The officials in attendance could not bear to see his sorrow and were in tears. Sadullah, Murshid Quli Khan and other senior officials lifted the coffin while the other ladies, their faces covered in veils walked behind. Hira and Aurangzeb's favourite spot by the lake, where they had spent many hours together, had been selected as the place for the burial. Aurangzeb walked along with his head bowed, his hand resting on Sadullah's shoulder for support. The tears continued to flow.

The mullah read out the *namaz-e-janaaza*, the prayers before the burial.

'Allah is the Lord of the earth. He is the merciful and the one who presides over the last day of the judgement ...'

Having said his prayers, he gestured that those who wanted to leave were permitted to do so. Sadullah said, 'Huzoor, you may return now. We will take care of the other formalities.' Aurangzeb did not move. The mullah was reading out the Surah-e-Yaseen and the Surah-e-Tabarak while Sadullah, Murshid Quli Khan and a few other officials lifted the coffin and placed it in the grave. Aurangzeb placed his palm on the coffin before it was lowered in. With tear-filled eyes, he uttered, '*minha khalaqnakum wa fiha nueedu kum wa minha nukhrijukum taaratan ukhraa*,' the last of the prayers before the burial.

It meant, 'We have created you out of this (dust) and we shall return you to it and it is out of the same that we shall revive you in the end.'

He managed to throw a handful of dust on to the coffin and then fell down unconscious. The servants hurriedly completed the job of the burial and then, placing Aurangzeb on to the royal elephant, got him into his quarters.

After coming to, Aurangzeb visited Hira's room. He sat on the floor, his head resting on the edge of the bedstead. Shamim Banu and some of the elderly ladies from the zenankhana gave him company. A few old women sat in one corner reading out the *Al Fatihah* from the Quran. '*Bismillah hir rahmaan nir Raheem,*' which meant, 'Allah is the only one, the wonderful, the omnipresent. He does not give birth to anyone nor is born of anyone. There is no one else like him.' The lines were repeated endlessly. The women in attendance tried their best to assuage Aurangzeb's sadness but, listening to the words from the Quran, he got more upset and started crying. After a long time he said, his voice hoarse, 'Please leave me alone. I don't want anyone here. Take away the Quran and leave me with my sorrows.'

This continued for a fortnight. Aurangzeb rejected all efforts to make him have his meals, let alone drink water. He was practically fasting himself to death. He would cry the whole night sitting next to her bed and shout, 'Hira, my dear Hira!' Anwar was the only one who would dare enter the room. He would somehow manage to coax him to take a small bite of fruit. In a fortnight, Aurangzeb looked like he had been ill for six months. His eyes were sunken, his face drawn; he had aged nearly ten years.

Eventually the grief abated and, one day, he called for Sadullah.

Sadullah came in with guarded steps. He had heard of Aurangzeb's state, but was shocked to see him in person. He said, 'Huzoor, some things do not return despite one longing for them with all one's heart. Any amount of sorrow would not get them back.'

'Sadullah, don't you think I understand? But the heart does not listen to what the mind says! I can feel her presence here. I can almost see her standing in front of the mirror or at the window. I cannot believe that her soul has left me. She is still here.'

'Huzoor, this old man has seen many a season more than others. I have seen near and dear ones pass away. Such illusions are common when someone close to the heart dies suddenly. But Allah is great. He gives the strength to overcome the deepest of the sorrows and continue living. That is why the world exists, Huzoor.'

Aurangzeb wiped his eyes and said, 'Sadullah, what is the point in living if one has to encounter sadness and nothing else? I had lived my life without discovering true love till I met her. I was in a different world for the past year and a half. She taught me how to love and how to understand humanity. But like someone plucking an unripe fruit from a tree, she was taken away rudely from my heart. I don't see any point in living. Does Allah want me to live like a madman?'

'Huzoor, why do you say so?'

'Sadullah, a man lives in the hope of something. I could never imagine her leaving me. What you are seeing is my body. The soul has left long ago. I have to now find a way to sustain this body.'

Sadullah tried his best to convince Aurangzeb. In order to divert his mind, he said, 'Huzoor, I have done some enquiries over the last fortnight. I have been trying to establish the cause of begum's death.'

'What is the point of it Sadullah? If investigation were to bring her back, would I have not spent my time doing that?'

'Huzoor, but it was my duty to do so.'

'And what were your findings?'

'Huzoor, her death was due to poisoning.'

'Who was responsible for this?'

'Huzoor, I could not investigate further, but I am sure she did not take the poison herself. She was poisoned by someone. There are many people who are jealous of her and she had many enemies. I will find out soon.'

Aurangzeb, despite his intense sorrow, was alert and confronted Sadullah. 'Sadullah, don't assume I have lost my ability to think because of my suffering. I am sure you have already found out who the culprit is. You are hiding from me.'

With his head bowed Sadullah confessed, 'Huzoor, I have found out who was behind this conspiracy. But I entreat you to start doing your regular activities and take charge of the subah. I shall let you know at an appropriate time.'

Sadullah was happy he had managed to divert Aurangzeb's attention, albeit for a little while. Taking liberties thanks to his age, he held Aurangzeb's hand and pulling him from his bed said, 'Huzoor, you should move to your mahal now. There are many things waiting for you. There is no end to sorrows and the only way to reduce their intensity is to engage oneself in other activities.'

Aurangzeb got up and, putting his hand on Sadullah's shoulder, walked slowly out of Hira's room.

⊰⊱ ⊰⊱

Activitites that had been at a standstill for months, started gathering pace. Within a month of Hira's death, Aurangzeb heard some good news. Shamim Banu came running in and, after a quick salaam, said, her face glowing with happiness, 'Huzoor, Khuda has been kind and has showered his blessings.'

'What is it, Shamim?' Aurangzeb asked, a little tersely.

'The messenger from Burhanpur arrived this morning with the news of Irani begum having delivered a boy.'

The birth of a son to the Irani begum helped soothe the pain that Aurangzeb carried in his heart. He exclaimed, 'This deserves a gift!' and saying so removed a pearl necklace from his neck and handed it to Shamim.

The news of a newborn son carried itself from the zenankhana to the officials and from then on to the markets outside. Soon, the whole town wore a festive look. Amaldars came in to congratulate Aurangzeb. Exchange of gifts from the royal palace to the officials and return gifts thereof continued for a few weeks.

In the late hours of the afternoon, wary of Nawab Bai's reaction, her maid Nargis broke the news to her. She was carrying a box of sweets. Muazzam and Sultan, her two sons, were present.

Sultan smiled and said, 'It is indeed good news; we have another brother now.'

'And I have another enemy,' Nawab Bai blurted.

Muazzam, busy unpacking a box of sweets, asked, 'Baiji, aren't you happy hearing the news? Abba Jaan has, in fact, declared a holiday and given leave to our Farsi tutor.'

Nawab Bai was about to react when Nargis rushed in saying, 'Begum Sahiba, Shahzada is coming in.' Aurangzeb entered her room with two servants in tow carrying a silver tray each. They put the trays on the table next to the bed and left. Aurangzeb indicated Nargis to step out. 'Begum Sahiba, you must have received the good news. I have got for you on this special occasion jewels ordered from Golconda.'

He uncovered the trays to reveal some exquisite jewellery. He expected Nawab Bai to show some excitement but instead saw her frowning. She said, 'You may have as well sent an enemy. That would have been better.'

Aurangzeb's face was grim. 'Begum, in this hour of happiness ...'

'Does anyone care about my happiness? You may celebrate the birth of your son the way you want. But you need not rub salt in my wounds by gifting me with these jewels.'

'Begum! Are you out of your mind?'

'I am in my senses. I am not a fool to realize that the birth of a son to the Irani begum makes my children orphans. They have no future now.'

'What do you mean by that?'

'I am aware of the fascination you have for your Irani begum. Now that she has borne you a son, I doubt you will give my sons their rights as your heirs.'

'Begum, your sons are elder and they have their rights which will not be denied to them. I give you my word; now does that make you feel secure?'

'I would have had no doubts if Huzoor were in the habit of keeping his word.'

'Are you suggesting I am in the habit of going back on my promises?'

'I don't have the right to make any suggestions. Anyway, I don't want to be a damp squib and spoil your happiness. I request Huzoor to inform the Irani begum that I share her happiness.'

Aurangzeb relaxed a little. He asked, 'How am I to know that you are really happy?'

'What proof can I give?'

'Won't you give me a gift on this happy occasion?'

'What can I give you? Whatever I have is yours. You may ask for whatever you want.'

'Begum, I don't want you to go back on your word later!'

Sultan stood nearby listening to the talk. He was a tall lad of fifteen or sixteen. Aurangzeb pulled him lovingly towards him and said, hugging him, 'He is a grown up boy now. You talk of his marriage, but I feel he has a lot to learn. I want to send him on an important task. He will have to stay away from you. I hope you won't object.'

'Stay away? If you are planning to send him on a shikar, I request you to send some experienced amaldars with him.'

'Don't worry, begum. I am sending him to the durbar at Agra as my representative. He will be given responsible tasks under my guidance. Till date, thanks to your love and pampering, the boys have not learnt anything. They cannot even speak Turkish properly or read the Farsi script. He needs to learn the manners of the court. He will be leaving tomorrow for Agra. I will consider this as a gift from you on this auspicious day.'

Nawab Bai ruffled Sultan's hair affectionately. 'It is fine with me. I could call them mine as long as they were in the zenankhana. Now they are under your supervision. I request one thing though; I hope the fact that the Irani begum has given birth to a son will not come in the way of these boys.'

'I have given you my word. I hope you won't ask for enemies to be sent instead of jewels on any such occasion.'

For the first time Nawab Bai burst out laughing.

⋅ଡ ଡ⋅

With nearly three thousand soldiers in tow, Sultan was despatched to Agra as Aurangzeb's representative. But within a matter of six months, he was recalled urgently to the Deccan. The political scene in the Deccan was taking on a different turn and Aurangzeb needed someone trustworthy to work with him.

Aurangzeb sat in his office looking into some papers, when he spotted something important. A huge amount was due from Golconda. He asked Diwan Murshid Quli Khan, 'Diwan, there are very large amounts due from Qutub Khan, but you have not bothered to alert me. Why so?'

The Diwan, well versed in administrative affairs, said, 'Huzoor, Qutub Khan's representative is here to meet you and has been seeking your appointment for the past few days. If you permit, I will ask him to present himself.'

'Go ahead.'

The representative was summoned to the office. He bowed and stood with his hands behind his back. His coat was bedecked with precious stones. Aurangzeb asked, 'How dare you stand here decked in jewellery when your state has not paid a sum of twenty lakh?'

Those in attendance were taken aback by the direct confrontation. The representative tried, 'Huzoor … we know we have not paid yet, but we will never default. Our Badshah has made a request to …'

'A mere zamindar of Golconda cannot be called a badshah. There is only one Badshah and he sits on the throne at Delhi. I suggest you choose your words carefully.'

The representative had not expected his Nizam to be trashed as a mere landlord. He said, licking his lips nervously, 'Your point taken, Huzoor. We are after all no more than a landlord in comparison to the Mughal Badshah. Please be assured we will fulfil our dues.'

'Diwan, since how many years have they not paid their dues?'

'Ten.'

'You have been dilly-dallying for the past ten years? Are you saying you could not afford to pay all this while? Don't be under the impression that I am not aware of all the revelry your landlord is indulging in Golconda and Hyderabad.'

The Diwan realized that Aurangzeb was in a mood to tick the representative off. He stepped in before the matter became worse. 'Huzoor, the representative has come precisely to work out a solution. You may state your conditions.'

'Then let your landlord know that he has three months to fulfil his obligations. If within ninety days the sum of twenty lakh does not reach me here, we will not be responsible for the consequences. Is that clear?'

'Huzoor, I request you to reconsider. Three months is too short a time to arrange for such a large sum.'

'That is not for the Mughals to worry about, I am told your men are mining diamonds out of the mines at Golconda and that they are sold to people as far as the Shah of Persia. Tell your Qutub Khan: if you are unable to pay the amount, we shall raid your port at Machilipatnam and take charge of your ships carrying diamonds.'

That very night, a spy sent by Mir Jumla, the wazir of Golconda, came to meet Aurangzeb. The secret meeting was organized by Sadullah. Seeing Aurangzeb enter the meeting room, the spy got up and saluted hurriedly. He said, 'I have been sent here by my master Wazir Mir Jumla with a special message.'

'How am I to know that you have come from his camp?'

The man put his hand into the pocket of his long overcoat and produced a large diamond. Handing it to Aurangzeb he said, 'This has been sent by Mir Jumla. A similar one was sent to you when he heard the news of your Irani begum giving birth to a son. You may compare the two.'

Aurangzeb did not need any further proof. 'Tell me what message your master has for me.'

'Shahzada, Mir Jumla is not in the good books of Qutub Khan any more. His wealth has become a source of discomfort for the Shah. Mir Jumla has requested your help.'

'What does he want?'

'He extends his hand in friendship.'

'What is your master willing to give in return?'

'The diamond mines of Golconda belong to Mir Jumla; you may take any number of diamonds you wish from them. In fact,' the man looked around to ensure no one was within earshot and then, lowering his voice, said, 'he is willing to lay the entire Golconda at your feet if you so desire.'

'I see! And all this to ensure the safety of your master?'

'Ji, Huzoor. My master, his son Muhammad Amin, and his entire family are worried. If the Shahzada takes care of them, my master is willing to give you whatever you wish.'

Aurangzeb pondered for a moment before saying, 'I will think about it.'

'Shall I tell him then, that you have agreed?'

'I can't say yes or a no right now. It is possible only when Mir Jumla agrees to work under the Mughals.'

'Work under the Mughals?'

'Yes, you heard it right. If he is agreeable to it, I will forward his request to the Badshah. I will take him under my command once the Badshah gives his consent. I am the subedar of the Deccan, but I cannot act on my own free will and do whatever pleases my mind. We have a protocol to follow.'

After the messenger left, Aurangzeb commented looking at Sadullah, 'It seems Allah has other plans for us. On one hand, Qutub Khan owes us a sum of twenty lakh and on the other, their richest man is asking for our help to save his life. The future looks interesting.'

⁓๑ౖ ౖ๑⁓

Aurangzeb had changed after Hira's death. The time in the company of Hira seemed like a beautiful dream now. It was as if Aurangzeb had woken up from a dream and now held a different perspective on life. He spent very little time in the zenankhana. In the beginning, he avoided visiting the zenankhana altogether as it brought back memories of Hira. He focused his attention on subedari work. He had to raise a bigger army and that meant arranging for funds to support the same. He believed in personally supervising all accounts and spent all his time doing that. He worked late into the night getting feedback from the spies who were posted in various parts of the region.

Dilras Banu, along with her young son and two daughters, shifted to Aurangabad. The living quarters were elaborately rearranged to ensure that Dilras Banu and Nawab Bai did not have to meet each other even inadvertently. Aurangzeb had named his newborn son Azam. For his daughters and Nawab Bai's ten-year-old Muazzam, Aurangzeb had nominated Sadullah's nephew, Aquil Khan, who had come in from Iran, as the tutor. His main task was that of the fort keeper of Daulatabad. Apart from the khojas, no males were allowed into the zenankhana. On special request made by Dilras Banu, her daughters were being taught both the Turkish and Arabic languages as well as reading books like *Gulistan* and *Bostan*, by Persian poet Sheikh Sa'di, and Firdausi's *Shahnama*.

Aurangzeb would enquire about the affairs of the zenankhana whenever he found time from his subedari work. Ever since he had heard of Golconda's riches, he was itching for an excuse to loot them. He needed a reason to raise a large army. It was unlikely that the Badshah would allow him despite his repeated requests. He knew his support to Mir Jumla would create a storm in Golconda. Then a new opportunity presented itself.

The kingdom of Vijaynagar had been divided and part of the Karnataka region was under Raja Shrirang. His Muslim neighbours, the sultan of Bijapur on the south and that of Golconda on the north, were keen to annex his territory. Realizing his fate, he had sent his messenger, Srinivas Rao, to Aurangabad pleading for Mughal support.

Aurangzeb, having mastered the art of politics, made Srinivas Rao wait anxiously for many days before granting him audience. Upon seeing Aurangzeb step into the room, Srinivas Rao flung himself at Aurangzeb's feet: 'Shahzada, we have been threatened by the sultans of Bijapur and Golconda and we fear for our lives. We have no one except you to help us. Please save us, Shahzada!'

Aurangzeb smiled at Srinivas Rao and invited him to sit down. He heard him patiently as Srinivas Rao described the atrocities being carried out by both the sultans. He could not believe his eyes that such a golden chance had presented itself. He was being handed his dreams on a platter. He said, 'Srinivas Rao, I have great respect for your Raja Shrirang. But you must understand I cannot offer you any help unless I have explicit permission from the Badshah. And you know Ala Hazrat; unless I am able to show some benefit to the Mughal Empire, he is unlikely to give me permission.'

'We are willing to offer any help you suggest.'

'What do you have in mind?'

'We will offer two-and-a-half crore rupiyas.'

It was a fabulous offer, but Aurangzeb did not show any excitement. On the contrary he made a face saying, 'That's all! A mere two-and-a-half crore?'

'What else can we give, Huzoor?'

'I am told there are a lot of elephants in Karnataka. How many can you present us?'

'We will give two hundred of them.'

'And …?'

'A lot more, Huzoor. Once Raja Shrirang is rescued we will welcome you to our palace and you can take all the jewels and jewellery that Raja Shrirang has inherited from the past five generations.'

'Oh! What sort of treasure is it?'

'It would fill more than a hundred sacks.'

'Hmm. Srinivas Rao, are you sure of what you are saying?'

'I am giving you my word. I am willing to stay here as your hostage till we fulfil our promise. Shahzada, I entreat you to make a decision fast. I am told both the sultans have already made plans to march upon us and could reach Karnataka any day.'

Aurangzeb's nonchalance added to Srinivas Rao's anxiety. 'Srinivas Rao, you have come to me begging for your safety when you see a threat from these sultans. What is the guarantee that once I offer you my help, you will not set up your kafir kingdom once again?'

'Huzoor, I was expecting this question. We have a proposal for you.'

'And that is?'

'Once the enemy is routed and we are safe, our Raja is willing to concede the territory to the Mughals and work under you. We will not function as an independent kingdom but will rule under the Mughal flag, for which we are willing to pay an annual honorarium. What else can we offer, Shahzada?'

'I hear you. I am fine with the proposal, but I need to get a formal approval from the Badshah. I shall let you know once I hear from him.'

'Shahzada, what shall I tell my master?'

'Tell him we shall act once we hear from Ala Hazrat Shah Jahan.'

'Shahzada, we need your immediate help. The enemy is threatening to reach us any minute. I am told the sultan from Bijapur has sent his troops across to attack Chandragiri. We cannot delay any more!'

Aurangzeb thought for a moment and said, 'You may return to Chandragiri and tell your raja that we will ensure the sultan's troops do not reach Chandragiri. You will not be touched by either of the sultans. We will ensure that.'

'What about the permission from the Badshah?'

'I will manage that. You may leave now. Please ensure that you have a better proposal for us when we meet next.'

'Shahzada, I would request you to be specific.'

'Please convey my message verbatim. You may not understand, but I am sure your maharaja would.'

Aurangzeb could hardly contain his glee. The opportunity was too good to be true.

◦◎◦ ◦◎◦

Under the able supervision of Aquil Khan, Zebunissa and Zeenat were learning quickly. Dilras Banu was not keeping well and rarely stepped out, but her daughters spent their free time in the private gardens every afternoon. Zebunissa, nineteen years of age, was a stunning combination of beauty and brains. Her youthful figure was amply evident through her dress of sheer satin, and her sister, though five years younger, matched her in beauty. It was Friday and a respite from the regular schedule. The sisters sat near the fountains, listening to a sarangi being played. Zeenat made a face saying, 'I am tired of music. I want to hear some interesting stories.'

One of the female teachers in attendance volunteered. 'I will tell you a story. What do you want to hear?'

'Anything interesting will do.' Zeenat, looking at her elder sister, asked, 'Is that fine, Apa?'

Zebunissa's finely arched eyebrows danced briefly as she pondered. 'Why not listen to a story from Sheikh Sa'di's book?'

The teacher opened a page from *Gulistan* and began, 'Once there was a maulvi ...'

'I don't want to listen to any stories about maulvis. How about *Laila–Majnu?*' Zebunissa blushed. The rose flowers on the creepers near the fountains vied to match the colour of her cheeks.

The teacher continued, 'Believe me. This story is more enjoyable than that of Laila–Majnu. Let me continue ... Once a beautiful woman asked a maulvi ...'

'*Hai Allah!* A beautiful woman? Now, it seems interesting.'

'The beautiful woman looked as lovely as the moon on the fourteenth day – a chaudhavi ka chand. Her eyes were liquid pools of blue. Her beauty was enough to arouse anyone.'

'I can imagine what the poor maulvi would have done. No one can stay away from such beauty.'

'I don't want to get into the details. Suffice to say such temptation would be most natural.'

The two sisters and the teachers were enjoying the light conversation. One of the teachers got up and returned carrying a few paintings. Showing one of them she said, 'This is the Badshah of Iran.' The painting showed an old man, almost a caricature of himself wearing a funny-looking cap. They all laughed seeing the painting. The teacher showed another one saying, 'This is Qutub Khan of Golconda.'

Zeenat looked at it for a brief moment and said, 'A donkey would have looked more handsome. I was told that he has sacks full of diamonds and gems. What an irony! Such wealth should be with Abba Jaan. What is the point in this fool having such wealth?'

They made comments on each of the portraits shown. A handsome man's portrait would generate some praise. They would practise copying the paintings for a while.

The teacher picked up a painting kept aside and said,' I had kept this for the end. It is a portrait of a kafir.'

'A kafir? Let me see.'

The picture showed a Maratha jagirdar. He had a small beard

and the tips of his moustache were pointed. The aquiline nose complemented the penetrating stare of the eyes. The bold horizontal strikes of white ash on his forehead added an aura to his personality. His turban was decorated with a string of pearls.

'Who is he?' Zebunissa said, clearly impressed with the handsome face.

'Our royal physician had visited Junnar recently. I managed to get this from him. He is a Maratha zamindar from Bijapur, called Shiva.'

'He is so handsome!' Zeenat exclaimed.

'Yes, he is!' Zeb agreed. She asked, 'Isn't he the same zamindar who recently attacked a lot of Mughal outposts?'

'*Ya Allah!* I don't know all that. I am told he is a Maratha by the name of Shiva Bhosale.'

'I will draw his picture next Friday. Help me do that.'

It was late in the evening when the two sisters, having spent their afternoons in the company of their teachers and ustads, returned to their quarters.

ঔৎ ৯৹

It was nearly midnight and Aurangzeb was being debriefed by Shamim about the day's events. There was nothing which escaped Aurangzeb's ears.

After hearing Shamim's account, Aurangzeb said, 'The fact is Shamim, parents rarely realize that their children have grown up. I feel I have been spending too much time in the subedari work and neglecting the family.' He moved the rosary beads for a while, lost in thoughts. He recalled the comments made by Zeb and Zeenat while discussing the maulvi's predicament on seeing a beautiful woman. Shamim's spies did not miss anything and would report promptly.

The next morning, he asked Sadullah, 'How are the security arrangement, in the zenankhana?'

'Very good, Huzoor. The khojas guard the outer circle while the Tartar women are inside.'

'Who takes care of the daily activities?'

'There are hundreds of maids, khojas and others, each carefully chosen. May I ask why Huzoor is having doubts today?'

'Sadullah, you are much older than me and hence I can afford to be direct. In the process of having our sights fixed on Golconda and Bijapur, we may have neglected some matters at hand, right here in the zenankhana.'

'Huzoor, I am unable to follow you.'

'Sadullah, ask the physician to check the khojas out once more. I don't want anyone to misuse their position there. We cannot afford to be lax. A wise bird, always careful, never forgets that the thorns below the rosebud could also be the claws of a falcon hiding there. The prestige of the Mughal zenankhana is in your hands. We have suffered once. I don't want any more lapses. I will not allow your old age to be a reason for being lenient.'

Aurangzeb had hit where it hurt the most. He was referring to Hira's death. Sadullah was aware that Aurangzeb had not taken any action against the murderer due to his own constraints.

'Shahzada, I never expected Mir Hasham to be a traitor. He has been in your service ever since he was young. I never imagined him taking such a step. I had doubted his integrity, but at the worst I thought he would pass on some secrets to the court at Agra. I knew he had gossiped about Zainabadi begum, but I never imagined he would stoop to this level.'

'Sadullah, a wise man learns from his mistakes. Those who repeat the mistakes are fools. I have learnt the lesson, but your age does not seem to have taught you. I am surprised you were in the dark about the plot to poison her.'

'I am guilty, Huzoor. I accept it. But I am surprised that despite knowing the crime Mir Hasham has committed, you allowed him to go scot-free.'

'It seems you have not learnt much in your life, Sadullah.'

'I beg your pardon, Huzoor?'

'Sadullah, it does not take much to insult Mir Hasham in public. He believes I don't know about his crime but would be emboldened to make all the happenings in the zenankhana public once I declare him a criminal. And it is a well-known fact that my enemies would be gladly welcomed by my elder brother Dara. I would be handing Dara a ready-made weapon to use against me. That is the reason I have been behaving as if I don't know of Mir Hasham's crimes.'

Sadullah looked at Aurangzeb with renewed respect. He never imagined him to have such foresight. He exclaimed, 'Shahzada! Despite my age and experience, I lose my control. I am amazed to see your composure. Where did you learn all this?'

Aurangzeb answered nonchalantly, 'Sadullah, that's why you are a mere mushrif while I am the subedar of the Deccan – Shahzada Aurangzeb. Please keep this in mind: I will wait for the right opportunity to teach Mir Hasham a lesson for life.'

৶৹৶ ৯৹৶

Dilras Banu sat looking outside a window that overlooked a private courtyard and where the maids were busy entertaining three-year-old Azam. Fountains gurgled while birds of various species flew around the gardens. The fine spray from the fountains created a cool and pleasant sensation. She was enjoying the sight when, seeing a ball of dust rising from the horizon, she glanced in that direction. She could hear a variety of noises; men shouting, a herd of camels approaching, and horses trotting. She craned her neck but could see nothing from where she sat. A few beads of sweat had gathered at her forehead. She would not normally show any interest in the affairs of the state. She turned away from the window to admire her slender figure in the mirror, now growing a little at the stomach. She was surprised to see faint dark circles around her eyes. Standing at the window with the sunlight streaming in had made her cheeks look redder than usual. She smiled at herself, enjoying the sight of her Persian beauty.

She rang a golden bell hung in one corner and, within moments, a maid came in. 'Send Shamim in. I have some urgent work to discuss.'

Within a matter of minutes, Shamim presented herself.

'Shamim, I have been hearing of some disturbances in the town since a few days. The movement of the soldiers and the cavalry was so frantic that I could see the dust rising on the streets from my window here. What's the clamour all about?'

'Did the Shahzada not tell you anything?'

'Do you think he would?'

'I am surprised, Begum Sahiba. I thought he visits you quite often these days. I wonder what he speaks to you about then.'

Shamim could take liberties with Dilras Banu due to her age and position as the daroga of the zenankhana. Aurangzeb, of late, spent a lot of his time in Dilras Banu's quarters enquiring about her daughters and Azam. Without taking offence to Shamim's comments, Dilras Banu said, 'Shamim, stop pulling my leg and tell me what is going on.'

'Begum Sahiba, there is a plan for a campaign.'

'Oh, I see! I thought everything was quiet on this side.'

'Shahzada is not fortunate enough to sit still for a long time. The Badshah has given his permission to attack the sultans of Golconda and Bijapur. I am told he is sending a large contingent under the supervision of Shaista Khan.'

'Is his zenankhana also going with him?'

'I am not sure but I suspect so. A separate haveli is being made ready for the stay of Gul begum.'

Dilras Banu made a face hearing Gul begum's name.

'Begum Sahiba, I see you are not happy hearing her name. May I know why?'

'Is it true that the Badshah Salamat Shah Jahan had called her into his zenankhana once?'

Shamim looked down at the carpet and answered, 'Yes, I heard so. There had been a lot of gossip in the zenankhana regarding this incident. Khan Sahab was very upset.'

Banu got up. Adjusting her dupatta in the mirror, she asked, 'Shamim, I want you to answer me without beating around the bush. Will you? And don't play with words. Tell me, is it not true that Badshah Shah Jahan made his daughter invite Gul begum into his zenankhana and that he tried to outrage her modesty?'

'It is true, Begum Sahiba. I was informed about this by the main khoja there.'

Dilras Banu had tears in her eyes. 'Oh, so it wasn't just gossip! One cannot trust anyone there now. I cannot believe that it is the same Badshah who built that beautiful Taj Mahal which, on a full moon night, looks like a rose flower in bloom.

'Begum Sahiba, don't torture yourself.'

'Shamim, I hate this hypocritical behaviour. Like Mumtaj Begum Sahiba, we Irani women give our heart and soul to the man we love. We sacrifice ourselves at their feet and all we get in return are such lowly acts of lust! What a shame that under the watchful eyes of the Taj, the Badshah should try to outrage the modesty of another woman. And how many of them! Jaffar Khan's begum, Shaista Khan's begum, the daughter of the subedar … the list is long! I am ashamed to say all this.'

Shamim consoled her, putting her hand on Dilras Banu's shoulder. 'Begum Sahiba, forget the happenings in Agra. Why should they bother you? Let us focus our energies here. It is good to see the Shahzada spending a lot of time with you these days. Azam will soon have a younger brother. I have been given strict instructions by the Shahzada to look after your health. I will be in trouble if he were to know that you were crying.'

ৡ৹ ৹ৡ

Aurangzeb got permission to attack Golconda on the pretext that the Shah of Golconda had captured Mir Jumla's son and wife. Aurangzeb's treasury was under stress having to feed a large army that had been sitting idle. He did not waste a moment after receiving the royal acquiescence and despatched Sultan with a large force.

Aurangzeb was being debriefed by the messengers each morning when Sadullah, standing next to him, said, 'You may recall the Mysore maharaja had sent his emissary to meet us.'

'Yes, I do. I know Raja Shrirang is very keen to see us defeat both the sultans of Golconda and Bijapur.'

'The emissary has been camping here for months now. He is getting anxious.'

'Why? Haven't we accepted his gifts and promised to take care?'

'He is worried we might form an alliance or have a pact with both the sultans. That will put him in a spot, he feels.'

'We have a right to get a treaty signed by them.'

'That is the reason he wants to ensure that we do not renege on our promise once we begin the campaign. In fact, he is willing to increase his offer.'

'He has literally emptied his coffers at our feet. What else can he give?'

Sadullah fiddled with the papers he held. He was not sure of Aurangzeb's reaction. Raja Shrirang's proposal was out of the ordinary and he was hesitant to read it aloud.

Noticing his hesitation Aurangzeb said, 'Sadullah, you don't need to hide anything from me. Please speak your mind.'

'Shahzada, if we agree to vanquish both Golconda and Bijapur, Raja Shrirang and his entire family are willing to convert to Islam.'

'*Ya Allah!*' Aurangzeb blurted out inadvertently, surprised and shocked at the good news. He looked at Sadullah carefully. He wanted to ascertain the truth behind his statement. There was no one inside the room. A few khojas guarding the room stood out of earshot. Aurangzeb asked, 'Sadullah, is it true?'

'*Ji*, Huzoor! His emissary Shrinivas Rao has personally proposed this to me on behalf of his raja. He said Raja Shrirang would like the Shahzada himself to read out from the holy book.'

'I don't understand why he is so desperate to see the kingdom of Vijaynagar being razed to the ground? They are already in dire straits. What does Raja Shrirang get from their downfall?'

'Shahzada, revenge is sweet. He is willing to pay any price for it.'

'Sadullah, a man obsessed with revenge forgets his balance. I can understand Raja Shrirang may be desperate to save his life and kingdom and hence may resort to any means. But let us not forget that we are here to rule and not create a spark which will engulf us tomorrow.

Nevertheless, I shall personally supervise the conversion of Shrinivas Rao to a Musalman. That will not only be an auspicious beginning but also satisfy Raja Shrirang that we intend to fulfil our promises.'

'I would like to bring to Shahzada's attention that not all the zamindars in the Deccan are supporting us. A few of them have been creating a lot of trouble of late.'

'Shiva Bhosale?'

'That's right, Huzoor. He is the son of Shahaji Bhosale, a mansabdar under the Bijapur sultan.'

'I know those details. Ever since I have taken charge of the subedari, I have been watching the kind of trouble he is creating from the Godavari till the banks of the Kaveri and the Tungabhadra. Send him a *shahi firman* with my seal. Tell him the Mughal army is marching against Golconda and Bijapur under direct orders from the Badshah. If he supports us in our campaign, he will receive our patronage in future.'

'I shall despatch the *firman* right away.'

It was late in the afternoon. Aurangzeb, on hearing the call of the muezzin, got up to read his prayers.

ೂಲ ೨ಿ

Aurangzeb was in the anteroom attached to the zenankhana looking into issues related to the harem. Ever since Hira's death some years ago, he had started spending time on these matters. Shamim was responsible for all issues like the appointment of maids and concubines and the allocation of duties to the various servants attached to each of the begums. There were the minor issues to be resolved like rewarding the maids for having done some good work and reprimanding some who had been slack in their jobs. Aurangzeb would look into these matters in the afternoon spending a few hours on them. The date for the campaign was nearing and Aurangzeb was keen to dispense with the matters at hand quickly so that he may get more time to spend with Dilras Banu.

Having issued instructions on various issues, he relaxed and reclined against a large pillow. Looking at Dilras Banu he said, 'Banu, you will have to excuse me for the next few months.'

'Why? Are you going somewhere?'

'I will be on a campaign. You will have to look into these matters in my absence.'

'Are you not planning to take the zenankhana with you on your campaign? Don't you recall the insults we had to bear in Agra when you left us alone and went off to Kandahar?'

'Banu, the situation here is different. And I am not handing over the charge to anyone in my absence. You are free to stay the way you wish.' Seeing that Dilras Banu was not convinced he asked, 'Why do you look so worried?'

'I don't want to trouble you with more problems. You have enough on your plate.'

'Tell me. I want to hear them.'

'Well, Zebunissa is nearly nineteen now. I am not sure how long you would be busy with your campaign. I wonder if the thought of her marriage has crossed your mind.'

'Oh! Now that you say so, Zeb is of marriageable age, isn't it?'

'You're so preoccupied with politics and campaigns, I would not be surprised if you don't remember that you have a daughter called Zeb.'

'Begum, I know Irani women are quick on the repartee, but you need not display the same each time we meet.'

Aurangzeb glanced around the room. Many maids hovered around the other side of the screen, their ears alert to catch any word spoken by him. He clapped once. Anwar Khoja came in and Aurangzeb instructed: 'Anwar miya, please ensure that there are no maids and laundis outside. Put a deaf khoja on guard and ask the others to move away.'

When he was sure the maids were out of earshot, he said, 'Do you have a suitable alliance in mind?'

'I do. And you know him too.'

'Whom are you talking of?'

'Suleman, your elder brother Dara Shikoh's son.'

'What? Dara's son?'

'I knew you would object. Dara's elder begum is from Iran and is very well mannered. The son too is known to be so.'

'Banu, are you not aware of my relationship with Dara?'

'I am. But what has this marriage got to do with politics?'

'I am a devout Musalman and I would want my daughter to be married to one such Musalman only.'

'What do you mean? Is Dara bhai not one?'

'He was born one, but his deeds do not make him so. He hobnobs with pandits, discussing their religion. He donates to their temples and reads their books which are nothing but blasphemous. He holds debates with their so called learned men.'

'So what's wrong with that? Even in Iran we …'

'Enough! Banu, I don't have the patience to hear another word of praise for your Iran. Do you realize my brother would not have hesitated to kill me had Badshah not been alive? I cannot allow Zebunissa to marry his son.'

Dilras Banu's disappointment was writ large on her face. She persisted, 'What's the difference between Dara and your other brother Shuja? Yet, you agreed to get Nawab Bai's son Sultan married to Shuja's daughter. Sultan is your favourite, but the moment I talk of my daughter's marriage, you bring up the issue of religion. I have to reconcile to my fate, unfortunately.' Dilras Banu's voice cracked as she was unable to continue, tears flowing down her cheeks.

'Banu! Don't get so emotional. You are not aware of the plots Dara is hatching against me. And regarding Sultan's marriage to Shuja's daughter, who told you it has been finalized?'

'All the maids and the khojas in the zenankhana are in the know of it.'

'Let me tell you something; that marriage will not take place.'

'What?' Dilras Banu asked wide-eyed, her fingers on her lips.

'We'll talk about it later. I am told you are not taking the medicines prescribed by the hakeem. You should not neglect your health.'

Dilras Banu realized Aurangzeb was trying to divert the topic. She did not want to push the issue further lest he lose all interest in her.

She looked down at the carpet and said, 'Shahzada, this hakeem does not know anything. I am fine and taking care of myself. I have given birth to two daughters, though they may not be your darlings. Now my heart says I am going to give Azam another brother.'

'Did you not visit the dargah of Sheikh Zainuddin at Khulabad and ask for his blessings?'

Dilras Banu blushed. 'I cannot hide anything from you!'

'Is it possible that anything can be hidden from Aurangzeb?'

'I request you to fulfil a small wish of this slave of yours. Please bear with me for a few moments. I know you have many things occupying your mind, but I need you to hear me.'

'Begum, what makes you feel I won't hear you? Tell me, what is troubling you?'

'Shahzada, I wish to see my daughters Zebunissa and Zeenat married. I may or may not be there, but they should have the good fortune of their father witnessing their marriage.'

'Begum! Don't get so worked up! I have to leave now. It is time for my afternoon namaz. You have prayed at the dargah of Sheikh Zainuddin and it won't go waste. I too will pray for your good health. Begum, I may be a Shahzada, but I am only a mortal. Allah is benevolent and he will ensure you get what you want.' For a change, Dilras Banu could feel an emotional tone in Aurangzeb's voice. She stepped forward and salaamed thrice with her right hand.

⋄⊚ ⊚⋄

It being Friday, official activities were closed. Aurangzeb stood in his room, looking outside the window. He had promised Dilras Banu to look after the daughters, but he was troubled by the burden of it. Anwar came in and said, 'Huzoor, the Shahzadis have asked for your audience.'

Stepping into Zebunissa's quarters, Aurangzeb asked, 'Zeenat, what's the matter? I was told you wanted to speak to me.'

'Ji, Abba Jaan. You never get time off from your work.' Zeenat was bold enough to speak to her father without any fear. Zebunissa stood at a respectable distance. Aurangzeb hugged his daughter and, holding her chin with his hand said, 'Zeenat beti, I know why you called me.'

'You do?'

'I had asked you to memorize the verses from the Quran. Today being Friday, you want to recite them to me, isn't it?'

'Abba Jaan, everytime you speak to us you enquire only about the chapters we have memorized from the Quran, how much Turki language we have learnt, what the old man in the Hadis says, and such things. We are not going to talk of all these today.'

'I am curious to see what you have for me today. But beti, please don't make fun of the Quran. You are young and will realize later.'

'Abba Jaan, please close your eyes.'

'Here, I have closed them,' Aurangzeb said, covering his eyes with his palms. Zebunissa gestured to Zeenat and she moved a curtain aside to reveal a few paintings kept for Aurangzeb's inspection.

'You may open your eyes now.'

Aurangzeb looked at the paintings and asked, 'Who has made them? Is it your teacher?'

'No. I painted them,' Zebunissa said, pride evident in her voice.

'Zebunissa!' Aurangzeb exclaimed.

'Don't you like them?'

Looking once again at the paintings he asked, 'Whose portraits are these?'

'Your enemies; this one is the Shah of Golconda and the other one Adil Shah of Bijapur. And here, the third one ...' Zebunissa pointed to a painting kept in a corner.

Aurangzeb looked at the painting intently.

'Can you guess whose it is?'

'Quite evidently it is some kafir's. Zeb, have you painted them yourself?'

'Why? Did you not like them?'

Kissing Zebunissa's long and delicate fingers he said, 'Zeb, it is not about liking them. I wish ...' He hesitated for a moment. Caressing her fingers with his rough hands he continued, 'I wish these hands are not put to such ungodly acts.'

Zebunissa's face fell hearing her father's disapproval.

'Abba Jaan, they are so beautiful and yet you say you don't like them? It is strange.'

'Beti …' Aurangzeb pulled her close saying, 'Allah has created human beings. What is the point in showing off to Allah that we can recreate his great work? Will he like it?'

'Abba Jaan, Allah is up there in the heaven. You are our Abba Jaan and we want to know if you like them or not.'

'Beti, how can Allah's servant like anything which Allah himself won't approve of?'

'But Abba Jaan …' Zebunissa held back her words. Aurangzeb was holding her hands. She quietly moved away saying, 'Abba Jaan, why would Allah not like what his creation creates?'

A faint smile played on Aurangzeb's lips. He said, 'Beti, I know where you are getting these ideas from. I know the Irani begum is proud of her lineage. But keep one thing in mind, dear; you should always listen to your elders. You girls should be spending your time reading the Quran and the Hadis. If you want something different, read *Gulistan* and *Bostan*. Spend time doing namaz. That is what will make you a better person. I don't want to disappoint you. Your paintings are really good, but I must add that you should never use these lovely fingers of yours to paint a kafir. By the way, who is he?'

Zebunissa was hurt and did not respond to his question directly. She said, 'It is a zamindar from the Deccan. One of the teachers got the painting from Junnar and I copied it. Abba Jaan, I am planning to visit the dargah of Sheikh Zainuddin tomorrow. I hope I have your permission to pray for your victory.'

'There is nothing more satisfying than praying at a dargah. I was informed by Shamim about your visit. I will give instructions to Aquil Khan. Do visit the Daulatabad Fort too.'

'Thank you for your permission,' Zebunissa and Zeenat said, getting up. It was time for Aurangzeb's prayers. They both saluted and left.

Aurangzeb did not leave but lingered for a while. He looked at the three paintings lying on the floor. The one with a Hindu ash mark on the forehead was the one which attracted his attention. He asked Anwar to pick up the painting and walked back to his quarters.

Aurangzeb had no time for himself. Regular *shahi firmans* giving instructions on the campaign were being received from Agra each day. The *firmans* were confusing in nature, at times asking him to slow down and other times urging him to show results. Sultan had been camping on the outskirts of Golconda with a large contingent. The two Badshahs of the south were a worried lot and had been sending their emissaries at regular intervals. Raja Shrirang would not hesitate to remind Aurangzeb of the promise made to him. Aurangzeb's uncle Shaista Khan was stationed at Aurangabad directing the war effort. He advised Aurangzeb on the changings aspects of the war.

One evening Shaista Khan came in unannounced to meet Aurangzeb. The meeting room was guarded only by deaf and mute guards. Nephew and uncle were thus able to confer without the fear of anyone overhearing them. Shaista Khan was around ten or twelve years older to Aurangzeb. He had the looks of a handsome Iranian. His expensive dress showed his inclination to things beautiful. His slim fingers were not meant for hard labour. But he possessed a sharp brain and he knew his nephew would be keen to take his counsel on matters of war.

Aurangzeb, after having heard his uncle speak at length said, 'Khan Sahab, I was not aware of the situation in Agra having turned from bad to worse. No doubt the *firmans* we are getting these days are all confusing and do not make any sense whatsoever.'

'Aurangzeb, I could have elaborated more, but you have got the gist. Mumtaz was my sister and the Badshah is my brother-in-law. All his four sons are dear to me, but I don't mind telling you that you are the closest. I found an excuse in the name of helping you in your campaign to meet you personally.'

'Khan Sahab, I never expected Badshah to be so partial to my elder brother. May I ask you something?'

'Please! Don't hesitate.'

'My brother Dara enjoys all the support of the Badshah. Why are you here instead of by his side?'

'I told you that you are closest to my heart, didn't I?'

'Yes, you did. But what about Shuja? And my brother Murad who is managing Gujarat? Don't you love them?'

'Let me be frank. I will have to be blunt, but please bear with me. Aren't you aware of the Mughal tradition?'

'What tradition are you talking of?'

'Badshah Salamat is not keeping well and it is a matter of time before the question of succession raises its head. A wise man prepares well in advance.' Shaista Khan did not elaborate as he knew Aurangzeb was perceptive enough to catch his drift. Aurangzeb kept a poker face and waited for him to continue. Shaista Khan said, 'It is a Mughal tradition that the person claiming the throne has to win it from his siblings. No one has claimed the throne based on birthright alone. The winner extracts his price from the rest. Badshah Shah Jahan did the same when he ascended the throne.'

Aurangzeb maintained his composure and asked, 'Khan Sahab, you know I am not interested in pursuing politics, and power does not attract me. Since Emperor Akbar's time the pure traditions of our religion have not been followed, rather we have allowed many practices of the kafirs to become part of our life. All I want is to follow the path laid down by Hazrat Muhammad and lead my life.'

'There is no doubt it is due to such inclinations of yours that all the old and orthodox mansabdars love you, Shahzada.'

'Khan Sahab, what has my way of life got to do with the mansabdars liking me?'

'Shahzada, you have been in politics long enough and know the art very well. Nevertheless, if you so desire, I shall speak without trying to beat around the bush.'

'I am not forcing you to; if you feel uncomfortable.'

'I would rather speak despite my discomfort. Else, there are many more dangers lurking around which could be disastrous,' Shaista Khan said.

He continued further, 'You know that the Badshah has announced your elder brother's name as a successor to the throne. He has been given the privilege to sit next to him in the durbar. Dara Shikoh may have a charming personality and behave well, but this sort of favouritism does not go down well with the orthodox mansabdars. Dara, following the tradition set by Shahenshah Akbar, favours and supports Hindu traditions, and hobnobs with the pandits. He encourages the mullahs to listen to the Hindu priests and participates in discussing the faults of our religion. And to make matters worse, he wears a ring which has the kafir word 'prabhu' engraved on it! If such a person were to sit on the throne, we are afraid it will soon become a Hindu kingdom. It will be the pandits, the priests, and the Christian preachers who will be advising the emperor on all matters. Our kazis, mullahs and maulvis will become a laughing stock!'

'Khan Sahab, I have heard something else though.'

Shaista Khan was hoping to see some reaction on Aurangzeb's face but to his dismay Aurangzeb continued his stoicism. He asked, 'What have you heard?'

'I am told the Rajput sardars favour Dara bhai. Thanks to the support extended by Raja Jaisingh and Raja Jaswant Singh, the other Rajputs from Bundelkhand and the Jats are supporting Dara. They are thrilled to hear that the next emperor will be their friend.'

'Shahzada, you may be right. But today's friends can be foes tomorrow, and vice versa.'

'Are you saying the mansabdars do not like my other brother Shuja who is managing the affairs in Bengal?'

'Everyone is aware of the way he is managing Bengal, spending most of his time in the zenankhana and leaving the affairs of the state to lower-level officials. A mere khoja can change his mind. No one can trust him and he has no qualities befitting an heir to the throne. Your other brother Murad in Gujarat – he is drunk most of the time. He does not deserve to be called a Shahzada. Complaints of his errant behaviour and debauchery have reached such levels that the Badshah himself is worried and does not know what to do with him. I have no doubt that in the event of a struggle for the throne, all the mansabdars will support you. They believe there is no one better suited than you, who leads by example and one who respects the maulvis and the mullahs.'

'Khan Sahab, that may be the popular opinion, but I do not think it is wise to usurp the throne.'

'Shahzada!' Shaista Khan's voice took on an edge. 'The question is not what you think. The question is of whether you will live or not!'

'I don't understand you.'

'Let me clarify: only one of the four Shahzadas is going to survive. This has been the Mughal tradition for generations. No one can change it even if one wants to. If you are not willing to fight for the throne you will have to accept defeat and death. It will be a pity if all the people who have shed their blood for Islam feel their sacrifices were in vain.'

Aurangzeb was silent for a long time. The evening had given way to night. The month of Ramzan had got over a few days back and the day of Eid had been celebrated with a lot of fanfare. The hangover was still visible on the streets where people were busy celebrating. After a while he said, 'Let us assume that what you say is likely to happen. If I were forced to fight against my brothers, what guarantee do I have that you will support me?'

'Are my words not enough?'

'You mentioned that today's friends could be foes tomorrow.'

'Let me assure you then; I will leave my zenankhana under your custody. You may release the zenankhana only after you are convinced of my loyalty. Does that give you comfort?'

Aurangzeb stifled his smile. He was satisfied, but did not allow his emotions to surface. He said, changing the topic, 'Let us bother about the throne at Delhi later. Right now, I have to worry about Golconda and Bijapur. Let us discuss how we should tackle them.'

'I believe Allah has given us a golden opportunity. Both the kingdoms of Golconda and Bijapur are sitting on tons of gold and enormous wealth. We have the support of people like Mir Jumla. The treasure we gather today will be of great use when we march against the Badshah tomorrow.'

Aurangzeb was now fully aware of the changes waiting to happen in the Delhi Durbar, but he displayed no sense of urgency as he said, 'Khan Sahab, I will think over what we discussed. But first we have to tackle the problem created by Qutub Khan of Golconda. He may surrender any day. I suggest I lead the campaign to its logical conclusion.'

'I would advise you not to lead the campaign yourself. Your begum, I am told, is not keeping well. It would be better if you don't leave Aurangabad at the moment.'

Aurangzeb sighed, 'Khan Sahab, the begum is not well nor is the situation around any better. I think we have no choice but to march on to Golconda. Let us see what happens then ...'

Things were happening at a rapid pace and there was no time for Aurangzeb to sit and contemplate. Within eight days of Shaista Khan's army marching out, Aurangzeb moved towards Golconda with his contingent. The effect was similar to that of ordinary animals in a jungle on hearing a tiger roar. The news of the Shahzada spearheading the campaign spread across the four corners of the Deccan within days. No one doubted that it meant the end of the two sultanates.

Within a few days of Aurangzeb's departure, emissaries from both Golconda and Bijapur arrived at his camp with heaps of jewellery, precious gems and jewels, and whatever they could get from their treasury to dissuade him from attacking. Aurangzeb chose to ignore their pleas and continued moving forward. He soon joined Shaista Khan's forces and ordered surrounding the Golconda Fort.

On the eighth day, Aurangzeb, while camping at Dharur, received a message. It was an emissary from one of the zamindars of Bijapur, who was seeking permission to meet.

'Who is the emissary? Whom is he representing?'

'The zamindar is a rebel and goes by the name of Shiva Bhosale. His emissary seeks your permission for a meeting.'

For a brief moment Aurangzeb's eyebrows knitted. He said, 'Present him in my tent.'

The daroga soon came in with a man, dark in complexion and wearing a local style turban.

'Tell me your name and whether you can speak Farsi or Hindavi.'

'My name is Krishnaji Bhaskar,' the man said in Hindavi, bending in salute.

'What is Bhosale's proposal? Join us or support Adil Shah?'

'My Lord has sent his greeting to you, Shahzada,' Krishnaji Bhaskar said, avoiding his gaze.

Interrupting him, Aurangzeb said, 'Answer my question. Are you supporting us or not?'

'I have a message for the Shahzada. I request you to hear me first.'

'I am listening. But please hurry.'

'May I request some privacy? I want to read out his message and also hand over a letter, my Lord.'

Aurangzeb scanned Krishnaji Bhaskar from head to toe, wondering whether he was armed and meant any harm. The cantonment was heavily guarded and there was no way to escape. The daroga, reading Aurangzeb's mind, said, 'I have checked him thoroughly before allowing him inside. Huzoor, you need not worry. You may meet him in private.'

'Let us go,' Aurangzeb said, turning to his inner quarters, a smaller tent, meant for his private meetings. Aurangzeb leaned back against the cushions and asked, 'What does your jagirdar want to convey?'

'Our raja wants to extend a hand of friendship to the Shahzada and at the same time ...'

'Raja? What are you talking of?'

'Shivaji raja; Shahaji raja's son. Shahaji raja is a jagirdar at Bijapur.'

'Adil Shah has crowned himself Badshah and is now giving titles to all and sundry, it seems,' Aurangzeb said. 'We consider Adil Shah a mere landlord of Bijapur. How can his jagirdar be a raja?'

'But ...'

'No buts; I recognize your Lord as Shiva Bhosale. If he agrees to work under the Mughals, I may consider requesting our Badshah to accord him the title of Raja.'

'Shahzada may recall that the reign of Adil Shah of Bijapur has been around for ages ...'

'Nonsense! We will soon see how long it lasts. Anyway! Let us come to the point.'

'Our raja wants the Dabhol port in Konkan, and the area around including the fort, to be under his control. It is, in reality, our territory, but the official recognition by the Mughals would help us. We are ready to work under the Mughals and our raja will be honoured to join the royal army along with his troops.'

'Oh I see! You are trying to take advantage of the situation and get your share of the territory from the Bijapurkars. I don't think one extends a hand of friendship in this manner.'

In response, Krishnaji Bhaskar took a letter out of a bag and placed it in front of the Shahzada: 'Raja has accepted all your conditions. It will be an honour if you can give us your blessings. The Mughal might is enormous while we are mere mortals. Nevertheless, our raja has written that in case you need our help at any time, we will be honoured to provide the same.'

Aurangzeb did not accept the letter in person. He glanced at an official standing nearby who came forward and took it. 'The Bhosales have been the jagirdars under the Bijapur rule for generations. What makes them ditch their Badshah and come to us for a deal?' he asked.

'There is no doubt that Shivaji raja is a mansabdar under the Bijapur kingdom. But the Badshah seems to have changed his mind and does not think twice before looting and plundering our territories. Our raja feels it is high time we stopped working under him.'

'And quite obviously, get all the associated benefits of such a change!' Aurangzeb remarked.

'How can we think of taking advantage of your situation? You have been our friend. Our raja thinks it is our duty to be of help to you when you need it,' Krishnaji Bhaskar persisted.

'Enough! Enough of this drivel. If Shiva Bhosale thinks he can spin the Mughal Empire on his finger as he does with Adil Shah, he is totally mistaken. He will have to pay a heavy price. You are going to face the wrath of the Mughals if you try to trick us.'

'I am flabbergasted, your honour. We are here to make a proposal.'

'All the while finding ways to trick us, isn't it?'

'Our conscience is clear. We are being unnecessarily ...'

'Come to your senses, emissary!'

Aurangzeb clapped once. A servant standing outside came in and at a nod from Aurangzeb, went out to return with a bag. Removing a letter from the bag Aurangzeb flung it at Shivaji's emissary and screamed, 'Krishnaji Bhaskar! Read this letter as proof of your betrayal. You come and talk of helping us while on the other hand you are looting our territories! Your people have attacked our camp at Junnar and after killing our soldiers, looted the treasury of nearly fifteen thousand gold coins, not to mention the horses, jewellery and other such treasures which your raja took away in the loot. And you have the audacity to stand here and offer your support?'

Sweat trickled down Krishnaji Bhaskar's face. Aurangzeb's penetrating stare seemed to cut him in half. He licked his dry lips nervously before saying, 'Something seems to be amiss. The news is flawed.'

'Krishnaji Bhaskar, it is your understanding which is flawed. Let your Shiva Bhosale know: we will not tolerate any such affronts. If you are under the mistaken belief that you can fool the Mughals, you will pay a heavy price for it some day. It will be a lesson learnt for life. You may leave now. I can't waste my time any more.'

On cue, the daroga standing nearby held Krishnaji Bhaskar's arm and escorted him out of the tent.

The very next day messengers were despatched with instructions for thanedars Nasir Khan, Kartabal Khan, Abdul Munim and others. The message was unambiguous:

Don't sit there just guarding the borders. At the slightest opportunity raid Shiva Bhosale's territories and push him back. Plunder his lands and

butcher his people. Don't show any mercy. The dust of Pune and Chakan
should be seen miles around. If any of the Patils and Kulkarnis, enjoying
our patronage, are found helping Shiva, behead them without any delay.

৵৶ ৶৵

The Mughal troops crossed the borders and within four days Aurangzeb received the news that his troops led by Muhammad Sultan had entered Hyderabad and that Qutub Khan was hiding in his fort at Golconda. Aurangzeb took an immediate decision. With just a few select soldiers in tow he rode on horseback towards Golconda.

It was nightfall by the time Aurangzeb reached the shores of the Husain Sagar Lake at Hyderabad; pitch dark all around. The cool breeze was a relief for the soldiers who had been riding non-stop for hours. Aurangzeb asked the troops to stay put while he rode into the city to meet his son. The loot, under the custody of various amaldars, was laid out for him to inspect. Elephants, horses, camels, gold, silver, jewellery, expensive clothes, vessels with gold inlay work, and other beautiful objet d'art collected by Qutub Khan from all over the world were on display.

Aurangzeb, walking along with his son Muhammad Sultan, could not believe his eyes. He had always believed that the riches of the Deccan were a myth. It was almost dawn by the time they finished their inspection.

The satisfaction of seeing the loot had diminished the strain of the journey. Sultan escorted him to the newly erected camp. Aurangzeb sat down, happiness clearly visible on his face. Sultan was pleased that his father had approved of his work. Auranzgeb, deliberately avoiding the topic of the loot asked, 'Where is Qutub Khan hiding? Why has he not surrendered yet?'

Sultan answered, 'There is no doubt about the complete victory of the Mughals. The moment Qutub Khan heard of our coming, he rushed into the Golconda Fort. He must have received the message of your arrival. I'm sure he will surrender in a few days. Our victory is guaranteed.'

'Sultan, you have done a commendable job till now. But the tough part is ahead of us. We need to penetrate the walls of the fort with our cannons. I will consider the victory complete only when you get me Qutub Khan in my camp with his hands tied behind his back.'

'*Inshallah*, that day is not far away!' Muhammad Sultan said in his soft voice. 'Shahzada must be exhausted by the long ride. I suggest you rest today. Tomorrow I shall show you how we have surrounded the fort.'

Raising his right hand Aurangzeb interrupted his son. 'I will rest inside the Golconda Fort. We shall leave once I am through with my morning prayers. In the meanwhile, send the details of the loot. I would also like to meet our spies whom we had deputed in Hyderabad earlier.'

Aurangzeb completed his morning prayers thanking Allah for granting him acesss to the enormous wealth of the Deccan. He returned to the tent erected for his meetings, where the amaldars and spies were in attendance. Accepting their salutes he asked, 'Is the loot complete or is something still pending?'

And old man, one of the spies, stepped forward, 'Huzoor, your son has personally inspected the havelis of Qutub Khan, his mansabdars and sardars. Only the poor people's houses remain untouched.'

'Don't spare them,' Aurangzeb thundered. 'Remember! Hyderabad should look like a ghost town once we're finished. The ryots should learn a lesson and never dare to raise their voice against the Mughals. If genocide would send the message, go ahead. Don't hesitate.'

'Your suggestion is absolutely right, Shahzada,' one of the maulvis agreed. 'Allah has his blessings on you.'

Ignoring his comment Aurangzeb turned to one of the generals responsible for intelligence gathering, 'I was told the Golconda mines have enormous riches. What I saw here seems nothing in comparison. What do you say?'

The question was a tricky one. Aurangzeb had been inspecting the loot wide-eyed at night. He had never expected such an enormous cache. Not wanting to reveal his inner happiness he had showed outward irritation. The old man answered on behalf of the Bakshi, the adjutant general. 'I am sure Huzoor is well aware that what we have captured in Hyderabad is nothing compared to the enormous wealth inside the fort. But we are sure to lay it at your feet the moment we capture the fort. We don't have an iota of doubt there.'

Aurangzeb's ploy had worked. The fact was too exciting to hide, yet he asked, narrowing his eyes, 'Miya, what is your estimate of the wealth held inside the fort?'

'Huzoor, it would be around …' he fumbled to find the right words and then said, 'even if you were to replace each brick of the fort walls with a gold one, it would not match the treasure inside. That is what I can say.'

Aurangzeb could not believe his ears. Taking a round of the fort with Muhammad Sultan, he quickly surmised that they needed enormous cannon power to be able to make a breach. He returned to the cantonment without further comments.

࿄ ࿄

Aurangzeb's fame had spread right across Hindustan. The might of his well-trained army and his rigid hold on the same had reached Qutub Khan's ears. Hiding in his fort with his wife, ailing mother and other sardars, he was at his wit's end. He had never expected Aurangzeb to personally march upon Golconda. Leaving his subjects to their fate, he had taken refuge inside his fort. The news from the guards at the ramparts that Aurangzeb had inspected the preparations alongwith Sultan shook Qutub Khan to the core. The sardars, fearing their lives, urged Qutub Khan to work out a pact with Aurangzeb.

The next day, two emissaries from the fort landed at Aurangzeb's cantonment where he was busy talking to Sultan. He said in a firm voice, 'Frisk them and then present them before me if they are willing to allow their hands to be tied behind.'

Within no time, two old men wearing long robes were presented before Aurangzeb. Long-flowing necklaces of precious gems adorned their chests, while their turbans sported pearls. Their legs trembled as they stood looking at Aurangzeb with fear-filled eyes.

'Huzoor, we have erred. Please pardon us,' they said falling at his feet.

Aurangzeb looked at them with contempt. 'I had not expected Qutub Khan, who calls himself the Badshah of the Deccan, to surrender so easily to the Mughal Shahzada. Get up! I would like to hear what conditions your Badshah has put forward for his release.'

'Our Badshah appeals to the large-heartedness of the Shahzada to pardon him,' one of the old men said, quivering in fear.

'It is too late for that …' Aurangzeb said, his voice taking on an edge.

'Our Badshah is willing to accept all the terms put forward by you,' the old man pleaded.

'What other option does he have? Don't put on this act of repentance. You were proud of your treasures and arrogant when we approached you in a friendly manner. You had no idea of the strength of the Mughals which has shown its prowess from the mountains of Kabul right up to the banks of the Godavari. You will understand only when you personally experience what the Mughals can do.'

'Huzoor, we have erred. Please don't punish us further.'

'There is no use of repeating the words. I need to hear your proposal in clear financial terms.'

The emissaries heaved sighs of relief. They were experienced in verbal negotiations and had come prepared to give only the bare minimum. They did not plan to show all their cards; their ploy was to approach and present the gains one at a time.

'We are agreeable to hand over our yearly collections, whatever little they are, to the Mughals.'

'We shall collect the taxes ourselves now. You need not trouble yourself for that. The time to make a treaty with ransom has long gone by. Despite knowing that Mir Jumla is under our patronage, you have had the audacity to capture him and his family and put them behind bars.'

'I was coming to that. We are willing to relieve Mir Jumla and his family immediately.'

Aurangzeb's words dripped with contempt. 'If you intend to speak in such a fashion I would not want this interview to continue any further. I am preparing to launch an attack on your fort. Once the cannons start booming, it will be a matter of time before the fort is devastated. I suggest you waste no further time and discuss the terms.'

'We have agreed to your demands for the revenue share as also the release of Mir Jumla. I am unable to understand what other terms you are referring to.'

'We want complete control of the sultanate.'

'The sultanate?' The emissary could not believe his ears. He had never expected such a proposal. He floundered for a moment before gathering himself and said, 'Hyderabad, the pride of the sultanate, is firmly in your hands. We have agreed on the annual revenue and are willing to pledge any collateral that will ensure that we do not default on the same.'

'Enough! I am tired of your political language. I want to know when you can present Qutub Khan here with his hands tied.'

'Ya Allah! Huzoor, my Lord is a Badshah after all. You should ensure his prestige is kept intact.'

'It is too late for that. He alone is responsible for losing his stature.'

Muhammad Sultan, sitting next to Aurangzeb, was listening carefully to the exchange of dialogue between his father and Qutub Khan's emissary. The emissary tried another ploy glancing in the direction of Mohammed Sultan. 'In order to prove our respect for the Mughals, our Badshah is willing to give his daughter's hand in marriage to Shahzada's son. There has been a custom to have Rajput begums in the Mughal zenankhana. We would like to propose our Badshah's daughter for your son. I request the Shahzada not to decline our proposal.'

The emissary was trying his best but Aurangzeb's mind was on the enormous wealth hidden in the Golconda Fort. He continued his arguments, making a show of not having heard the marriage proposal: 'I am giving you four days to rethink the terms. In case Qutub Khan does not surrender to me in my tent here with his entire zenankhana within these days, I will have no option but to order the cannons to start firing. It will then be a matter of days before you stare at total destruction.'

The emissary, dejected at having failed in his attempts, left the tent with his head bent low. Aurangzeb heaved a sigh of relief and turning towards Sultan said, 'Sultan miya, it seems others are more concerned of your marriage than I am.'

Sultan did not respond but continued looking down at the floor.

৵৹৻ ৻৹৵

A week passed. In this while, Shaista Khan and Shahnawaz Khan had reached the banks of the Husain Sagar Lake with their armoured batallions, and placed the cannons in strategic positions.

If was only after a fortnight that Aurangzeb got some time to breathe. He returned to his tent a little earlier than usual. He lay on the bed but sleep eluded him. His spies, spread across the entire country, fed him regularly with the latest news, but of late, many of those had been worrisome.

Aurangzeb's mind was troubled. Thoughts whirled as he worked out various scenarios in his mind. The success of his campaign against Qutub Khan was within sighting distance. He knew that the victory was sure to make all his brothers jealous. The Badshah, in the meanwhile, had continued to ignore his repeated messages. He was sure that the news of the enormous wealth of Golconda would have reached the Delhi Durbar through various channels and knew that there were many who would twist the news to their advantage while conveying it to the Badshah. He remembered the way the news of his flirting with Hira Bai in the Zainabadi garden had reached the Badshah's ears. There were many in Delhi who would want to poison the Badshah's mind: mansabdars and close confidants of the emperor, Aurangzeb's elder brother Dara, and his elder sister Jahanara Begum. Aurangzeb was worried of the conspiracies being hatched in Delhi on the one hand and of his Begum's health on the other. Added to it was a doubt that the Badshah of Bijapur may rush in with his troops in support of Qutub Khan. His sleep was fitful.

৵৹ে ৩৹

Winter was receding on the Deccan plateau and it was getting warmer. Thankfully the cantonment, situated on the banks of the Husain Sagar Lake, enjoyed the cool breeze soothing the tired soldiers. Several months passed by. Hopes and disappointments played hide-and-seek while slippery emissaries sent in by Qutub Khan continued to enagage Aurangzeb in various dialogues. The cannons were ready to fire but they were yet to receive explicit instructions from Agra. Aurangzeb did not want to take any chances unless he had clear instructions from the Badshah. He was frustrated to the core but continued to maintain his calm demeanour.

He took a bold decision one day and agreed to the proposal to get his son married to Qutub Khan's daughter. The marriage was celebrated with pomp and show in the cantonment. Qutub Khan had sent exquisite jewellery as a gift to Aurangzeb. The bride came into the cantonment in a palanquin decorated with rare gems and pearls. But Qutub Khan did not venture out of the fort. In the midst of all these events, the news of the Irani begum having given birth to her second son reached Aurangzeb.

Aurangzeb was pleased and presented the messenger with a diamond ring. This was another occasion for the others to shower Aurangzeb with gifts. The celebrations continued for many days. Aurangzeb sent a word to Aurangabad with his wish that his son may be named Muhammad Akbar.

The celebrations distracted his mind for a while but he had a niggling doubt that things were not right. He was worried of treachery and was on guard all the time. The news of the sudden death of Adil Shah of Bijapur presented another opportunity to Aurangzeb. Adil Shah did not have any heir and all it required was a little bit of arm twisting to annex his territories right from the southern banks of the Narmada up to the seashores of Rameshwaram in one swoop. Aurangzeb was well prepared with his thirty thousand and more soldiers, a trained cavalry, and his powerful armoury of cannons. All he needed was the *shahi firman*. Aurangzeb was eagerly waiting to see the Mughal flag fluttering on both the sultanates of Bijapur and Golconda.

The royal *firman*, over which Aurangzeb had spent many a sleepless nights, landed itself in a totally unexpected manner.

While returning from inspection one evening, Aurangzeb got a message for an urgent meeting. He directed his horse towards his tent where he found Shaista Khan and Shahnawaz Khan waiting for him. It was evident, looking at their creased foreheads, that the news was not good.

'Khan Sahab, what is the reason for a request for such an urgent meeting. You are aware it is time for my namaz.'

'You must have noticed during your inspection that some sections of the cavalry and the armoured troops are missing.'

'I did notice. In fact, on not getting a satisfactory answer from anyone, I commanded the guards to arrest the amaldars responsible for those units.'

'Shahzada ...' Shahnawaz Khan hesitated before continuing, 'I doubt whether your orders will be implemented.'

'What do you mean?'

'The troops left with the amaldars leading them.'

Aurangzeb could not believe his ears. His insistence on discipline was well known. For someone to have the courage to tell him that the troops had not only vacated their positions but had left the cantonment without his permission was akin to flirting with death.

'Khan Sahab, how is this possible?'

'It is the hand of your enemy in the royal durbar.'

'You mean Dara bhai?'

'Yes. While you waited for the *shahi firman* to capture the two territories, your brother Dara has managed to convince the emperor that you have committed a grave mistake and has, in fact, sent a letter of apology to Adil Shah and Qutub Khan!'

'What? Ala Hazrat has sent a letter of apology, and that too without my knowledge?'

'Adil Shah and Qutub Khan had sent their emissaries to Delhi complaining against you. They managed to get the *firman* acknowledging our mistake. Now that they have a letter from the emperor himself, our threats are of no value to them.'

'I am the subedar of the Deccan! I had explicit permission from the Badshah to attack these two territories. How can the Badshah send his apology without taking me into confidence? Don't I have any say here?'

'Shahzada, we have tried to warn you often that the people there are poisoning the Badshah's mind against you. Unfortunately, you did not heed to our warnings.'

'I am really amazed! What crime have I committed? All I have done is manage the Deccan as per the orders given to me.'

'Shahzada, please don't mind my being blunt. Dara is least bothered of the territories you annex to the Mughal Empire. He is jealous of the way you are being treated here and the wealth you have amassed. He has managed to convince the Badshah that you may declare yourself the Badshah of the Deccan one day and break away from the Mughal Empire.'

'Shaista Khan Sahab, it would be my misfortune were the emperor to misjudge my actions. Tell me, how did the amaldars have the courage to leave their positions without my permission?'

'Shahzada, please pardon my saying so but the issue is not between you and the emperor.'

'What do you mean by that?'

'Badshah Salamat is an emperor for the name's sake. The real power rests with your brother Dara now. He is the one who sent direct orders to the amaldars here.'

'Oh!' Aurangzeb blurted out. He never had had any doubt of the love lost between the two of them, but he always believed that Dara would respect protocol, give weightage to his authority, and not bypass the chain of command. He had never expected Dara to throw caution to the winds and insult him by sending direct orders to his amaldars.

Aurangzeb realized then that things had changed beyond his belief. He said, 'I agree that Darabhai and I don't see to eye to eye on many things. I had my wish to see the borders of the Mughal Empire stretch from Kabul in the north-west to the ocean shores in the south. We have lost a golden chance and I am not sure whether we will get such an opportunity in the future. Send a message to Qutub Khan, hiding in his fort like a scared woman, that I am leaving for Aurangabad due to pressing concerns regarding Irani begum's health. But warn him that he should continue to send the yearly amount as promised. If he fails to do so, let him know that we will take strict action.'

The huge army lumbered its way back to Aurangabad; elephants, camels and horses laden with the riches of the loot. Aurangzeb, sitting atop an elephant, had a dejected look as he rode back to Aurangabad. Despite having amassed so much, he was saddened by the fact that his dream to expand the Deccan subah had not been fulfilled. One dream had been snuffed while other sparks had been ignited. It was now a matter of time before the sparks would create an inferno.

๑๐ ๑๑

On his way back to Aurangabad, Aurangzeb sent letters to his brothers Shuja in Bengal and Murad in Gujarat. As expected, they too were not happy with the way Dara had managed to tighten his grip on the Delhi Durbar. Aurangzeb had camped at the borders of Aurangabad and had plans to complete innumerable pending tasks before entering the city, but an urgent message made him change his plans and he mounted a horse with a few select horsemen in tow and rushed towards the royal palace. Ignoring the usual protocol offered by Sadullah, Murshid Quli Khan and other amaldars he asked, as soon as he climbed the steps to the haveli: 'Is Begum Sahiba's health deteriorating ?'

'Ji, Huzoor,' Sadullah answered, looking at the floor. 'For the past month and a half, the hakeem has been trying different medicines to reduce the puerperal fever, but to no effect. The moment Begum Sahiba came to know that you have camped outside the city, she called for you.'

He walked swiftly towards the zenankhana where Shamim waited at the door to Dilras Banu's room. Aurangzeb turned to see that his father-in-law, Shahnawaz Khan, had not accompanied him. Dilras Banu may have been his daughter but as per protocol, only Aurangzeb had the right to enter the zenankhana. Aurangzeb sent a word through Shamim asking Shahnawaz Khan to meet his daughter.

Dilras Banu, emaciated with constant fever, lay on a high bed. Her cheeks had lost their pink glow land her eyes and cheeks were sunken. Her lips were dry and pale. Zebunissa and Zeenat stood on either side of her bed. Two maids in attendance were fanning her while another one prepared the medicines. On cue, the attendants left the room as soon as Aurangzeb entered. Zeenat looked flustered, glancing alternately in the direction of her mother and at the tanned face of her father. She could not hold back her tears and hugged her father. Through her sobs she somehow managed to utter, 'Abba Jaan! Abba Jaan! We have been waiting for you. Ammi Jaan is very ill.'

Aurangzeb gently extracted her arms from around his waist and patted her back affectionately, then went and sat next to Dilras Banu. She opened her eyes and it took her a while to recognize him. She exclaimed, 'Huzoor, aap aaye!' Speaking was an effort for her and she gasped for breath. Aurangzeb touched her forehead with the back of his palm and felt her burning with fever. He raised his eyebrows questioningly at Zebunissa.

'The fever does not seem to abate. Hakeem sahab has tried different medicines but there does not seem to be any improvement whatsoever,' his older daughter said.

Shahnawaz Khan entered the room and stood near the bedstead. Aurangzeb gently patted Banu's cheeks saying, 'See! Your Abba Jaan too has come to see you. Open your eyes now.'

Dilras Banu took a while to open her eyes. They had lost their shine. Shahnawaz Khan was seeing his daughter after a gap of many years. It was a terrible shock for him to see her in her fragile and emaciated state. He could not hold himself back, and putting his head on her chest wailed, 'Beti! Beti! What have you done to yourself?' He caressed her face tenderly while the tears flowing down his cheeks lost themselves in his grey beard.

Aurangzeb patted Shahnawaz Khan's back, then addressed his wife, 'Begum, I have returned from my campaign now. I pray you get well soon.'

'Huzoor, I had made a request before you left for your campaign. I have been holding on to my life to remind you of the promise made by you,' Dilras Banu whispered.

'Please don't say that, Begum! Everything will be fine!' Aurangzeb's voice quivered as he held her hand. Dilras Banu could not sense the anguish in Aurangzeb's voice. She said, 'I don't think medicines can help me now.' She tried raising her hand to beckon her daughters closer. Putting their palms in Aurangzeb's she slowly said, 'Huzoor! My Lord! These two daughters are part of me … Even if I die … my soul will pine … for them. I will know peace only when their marriage procession … leaves from my haveli.'

'Everything will be as per your wishes, I promise you.'

'I would … like to speak … to you in private …'

Shahnawaz Khan and his granddaughters left the room. For a brief moment, Dilras Banu's face seemed to brighten up. Her grip on Aurangzeb's hand tightened as she spoke with great difficulty, 'Huzoor … I have tried my best to please you … since the time I came into your life. You were upset … I gave birth to two daughters … Now I have given you two sons. I hope you will pardon me if I ever … hurt you …'

'Begum, Begum …' Aurangzeb voice was filled with anguish.

Dilras Banu continued, 'Please … tell me you have pardoned me. I am waiting to hear you say that.'

It took a lot of effort for Dilras Banu but her eyes penetrated Aurangzeb's gaze. He looked at her once and said, 'I pardon you. I pardon you, I pardon you!'

Within moments the eyes lost their sheen and then her hand went limp.

ംരെ ളo

The royal palace was engulfed in a pall of gloom. For a month, all official duties were on hold as the court was in mourning. In the meanwhile, letters of condolence were sent by the Badshah, Dara, Jahanara Begum and Roshanara Begum, sisters of Aurangzeb. It hurt him that all the letters, except the one sent by Roshanara Begum, were clearly a formality.

Aurangzeb stepped out of the palace on a Friday to pray at the mosque. He planned to perform his namaz at his favourite dargah – that of Sheikh Zainuddin at Khuldabad. The royal elephant stopped near the steps and Aurangzeb dismounted, then glanced up at the tall minarets before climbing the steps. Each step seemed a Herculean effort to him. It reminded him of each step in his life that had gone by ...

Dilras Banu had been just fifteen when Badshah Shah Jahan had lovingly chosen the Iranian beauty from his extended family for Aurangzeb. Aurangzeb was then the subedar of the Deccan and the thought that his father cared for him had soothed his soul. The next ten years had passed off in dream-like happiness. The independence of being a subedar and the accompanying powers, the ever alert and fawning amaldars, and his beautiful begum – all these had created a sense of wonder and awe. Life and its accompanying mysteries seemed easy to solve. Within a few years of marriage, he had had children. The years passed by in a blink. He remembered the encounter, in his earlier years, with a drunken elephant at Burhanpur and his first brush with death. It was only later he came to know that it had actually been a ploy to kill him. His father had been in attendance, watching the spectacle. The elephants had been fed the juice of kusumba flowers while he was astride a horse with a small spear in hand. As one of the she-elephants charged, he had flung the spear in her direction to no effect. The elephant's blow, on the other hand, had flung him high in the air. His brothers, standing nearby, had run away rather than try and help him, leaving him to his own fate. Since that day he had lost faith in people and could not trust anyone. He had seen people being betrayed. It was then that he realized that he had been insulted, betrayed and defeated multiple times. A simple action of his would be interpreted differently. His Abba Jaan and his elder brother felt his presence was a bother and had despatched him to the Deccan as a subedar. In order to ensure that his humiliation was complete, his zenankhana had been deliberately held back in Agra while he was asked to march on to the Deccan. He had swallowed all insults. He could not forget Dara's treachery when he had got the two badshahs in the Deccan to their knees. His love for Hira had opened up another universe and he had felt genuine love for the first time. But fate had other plans for him. His enemies ensured that he would not be able to enjoy the pleasures for long. It was here in Aurangabad that he had cremated his dear Hira … and it was here that he had buried Banu too. He regretted he had not been able to express his love to Banu as much as to Hira …

Thoughts raced through his mind … He soon reached the last step and turned back to look at the wide expanse of the city below. It had been fifteen years since he had taken charge of the Deccan. He had helped build many mosques and dargahs and could see their minarets kissing the skies. He should have felt proud, he thought. He mused, 'This is the place I always visited with a lot of hope. But happiness has eluded me. I, who at one time roamed around freely under the cool shade and patronage of the Badshah, am now being burnt under the bright heat of suspicion. Dara fears me. One, who does not have confidence in his own self, sees an enemy in each person. Dara is able to get away thanks to the implicit support of the Badshah. It is my fate! If Allah believes that Aurangzeb should not find love, peace or happiness anywhere, so be it! Jahanara Begum, my elder sister, who is the apple of the emperor's eye, does nothing when Dara insults me. Roshanara Begum is only one who sends me news from Agra and seems to favour me, but I am not sure whether she supports me out of love for me, or to spite her elder sister. I don't think this place will give me happiness any more. I can only see darkness ahead …'

Aurangzeb lightly brushed his palms over his eyes before entering the dargah. He indicated to the mullah and maulvis to step out and knelt near the grave of Sheikh Zainuddin. Touching his forehead to the ground and raising his palms in the air he recited, 'La ilahi illilah, Muhammad rasool lillilah'.

જી ૭

Fate had delivered multiple blows and hardened Aurangzeb beyond recognition. He had lost all his finer sensibilities now. He was engrossed in the affairs of the state, with Murshid Quli Khan giving him an account of the revenues collected and Sheikh Sadullah describing the matters of internal security. Aurangzeb had called for a meeting and Danishmand Khan and Bahadur Khan had come over from Agra. Shaista Khan too was present. Aurangzeb's gaze was focused on a particular document. Putting it aside he said, 'We shall conclude work for the day. I have to spend some time with Danishmand Khan in private now.'

When they left, Aurangzeb said in a low voice, 'My informant says that Badhshah Salamat is unwell and that Dara Shikoh has taken charge of affairs.'

'That's not news. Your brother managed affairs earlier too. Now that Badshah is not well, he will make your life miserable.'

'I had been expecting this for the last few months. But I have a doubt … I am not sure if Hazrat is ill or whether he is already dead.' Aurangzeb spoke without a trace of emotion.

A shiver ran down Danishmand Khan's spine. He had heard a lot of rumours in Agra but was not sure whether he should share them with Aurangzeb. He said, 'Shahzada, you may rest assured that Badshah is alive in Agra.'

'How do you say that?'

'I know what illness he is suffering from; and it is not fatal. I heard it from one of the guards in the zenankhana. It was an event which occurred a fortnight ago. Badshah was in his room enjoying his beauty in the mirror, dyeing his hair. Of late he has this habit of twirling the ends of his moustache. He was busy doing so when a young maid came into his room. She chuckled seeing that the Badshah, despite his advancing age, was still keen to look young. Seeing her chuckle, the Badshah ...'

'Pray, continue. Do not stop.'

'Shahzada, I am a mere khoja but what happened next is shameful for me to tell. Badshah grabbed the maid and, as a punishment for her impudence, threw her down on the bed. He tried to force himself on her when he realized that he had lost his manhood. The realization that the mind was willing but the body was not upset him. He called the royal physician who gave him a strong medicine. Within a few days boils erupted all over his body. He was barely able to breathe, and to add to his misery, he was unable to pass urine. I conveyed the message to the French hakeem, who prescribed certain medicines which alleviated the pain to a great extent. Badshah was recovering slowly when I left Agra.'

Aurangzeb listened to Danishmand Khan wide-eyed. He had heard stories of his father's sexual escapades within a few days of Mumtaz Begum's death and had lost all respect for him. A sudden doubt crept in his mind: *Could Dara have taken advantage of his weak health and put him to death?* There was no doubt that even if Badshah were to be alive, he would be a mere puppet in Dara's hands. There was not much time for Aurangzeb to act, if he had to survive. He exclaimed, 'So that's it! I don't think I will be able to live long if I continue to stay in the Deccan.'

෯෬ ෨෯

Aurangzeb's fears turned out to be true. Ever since Badshah had been taken ill, he had not been seen by anyone. All kinds of rumours made the rounds, from his death having occured a fortnight back, to his body having been buried secretly in a grave at the Agra Fort. Aurangzeb heard that Dara had sent a large contingent of troops to prevent him from marching up north and the spies soon reported that Dara had given orders to ensure Aurangzeb never reached Delhi.

It was impossible for Aurangzeb to sit quiet now. He had to take action. He called for his confidants, Shaista Khan, Shahnawaz Khan,

Murshid Quli Khan and a few other amaldars. The news of Badshah's illness was all over the Deccan. The murmur could be heard in the bazaars and the streets of all towns and there was a lot of speculation on who would succeed him. Aurangzeb consulted his team and asked, 'The question is whether we wait here and be at the mercy of Dara's troops who will spare no one, or take a chance to march up north and present ourselves to the Badshah Salamat. If he is alive it will not pose a problem. We can ask for pardon. But if he is already dead, fate will decide whatever is in store for us. Those who are with me may please say so. Those who cannot support me may leave right away. I want to ensure that there is complete loyalty once we commit to the act.'

Aurangzeb's quiet demeanour was uncomfortable to those in attendance. The amaldars did not react immediately but squirmed in their seats. Shaista Khan was the first one to respond. He said, 'Shahzada, you should have taken this decision much earlier. You have my complete support. The moment you cross the Narmada, my troops will join you. Please rest assured.'

Others quickly joined in to offer their support pledging complete loyalty placing their hands on the holy Quran. They spent the next few hours discussing the strategies of warfare. At the end of the meeting, Aurangzeb got up, determination writ large on his face. It was now a question of 'do or die'.

৯৫ ৯৯৯

The decision had been taken and orders were issued quickly for Muhammad Sultan to march with a large contingent. His job was to guard the banks of the Tapi and the Narmada. The zenankhana and one-year-old Akbar were safely ensconced in the Daulatabad Fort. Leaving the affairs of the Deccan under the charge of his younger son Muazzam and some senior officials, Aurangzeb marched northwards within a month.

Dara had sent a large force to confront Aurangzeb's troops under the leadership of Jaswant Singh and Kasim Khan. They saw Aurangzeb and his contingent at the banks of the Shipra near the village of Dharmat. Jaswant Singh was in a dilemma: Aurangzeb had clearly stated he was en route to seek attendance with the Badshah and, in such a situation, an attack would look vindictive. But the instructions from Dara were to capture Aurangzeb 'dead or alive'. He was left with no choice but to attack. Aurangzeb and his troops made a surprise counter-attack on Jaswant Singhs's troops by crossing the river at an unexpected place and catching them unaware. The troops ran for their lives. Jaswant Singh had to get down from his elephant and fight bravely with swords in both his hands. His troops managed to rescue him and they all fled. Aurangzeb's troops celebrated their victory that evening.

Aurangzeb had enough experience not to get excited over this victory. He was aware that the entire royal force was under Dara's command and that he would have to confront them sooner than later. Nevertheless, the victory was a good omen.

He camped near the Shipra for a month, corresponding with his other two brothers in the meanwhile. They too were uncomfortable with Dara's behaviour and were itching to take action. Fatwas, issued by the maulvis, proclaiming Murad in Gujarat and Shuja in Bengal as the Badshahs, were circulated across Hindustan. Murad sent his contingent to join Aurangzeb's forces near Depalpur with a request to help him ascend the throne. Aurangzeb was amused at the eagerness his brothers showed in proclaiming themselves the next Badshah but kept his feelings to himself. He marched onward towards Delhi.

In the peak of summer Aurangzeb received the news that Dara Shikoh had left Delhi with a contingent of nearly a lakh soldiers in tow.

The contingents were at sighting distance from each other near Samugadh, a few miles south of Agra. Aurangzeb consulted with his officials on the strategy for attack and spent the night working out plans. Many amaldars, who had bowed in salaam seeing Aurangzeb, were now on the other side supporting Dara. Aurangzeb had staked his future to his fate. There was no looking back now.

After finishing his morning prayers, Aurangzeb issued instructions for the cannons to start pounding. He personally supervised the battle sitting atop an elephant. The attacks and counter-attacks continued till noon with both sides barely giving in. In the afternoon, Aurangzeb's troops managed to find a breach and entered the enemy lines. Dara, personally supervising the attack on the other side, charged into Aurangzeb's troops. He got off his elephant to fight and victory seemed within reach. But a strange situation developed while Dara was busy pushing back Aurangzeb's troops. Dara had jumped from his elephant to stop the breach. His troops, in the meanwhile, presumed that Dara had fallen and the rumour spread like wildfire. Large parts of his army started retreating. Aurangzeb, watching from a distance, took advantage of the situation and charged into the battle. Dara tried in vain to stop his amaldars who were running for their lives. His throat, hoarse with shouting, was of no use as the amaldars, seeing death hovering over their heads, ditched the battlefield.

By evening Dara's forces suffered a major jolt. A force of more than a lakh soldiers had been routed. By the time the evening sun dissolved into the western horizon, it was clear that a new sun was going to rise over Hindustan.

Aurangzeb, amidst the clamour of the battle and the shrieks of the wounded soldiers, calmly got off his elephant and performed his namaz. Raising his hands heavenward, he thanked Allah for his mercy.

He asked his officials to sound the cannons announcing his victory. Nearly ten miles away, sitting in Agra, the Badshah wondered who had won. The cannons continued for an hour and the news soon spread across the town that the royal forces had been routed in the battle at Samugadh. Dara had run away. Aurangzeb could stake his claim on Hindustan now.

ഛര ളഌ

Aurangzeb spent the night on the battlefield. He instructed his men to ransack Dara's cantonment. They returned with whatever riches they could lay their hands on. All that was left behind were torn tents and some maids and khojas, who sat cowering in a corner fearing for their lives.

Aurangzeb reached Agra the next morning and camped on the outskirts at Noor Manzil. Amaldars, who had been sitting on the fence without supporting any of the camps overtly, hurried to pay their regards and show their loyalty. Aurangzeb sent a message to the Badshah stating clearly that the sole purpose of his visit had been to meet him. Shah Jahan sent Fazil Khan and the main kazi Saiyyad Hidayatullah to meet Aurangzeb. They informed Aurangzeb that the Badshah was waiting to meet him at the Agra Fort. A specially made sword was presented to him as a welcome gift.

Aurangzeb received the sword with great excitement. He looked at the words carved in the handle. The letters, carved in Persian, read 'Alamgir' – the conqueror of the world. Seeing Aurangzeb's reaction Saiyyad Hidayatullah added, 'The Hazrat has sent this as a special gift. He wishes that you succeed in all your ventures and emerge victorious.'

The Badshah had also sent precious gems and jewels for his son. Aurangzeb received the officials warmly but did not commit to a date for the meeting with the Badshah giving an excuse of having to look after his wounded soldiers.

Aurangzeb was in a dilemma. He had been victorious in the battle and most of Dara's troops had already joined him but he was not sure of the Badshah's mind. He spent the whole day trying to get information from various sources. That evening he called for a meeting with Khalilullah Khan, the Badshah's chef.

Aurangzeb asked, 'Khan Sahab, you are well aware that I am here with my troops and it will not take me any effort to capture the fort itself. But I don't intend to insult the Badshah by doing so. I am told the Badshah is waiting to see me. You are one of his oldest confidants. I would like you to place your hand on the holy Quran and tell me whether the Badshah really intends to meet me or he has other treacherous plans. If you tell me I have nothing to fear, I will walk in barefoot and meet the Badshah.'

Khalilullah Khan was old and bent with age. His previous two generations had been in the service of the Mughal emperors. In his youth he had seen Shah Jahan leading a revolt against his father.

History seemed to be repeating itself. He had an inkling of the events to come and was aware of the reason for the Badshah to invite Aurangzeb into the fort. He hesitated to place his hands on the holy book. Aurangzeb, watching him intently, noticed the hesitation and said, 'It is amply evident that there are plans to execute me in the fort. You have been a personal advisor to the Badshah. You have nothing to fear. Tell me, Khan Sahab, are the Badshah's intentions pure?'

Tears flowed down Khalilullah Khan's wrinkled eyes. He placed his trembling hands on the Quran and said, 'Shahzada, you have put me in a dilemma. I have been under the patronage of the royal throne. Like me and my earlier generations, my sons and grandchildren too will live under the Mughal patronage. I cannot tell a lie when I have to face the Allah in his court soon. Let me tell you the fact straightaway: Shahzada, the Badshah does not trust you one bit. His favourite is Dara. He has plans to invite you and finish you off in the fort or else ask your brother Murad to do the same in the cantonment. Shahzada, this servant of yours has seen a lot of royal blood spilled in his youth. But I am old now and want to spend my time reading the namaz five times a day. I don't have many days left. I wish I don't have the misfortune of seeing the old events being repeated.'

Aurangzeb could not believe his ears. Despite the fact that Dara had been routed and the royal troops had been vanquished, he was shocked to know that the Badshah had no love lost for him. Aurangzeb was aware of Khan's loyalty to the emperor. The fact that he had spared no details also meant that the plans would not remain secret for long. Taking Khan's hand into his he said, 'Khan Sahab, you have been of great help. In fact, you have saved my life in a way. I fear that your life may be in danger if you return to the Agra Fort. My father, who has lost all his balance in favour of Dara, may not care about your old age and will not hesitate to act against you. I feel your presence here will be of much use to me. I need an elderly and experienced advisor like you. I would like to appoint you as my advisor and the royal chef from today, if you are willing.'

Khalilullah Khan said, extricating his hand gently out of

Aurangzeb's, 'Please don't force me, Shahzada. I have committed a crime by speaking against the emperor, under whose patronage I have spent my entire life. Now, if I am going to be killed for that, I am ready for the same. I leave it to Allah. I would like to seek your leave, Shahzada.'

Aurangzeb had no words. He looked at Khalilullah Khan for a few seconds and said, 'As you wish. *Khuda hafeez!*'

⋰⊚ ⊚⋱

It was not possible for Aurangzeb to rest while the Badshah was managing affairs from Agra Fort. An inordinate delay could lead to the mansabdars switching their loyalties. He took a bold decision – he ordered that Agra Fort be surrounded. One cannon was placed near Jama Masjid and another at a haveli on the banks of the Yamuna facing the fort. Both the cannons started bombarding. The fort was under attack.

Despite shelling the whole day, the cannons could hardly make a dent. Aurangzeb realized that surrounding the fort may not lead to immediate results. He had also received the news of Dara gathering his troops in Punjab while Shuja was on his way from Bengal. He had, of late, also realized that he could not trust his younger brother Murad completely. It was important to put the Badshah in his place at the earliest.

After deliberating through the night, he found a solution that was ingenious and simple. The water supply to the fort was through a well dug on the banks of the Yamuna. He sent a few troops to take charge of the well. He waited to see how long the residents inside would be able to survive without water. On the third day the doors of the massive fort were opened. Khalilullah Khan, waving a white flag of peace, marched out of the fort and presented himself before Aurangzeb.

Aurangzeb sent his son Muhammad Sultan along with a few soldiers to take charge of the fort. The moment they entered the fort, the guards dropped their weapons and surrendered. Sultan took charge of the royal treasury and went to meet his old grandfather. Bending in salaam he said, 'As per instructions issued by my father and your son Shahzada Aurangzeb, you are hereby informed that you are not permitted to leave the fort and that you will be allowed to remain in your palace with your zenankhana. You are not allowed to correspond with anyone. The city of Agra and the fort are now under the command of Shahzada Aurangzeb.'

The emperor's lips quivered but he was unable to speak. Lifting his right hand a little, he managed to utter a single word, 'Ameen!'

Aurangzeb's reign in Agra had commenced.

BOOK TWO

Delhi! It was a city that Shah Jahan had made his capital and whose beauty matched that of Agra. The lovely buildings and havelis of Shahjahanabad were decorated to receive Aurangzeb. There were celebrations in all corners – at Chandni Chowk, Lahori Darwaza, Ajmeri Darwaza, Khwaja Nizamuddin's dargah and Amir Khusrau's dargah. People were tired of wars that had been waged continuously over the past three years across Hindustan. Thousands had lost their lives, not to mention the loss of elephants and horses, and the constant burden on the exchequer. It seemed that finally peace had descended. Aurangzeb left Agra to take his seat at the Takht-e-Taus, the Peacock Throne, and declare himself the Badshah of Hindustan. The celebrations at Aurangzeb's temporary camp set up at Khijrabad near Delhi continued till the wee hours of the morning.

The summer morning air was warm. Aurangzeb's caravan proceeded at a slow pace towards Delhi. The caravan was led by trumpeters who heralded their arrival. Following them were richly caparisoned elephants. Golden posts hoisted on the elephants' back sported the Turkish colours. Persian and Arabian horses cantered behind the elephants. Behind the few hundred horses, a select herd of elephants walked slowly, small cannons strapped to their backs. Swords and other weapons dangled from their sides; wazirs, amaldars, mansabdars, and other officials of the Mughal Empire, dressed in their finery, followed the elephants, sitting astride their horses with pride. The royal elephant carrying a golden howdah was the centre of attraction, its trunk decorated with colourful gems. The pillars of the howdah were decorated with precious stones. Sitting in the howdah was a man who had been engaged continuously in battles for the past three years and who now had stars in his eyes. It was Shahzada Aurangzeb.

Aurangzeb was in his early forties but the battles had taken a toll on him, giving him a hardened look. He was slim and tall. When he had left Delhi to take charge of the Deccan he looked like someone used to the luxuries of life. On return, people were seeing a very different Aurangzeb with a small beard and the odd white hair visible in it. His forehead was not creased but his penetrating eyes seemed capable of reading anyone's mind. The eyes did not know fear and never showed a glimpse of anxiety. There was not a hint of gentleness or compassion in them. They observed everything as he rode the elephant on the way to his coronation. His soldiers – those who had been loyal to him having fought alongside and survived many battles – marched in flanks beside him. The wives of the amaldars and other officials eagerly waited behind the curtained windows of the havelis along the route to catch a glimpse of the man who had successfully managed to get two Badshahs in the Deccan to their knees. They were seeing the Shahzada in a new avatar having put Badshah Shah Jahan, who had ruled the country as an emperor for more than thirty years, under house arrest at the Agra Fort. The crowds were curious to see the warrior who had managed to rout the huge forces of Dara and Shuja in no time. Aurangzeb sat in the howdah, throwing fistfuls of gold coins as his elephant lumbered its way forward. Crowds gathered on the street went berserk trying to catch the coins. The procession, after crossing Chandni Chowk, finally reached the Red Fort. The amaldars leading the procession dismounted and made way to welcome the eleventh successor to the Mughal throne, in an unbroken line since Timur. The elaborate ceremony in the Diwan-e-Aam was about to commence.

The Diwan-e-Aam, the hall of the commons, was resplendent in preparation for the coronation ceremony. The forty-odd pillars in the hall were covered with bright red Persian satin cloth, some of them with flowers embroidered in Gujarati tradition. A square portion of the hall was marked out, the famous Peacock Throne placed in the centre and adorned with thousands of gems, diamonds and other precious stones. The narrow pillars of the throne, supporting the umbrella, too were bedecked with gemstones. Small pillows, kept on each side of the seat, were decorated with gem studded cloth. The entire hall was covered with thick Persian carpets with an exquisite interplay of colours and design. The royal guests had a special enclosure with silver railings. The doors and the walls of the entire hall were draped with Turkish and Chinese curtains, decorated with fine embroidery that further enhanced the grandeur of the hall.

The mullahs and the maulvis sat in a corner dressed in their finest. A group of pandits stood in another enclosure wearing silk dhotis and angavastrams. A copper ghatika patra, a water clock, was placed in a gold tray to announce the correct time for the coronation. In addition, an imported valuka yantra, an hourglass, filled with sand, hung on a nearby decorated pillar.

The maulvis and the kazis, after consultation, had declared an hour after noon as the auspicious time for the coronation. As soon as the maulvis raised their hands signalling the appointed hour, the trumpeeters began, their sound piercing the skies. A silk curtain hung behind the Takht-e-Taus, the Peacock Throne. At the sound of the trumpets, the curtain was raised and Aurangzeb, deserving successor to the tradition established by Timur, and a descendant of Babar, stepped forward dressed in his finest royal clothes to sit on the Peacock Throne. Shouts of 'Allah o Akbar' and verses from the Quran were heard. The pandits recited verses from the holy books in their distinct and clear Sanskrit pronunciation.

As soon as Aurangzeb sat down, a group of dancers, waiting in a corner, stepped forward and, bending in elaborate mujra with their right hand almost touching the floor, began their performance. They danced for over half an hour and then retreated, taking care not to show their back to the Mughal throne.

The head kazi climbed up the steps of a specially erected platform adjusting his flowing robe and read out the khutba, the sermon, praising Aurangzeb. He read out lines in praise of the work done by Aurangzeb's father Shah Jahan and his grandfather Jahangir. The kazi paused for a moment to glance in the direction of Aurangzeb before reading out his official name: *Abdul Muzaffar Muhi-ud-Din Muhammad Ghazi Aurangzeb Bahadur Alamgir Badshah-e-Hind!*

The moment the kazi announced the name, he was showered with jewels and gems. The mansabdars in attendance, hearing the name of their newly coronated Mughal emperor raised their hands shouting *'Karamat! Karamat!'* Shouts of *'Allah o Akbar'* rang through the hall.

Another hour was spent distributing clothes and gifts to the officials in attendance. A rich fragrance spread through the hall as the servants, holding trays of paan and a rose water sprinkler moved around. The newly coronated Badshah of Hindustan watched the goings-on as he sat on the Peacock Throne. Alamgir Badshah had already made his first announcement, issuing a new coin in his name. The words on the coin read: 'This coin shining like a full moon has been issued by Alamgir Badshah'.

Alamgir spent the next hour issuing *shahi firmans* to be despatched to various corners of the country. He then got up to move towards the zenankhana. It was a signal to those present that the ceremony was over.

The first one to meet the newly crowned Alamgir Badshah, as he sat down in a specially created seating arrangement at the zenankhana, was his sister Roshanara. She was the one who had been diligently conveying all the happenings in Delhi and Agra to her brother when he was posted as the subedar of the Deccan and had tried her level best to ensure that Shah Jahan's views about Aurangzeb were not biased. Seeing her brother in the new avatar, her happiness knew no bounds. Her elder sister, Jahanara, was imprisoned with Shah Jahan in the Agra Fort. It was a soothing thought for Roshanara to know that her jealous sister was out of her way and that her favourite brother was now the emperor at Delhi. Aurangzeb looked admiringly at his sister as she, dressed in her finery, bent in salaam and said, 'Salaam, Huzoor-e-Ala Hazrat! Salaam!'

'Roshanara Begum, I am really pleased with you. As a token of my happiness, I am offering you a sum of five lakh rupiyas.'

A maid in attendance stepped forward holding a golden tray. The

Badshah touched it lightly before she handed it over to Roshanara. Zebunissa and Zeenat too were recepients of two lakhs and one-and-a-half lakh rupiyas respectively, apart from expensive clothes and jewellery. After handing over the gifts to his sister and daughters, the Badshah looked around. Roshanara, noticing his glance, clarified, 'Begum Sahiba is not well.'

'Oh! I will pay her a visit then,' Aurangzeb said.

It was the turn of wives of the senior officials to pay their regards to the newly crowned emperor with gifts befitting their status and hierarchy. Aurangzeb received them patiently, spending the next hour or so. His sons Muazzam, Azam and Akbar were waiting for him in the Diwan-e-Khaas along with the aged Wazir Jaffar Khan and the main kazi Inayatullah. They too offered their gifts to the Badshah and in return, were rewarded with cash and expensive clothes as per protocol and hierarchy.

Late in the afternoon, the entire city assembled on the sandy banks of the Yamuna abutting the fort to have a glimpse of their new Badshah. A loud roar erupted from the crowds the moment Aurangzeb was visible at a window. A veritable ocean of people had gathered to welcome him. A small entertainment area, cleared in the middle of the crowds, was featured elephant fights and various attractions till sunset. The pyrotechnics display, at sundown, was a sight to behold. The waters of the Yamuna shone with reflected light as fireworks lit up the sky. Amirs and other wealthy merchants joined in the celebrations as they crusied along the river in their specially designed boats.

After enjoying the spectacle for a while, Aurangzeb got up.

Roshanara and the daroga led him upto the zenankhana and waited at the entrance as Aurangzeb entered Nawab Bai's chambers. Aurangzeb could not fail to notice that there was no joy or pride on Nawab Bai's face on seeing him in his new avatar as the Alamgir Badshah. He asked, 'Begum, the city of Delhi is going wild with celebrations, but I don't see an iota of happiness on your face. Are my expectations beyond reason?'

'I don't feel comfortable that the Badshah of Hindustan stands while talking. I request him to take a seat.'

Sitting down Aurangzeb said, 'Begum, you have not answered my question.'

'I am not sure if the Badshah of Hindustan would be able to accept my answer.'

It was clear that Nawab Bai was hurt. Aurangzeb knew the reason but events had unfolded at such speed that he had had no choice but to act in a manner which was not palatable to all. He said, 'I can see that you are deliberately trying to insult me by referring to me formally as the Badshah of Hindustan. You know I have not come into the zenankhana in that capacity. Please speak your mind.'

Tears flowed down Nawab Bai's cheeks. She said, her voice choking with emotion, 'Huzoor has occupied the throne in all pomp and glory. But my Sultan …' A sob escaped her lips.

'I understand your agony at Sultan being thrown behind bars. I had sent him with a large contingent to fight my brother but what did he do instead? He joined them! Now you tell me; what else other than a jail does he deserve for such a treacherous act?'

'I can't tell Huzoor what is right or wrong. All I know is that Sultan is my son. He may have committed crimes but he doesn't deserve to be treated like ordinary criminals and thrown into a prison at Gwalior. You are celebrating here while he sits in his small cell looking out of the window cursing his fate. Can you expect me to smile when I imagine his situation?'

'Begum, you don't understand politics.'

'Huzoor, you are incapable of even imagining the trauma a mother goes through.'

'Begum, let me make it clear; I would never have been able to conquer the throne had I been swayed by such emotions. I can very well understand your heart reaches out for him, but experience has taught me that these are the very emotions one must guard against. I was disappointed when you had borne me sons while the Irani begum had had daughters. But my disappointment has multiplied manifold with the way your son has acted. I never expected him to play such a dirty trick. Let me say this: you have your place and position in the zenankhana being the senior most. It is up to you to enjoy your stay here. Else, you will suffer for the rest of your life.'

Aurangzeb tried his best to pacify Nawab Bai but to no avail. The world outside was celebrating but her world had crumbled. The last memory she had of Sultan was when he had come in to take her blessings before leaving for the campaign. Roshanara, standing at the door, strained her ears to hear their conversation but was unable to. After a while, Aurangzeb left Nawab Bai's quarters.

The sobs from Nawab Bai's quarters were heard for a long time in the silence of the night.

⚬⚬ ⚬⚬

The next twelve months kept the Alamgir Badshah busy. Emissaries from various countries in Asia and Europe came in with exquisite gifts, which were received graciously and the guests sent back with appropriate return gifts.

While Aurangzeb's eldest son languished in Gwalior prison, Muazzam was sent across to the Deccan to take charge as the subedar. Azam, ten years old, would sit with Aurangzeb while he presided over meetings in the Diwan-e-Khaas and Diwan-e-Aam. Being the Irani begum's son, he was Aurangzeb's favourite. Roshanara, as a reward for her loyalty, was given the responsibility of managing the zenankhana and overseeing the education of the girls, Zeenat and Zebunissa, as well as that of Azam and Akbar. Roshanara's beauty, matching that of her mother Mumtaz Begum, was being wasted as she busied herself in the affairs of the zenankhana. A keen observer could sense that she was trying to suppress her bodily desires and passions. The complete charge of the zenankhana and the faith reposed by the Badshah in her had given her a new lease of life. She managed the affairs with a firm hand and had complete freedom to do so.

Roshanara was yet to sort out a few critical issues in the zenankhana. She waited for an opportunity to speak to Aurangzeb.

When he visited the zenankhana with Azam, Roshanara asked Shamim to leave. There was no fear of Nawab Bai's presence as she would avoid meeting the Badshah in the zenankhana unless she was explicitly called for. Roshanara said, 'Bhai Jaan, I am unable to resolve a tricky issue. I need your advice.'

Aurangzeb had been incredibly busy ever since he had taken charge as the emperor. Despite being of robust health and possessing enormous stamina, the strain of the last few years showed on his face. He rested against a pillow and said, 'You have been given complete authority to do whatever you feel like. Your command is as good as mine. What is it that you are unable to resolve?'

'Bhai Jaan, I have streamlined everything except for one; I am unable to discipline Dara bhai's daughter Jahanzeb Banu. She is very adamant.'

Aurangzeb was aware of his niece's nature. 'What is new about it?'

'Bhai Jaan, I ignored her behaviour thinking that she would learn the ways of life in the zenankhana. She was young when she came in, but has become even more of a brat now. She speaks ill of the Badshah in front of the maids, the khojas and other laundis. She has no respect whatsoever for you. It would have been better had she been sent across along with her brother to the prison at Gwalior.'

'Roshanara, do you realize how the elders here would have reacted had I thrown a young girl behind bars? I removed Dara Shikoh from my path but many here do not like that I sent his son to prison. They may agree that the son could eventually become a threat like his father but sending his innocent daughter to prison is ...'

'Innocent? Bhai Jaan, she may be young but surely not innocent. Her presence here is akin to keeping burning embers near a haystack. You never know what she will do.'

Roshanara's nostrils quivered with emotion. She tugged at the edge of her dupatta as she waited for her brother to react.

Fo a while Aurangzeb was silent. He said, 'I would like to meet her in person before I decide her fate.'

'I would not recommend that. She does not know how to control her tongue.'

'If that be the case, I will surely like to meet her! Let me understand what she has in her mind.'

Roshanara was about to object again when Aurangzeb said, 'It is decided then! Present her before me right away. I am sure Shahezada Azam too wants to meet his cousin. Don't you?' Aurangzeb asked, kissing Azam's cheeks lovingly.

Soon after, Shamim came in with two maids followed by Jahanzeb Banu. Aurangzeb observed that Jahanzeb had inherited her good looks from her parents. Her delicate eyebrows, aquiline nose and pink complexion added to her beauty. The red eyes indicated that she had been crying for some time. Aurangzeb looked at her for a few moments and then turned his face to look out of the window when Roshanara prompted her saying, 'Banu, you are in presence of the Badshah. You need to salaam.'

Jahanzeb refused to acknowledge her aunt's advice. Roshanara repeated, 'You are meeting the Badshah for the first time. Please salaam thrice. That is the protocol.'

'Which Badshah are you referring to?' Jahanzeb asked, her sharp voice showing a mixture of anger and arrogance. Aurangzeb continued to gaze out of the window.

Roshanara patted her back affectionately and touching her chin said, 'Beti, don't be so adamant. Please show respect to the Badshah.'

Jahanzeb looked up and pointing her finger at Aurangzeb asked, her voice quivering with emotions, 'Is he the Badshah Salamat? He is my Chacha Jaan – the one who murdered my Abba Jaan.'

Roshanara cupped Jahanzeb's mouth saying, 'Beti, please check your manners.' Brushing her hand off Jahanzeb said, 'My Abba Jaan, my Ammi Jaan; he is the one who …' She was unable to continue as sobs wracked her body.

Aurangzeb turned to face her and said, looking at Azam, 'Beta, won't you pacify your sister?'

Azam got up and tried to wipe her tears. Without warning, Jahanzeb slapped hard across Azam's cheeks. The impact was so great that Azam fell down on the carpet. Her nails had scratched his cheeks and blood streamed down.

Aurangzeb did not react but his eyes bored into Jahanzeb. Roshanara gave Azam a helping hand wiping his cheek with her dupatta. A maid ran forward to grab Jahanzeb Banu's arm, but Aurangzeb indicated with his hand to stop. Roshanara shouted, 'Do you realize you have committed another crime by hitting Azam? You have no option but to ask for pardon.'

'I don't need to,' Jahanzeb replied, her voice stubborn.

Aurangzeb tried his affectionate tone, 'Beti, do you think what you did was right?'

'Chacha Jaan, do you think you were right in getting my father killed?'

'Beti, you are too young to understand everything.'

'Chacha Jaan, you are old enough. Let me ask you something: a mere drop of blood on Azam's cheeks disturbed my aunt. The murderers, sent by you, spared no mercy when my father pleaded for his life. What kind of justice is this?'

'Beti, you will understand the politics of the state when you grow up and decide whether what we did was right or wrong. You are too young right now.'

'Chacha Jaan, you are trying to pacify a young orphan, whose parents were mercilessly killed and whose brother has been thrown in jail. A few days ago I was a free bird. If you feel that a salaam will make you feel happy, I bow in salaam to the emperor of Hindustan.'

Aurangzeb's heart was touched and he was unable to fathom the maturity shown by a girl at such a young age. He got up and taking Banu's hands said, 'Beti, I can understand your pain and I know you believe I am responsible for it. The Quran teaches one to pardon. I ask you to pardon me. This Badshah of Hindustan is bowing his head to salaam you and asks you for forgiveness.'

'Abba Jaan! Should she not be punished for what she did to me?'

'Beta Azam, for a moment I forgot that you are a Shahzada now. Why don't you decide?'

Azam rubbed his cheek for a moment contemplating what he should say. He said, 'I will check with the kazi; he will tell me what punishment should be given to a person who has the audacity to slap a Shahzada.'

Taking it as a cue, Shamim led Jahanzeb out of the room.

ஒ௦ ௦ை

It was a daily ritual for Aurangzeb to sit at a window and allow the people gathered on the sandy banks of the Yamuna an opportunity to see their Alamgir Badshah. Select mansabdars would use this opportunity to display their cavalry.

One such day, sitting with Prime Minister Jaffar Khan, he noticed a group of horsemen sporting coloured turbans. The one in the lead held a saffron flag, a symbol of the Hindus. Pointing at them he asked, 'Wazir, who are these horsemen?'

'They are Raja Jaswant Singh's troops.'

'Raja Jaswant Singh? Isn't he the one who waited for me on the banks of the Shipra?' Aurangzeb frowned.

'*Ji*, Huzoor.'

Aurangzeb thought for a moment caressing his beard. He said, 'Ask Jaswant Singh to present himself in the Diwan-e-Aam.'

'As you command,' Jaffar Khan said, bowing down in acknowledgement.

At the morning durbar, the broad-shouldered Jaswant Singh, with an upturned, Rajput-style moustache, came into the hall when Jaffar Khan whispered, 'This is Jaswant Singh.'

The other mansabdars in the Diwan-e-Aam in attendance stood with their hands held behind their backs and head bowed. There were Rajputs, Bundels, Jats, Mughals and others. Telling the beads of the rosary, Alamgir said to no one in particular, his voice deliberately loud, 'So that's Jaswant Singh, is it? The one who dared confront my troops on the banks of the Shipra.'

Jaffar Khan pointed at Jaswant Singh saying, '*Ji*, Huzoor, he is Jaswant Singh of Marwar. Three generations of his have served the Mughals.'

'I am surprised that despite having served for three generations he dared to fight my men.'

There was a pin-drop silence in the hall. Jaswant Singh did not respond but continued to look down at the floor.

'Ask Raja Jaswant Singh whether he is willing to accept his crime.'

Jaswant Singh did not wait for the Wazir to repeat. He said, 'I am a mansabdar under the Mughal Empire and was merely following orders given to me, Ala Hazrat. I had no choice.'

'Wazir, I would like to know where he has learnt to speak the truth and lies in the same sentence.'

Jaswant Singh glanced up for a moment and said, looking down, 'Huzoor-e-Ala, the Rajputs do not have a tradition of telling lies in presence of the Mughal throne.'

'So! I have to learn your traditions now. Wazir, tell him he should answer only when asked. I wonder why he ran away from the battlefield, when the emperor had ordered to confront me and, if possible kill me and present my head. Is that a Rajput tradition too?'

'Jahanpanah, I was in a dilemma. On one hand I was following the orders of the emperor and on the other it was the Shahzada himself against me. I had no choice but to follow the emperor's orders.'

'Wazir, ask him how his queen welcomed home a soldier who had fled from the battlefield?'

It was an insult difficult for Jaswant Singh to swallow and a direct blow to his pride. The news of the insults he had had to bear on returning home was a topic of juicy gossip which had now spread across the country. His queen had apparently refused to allow him to enter the town and had ordered the doors to be closed. Jaswant Singh was acutely aware that the mansabdars present in the hall knew how he had been booted out of his city by his own queen.

Realizing that his words had had the desired effect, Aurangzeb issued the orders, 'Wazir, please issue a *firman* that Jaswant Singh is hereby not allowed to leave the city till further instructions. We will decide what punishment he should be given for having betrayed us. If he does not follow the *firman*, he will be arrested.' Aurangzeb spoke in a deliberate slow voice for maximum impact.

Another Rajput sardar stepped forward, saluted thrice and introduced himself saying, 'I am Raja Jai Singh; generations of mine have served under the Mughals.'

Aurangzeb said, 'Please ask Raja Jai Singh to present his request.'

'Huzoor-e-Ala, I beg to state that the punishment given to Raja Jaswant Singh is too strict. The Rajputs have been ardent supporters of the Mughal Empire and have laid their lives for the cause. Raja Jaswant Singh is senior-most amongst the Rajputs. The sultanate does not stand to gain anything if such a senior sardar is insulted in the royal durbar.'

'Wazir, you need to explain to the raja that we have in fact been lenient.'

'I beg you to reconsider. Unlike other Rajputs, he is a close family member of Ala Hazrat. He ...'

'Enough! Wazir, please tell Raja Jai Singh that I am not interested in hearing a plea on behalf of Raja Jaswant Singh. He cannot take advantage of the fact that he is related to me. I know my sister is one of his begums but that does not give him the liberty to act in any manner he wishes. My orders are final. The Rajputs need to know whom they are dealing with. This will be a lesson for them.'

Aurangzeb closed his eyes and moved the beads in his rosary. Seeing that Raja Jai Singh's plea had fallen on deaf ears, other mansabdars did not dare to speak. Jaswant Singh stepped out of the hall walking backwards a few steps. Two guards followed him.

The news of the punishment meted out to Raja Jaswant Singh spread like wildfire across Rajputana. They were unable to believe that their loyalty to the Mughal throne had been rewarded with such a punishment. Aurangzeb heard some murmurs of a revolt but chose to ignore them and instead, issued strict orders that Raja Jaswant Singh should not be allowed to step out of the city under any circumstances.

The Rajputs, in the meanwhile, were urging Raja Jai Singh to appeal. Finally, one summer afternoon, Jai Singh's palanquin stopped outside the haveli of Shaista Khan.

Shaista Khan was resting in the zenankhana but the moment the khoja delivered the message, he came out to receive the Rajput sardar. 'Rajaji, why did you take the trouble to come here on such a hot afternoon? Is it something urgent?'

Jai Singh knew Shaista Khan had played an important role in Aurangzeb's accession to the throne. He was, after all, Auragzeb's uncle and was one person who could possibly convince the emperor. Jai Singh did not come to the point directly. 'Khan Sahab, we have been serving the Mughals since the time of Badshah Akbar. Now with the change of guard, we are worried that our prestige will be diminished.'

Shaista Khan was an old fox, well versed in politics. His messengers would convey the events of the durbar each day. He had already worked out the reason for Jai Singh's unannounced visit. He said, 'I understand. I had, in fact, sent a secret message to Jaswant Singh that he should not heed Dara's orders. But he did not take cognizance of my message. You know Badshah Salamat for long now. He doesn't forgive the smallest of crimes. As far as Raja Jaswant Singh is concerned, it is unfortunate that he lost the battle and that Aurangzeb became the emperor. He has no choice but to bear the cross.'

'Khan Sahab, I had come here with great hopes. A man may commit mistakes but keeping the conditions in mind, you would realize that anyone else in Raja Jaswant Singh's position too would have erred. To top it all, he is married to the Badshah's sister. He should not be treated like an ordinary criminal.'

'Rajaji, it is not easy to change the Badshah's mind.'

'I have come with a request that he should consider us his allies right now. I hope you are able to put in a word soon.'

'I will. *Khuda hafeez. Inshallah, phir milenge.*'

৵৶ ৶৵

Winter came in faster than expected. The days were shorter and cold winds from across the Yamuna blew into the city. Zeenat was busy reading the Quran one evening when the maid Yasmeen came in to light the lamps. She sat next to Zeenat who, after finishing her reading, wrapped the book in a satin cloth and placed it carefully in a corner. Seeing her get up and sit on the bed, Yasmeen asked, 'I have seen you read the namaz three times a day. Even the Badshah, impressed with you having memorized the entire book, has gifted you one lakh rupiyas. May I ask you something?'

Zeenat replied, 'You may, what is it you want to ask?'

'I have read that even Hazrat Muhammad got his daughters married. Why then does the Badshah Salamat not think of getting his own daughters married?'

Zeenat frowned as she raised her eyebrows. 'Is that the only thing you picked up from the Quran?'

'Please pardon me for asking. I am but an uneducated maid but the woman in me wonders whether Allah, who bestowed you with such beauty, would want it wasted. I am sure it is not against the Quran to get married and the Badshah too would agree.' Changing the topic, Yasmeen continued, 'With your permission, may I mention something else?'

'You may.'

'Young Shahzada Akbar prefers to remain in the nude these days and wanders around without any clothes all the time.'

'*Tauba! Tauba!* Is that so?'

'Last week, en route to Chandni Chowk to read his prayers, he spotted a naked fakir. It seems the fakir mesmerized him. Since then he too has decided to shed all his clothes.'

'*Ya Allah!* What is Akbar up to?'

'He also mentioned that he is the one who will succeed the Badshah as the emperor. He says he is destined to do so.'

At that moment one of the khojas came running in. 'Begum Sahiba, Shahzada Akbar is here.'

Akbar was ushered in. Seven years of age and extremely fair, he looked around the room with wide-eyed curiosity. He bowed in salaam. Zeenat noticed that he was wearing just a thin satin kurta. Holding his hand Zeenat remarked, 'Shahzada, it seems you have forgotten the dress code one needs to adhere to before entering the zenankhana.'

'Begum Sahiba, the other day on my way to offer my prayers, I met a naked fakir. A crowd had gathered around him. His eyes had a certain magnetic quality that attracted me. I got off my palanquin and he hugged me affectionately.'

'*Hai Allah!* Are you saying that naked fakir hugged you?'

'He may be naked but he was not unclean. In fact his body emanated some kind of fine smell, like a mild scent. He also kissed me on my cheeks. A shiver ran through my body. It was unbelievable. You should have been there.'

'Why?

'He would have hugged you too.'

'Please mind your language, Shahzada!' Yasmeen could not stop herself from interrupting. 'It is not appropriate to discuss naked fakirs in the presence of Begum Sahiba. If Ala Hazrat comes to know of it all the maids here will be punished.'

The innocent Akbar was unable to fathom the transgression Yasmeen was referring to.

'I suggest you don't meet the naked fakir again. You are too young right now. Promise me you will wear your regular clothes. And one more thing; never speak about the succession to the throne. Is that clear?' said Zeenat.

One of the khojas came in to announce the arrival of Zebunissa. Zeenat was worried. Her elder sister would not appreciate Akbar's half-naked appearance. Looking around, she found a pashmina shawl which she quickly draped around Akbar. Akbar feared his Zebunissa Apa, a strict disciplinarian. Zebunissa walked in and seeing Akbar wrapped in a shawl commented, 'Oh, so the news I heard is correct. Akbar miya does seem to be going around without any clothes. What has got into your head, Akbar?'

Akbar could not bear to stand there any more and ran out of the room. A few khojas followed. Both the sisters had a hearty laugh when Zebunissa said, 'He is still young. Had he been older, Abba Jaan would not have spared him. Mother died at his childbirth and Abba Jaan has a special soft spot for him.'

Zeenat said, 'That's true. Nevertheless, I have convinced him not to try out such wild things. I am sure he will listen. But what he told me about the naked fakir is surprising; that people gather to listen to him.'

Zebunissa said, 'One of the khojas was telling me that the fakir's eyes are magnetic and people are mesmerized listening to him. I too feel like visiting him once.'

'*Ya Allah!* Can we meet him?'

'Sure we can. People don't see him as a fakir. They think he is an aulia or a dervish. Abba Jaan always says we should take the blessings of aulias, isn't it? Let us ask Ala Hazrat for his permission. If he says so, we will go.'

'I don't want to. I am scared.'

Zebunisssa could not understand what Zeenat feared.

⁘⊙≈ ♔≈⊙⁘

Crowds had gathered in Chandni Chowk. People, wanting to get a better look, had climbed on to rooftops of buildings nearby. A dervish, with long hair and a beard flowing till his chest stood stark naked talking to the people assembled. A little distance away stood a young man in his twenties. The dervish seemed to be pointing at him as he spoke.

'He is the fakir Sarmad, you know,' one of the men told his neighbour in the crowd. 'He was a great favourite of Shahzada Dara and Badshah Shah Jahan.' The other man looked around to ensure he was not in earshot of anyone else and said, 'But isn't he same person who had predicted that Dara would occupy the throne at Delhi? Dara not only did not get the throne but he and his begum had to pay with their lives.'

The other person asked, 'Who is the other young man standing there? Is he his disciple?'

'Yes. His name is Abhay Chand.'

The crowds were increasing. Sarmad looked lovingly at his disciple standing a little distance away. His eyes were filled with compassion and his face looked radiant when he welcomed his disciple saying, 'Abhay Chand, come here.'

The youth walked in a trance and the moment he reached him, the fakir hugged him tightly. Seeing them the crowd burst out shouting, 'Aulia fakir Sarmad zindabad! Zindapir Sarmad zindabad!'

Sarmad looked at the crowd and said, 'La ilahi illilah!'

The crowds repeated, 'La ilahi illilah!'

Sarmad raised his right hand and said in a solemn voice, 'Brothers, don't say the next kalma. The first one is enough.'

'Why do you say so? Our kazi has taught us to read both together: La ilahi illilah, Muhammad rasool lillilah.'

'That is true. The first part is true; it means there is only God. But the other part is false. It says Muhammad is the only prophet.'

'Are you saying that the Quran Sharif is not correct?'

'It is all humbug!' Sarmad raised his hands and said: 'It is a cunning trick of the mullahs and the maulvis to fool you.'

'Are you saying Hazrat Muhammad is not the prophet of Allah?'

'Of course, he is. But he is not the last one. That is not true.'

'Who's the one after Muhammad?'

'Why, don't you believe me? Arre, there is one standing right here – me! I have nothing to hide. I am not even wearing any clothes. I am standing the way I was sent into the world.'

A few men had gathered to take potshots at the naked fakir. One of them said, 'My dear aulia! How are we to know what you do when alone? You say you are speaking the truth, but did Allah send you into this world with this long beard?'

Sarmad smiled indulgently. He looked around and said, 'I agree I may not have had the beard when I was born. But I am not hiding it. But look at the men who asked me the question; how much are we hiding from others? That is the question we have to ask ourselves.'

⚬⚬ ⚬⚬

Aurangzeb's spies ensured that he was updated on everything that happened in the town. He knew how people had reacted when Dara Shikoh had been put to death and also when his son had been thrown into prison along with Aurangzeb's younger brother Murad.

The network of spies penetrated the bazaars, mosques and havelis. Most of the amaldars had shifted their loyalties to Aurangzeb. Dara's religious teacher Mullah Shah, despite his ardent pleas, was not spared and given capital punishment. For a while after taking over, Aurangzeb had been busy getting the affairs of the state in order. Now with those in place, he focused his attention on other issues. Aurangzeb had heard of the naked fakir's teachings and had dismissed them as a madman's rant. There were many mad fakirs who considered themselves descendants of the Paigambar. But a casual conversation with Shamim led him to understand how Akbar had been under the influence of the naked fakir. Aurangzeb, suspicious by nature, waited for an opportune moment to make his move.

Aurangzeb was hearing petitions one afternoon in his durbar. The cool winds from across the Yamuna created a pleasant ambience. Some mullahs and kazis had come in to complain. One of the kazis, his lips quivering with anger said, 'Huzoor-e Ala, it is getting impossible! Sarmad, a naked fakir, has the audacity to stand in the middle of Chandi Chowk and declare himself a descendant of the Paigambar. He asks people not to recite the entire kalma.'

Aurangzeb sat impassively, moving the diamond beads of his rosary while he silently recited the kalmas. Putting the rosary aside he asked, 'Who is this aulia?'

'His name is Sarmad.'

'Are you saying people listen to him?'

'It is not just the common man who listens to him, Huzoor. He was a favourite of Shahzada Dara and Badshah Shah Jahan. He is the one responsible for taking people away from our religion. He says it does not matter whether one prays to Allah, Prabhu or Jesus. They are all paths which lead to heaven.'

Aurangzeb was disturbed but was careful not to show his feelings. He asked, 'What else does this fakir say?'

'He says there is no need to read the Quran. Love is more important. A man should love another man. Love will lead to God, he says.'

Another kazi, his beard flowing to his waist, nodded vigorously and added, 'Ala Hazrat, it is impossible to repeat his words without insulting this august gathering. We cannot dare to repeat the blasphemous words he utters.'

'Please don't hesitate.'

'We cannot dare to utter those words even if you order us. He has even managed to influence a young lad who is hugged and kissed by that naked fakir. Ala Hazrat is perceptive enough. We need not say more.'

The people in attendance were stunned. The maulvi had managed to convey a lot without uttering Shahzada Akbar's name. Those standing a little away could indulge in a smile.

Jaffar Khan, standing next to the throne, said, 'If Huzoor orders we shall punish the fakir. Huzoor need not involve himself in such a trivial matter.'

'It is not a trivial matter when he goes about rousing the people against our religion. If the issue is not nipped in the bud, there will be hundreds like him in no time. Tomorrow is Friday. When I visit the Jama Masjid to offer my prayers, please bring this fakir before me.'

The next day after the prayers, Aurangzeb sat along with his select men when Jaffar Khan announced, 'If Huzoor so desires we can present the fakir here.'

Aurangzeb waved his hand giving his approval.

The Wazir did not move immediately. 'But Huzoor …'

'What is it?'

'He is naked. We asked him to cover himself but he refused.'

'Bring him in.'

Jaffar Khan, used to protocol, could not believe his ears. He hesitated for a few more moments and then ordered the khojas to present the fakir. The naked fakir came in and stopped twenty steps away from the Badshah. He looked the emperor in the eye. Aurangzeb returned his stare with equal intensity. For a while both the men assessed each other. Aurangzeb detected a strange zeal in the fakir's eyes.

Itimad Khan, well versed in religious arguments, stood in one corner. Looking at him Aurangzeb asked, 'Khan Sahab, ask this man, who has the profanity to stand here stark naked, what the Quran has to say about a man not hiding his modesty.'

Danishmand Khan and Itimad Khan were well known for their arguments and Aurangzeb would often invite them for a discussion. The main kazis and ulemas were a little disappointed that the emperor had not given them the opportunity to question the fakir.

Sarmad had an indulgent smile on his face. Looking into Aurangzeb's eyes he said, 'Where does religion say that we need to cover our bodies? We all know of a messiah who roamed around naked in his final years, is considered one of the Paigambars. Why then should one be forced to wear clothes?'

'Itimad Khan, ask this insolent person whether all Muslims who have worn clothes for thousands of years are fools.'

Itimad Khan repeated the question. Sarmad had his answer ready. 'It is quite evident that people wear clothes to hide their sins. I wear the clothes of purity that Allah has given me. Those who need to hide have to dress in clothes. The Badshah Salamat himself ...'

'Khabardar! Hold your tongue!' Jaffar Khan erupted.

'So are you suggesting we who wear clothes are not Allah's favourties?'

Sarmad replied, 'I know I am Allah's favourite. Allah is not bothered if I am naked. He loves me.'

The court was stunned hearing Sarmad's response. The ulemas and the kazis present were itching to grab his throat. They restrained their emotions as the Badshah himself had not reacted. Sarmad, on the other hand, seemed to be enjoying his dialogue.

The next question was: 'You ask the people to recite only one kalma. Why so?'

'It is simple; the first one states there is only one God. The next one is not true. It says Muhammad is the last prophet. I have not seen him and I don't want to be seen telling lies.'

'So are all other Musalmans lying?'

'Of course! I can't utter what I don't believe in. I will otherwise be a hypocrite. I ask people not be hypocritical, that's all.'

'Huzoor-e-Ala ...' the main kazi shouted, unable to hold himself back. 'He has the audacity to insult the religion and that too in your presence. *Tauba, tauba!* It is better that we are dead than listen to his prattle. We request you to stop this tamasha. We are being insulted. He is insulting the Badshah himself.'

'I am here to deliver justice. Therefore, I will listen to his views before giving my verdict,' Aurangzeb said.

'Huzoor, you must have been convinced by now that the person is a sham. He is an enemy of our religion. He deserves a punishment which pulls out his blasphemous tongue and then hangs him to death.'

'Kazi, I cannot hang a person just because he roams around naked. There is a question of the Mughal Empire's reputation at stake. I am going to ask a few straight questions to the fakir. I will decide only after I hear his answers.'

Aurangzeb looked at Sarmad and asked, 'I shall ask you a final question. Please answer after careful consideration.'

'I will answer right away; please ask.'

'This is my question: Hazrat Muhammad Paigambar is the last prophet as per the Quran Sharif. All Musalmans believe he went to heaven to meet Allah. Why do you tell people that this is a lie?'

'It is an insult to Allah to say that the Prophet went to heaven.'

'What do you mean?'

'Aurangzeb, it is not something you would understand easily but as a Shahenshah of the earth, you have asked me this question, so I am forced to answer. Muhammad Paigambar is not the last prophet. There is nothing called the end. It is childish to believe that he went to heaven to meet Allah.'

'Childish?'

Sarmad chuckled and looked straight into Aurangzeb's eyes without blinking. He said, 'Aurangzeb, I know you are not ignorant about religion. You have been blessed with the ability to read people. I know you have the discerning ability to understand religion in its true sense. Nevertheless, I will answer your question. It is an insult to say that Muhammad Paigambar had to go to heaven to meet Khuda. Khuda is omnipresent. Where is the need to go anywhere? What the Quran meant was that he merged with the consciousness, the ever-present power which we call God. Aurangzeb, it is your ego which makes you ask this despite your deep knowledge. I have nothing else to say.'

Aurangzeb kept staring at Sarmad for a few moments. He said, 'Do you have to say anything in your deposition before I pronounce the verdict?'

'Deposition?' Sarmad opened his half-closed eyes and asked. 'Aurangzeb, you know my answer. There is no point in giving a deposition to someone who does not understand. I am Allah's banda. Let *Him* decide my fate.'

Aurangzeb closed his eyes in contemplation. His fingers moved the beads of his rosary for a while. He glanced at the people in attendance and then told the Wazir, 'You have heard Sarmad. I would like to ask the ulemas and the maulvis for their verdict.'

The ulemas consulted amongst themselves for a while. Jaffar Khan heard their verdict and then, nodding his head, said in a loud voice 'After consulting the Quran Sharif and the Hadis, the ulemas have come to a conclusion that the naked fakir has insulted the Paigambar and the holy books. His faith in religion is questionable. It is a crime to interpret the meaning of the kalmas the way he does. We propose that he should be beheaded at the same place, Chandni Chowk, where he gives his so-called sermons to the people at large.'

The people in the durbar turned to see Sarmad's reaction. He continued to smile as before, the pronouncement having had no effect on him. He seemed lost in his own world.

Aurangzeb raised his right hand and proclaimed: 'I am agreeable with the verdict given by the ulemas. This criminal shall be beheaded before sunset tomorrow. A true Musalman will be relieved. Let the common man know that he should stay away from the company of such profane and unholy fakirs.'

ஒ௮ ௮ஒ

The punishment was duly carried out in Chandni Chowk the next day.

It had been a week since the event. Danishmand Khan sat in his haveli poring over an Arabic manuscript when the servant informed him of Sheikh Sadullah and Kazi Abdul Wahab's arrival.

The guests were ushered into Danishmand Khan's library. Danishmand Khan set aside the book he was reading and got up to receive Sheikh Sadullah hugging him in the traditional manner. Danishmand Khan was a little surprised seeing the two elderly and high-ranking officials in his home. He was not used to socializing with the amaldars and kept to his research and study of religious books. Knowing well that they would come to the point soon, he began by discussing the weather.

Sheikh Sadullah was a little impatient and asked, 'Khan Sahab, I am sure you have heard of the punishment meted out to the fakir Sarmad.'

Kazi Abdul Wahab added, 'We were expecting the matter to end there. But things have turned out differently.'

'I have been busy reading some of the books which my friend, the French physician, has sent from Europe.'

'*Tauba! Tauba!* Are you saying you read books written by infidels? Does the Quran Sharif not have enough wisdom? Why do you need to read anything else?'

Danishmand Khan smiled. He tried, 'Kazi Sahab, what else is there for a person like me to do? The mansab given by the Badshah gives me enough to take care of my expenses. I don't have a zenankhana like others, nor do I have interest in going out and meeting people. I spend time reading these books. I hope you won't take that away from me?'

'There was a strange event at the beheading. The fakir's head rolled down the floor and spouted the entire kalma "*la ilahi illilah,*

Muhammad rasool lillilah". The very kalma that Sarmad did not want to utter was now being recited by his severed head.'

'Not just that,' the kazi continued. 'After a few minutes, the body got up and picking up the head started walking down saying, "I am the Parmeshwar, I am Allah and Jesus", leaving people speechless.'

'The worry is, Khan Sahab, that the fakir was better off being alive. He has been made into a Pir now. And there are murmurs against the Alamgir in the bazaars.'

'We should have thought about this before we gave the orders for his execution. There is precious little one can do now.'

Abdul Wahab and Sheikh Sadullah looked at each other for a moment. They were reluctant to speak up. Sadullah felt it was the kazi's responsibility, it being a religious matter. Finally, the kazi said, 'Khan Sahab, the people believe that the Badshah is a devout Musalman. His elder brother was almost half Hindu. Years have passed by since his coronation but the Badshah has done nothing in favour of Islam. This is the first public execution since he came to power and a Musalman is beheaded. The people are angry.'

'Public memory is short. One need not be worried,' Danishmand Khan said.

Quite obviously the two gentlemen had not come in to listen to Danishmand Khan brushing aside the issue as trivial. They said, 'Isn't it the duty of the Badshah as a true Musalman to eradicate the religions of the kafirs? Unless the people of Delhi see some proof in this regards, they won't feel comfortable.'

'The question is quite straightforward,' Abdul Wahab continued. 'Despite having a devout Islam lover like Alamgir Badshah on the throne, the Hindus are busy building more temples and worshipping idols. The Badshah continues to ignore these practices. We believe he should teach these kafirs a lesson to make the Musalmans happy.'

'What can I do? I am just a mere mansabdar in this vast empire. I spend my time reading these books. What advice can I give the Badshah?'

'The Badshah always considers your opinion before taking any important decision. We want to know if you would support us, in case we declare a jehad against the kafirs. We have come here asking for your support.'

'But you must know that the Badshah has a mind of his own. He takes his own decisions though he may consult many.'

Sheikh Sadullah was clearly disappointed. He made a last-ditch attempt. 'We would not force you against your will. I need you to promise us something; if a situation so arises I hope you would not oppose it and advise the Badshah against it.'

'I can promise you that. I hope I am on my way to Mecca but if I do stay back I will not involve myself in these affairs. Does that satisfy you?'

'Yes. It does.'

The guests got up and, accepting the traditional paan and betel nut, left Danishmand Khan's haveli.

৩৫ ৩৫

Ever since his beheading, Sarmad's popularity rose like never before. People now considered him a Pir. Many Muslims were angry at Aurangzeb for having mercilessly killed their favourite aulia. The Rajputs, with the house arrest of Raja Jaswant Singh, were already a disgruntled lot. To add to it, the behaviour of Kazi Abdul Wahab had made the Bundels and the Jats uneasy. The maulivs, mullahs, ulemas and other religious leaders were constantly finding excuses to complain against the Hindus. Alamgir Badshah listened to them silently without giving his views. No one could fathom his mind.

A few months passed by. The unrest in Delhi seemed minor compared to the news the spies had just brought in. Aurangzeb called in for Shaista Khan to confer with.

They met that evening in their secret meeting room. The open windows brought in the soft noise of the waters of the Yamuna crashing against the sandy banks. Shaista Khan came and bent low in salaam. Aurangzeb, waving the papers brought in by the spy, said, 'Mamu Jaan, the news is worrisome. We had left an enemy behind when we moved away from the Deccan, you remember?'

The past few years since Aurangzeb's accession to the throne had been easy ones for Shaista Khan. It took him a while to get the gist of Aurangzeb's statement. He said, 'I thought you had only two enemies in the Deccan; Qutub Khan of Golconda and Adil Shah of Bijapur. But they have been sending in their annual share of revenue as promised.'

Aurangzeb stood up and went near the window. The Yamuna flowed silently. He said, looking out of the window, 'Mamu Jaan, I am talking of the Maratha rat. You must have heard of the way he killed Bijapur's Afzal Khan treacherously.'

'Yes, I did. I can't call someone brave if he resorts to such tricks to kill.'

'The point is not about his bravery,' Aurangzeb said, turning away from the window. 'I am worried about his cunning. He has managed to rout Afzal Khan and Siddhi Johar, two of the most capable generals of Bijapur. I am told Adil Shah is a worried man these days.'

'Adil Shah's reputation does not make him a very courageous fellow, does it?' Shaista Khan commented.

'You may call him impotent but I am worried about the fact that this Maratha fellow is now testing us by raiding into our territories. He looted Junnar and our amaldars could do nothing. It is time to show our manhood, Khan Sahab.'

Shaista Khan did not get the drift of Aurangzeb's words and added casually, 'Sure. Why not send one of our capable mansabdars? They will capture this troublemaker and present him to you. You may then decide the punishment you want to give him.'

'Aren't you too a mansabdar?'

'Of course, I am!' Shaista Khan replied and then realized, a little later, the direction in which Aurangzeb was pointing. Aurangzeb continued before Shaista Khan could reply. Putting his hand on his uncle's shoulder he said, 'Mamu Jaan, I want you to take on this responsibility.'

'Me?'

'Why not, you have Irani blood flowing through your veins. You know how to teach that mountain rat a lesson.'

Shaista Khan recovered quickly from the surprise thrown in by Aurangzeb. He said, 'Of course! It would be my honour, Huzoor. I have but a request to make.'

'Please speak your mind.'

'The troublemaker is a kafir. You have always believed that only a diamond can cut a diamond. It would be of great help if I have the support of a capable Rajput sardar.'

'Which sardar are you thinking of?'

'May I suggest someone? I hope Huzoor won't get upset.'

'Why should I? Whose name do you want to propose?'

'Raja Jaswant Singh.'

Aurangzeb regarded Shaista Khan for a few moments. He said, 'You know he has stabbed me in my back. Do you still want to propose his name?'

'Huzoor, he has committed a crime against the throne, I agree. But he has suffered a lot already. This responsibility would be, in a way, another punishment for him.'

'Khan Sahab, I will accept your request. I will cancel the orders regarding his house arrest and issue a *shahi firman* ordering him to march with you to the Deccan. But beware! It should not happen that you land up getting the punishment meant for Raja Jaswant Singh.'

'I don't get you, Huzoor.'

'Mamu Jaan, I have spent my life reading people's minds. I don't underrate any enemy of mine. You may leave as soon as possible. I will be waiting for the good news.'

'Huzoor …'

'That is all for the moment, Mamu Jaan. I will explain some other day what I meant.'

It was a cue that the meeting was over. Shaista Khan bowed and left.

৩৫ ৯৯

Jaswant Singh was invited to the durbar the next day and greeted by the Badshah. He was cordially welcomed back into the fold and presented a mansab of five thousand. Shaista Khan too was received by the emperor and both of them were then given the task of capturing the Maratha troublemaker.

Aurangzeb left for a hunting trip in the jungles adjacent to the Yamuna. He had been on a trip after a gap of many years. It was a contingent of nearly two thousand men. He managed to shoot a few small animals but luck turned in his favour when, sitting atop his elephant, he shot two tigers and another one shortly while riding a horse. The trip was cut short when he fell ill.

He returned to Delhi after nearly a fortnight, his body burning with fever. But he continued his usual activities and did not let others know of his ill health. Roshanara, managing the affairs of the zenankhana, was soon informed of the Badshah's condition and rushed to see him one afternoon when Aurangzeb returned from his durbar for a siesta.

Entering his room she exclaimed, '*Hai Allah!* You are burning with fever. What's the need to spend time in the Diwan-e-Aam when you are not well?'

'Begum Sahiba, it is just an ordinary fever. I wasn't here for two weeks and work has piled up. How can I afford to rest?'

'*Tauba! Tauba!* Is it not better to rest now rather than allow the situation to become worse?'

Aurangzeb's forehead was glistening with sweat. He felt weak. She patted his forehead with a satin handkerchief. Aurangzeb said, 'Begum Sahiba, why should I be worried of an ordinary fever when I have someone like you to take care of me?'

'You call this an ordinary fever? I am worried,' Roshanara said, holding his wrist to check his pulse.

'The hakeem said it was due to excessive strain of the shikar.'

'The hakeem does not know anything, Bhai Jaan. I know the reason for this fever.'

'What is it?'

'As long as the cursed woman is alive ...'

'Begum Sahiba, please mind your tongue. Whom are you referring to?'

'I am talking of your elder sister Jahanara Begum Sahiba,' Roshanara said, her words spitting poison. 'Badshah Shah Jahan still believes that he is the Shahenshah. Jahanara stayed back in the fort to take care of him. With the help of aulias and other fakirs, she is trying out various voodoo practices to hurt you. Your fever is a result of such things.'

Aurangzeb was aware of the hatred between the two sisters. He could see that Roshanara was visibly disturbed. He teased her saying, 'If that be the case, why don't you try some reverse voodoo magic?'

'On whom?'

'On the royal prisoner at Agra Fort?'

'*Hai Allah!* You mean Shah Jahan Badshah?'

'Why? Won't your magic work on him?'

'Where's the need for it? Bhai Jaan, listen to me. It is a question of time; our father, if he remains imprisoned in the fort like an ordinary criminal, would die of heartbreak within no time.'

Aurangzeb knew Roshanara was speaking in riddles. He said, 'Our father is enjoying the life of a Badshah within the four walls. He has all the luxuries, not to mention the constant care provided by Jahanara. Dara's daughter, his favourite granddaughter, Jahanzeb Banu too is his companion. Where is the opportunity for my father to lament his condition?'

'I have something to share with you. I am told he sits at a window watching his favourite Taj Mahal for hours together. I am convinced that is what is keeping him alive.'

'Is that so?'

'My advice is to seal the window which keeps alive the memory of Mumtaj Begum. I am confident he will wither away in no time, once the sight is removed from him permanently.'

It was a suggestion that shook Aurangzeb for a moment. He kept a strict control on the amount of liberties given to the royal prisoner in the fort. The thought that he needed to do something more never occurred to him. The suggestion to remove all his liberties one by one to ensure his death had been made by his own daughter!

He watched his sister without saying anything. Noticing his silence Roshanara said, 'Don't you like my suggestion? Bhai Jaan, please keep it in mind as that as long as our father is alive, you can never consider yourself the emperor in the true sense. Jahanara Begum is looking for every possible opportunity to rouse public opinion against you. You must be aware of the amount of dissent she managed to stir up when you executed the fakir Sarmad.'

Encouraged by his silence as an implicit approval, she asked, 'Are you aware that Jahanara was a disciple of the naked fakir and often met him in private??'

Roshanara felt proud that she had conveyed an important but hitherto unknown information to Aurangzeb, but seeing no reaction from him she was a little disappointed and said, 'It seems you don't believe me.'

'Begum Sahiba, I always believe you. I have always acknowledged your help in getting me this throne. But those are things of the past. I don't expect my sister in Agra Fort to cause any trouble. By the way, is everything fine in the zenankhana?'

She said, 'Bhai Jaan, I hope you don't mind me saying something regarding the zenankhana, given my seniority there.'

'No. Please go ahead.'

'Bhai Jaan, you are now the Badshah of Hindustan. You prestige is spread far and wide. But I wonder if there is a begum in the zenankhana.'

Aurangzeb realized the direction in which Roshanara was pointing but pretending not to have understood her he asked, 'Why? What about Nawab Bai?'

'What the emperor needs is a begum who showers her love on him. Nawab Bai is only concerned with her son Muazzam. Ever since her older son Sultan has been imprisoned she has refused to step out of her mahal.'

'That is her wish. She has decided not to speak to me since the Irani begum delivered two sons. She has to suffer her own fate.'

'Bhai Jaan, I was referring to the maid in Dara's erstwhile zenankhana. Udaipuri has now come of age,' Roshanara blurted out.

Roshanara was aware that Aurangzeb had an eye on Udaipuri, a concubine in Dara's harem, since long. The Mughal tradition was to merge the two zenankhanas, but Aurangzeb had deliberately delayed the same knowing that there were many people in Delhi who were partial to Dara. Dara's Irani begum had died in the skirmish while his other begum had committed suicide. Udaipuri was very young then and had been housed in a haveli at Suhagpura. Time had healed the shock of Dara's death. It was clear that there was no love lost between Aurangzeb and Nawab Bai. Aurangzeb, now in his forties, missed having someone in the zenankhana who would shower love on him. Udaipuri, a girl of Georgian descent whom Dara had specially recruited into his harem, was a rare beauty. Roshanara had touched a raw nerve. She asked, 'Bhai Jaan, don't you like Udaipuri?'

'That is not the question. The question is about what she wants.'

'Bhai Jaan, I also wanted to get something to your notice. I have information that Zebunissa and Zeenat roam around the city hidden behind their hijab, ogling at men in the bazaars.'

'Aren't you being too harsh? My daughters are beautiful and young and it is quite natural that their instincts would lead them to explore the world but I am not willing to believe that they are lusting for bodily desires.'

'I am responsible for the zenankhana and it is my duty to bring things to your notice.'

'I know, I know,' Aurangzeb muttered.

Roshanara added casually, before getting up to leave, 'Hazrat, I have sent orders for the window at Agra Fort to be sealed. This is just for your information.'

Aurangzeb barely heard her. He was lost in thoughts; on one hand his beautiful daughters were gallivanting in the bazaars incognito while on the other, the temptation to get Udaipuri to his zenankhana had stirred new emotions.

ೕഇ ഇஐ

Aurangzeb attended the Diwan-e-Khaas despite having fever. He had adjourned the practice of holding the general durbar in the Diwan-e-Aam. The tradition of sitting at the window for the common public to have a view of their emperor continued each morning.

After taking his medicines in the afternoon, he moved into the Diwan-e-Khaas when Jaffar Khan said, 'Huzoor, if it is not a trouble, may I ask your ustad since your childhood, Mir Hasham, to meet you?'

Aurangzeb's sharp eye had seen Mir Hasham the moment he had entered the durbar. He asked, 'So is the old ustad Mir Hasham still alive? What is his request?'

'Huzoor, he would like to present his request himself.'

'Jahanpanah,' Mir Hasham began.

'You can call me Aurangzeb. You are, after all, my ustad. What is it that you want?'

'What request can I make, Huzoor? Ala Hazrat was my student at one time but now sits on the Mughal throne. It would be kind of him if this old man is granted a mansab to take care of his remaining years.'

'Mansab? Why should that be granted to you?'

'Huzoor, this old man has spent all his life teaching his young student. My back is bent poring over the religious texts that I taught you.'

'Really? What exactly did you teach me?'

'Huzoor, I taught you everything – from writing the Persian script, to reading the Quran and the Hadis.'

'What else?

'I taught you the Turkish and Arabic tongues. I believe I made you eligible to sit on the Mughal throne. What more do you expect?'

'Let me tell you what I learnt. If I miss out something let me know.'

'Sure. Please tell me,' Mir Hasham said proudly.

'You taught that the entire world outside of Hindustan is a small group of islands where the Portuguese or the English people stay. You said there is no one comparable to the Badshah of Hindustan.'

'That is absolutely correct.'

Ignoring him, Aurangzeb continued in a measured tone, 'You taught me that the emperor's word is the law and the amirs of Persia, Uzbek or Kashgar fear the Badshah of Hindustan.'

'That is the kind of scare your word creates,' Mir Hasham said proudly.

'*Waah!* I wish you had known world affairs better. Was it not your duty to teach me how the mighty powers interact with each other?'

'But ...'

'Enough! You never taught me how to deal with other powers. You did not bother to make me understand the power of the army and how the Badshah should control it. You taught me to speak Arabic. What use is it here? You never explained the good things the earlier Badshahs had done for the people. Yet you believe you made me capable of sitting on this throne?'

'Huzoor, you are being too harsh. I taught you what I knew, as per my calibre. I have been sincere in my teachings.'

'*Khamosh!* Stop your nonsense! Had you taught as per your knowledge, I would not have any objection. I have been given enough intelligence to assess a person's capabilities. You, on the other hand, made the Shah Jahan Badshah believe that you are being a great teacher to me. You told him I was being imparted world knowledge when all you did was teach me useless languages like Turkish and Arabic. You did not tell me the way a Badshah should deal with the ryots, the way he should manage administrative affairs.'

'But Hazrat Salamat ...'

'I don't want to listen to your defence. I am fully aware of your capabilities. I am telling you in the presence of other mansabdars here. I knew you would come in here begging some day or the other. Your punishment is long due. You seem to have forgotten the days of Aurangabad, ustadji!'

Mir Hasham muttered, 'I remember, Huzoor.'

'You may have forgotten. Let me remind you; you were under my patronage but you stabbed me in the back. You are a haramkhor. I am ashamed to utter the word. Seeing you here makes my blood boil. I can't even utter the crimes you have committed. I made a few mistakes in my youth. You, on the other hand, under the garb of showing sympathy, were busy collecting evidence. That is how the blouse that was pierced by the Zainabadi begum showing off her archery skills in the deer garden reached the Badshah at Agra. You were responsible for showing me in a bad light.'

Mir Hasham did not dare look up. His body was shivering. Aurangzeb continued, 'Your treacherous acts did not end there. You encouraged the fakirs to revolt against me and encouraged them to loot the temple. How can you expect me to help you when you have done all this?'

Mir Hasham stood with head bent low. He had never expected Aurangzeb to openly berate him. Jaffar Khan, seeing the old ustad shivering with fear said, 'Huzoor, the ustad has committed crimes no doubt. But seeing his age, I appeal to your good sense.'

Aurangzeb glanced in the direction of Jaffar Khan and said, his voice taking on an edge, 'I shall surely show some sympathy. Instead of putting him in chains, I am allowing him to walk free. He dare not show his face here again.'

Aurangzeb got up from his throne. The fever had made him weak and his hands were trembling. Putting his hand on Anwar Khoja's shoulders he walked away towards the zenankhana.

જીલ ભૂભ

Aurangzeb's face was red with anger. The fever had taken a toll on his health and now Shamim had brought disturbing news from the zenankhana.

It was past midnight when, after having got the latest update from the spies, he sat with Shamim. He asked her repeatedly, 'Shamim, are you sure? Is that true? Why have I not been told of it till date? Were the guards sleeping?'

'Huzoor, it is true? I have told you the facts.'

'I cannot believe Roshanara Begum can do this. Have you seen it yourself?'

'I have seen both men myself.'

'Two men come into the zenankhana and stay with Roshanara in her mahal. How is it that I am the dark?'

'They came in wearing a burkha and a black gown. And on top of it there were written orders to allow them in.'

'Written orders? What do you mean?'

'The orders had your seal on them.'

'What nonsense you are talking, Shamim! You think I would give permission for these two men to enter Roshanara Begum's mahal?'

'That's what stumped me. The guards allowed the men only after confirming that the letter had your seal and signature.'

'*Tauba! Tauba!* Shamim, I never expected Roshanara to stoop to this.'

'Huzoor, the maids and others are scared of her. She runs the zenankhana with an iron hand. Many maids and khojas have been punished; some losing their arms and legs and some have had their eyes gouged out, while others have been whipped. No one dares complain. It took me a while to get a khoja into confidence to extract this information.'

'Shamim, it is shameful that Roshanara Begum should indulge in such activities. She is older to me in age. Her actions are a blot on the Mughal Empire's reputation.'

'Huzoor, pardon my impertinence but the Mughal Empire has been cursed for generations.'

Aurangzeb asked, 'What curse are you referring to?'

'The curse that the men born in the family have to give up their lives for the sake of one emperor while the girls have to suppress their desires and live a life trapped in the zenankhana. No girl born in this family has had the pleasure of leaving the zenankhana as a bride. She has left this zenankhana in a hearse. This is the curse I am talking of.'

'People should know how to curb their desires. I have provided them whatever they need.'

'I can't spell out what you have not provided, Huzoor.'

'Please be specific, Shamim.'

'Huzoor, a man cannot suppress his physical desires. Nature will finally have its way. It is a question of time before Roshanara's nieces learn of her behaviour. Huzoor can imagine the impression it will create on their minds.'

'Shamim, Zeenat and Zebunissa are different. Zebunissa is engaged in her poetry and music while Zeenat is all the time immersed in the Quran.'

'Human emotions cannot remain suppressed for long. Especially when such behaviour is displayed around, it takes very little for them to show their true colours.'

'Shamim, this is the difference between a daroga and a princess. We teach manners and religious practices so that one can control one's desires. Is is unfortunate that Shah Jahan Badshah, at seventy, was dragging a sixteen-year-old to his bed. I kept quiet as I believe Khuda has given each one a mind to use it wisely. Tell me, have I not controlled my desires?'

Shamim realized she was not making any headway. She said, 'Huzoor, your case is different. I am talking of ordinary humans here.'

'I cannot tolerate Roshanara's behaviour. I am going to look into the matter tomorrow and ...'

He paused for a moment and then continued, 'I have to ensure that this matter is nipped in the bud. It is a question of our prestige. The irony is I have to live with it. *Ya Allah! Ya Khuda!*'

Aurangzeb covered his face with his hands in anguish.

જ્હ ૭૯

Aurangzeb did not have anyone to share his thoughts with. Ever since Roshanara had taken charge, the people at large had not been privy to any gossip emerging out of the zenankhana. Roshanara ruled like a tyrant. Aurangzeb owed a lot to his sister who had worked tirelessly to ensure he became the emperor. It was the month of Ramzan and Aurangzeb spent all his time reading the Quran, observing fasts and remaining aloof. The official durbar was closed for the month. Except for stepping out with the maulvis and the mullahs to the Jama Masjid across the road for his evening prayers, Aurangzeb kept to himself. He would have a frugal meal at sunset and then spend the night praying. *'I have occupied the Mughal throne as per your wish. You have bestowed upon me a huge responsibility but this devotee of yours is helpless. I am but a tired soul. You have given me the task of making people realize the true value of our religion. My mind is confused. Please take care of my family, my daughters; it is in your hands.'*

In the solitude of dawn, Aurangzeb sat with his hands together praying to Allah. Tears flowed down his cheeks. The only witnesses to his inner turmoil were the curtains on the windows.

The rigorous fasting had taken a toll on his health and two days before the end of the Ramzan month, Aurangzeb fell ill. Anwar found him unconscious when he came in the morning with the water for his bath. He shouted for the royal hakeem who came in immediately. Putting his hand on Aurangzeb's forehead he said, 'He has a high fever.' His voice sounded grave.

Hearing the commotion, Roshanara came in. The hakeem told her that he suspected an attempt to poison the Badshah. He was tense, not knowing what cure would work. Roshanara immediately issued instructions to not allow anyone else inside the chambers. Ordering Anwar to move out, she got in her own trusted maids and khojas to guard the room.

No one outside was privy to the status of Aurangzeb's health. But gossip has its own way of reaching the people and by afternoon the news of his illness had spread across the city. People in the bazaars, lanes and bylanes arrived at their own conclusions and many assumed that Aurangzeb was dead. The gossip that Roshanara was hiding his dead body in the zenankhana spread like wildfire. Similar news had done the rounds a few weeks back when Shah Jahan had fallen ill. People at large were worried about large-scale violence, loss of property and vicious battles if Aurangzeb were to die. The victim of the clamour to the throne would be the poor man on the street.

Roshanara kept a strict vigil on Aurangzeb's health. She was aware of the fact that her brother knew of the two men she was hiding in her mahal. She was familiar with his anger and the fact that he could resort to anything to ensure that the zenankhana's prestige was upheld. But the lure of carnal pleasure had not allowed Roshanara to let the men go. Aurangzeb's sudden illness was a god-sent opportunity as it gave a chance for the men to escape.

By nightfall, Aurangzeb's fever had increased. The hakeem feared that the Badshah might start mumbling deleriously if the fever did not abate.

The people, not finding the Badshah at his window next morning, were convinced that something was amiss. The rumour-mongers were spreading the news of his death and masses of people gathered at the banks of the Yamuna. Roshanara ordered Sheikh Sadullah to disperse the crowds.

The day passed without much improvement in Aurangzeb's health. Nawab Bai's maid Nargis and the Khoja Daulat informed their mistress about the latest developments.

'Begum Sahiba, Huzoor-e-Ala's health is very bad and your enemy Roshanara Begum has taken charge. There is a danger to your life. You need to be careful.'

Daulat was sent to get first-hand information but he returned with a sour face. He had not been allowed anywhere near Aurangzeb's quarters. But he surmised, hearing from some of the khojas, that the Badshah's death was just a matter of hours away.

Nawab Bai sank down on her bed stunned at hearing this. She knew that the Badshah did not love her and that her first son had been imprisoned, but her second son, now eighteen years of age, was the rightful heir to the throne. She knew that Aurangzeb was affectionate towards him. The news of his impending death was too much to bear and she started sobbing. The maids around tried to pacify her.

She said, 'Nargis, I know that if the Badshah dies I will be treated worse than a dog. I would have to live the life of a maid.'

'Begum Sahiba, I have an idea; please ask Shahzada Muazzam to return immediately. His presence will be a great help.'

Nawab Bai removed a ring from her finger and handing it to

Nargis said, 'Please take this ring and ask Muazzam to meet me at the earliest.'

Nargis and Daulat left her quarters with the task at hand. Nawab Bai, thinking the worst, could not stop her tears from flowing.

ॐ ॐ

Muazzam had been enjoying his freedom away from his disciplinarian father, having taken charge of Dara's erstwhile haveli, a little away from the Red Fort. But the news of the Badshah's illness and the impending rumours that he may not be the rightful heir to the throne shook him to the core. The fact that his mother was a Rajput could come in the way of his staking a claim to the throne. The rumours also suggested that Roshanara Begum had proposed Azam to be crowned the emperor.

He visited the only Rajput mansabdar he could trust at midnight, dressed in the guise of a commoner. Raja Jai Singh, seeing the Shahzada at that odd hour rushed out to meet him. Ignoring protocol, Muazzam got off the palanquin and put his forehead on Raja Jai Singh's feet.

Raja Jai Singh, confused at his behaviour, asked, 'What is the matter, Shahzada? What brings you here at this hour?'

'Raja Sahab, the situation is such that I had no option but to meet you. You must have heard of the Badshah's health.'

'Yes, I have.'

'Well, I am told he is dead and that Roshanara Begum has taken charge. She is trying her best to crown Azam as the next emperor,' Muazzam said, his voice quivering.

Raja Jai Singh was a man of experience. He was a little amused seeing the young Shahzada emotional. Many years back, he had sent his troops to support another Shahzada, who later occupied the throne. Today his son was asking for his help. But he knew that the situation was not similar. Patting his back, he said, 'Shahzada, don't worry. Anyone can fall ill. Don't give much weightage to the rumours you hear in the bazaars.'

'Raja Sahab, I got an urgent message from my Ammi Jaan asking me to meet her.'

Jai Singh found the entire episode somewhat funny but he did not reveal his thoughts. On the contrary, he said in a serious tone, 'Your mother does not have experience of such political intrigues. But you have been personally trained by the Badshah himself. You should not allow the rumours to affect you.'

'Raja Sahab, you know Roshanara Begum would not hesitate to behead me the moment Azam is made emperor. And yet you are asking me to remain calm.'

'Gather yourself. My spies told me that the Badshah has high fever and is unconscious. The hakeem has given him some medicines and is expecting him to recover in a few days. There is no cause of worry.'

Muazzam let out a deep sigh of relief. 'I wish my father lives long but I want to ask you if such a situation were to arise tomorrow, would you do one thing for me?'

'Please tell me.'

'Would you rush to Agra and release my grandfather from captivity? I feel he should be made the emperor again. I fear, otherwise, not for my life alone but for the lives of countless men in Delhi.'

Raja Jai Singh did not answer immediately. He watched Muazzam carefully. He knew that Muazzam had proposed a tricky situation. Muazzam was under the impression that the crowning of Shah Jahan as the emperor would not only be welcomed by the people at large but also ensure that Azam did not become a threat.'

Raja Jai Singh said, 'Shahzada, it is strange but true; a man under stress gets all kinds of wild ideas.'

'So you think my idea is fanciful?'

'Shah Jahan Badshah has been imprisoned for years now. Do you think he would be forgiving once he takes charge? He will be like a hungry lion who has escaped from its cage. Remove the idea from your mind. Don't even think of releasing the Badshah from the Agra Fort.'

Muazzam was confused. His mother was worried sick while the Rajput sardar was asking him to relax and not get unnecessarily worried. He asked, 'There is one more thing; in case of a fight for the throne, would you support me?'

'You are naive. Such a situation will not arise.' Raja Jai Singh avoided giving a direct answer.

Muazzam was not one to give up easily and repeated, 'Raja Sahab, please tell me; I want to know whether you will stand by me.'

'My men and I will stand by your side. Please rest assured.'

Muazzam was visibly relieved and hurriedly took leave.

It had been three days but the fever had not abated. Alamgir Badshah continued to be unconscious. Roshanara was at his bedside night and day. She would send instructions to the hakeem who would then prescribe the medicines. The hakeem too was not allowed to enter the quarters. While all this was going on, Roshanara sent out a *shahi firman* which was despatched to all across the country. The *firman* stated that in case of the Badshah's death his younger son Azam was to be crowned the emperor. It also said that as the young prince had not reached adulthood, Roshanara Begum would manage the affairs till he reached adulthood.

The news created turmoil all over. Nawab Bai heard of it that afternoon and sent urgent word to Muazzam. The entrance to the fort was now closed for all. She decided to find out the status of Aurangzeb's health by checking on him first-hand. Roshanara, upon hearing of her arrival, rushed to meet her at the door. Peeping through the door, Nawab Bai was able to get a glimpse of Aurangzeb lying on his bed. She saw him move his hand and mutter something.

She knew he was not dead and was a little relieved. Confronting Roshanara about the *shahi firman* she asked, 'What is the meaning of this? When the Badshah is alive, how dare you send false *firmans* in his name?'

Roshanara Begum tried glaring at her to stop her tirade. 'Please maintain silence. You know the Badshah is not well; yet you come here and shout at the top of your voice?'

Nawab Bai was not in a mood to be pacified. She pushed her aside and approached Aurangzeb's bed. Incensed at her bold behaviour, Roshanara grabbed Nawab Bai and dragged her out of the room shouting, 'Don't throw your weight around thinking you're a begum.

Your position is no more than that of a maid here, is that understood? Don't you dare come here again without my permission!'

'I was trying to be civil so far but you forget that I am, after all, the Badshah's begum. I have been with him through thick and thin in the Deccan when you were busy playing political games in Agra. Don't make a show of your concern for his health.'

Roshanara was not one to take insults lying down. She screamed, 'What temerity! A mere laundi from the zenankhana has the gall to shout at me?' Saying so, she raised her hand and slapped Nawab Bai. Then, holding her by her hair, she dragged her through the corridor. The khojas and the maids in attendance were shocked beyond belief. Flinging Nawab Bai on the floor, she turned and walked back to the royal chambers. The begum, mother to Badshah's eldest son, sobbed as she lay on the marble floor.

୶ଔ ଓ

The next few days were tense. Despite Raja Jai Singh's assurances, Muazzam was not able to relax. He sent out messages to key sardars and started assembling an army. But an event changed everything.

The amirs and the sardars routinely assembled at the Diwan-e-Khaas despite the Badshah being ill. They would wait for an hour or two and then, on an indication from Jaffar Khan, disperse. They had assembled that day too and to their surprise, the curtain in front of the royal throne was raised to reveal Alamgir Badshah sitting there. Those present were stunned. The Badshah looked a little pale, having lost weight. His hands trembled a bit but the piercing eyes carried the same intensity as always. He sat for a quarter of an hour and then the attendants dropped the curtain. The mansabdars left the court with shouts of glory.

The next morning, Alamgir Badshsah sat at the window facing the Yamuna banks for a quarter of an hour. A wave of joy spread all over. The mullahs and maulvis held special prayers in the mosques for the good health of their Badshah.

Muazzam, on the other hand, was restless. He had been living on

the edge for the past ten days. He was overjoyed to know that his father
was well. Unable to control his emotions, he barged into Aurangzeb's
room one afternoon, ignoring the usual protocol. Aurangzeb was
surprised to find his son standing at his bedside. They looked at each
other for a moment. Overcome with mixed feelings, Muazzam held
Aurangzeb's feet and started sobbing.

Aurangzeb had not fully recovered and was weak. He asked,
'Shahzada, what is this? I am fine now. Why are you crying?'

Muazzam looked up. For a brief moment he thought he might
have inadvertently crossed the line by hugging the Badshah's feet
without permission. He withdrew quickly and standing next to the
bed said, 'Abba Jaan! I apologize. You do not know the turmoil I was
going through. Abba Jaan, I was in hell!'

Aurangzeb looked at him saying, 'Shahzada, you are the eldest. If
you behave thus what example will you set for others?'

'Abba Jaan, I was worried sick fearing my life. I lived in mortal fear.'
'But why?'

'My aunt Roshanara Begum had made plans to declare Azam the
next emperor in anticipation of your death.'

Aurangzeb looked at his son. He was trying to ascertain whether
he was lying. He said, 'Shahzada, you should not say such things
without proof. Are you sure of what you accuse Roshanara Begum of?'

'Abba Jaan, I would not lie in such matters. I have personally seen
the royal seal and signature on the *shahi firman*.'

Hearing him, Aurangzeb felt his left arm and found the royal
seal, that was usually tied there, missing. He was taken aback but
maintained his composure and looked at Muazzam who stood there
shivering. 'Abba Jaan, I hope such a calamity never befalls me. But if
it were to happen, I would wish to die at your hands.' Muazzam said
tremulously.

Aurangzeb said, 'Shahzada, such words of cowardice do not suit
you. You are my son, after all.' Pausing for a breath he continued, 'I
have taken congnizance of what you said. I will look into the matter
soon. Now, go and reassure your mother that things are fine. And

please ensure that you wipe your tears before you leave this room. I cannot tolerate the servants seeing a Shahzada in tears.'

♠ ♠ ♠

Within a month Aurangzeb had recovered fully. His return to good health was celebrated with a grand function in the shahi hamamkhana. The next few weeks were spent attending dinners and lunches organized by various mansabdars.

The summers had nearly ended. One day Danishmand Khan met Aurangzeb in private. He said, 'Allah is great. No doubt you recovered because He wants you to accomplish more.'

Smiling at his comment Aurangzeb said, 'I see at it differently. Allah has taught me a lesson and made me get down from the perch of pride.'

'Why do you say that?'

'It is simple. The moment I ascended the throne I thought nothing was beyond my reach. It took Allah just a simple fever to prove me wrong. He has the power to put me on the throne and also take me away from this world. He showed me a glimpse of his infinite power.'

'Hazrat Badshah has been toiling day and night. It is an indication from the Allah that you need to take rest. The illness was a mere signal to you to take it easy.'

'It seems you are stating your mind quoting Allah.'

'You may assume that for a moment. I have a request – Kashmir is considered heaven on earth. Since Badshah Jahangir's times the gardens there are considered a sight to behold. It is as if nature has bestowed her best in the valley of Kashmir. I am sure a few months' rest there will make you more capable of fulfilling Allah's will.'

Aurangzeb looked at Danishmand Khan. Had it been anyone else he would have been suspicious. But he was certain that Danishmand Khan meant well. He was trustworthy. He said, 'I think there is no place for me to rest. Perhaps Allah wants Alamgir to work till his last breath.'

'Huzoor, don't be so dejected. Please believe me; the recuperation there will work wonders for you.'

Aurangzeb had a nagging fear which he now voiced: 'And give a chance to my enemies, who are waiting for an opportune moment along with many others, to take charge here?'

'Huzoor, I don't think your fear is rational. There is prosperity everywhere. Why would anyone want to disrupt your reign?'

'I don't agree. As long as there is power in other people's hands, there will be many who want to use it to their benefit. Danishmand Khan, Agra is your responsibility from now on. You must take all precautions.'

'Me? I am honoured, but I believe there are enough experienced men who can handle this responsibility. I am, after all, a scholar.'

Aurangzeb smiled. He said, 'I want you to do a task for me. There is no one else who is capable of doing it.'

'What is this task you want to entrust on me?'

'I have sinned against the Badshah Shah Jahan. I don't want his curse to affect me. I want you to visit him on my behalf and ask for mercy. Get a letter stating he has forgiven me. You are one of the people he trusts.'

'Hazrat, you have put me in a great dilemma. I was planning to leave for the Haj pilgrimage.'

'You can go later anytime. In fact, I too want to visit Mecca and I would want a scholar like you to accompany me.'

'Huzoor, I had made all arrangements. The ship is being readied at Surat soon.'

'The situation in Surat is not very good at the moment. I urge you to defer your plans.'

'I am at your command. I request you to consider my suggestion of visiting Kashmir while I take care of Agra.'

'Ensure that you take my elder sister Jahanara into confidence and win her heart too.'

Aurangzeb and Danishmand Khan sat talking for a long time. Aurangzeb had finally found a person in whom he could confide and felt relieved.

As the rains abated, Aurangzeb left for Kashmir with a huge caravan in tow. Jaffar Khan was bestowed the tile of Umdat-ul-Mulk.

He and his key sardars joined the caravan along with their respective zenankhanas. Shaista Khan, managing the affairs of the Deccan, was given the title of Amir-ul-Umrao. Till Aurangzeb's return, Shaista Khan was asked to stay put in Delhi. The royal entourage camped in the vineyards of Lahore till the end of winter. By the time summer arrived, the advance parties had reached the valley of Kashmir and were awaiting the arrival of Alamgir.

A messenger reached the gardens at Lahore with an urgent message for the Badshah. The message was immediately received by Jaffar Khan to be delivered to Aurangzeb who was about to leave for his evening conference with his select amaldars. He was surprised to find Jaffar Khan there and asked, 'Is there some problem in Agra?'

'No, Huzoor. That would have been easier to manage. It is regarding Shaista Khan, whom Huzoor had entrusted to capture the Maratha rat.'

'Why? Did that Maratha sardar escape?'

'Huzoor, the matter is much worse. Pune was under Raja Jaswant Singh's command, but the Maratha rat, under the darkness of the night, managed to climb into Shaista Khan's haveli and attacked him. He lost his fingers in the melee that ensued. Many of his begums were killed. Khan Sahab lost his son in the attack.'

'I wonder how Mamu Jaan could be so casual in his security arrangements. And what was Raja Jaswant Singh doing?'

'Huzoor, the attack was sudden.'

'The enemy is expected to attack suddenly. If my Mamu Jaan was expecting the enemy to give advance notice, he is badly mistaken. My mansabdars have become lazy and incompetent staying in Delhi doing nothing for years. My Mamu Jaan cannot protect his own zenankhana! What a shame! Get me all the details in the next four days. I will then decide the next step.'

'But Huzoor, Shaista Khan will be waiting for support from the royal troops. Should we not despatch them without any delay?'

'It will be a waste of resources. I am familiar with the territory of the Deccan. I will decide what we need to do, within a week.'

Jaffar Khan could not counter Aurangzeb. He saluted and took leave.

❧ ❧

Aurangzeb had promised to look into the matter and take a decision within a week, but a month had passed since the news of Shivaji's attack on Shaista Khan. Aurangzeb's caravan moved at a snail's pace towards Kashmir. Nature, shikar and sumptuous delicacies diverted Aurangzeb's mind. Shaista Khan, on the other hand, was persistent and sent message after message requesting him to give him another chance to prove his merit. Shaista Khan was worried that Aurangzeb was upset and might punish him. He pleaded to the Badshah to allow him an opportunity to prove his superiority in bringing the Maratha rat to his knees.

Two months had passed when Aurangzeb finally sat down to discuss the matter with Jaffar Khan and Muazzam. Aurangzeb, despite being far away in the valley of Kashmir, was fully clued into the happenings in the sultanate.

Looking at Jaffar Khan he said, 'Wazir, send a *shahi firman* to Shaista Khan that he has been terminated from the subedari of the Deccan.'

'Terminated? Huzoor, isn't that too stringent a punishment?'

'He is getting away with a mild punishment as he is my Mamu Jaan. Anyone else in his place would have been thrown behind bars. He does not know how to protect his own zenankhana. What kind of a leader is he?'

'Huzoor, he has been an old and trusted servant of the sultanate. Can't you pardon him just this time? And if you do intend to punish him, may I suggest something?'

'What do you have in mind?'

'Why not send him to Bengal as the subedar there? For someone with his seniority, it is as good a punishment!'

Aurangzeb closed his eyes in contemplation for a while and said, 'I agree. Send a *firman* stating he should depart for Bengal right away.

Please also mention that he should not try for an appointment with me as it will be refused.'

Jaffar Khan's intervention had prevented Shaista Khan from being publicly humiliated.

But the question of the Deccan was unresolved. Till Shivaji's men were routed, the danger remained. Aurangzeb's plans of integrating the regions of Golconda and Bijapur into the Mughal Empire were pending. He had to make a long-term plan to succeed.

Muazzam stood nearby listening to the conversation. Aurangzeb looked at him and said, 'Shahzada, sometime back in Delhi you had shown that you were weak at heart. I am going to test you now. If you pass this small test, I will be assured that you are ready to take on larger responsibilities.'

'Huzoor, I am waiting for your command.'

'Look outside,' Aurangzeb said, pointing towards the undulating valley, with the chinar tress in the distance. Muazzam looked askance.

'Shahzada, I am told a tiger has been spotted nearby. I want you to go and capture him before the end of day tomorrow. If you are successful, I shall appoint you as the subedar of the Deccan to capture that Maratha tiger.'

Muazzam, bored of being under the constant supervision of Aurangzeb, swelled with the thought of the golden opportunity within grasping distance now. The thought of being made the subedar of the Deccan was exciting.

Aurangzeb read his mind and said, 'Shahzada, the Deccan is still far away. Please focus on the task at hand. I will see you tomorrow once you are successful in your mission.'

By next afternoon a group of drummers followed by a victorious Muazzam reached Aurangzeb's tent with four dead tigers. Within a few days, Muazzam departed with a huge force to take charge of the Deccan as the newly appointed subedar.

෴

Two monsoons had passed by the time Aurangzeb returned from his visit to the Kashmir Valley. He looked fit and within two months of his arrival, Roshanara Begum started the preparations for his marriage ceremony. There was a buzz of excitement amongst the common people who were to witness the marriage of an emperor after a long time.

The marriage rites of Aurangzeb with Udaipuri took place amidst extensive celebrations that lasted for weeks. The royal couple enjoyed watching a display of pyrotechnics sitting at a window overlooking the Yamuna. On Roshanara's ardent request, Aurangzeb had dropped his usual reluctance and had allowed celebrations that included song and dance. The entire winter was spent in lavish invitations from various amaldars. Everyone, down to the smallest mansabdar was presented with a royal gift. In the meanwhile, Shaista Khan had formally taken charge as the subedar of Bengal.

One day Jaswant Singh presented himself at Aurangzeb's court. Aurangzeb had not forgotten the way he and Shaista Khan had been taught a lesson by the Maratha rat. The defeat had further deepened Aurangzeb's distrust of the Rajput sardar.

Jaswant Singh bent thrice in salaam and presented three large diamonds. Other mansabdars stood respectfully at a distance, their hands behind their backs. Jaffar Khan announced in a soft voice, 'Huzoor, Raja Jaswant Singh has come in to pay his respects.'

'I hope he has come with good news.'

Aurangzeb's taunt was not lost on Jaffar Khan. The news of Shaista Khan's defeat was well known throughout the country. Aurangzeb was using this opportunity to insult the Rajput sardar. Jaffar Khan said, in defence of the Rajput, 'Huzoor, Raja Jaswant Singh is one of the most loyal and hard-working mansabdars.'

Jaswant Singh knew he had no defence. Keeping his head low, he said, 'I am here to beg your forgiveness. I have not been able to fulfil the task for which you had deputed me.'

Aurangzeb continued to address Jaffar Khan, 'Wazir, please ask this Rajput sardar how I am to believe that the mountain rat Shiva could not be flushed out.'

Jaffar Khan continued his plea on behalf of Jaswant Singh. 'Huzoor, there is no doubt that Shiva is a wily and cunning enemy. There was an error in judgement and Shaista Khan Sahab and the raja were taken by surprise. I have no doubt they will fulfil the task at hand sooner than later.'

Aurangzeb, turning the beads of his rosary, said, 'I agree. By the way, what mansab is Jaswant Singh holding right now?'

Jaffar Khan answered, 'A mansab with five thousand troops, Huzoor.'

'So it seems Shahzada and Raja Jaswant Singh are both of the same hierarchy.'

'I could not get you, Ala Hazrat.'

'Wazir, you may not be, but I am ashamed that a mansabdar, holding a mansab of five thousand, runs away from a puny enemy like Shiva. Henceforth the Rajput sardar will hold a mansab of a thousand troops.'

The pronouncement shocked those in attendance. Raja Jaswant Singh's father had served under Badshah Akbar. A mansabdar managing a mere thousand troops was considered an ordinary official and far below the prestige of someone like Raja Jaswant Singh.

Raja Jai Singh and his son Ram Singh stood nearby. Raja Jai Singh stepped forward and said, 'Badshah Salamat is quite justified in his anger. The crime deserves such a punishment. But Huzoor-e-Ala, I request you to give weightage to the fact that Raja Jaswant Singh and his family have served the Mughal emperor for generations. The smallest of the mansabdars in Rajputana has a mansab of two thousand. Asking Raja Jaswant Singh to manage a mere thousand soldiers is an insult to him.'

'Wazir, you may please inform Raja Jai Singh that I am bothered about the insult to the Mughal throne and not to any mansabdar.'

Raja Jai Singh persisted, 'Badshah Salamat, both Shaista Khan and Raja Jaswant Singh have been equally responsible. But I find that Shaista Khan Sahab has been sent to Bengal as a subedar while Raja Jaswant Singh is beng punished. I earnestly urge Your Highness to reconsider the punishment and not insult the Rajputs.'

'Wazir, you may please explain to Jai Singh that we do not differentiate between a Mughal and a Rajput mansabdar. But he needs to keep in mind that Shaista Khan is not only a Mughal mansabdar but also close family. I do differentiate between the Mughal family and Hindu families.'

Jaffar Khan had been a silent observer and had not commented till then. He too was related to the Badshah. He blurted out a little too late, 'May I take the liberty to remind Ala Hazrat that Jaswant Singh too is equally a close relative of yours.' Shah Jahan had given his daughter in marriage to Jaswant Singh. It was not something Aurangzeb wanted to be reminded of. Aurangzeb's fingers, telling the rosary stopped for a brief second. Recovering quickly, he replied, 'I don't need to be reminded about that. I have pronounced the punishment. Let Jaswant Singh be sent on a campaign to Kabul. If he does something remarkable there, I will reconsider my decision. Till then, he need not take the trouble of attending the durbar here.'

The Badshah dismissed the durbar as he got up and left.

⁂

Udaipuri begum's mahal shone in the light of lamps covered with multicoloured shades of glass. It gave the room an ethereal feel. Shamim peeped into the mahal before walking into Aurangzeb's room. Aurangzeb stood with his hands behind his back watching the reflection of the moon on the surface of the River Yamuna. Hearing Shamim's footsteps he turned when she said, 'Huzoor, Begum Sahiba has been waiting for you.'

Aurangzeb was dressed in a satin kurta and a flowing pyjama. His bright red velvety mojadis were embellished with pearls. Caressing his beard, he indicated Shamim to lead. Shamim, walking briskly in the corridors stopped outside the large door leading to Udaipuri begum's mahal. She bent in salaam and said, 'Begum Sahiba is waiting. Please enter.'

Shamim gestured to the khojas who dispersed immediately and

were replaced by maids. Aurangzeb took out a pearl necklace and handed it to Shamim who took it with gratitude adding, 'Mubarak! Ala Hazrat, Mubarak!'

Udaipuri begum stood expectantly on a bright red Persian carpet to welcome the Badshah. She was Dara's find but since the day she had stepped into his zenankhana, he had been running from pillar to post. Destiny, it seems, had other plans. It had taken Shamim and Roshanara some effort to convince her to marry Aurangzeb. She now stood decked from head to toe, her kohl-lined eyes fluttering as she looked at Aurangzeb entering her room. She briefly scanned him as he walked towards her and then bent slightly at the waist.

Holding her henna-decorated hands, Aurangzeb said, 'Janeman, Allah has not made these delicate hands for saluting.'

'But Shahenshah ...' Udaipuri begum blushed.

'No dear. I am not the Shahenshah here. I am your Aurangzeb.'

'Huzoor ...'

'Oh! You won't understand, my sweetheart. These lips are not meant to say such things. Let me punish them.'

Saying so, he locked her lips in a passionate and lingering kiss. Looking into her eyes he said, 'Begum, don't call me Huzoor.'

Udaipuri put her hands around Aurangzeb's neck saying, 'If Huzoor is going to punish me like this for saying so I would like to say it a hundred times. Huzoor, Shahenshah, Badshah, Alamgir ...' Snuggling close to Aurangzeb she said, 'The day I agreed to marry the Badshah of Hindustan I was prepared for any punishment but I never expected it to be such a sweet one.'

Aurangzeb glanced around the room. A few musical instruments were arranged in one corner and a table with bottles of wine and crystal glasses stood in the other.

Resting her head on Aurangzeb's chest Udaipuri said, 'I know Huzoor does not approve of wine. But I hope he would not disapprove of these things in my mahal.'

Aurangzeb held her face in his hands and showering kisses on her said, 'I would not have married you if I wanted to remain sober enough to say what is approved and what is not. You are the begum here and you have a right to do what pleases you in your mahal.'

'Really? I can't believe my ears.'

'Ask what you want and it shall be yours.'

'Won't Huzoor get upset?'

Hugging her again Aurangzeb said, 'How can I be when I have you here? What is it that you want?'

'Huzoor, you have such a huge zenankhana but the person ruling it is your sister Roshanara Begum.'

'What about her?'

'I would want my word to rule. I want the zenankhana under my command.'

Udaipuri was in the peak of her youth. She had ingited a passion in Aurangzeb which he had long forgotten. He was mesmerized with her eyes and the touch of her luscious lips. Yet, the demand for power made him alert. He loosened his grip on her. Sensing it, she asked, 'Is Huzoor angry at me?'

Aurangzeb said, 'Not at all. Why should I get angry? I understand you don't like the way Roshanara manages the zenankhana.'

'Huzoor has come into my mahal for the first time. I would not want to speak about these things today. If Huzoor does not like what I said, I will not speak about it at all.'

Aurangzeb sensed Udaipuri was hurt. He tried pacifiying her. 'That is not the case. There are two Shahzadis here who are older to you, not to mention the Kashmiri begum. Managing the zenankhana is not an easy affair. You need someone experienced ...'

'Your daughters are my daughters too. And as far as the Kashmiri begum is concerned, she has her place as the mother of the eldest son. But if Huzoor does not want, then ...'

'Dear, don't get upset. Roshanara has been managing this for such a long time.'

'I think the time has come for her to leave for Mecca.'

Aurangzeb threw a surprised glance at her. He was seeing a

different image of the sensual beauty. He had never imagined that she would propose such a drastic step at their very first meeting. His ever cautious and suspicious mind did not agree with her proposal but his heart was tempted. She had ignited his passions where logic failed. Finally sensual desires won.

Aurangzeb got up and led her to the bed. The light of the lamps reflected in the chandeliers creating a surreal effect. Very soon, they fused in each others arms.

The lamps had burnt themselves off in the night. The distant call of the muezzin from the Jama Masjid woke up Aurangzeb. The embers of the passionate night had not yet been doused. It was a rare morning to see the Badshah miss his morning prayers.

🙰 🙲

The marriage to Udaipuri and the celebrations thereafter were now a distant memory. Zebunissa sat in her garden at the edge of the fountain looking at the golden fish darting around. Her mind was not at ease when she heard Shamim call out her name. 'Begum Sahiba!'

She turned to see her maid Saloni with Shamim.

'I apologize for disturbing you. Your maid here has committed an act which deserves a severe punishment. She was caught taking this out of the mahal.' Shamim put forth her hand showing a piece of paper.

Shamim read the words written on the paper, '*Tum pas nahin to koi pas nahin.*'

'*Ab muzhe zindagi ki aas nahin,*' Zebunissa blurted out the other line.

Shamim looked up in surprise to see tears in Zebunissa's eyes.

'Shamim, I am the one who wrote it. It seems Saloni got hold of the paper. It is my crime but she is being punished for it.'

'May I ask what made you cry Begum Sahiba?'

'Shamim, I am missing my Ammi Jaan today. It was in Aurangabad; I remember her ardently wishing to see my marriage procession leave the royal palace one day. But I don't think her wish will ever be fulfilled.'

Zebunissa's face glowed in the light of the slanting rays of the evening sun. She shielded her face with her palms when Shamim said, 'Begum Sahiba, there is no tragedy bigger than being born a Shahzadi to a Shahenshah. The sons kill themselves in the race to the throne and the daughters have to live their entire life in the zenankhana. But look around; there are many women like you. Don't lose hope. You are not even twenty-five yet. I know it is easy to say than do. But nothing is impossible.

The setting sun had set the western sky ablaze. Zebunissa, preoccupied with other thoughts, did not stay in the gardens to enjoy their beauty and walked back slowly to her quarters.

৩ৎ ৎ৩

It was the month of Ramzan and the festival of Eid was celebrated with gaiety across the city. Amirs and other officials busied themselves exchanging gifts.

Raja Jaswant Singh and Jai Singh's palanquin stopped at the doorstep of Jaffar Khan's haveli. Raja Jaswant Singh's stature had been reduced in hierarchy thanks to the diktat issued by Aurangzeb, but Jaffar Khan was sensitive to the fact that Raja Jaswant Singh still carried a huge respect amongst the Rajputs. He personally welcomed them with a traditional embrace as they greeted each other 'Eid Mubarak'. They moved to the living room where an Irani dastarkhan, a traditional cloth on to which food was served, was laid out for the guests. Apart from the plates of dry fruits and sweets, there were wines from Shiraz and Istanbul in long-necked pitchers.

The khojas served the wines to the Rajput guests. Seeing Jaffar Khan sip wine with hesitation, Raja Jaswant Singh commented, 'I am sure the Badshah won't appreciate your enjoying the wine.'

Jaffar Khan replied, 'It is not a newly formed habit. We have been used to it for generations. It would not be an exaggeration to say that this old man is able to perform his duties towards the sultanate thanks to the energy this wine provides.'

'Khan Sahab,' Jaswant Singh said, keeping his tumbler in a tray,

'Badshah Salamat's marriage celebrations led to a lot of pardons, including diehard criminals being released. It seems everyone else except me is enjoying his benevolence.'

'Let bygones be bygones, Raja Sahab,' Jaffar Khan said. 'Why don't you enjoy this wine ordered especially from Shiraz?' He downed the tumbler in one swig and dabbed his beard with a satin handkerchief.

For a while they were silent, all others except Jaswant Singh enjoying the wine without speaking a word. Noticing his silence Jaffar Khan said, 'Maharaj Sahab, I have tried my best but Ala Hazrat refuses to change his stand.'

Jaffar Khan was a little drunk. He leaned against the pillows and continued, addressing Jai Singh, 'Raja Sahab, it is not the only crime our Maharaj Sahab has committed. He had taken up arms against the Shahzada when he had marched from the Deccan, remember?'

'Was that a crime?' Jaswant Singh asked angrily. 'The elder Shahzada Dara had called for my services and I was under the direct command of Shah Jahan Badshah himself. What did you expect of me? To obey the Badshah's command or support an upstart Shahzada who was challenging the emperor?' Jaswant Singh twirled the ends of his moustache waiting for Jaffar Khan to reply. He was in a confrontational mood.

Jaffar Khan was a seasoned politician and knew that certain rhetorical questions were best left unanswered. He kept quiet. Raja Jai Singh added, 'Khan Sahab, there is no point in raking old issues. Those were uncertain times and the loyalty of a person cannot be judged by the actions taken then. We Rajputs have always been loyal to the throne. Alamgir is on the throne now. Raja Jaswant Singh is our leader and any injustice to him will be an indication to the entire Rajput community that they have been denied justice just because they are Hindus. This has not happened since Badshah Akbar's time. We need your help to make the Badshah understand how his actions are hurting the the feelings of the entire Rajput community.'

'I had not spoken till now but let me tell you the truth Khan Sahab,' Jaswant Singh said, downing his wine in one gulp.

He continued, 'The Badshah would be surprised if he hears the true story. He has been blaming me, making me out to be the sole cause of Mughal defeat but the fact is we have all been responsible.'

'What do you mean?'

'Let me explain. I realized that the two Badshahs of Golconda and Bijapur had been reduced to a mere fraction of their earlier strength. The only troublemaker was the small upstart zamindar who called him Shivaji Bhosale. I knew, that in order to capture the forts under Shivaji's command, I needed the full backup of the Mughal forces, especially the cannons. Each time I raised the topic Shaista Khan Sahab would find an excuse and not send the armaments on time.'

'I don't understand why he would try such delaying tactics,' Jaffar Khan said.

'It is simple. The Mughal Empire had but one enemy in the north-west, in the treacherous mountains of Afghanistan. Other than Yusuf Shah of Kabul, the empire had literally no resistance. The two Badshahs in the Deccan were likely to surrender sooner than later. Shiva Bhosale was one irritant. If that was removed quickly, the likelihood of the Badshah sending Shaista Khan Sahab to fight against Yusuf Shah was very high. Quite obviously, it was not an exciting prospect, and the more he delayed, the more time he got to spend in the Deccan enjoying the luxuries. When I asked him the reason for his dilly-dallying he said he was convinced that the Rajputs may be strong, loyal and be willing to fight to their death but they could never beat the Mughals in their cunningness. I was surprised to hear him say that. I was confident of capturing the Maratha zamindar but Shaista Khan Sahab deliberately did not allow that to happen.'

Jaffar Khan let out a deep sigh as he emptied the tumbler of wine. 'I am not surprised to hear this. Shaista Khan has managed to escape going to Kabul. Instead you have been penalized. I request you to have patience. I will, at an appropriate time, apprise the Badshah.'

'I hope you will be able to help me. If not I may as well call it a day. I don't have any children. I would rather spend my remaining days in Jodhpur in the service of the Lord.'

The afternoon turned to evening as Jaffar Khan and the two Rajput sardars conferred, talking of various things. Jaffar Khan wanted to make sure that the Rajputs would not revolt. Cold winds swept the streets of Delhi as the Rajput sardars returned home.

It was a holiday on account of it being a Friday. Aurangzeb, alongwith the chief kazi Abdul Wahab, a few key officials and Jaffar Khan sat in an office next to Moti Masjid. The Badshah supervised the arrangements of some of the key amirs who were planning to make the pilgrimage to Haj.

Abdul Wahab, sensing an opportunity began, 'The ulemas and maulvis are very happy to see you occupying the throne at Delhi.'

Aurangzeb was aware the kazi wanted to suggest something else. He brushed aside the praise saying, 'What's so great about that? Someone else would have been ruling had it not been me. It could have been my elder brother Dara, for that matter.' The kazi, pondered for a moment and said, 'But it is different when someone as devout as you takes charge.'

'I am not interested in small talk. Do you have any advice for my pilgrimate to the Haj?'

'The Quran says you need not go. The very fact that you are a Shahenshah and are spreading the word of Islam is equivalent to visiting the Haj ten times.'

'Does the Quran say that?'

The kazi looked at one of the ulemas, who sat a little away reading the holy books. He said, 'Yes, Huzoor. The Quran and the Hadis say that the job of the emperor is to spread the word of Allah. He need not go for the pilgrimage.

'I am doing that in any case. What else did you want to say?'

'Huzoor, your father Shah Jahan and your brother Dara Shikoh were competing with each other to do things against our religion. Allah has given you the opportunity to ascend the throne. We feel you should create some special rules for the Muslims in our country.'

'Please be specific.'

'Consuming alcohol or wine is prohibited as per Islam. We would want Badshah Salamat to issue strict orders against the same.'

'I am hearing a good suggestion for the first time. It has been nearly ten years since I took charge. I am against any habit-forming substance. Please issue orders on my behalf immediately.'

'Huzoor, the Hindus have built temples all around. We request the Jahanpanah to issue orders to destroy all of them.'

'Why?'

'Islam prohibits idol worship. The sounds of the temple bells are a disturbance to a pious Musalman.'

'Kazi Sahab, the Mughal throne has dealt with such issues in a different manner ever since the time of Shahenshah Akbar. Let the kafirs practise what they believe in and let the Muslims lead the way Islam suggests. Of course we will not allow their practices to interfere with our administration.'

The kazi was not the one to give up easily. He said, puffing out his chest, 'Huzoor, the world expects the common man to behave as per the rules of the Quran ever since you have come to power.'

Aurangzeb was tired of the discussions. He said, 'If you need to issue *firmans* to ensure that the common people behave as per the laws of Islam please go ahead. I will honour your *firmans*.'

Kazi Abdul Wahab was overjoyed. He said, 'Such an assurance is enough for me. I was sure the Badshah Salamat would encourage us to spread the word of Islam.'

'But please ensure one thing,' Aurangzeb said, his eyes half closed in contemplation. 'Let it be known that the rules you put forth for the common man apply to each and every one equally. You know I offer my prayers along with the common people at the masjid. Islam does not differentiate between a Badshah and a fakir.'

The ulemas raised their hands up saying, '*Qayamat! Wallah, kya baat hai!*'

Aurangzeb smiled indulgently. He got up saying, 'If there is nothing else, I would like to end this discussion.'

ᴐᴈ ᴈᴐ

Freezing cold winds blowing across the Yamuna made the life of the people staying in tents and shacks miserable. Small fires could be seen lit at various street corners where the fakirs and the homeless sat around trying to keep themselves warm. Discussions, whether in the warm havelis of the amirs or around the bonfires on the streets, were about the people who had left for the Haj pilgrimage.

A chilling news, enough to freeze the blood of those who heard, spread across the city. Within no time the fakirs, the amirs or anyone who heard were seen asking, 'Is this true?' Soon the news reached the royal palace. They wondered whether the ships docked at Surat had departed.

The activities at the Diwan-e-Aam were proceeding at their usual pace. The Wazir, old and bent with age, found an opportune moment to interrupt. 'Huzoor, there is some disturbing news which we have just heard.'

Aurangzeb raised his hand a little indicating the Wazir to continue.

The Wazir said, 'The Haj pilgrims had assembled at Surat ready to depart. Surat's mansabdar Bahirji Bohra and Haji Saiyad Baig were given the task of managing the few lakh gold coins presented by the Badshah himself for the purpose of the pilgrimage. The Marathas, in a surprise raid, managed to loot the entire amount, including the havelis of the merchants there. Saiyad Baig managed to escape and hide in his fort but lost all his wealth including precious gems and jewellery. The ships, which had left Konkan, were intercepted midway and drowned. The Marathas managed to destroy the port too. It was total chaos.'

Jaffar Khan stopped for a moment to see Aurangzeb's reaction who continued to listen with his half-closed eyes.

Jaffar Khan waited for instructions. He had recounted in brief the way the Marathas had looted and ransacked Surat. He said, 'Huzoor, the Marathas have plundered the city. The people there are clamouring for justice and some of their representatives are marching towards Delhi to appeal for help. Please instruct what we should do.'

Alamgir raised his right hand and asked, 'Is there any other task pending for the day?'

Jaffar Khan was surprised that the Badshah had not shown any apparent anger at the way Surat had been looted. He said, 'Huzoor, the news from Surat has disturbed all of us. Each one of us is worried. We have nothing more important to discuss.'

'Then I dismiss the durbar,' Aurangzeb said, and left without turning back. The satin screen was dropped immediately. Aurangzeb walked towards the Diwan-e-Khaas. He turned towards a gurzbardar, the mace bearer, standing nearby and said, 'Ask the Wazir to meet me in the personal chamber.'

Aurangzeb continued walking down the corridors towards the khalbatkhana, the room designated for meetings held in private. Jaffar Khan soon followed. He asked Jaffar Khan to take a seat and said, 'What was our Shahzada Muazzam doing? How did this Maratha sardar manage to reach Surat without being detected en route?'

'Shahzada was engaged in a shikar deep in a jungle. But it is still surprising that the Maratha sardar and his men managed to evade all the posts on the way.'

'I am told it is Shiva Bhosale, the same Maratha sardar who made life miserable for Shaista Khan. He seems to have become a bigger nuisance in the last few years. His mischief is increasing day by day.'

Aurangzeb took a minute to gather his thoughts. He said, 'Wazir, I had heard of his cunning when I was the subedar at the Deccan. He tried to trick me then by engaging me in a dialogue of reconciliation while attacking our other camps at the same time. I called his bluff and gave him a strict warning. While leaving for Delhi I had given instructions to keep an eye on his activities, but it seems no one has bothered.'

The wazir, in defence of the current subedar, said, 'Shahzada may have ignored him thinking he was a small fry.'

'Should he not have assessed the enemy more accurately after seeing what he did to Shaista Khan? I cannot allow this rebel to harass our people going to Haj. He has looted Surat. He needs to be taught a lesson.'

'I suggest we send a large army to support the thanedar at Surat.'

'You expect Shiva to stay put in Surat for such a long time? These people are well known for their guerrilla tactics. By the time the news reaches us, he and his men would have reached the mountainous region with the loot.'

'I am told our forces are marching towards Surat and they plan to intercept them. I am sure the Marathas will not be able to get away.'

'I wish it happens that way. I have a different view though. I feel I have ignored the Marathas. The two Badshahs are quite old and unlikely to create any problems in future. But this Maratha sardar is now emboldened with his success against Shaista Khan. I have thought of a game plan that I shall disclose at an appropriate time.'

Alamgir was clearly disturbed. He asked after a pause, 'How much did he manage to loot in Surat?'

'Huzoor, I am told that both Bahirji Bohra and Saiyad Baig had a wealth of more than eight crore each.'

'It is unthinkable that an ordinary Maratha sardar thumbs his nose at us and manages to get away. Even if he was to be intercepted and the loot recovered, we cannot forget the way he snubbed us. We will have to find a way to take our revenge.'

'I am unable to follow you, Huzoor.'

'He needs to be insulted in the same manner.'

'Huzoor, what importance does a small-time rebel like him have for us to want to insult him?'

'You are mistaken. Each person has a different perspective on where his prestige lies. We have to hurt him where it matters. The value of it will be much more than a hundred crore of loot. Once he is hurt at the right place he and his future generations will not dare raise their heads against the Mughal might.'

Jaffar Khan was confused. He thought it wise to keep quiet. Aurangzeb did not elaborate further. Jaffar Khan saluted and left silently.

A couple of months passed by and the lack of any retaliation from the Mughal emperor upset the amaldars but they were wise enough not to voice their opinion to their master.

One day the news that the temple at Somnath had been plundered spread all over. The temple housed wealth collected over hundreds of years. Scores of temples from the port at Veraval to Khambat were razed to the ground. The quantum of loot was such that it took more than a month for the officials at Delhi, entrusted with the task of classifying and noting down the wealth, to account for it. The Rajput sardars were fuming silently but were unable to openly voice their dissent.

⊷❧ ❧⊶

Kazi Abdul Wahab, having been given a go-ahead by the Alamgir, managed to issue a number of *firmans* instructing the general public on the dos and don'ts related to daily life. Consumption of alcohol was banned for all. The ban extended to all products that were bitter in taste. Instructions were issued on the dress code for men and women. Women were warned not to show any part of their body as it was against Islam. The fatwas also mentioned that men could not grow their beards more than four inches below their chins.

The main kazi appointed amaldars to ensure that the fatwas were carried out. Anyone found drunk on the road was punished with whiplashes. The kotwal and their prosecution officers would randomly check people on the streets. Women were forced to remove their burkhas during such checks. Officers would stop any man they wished to measure the length of his beard. The mohtasibs, or the investigating officers, being given complete power by the main kazi at Delhi, zealously implemented the fatwas, the heat of which was being felt right across the subcontinent whether in Delhi, Agra, Allahabad, Lahore, Ahmedabad, Aurangabad or Dhaka. The mohtasibs patrolled each lane and bylane of Delhi, the capital of the Mughal Empire. The maulvis were finally content that they had a true follower of Islam as their emperor.

The job of making people live by Islamic code of conduct was followed earnestly for a couple of years. As expected, complaints

against the excesses being carried out
increasing with each passing day.

❦

Danishmand Khan and Asad Khan, husband of A
waited for a meeting in the private room. They had
personally meet Shah Jahan at Agra fort and were retur.
stay of nearly three months.

On way to Moti Masjid for his evening namaz, Aurangzeb s
by to meet them. Without preamble he asked, 'Danishmand K.
how was your visit to Agra? I hope my Waalid Sahab Badshah
keeping well.'

Asad Khan was married to Shah Jahan's sister and thus was high
in the hierarchy. He said, 'Huzoor-e-Ala, we did meet the Badshah as
per your orders. He is very ill.'

'I am told that despite his age, he is quite active otherwise,'
Aurangzeb's voice wore a sardonic tone when referring to his father.

Asad Khan licked his lips nervously. He was not sure how to state
the facts. 'Huzoor, Badshah's body may be weak but he cannot resist
the young maids and concubines there.'

It was evident that Aurangzeb had nothing but disgust for such
behaviour. He said, 'The house arrest does not seem to have changed
him one bit. Old habits die hard. As an emperor he abused all his
powers and I wonder whether he will ever change.'

'The body is used to certain things, Huzoor. It takes time.'
Danishmand Khan tried.

'Many of the mansabdars were hurt that I put him under house
arrest. But many also accuse me of tolerating his wayward behaviour.
I am told he is in touch with the Badshahs of Golconda and Bijapur.
Is this true?'

'Apparently he manages to send letters to them through the maids.
He has also been in touch with Shiva Bhosale.'

'Could you get any written proof?'

ried a lot. I tortured a few slaves and threw them in the dungeons. no one was willing to speak.'

How can you be sure of the correspondence with the Maratha dar?'

'I enquired and found that the Badshah had played a role in Shiva's attack on Surat last year.'

Aurangzeb turned his gaze on Asad Khan. 'I had sent you to gather information on a specific subject. Were you successful?'

Hesitation and embarrassment were writ large on Asad Khan's face. He said, 'Huzoor, it is a very embarrassing situation. Jahanara is after all my begum's sister's daughter. She spends all her time with the Badshah.'

'So what I have heard is true, isn't it?'

'I am not sure, Huzoor. She spends all her time reading the namaz or praying to Allah for her father's health.'

'But the rumours …'

'I checked. There were a few people who are sure that what you fear is true.'

'You are not being clear. Please be more specific.'

'It so happened one day that Jahanara Begum came to visit the Badshah at around midnight.'

'Midnight? Why at such an odd hour?'

'He had been indisposed since morning. Jahanara Begum prayed in the masjid for his health where an aulia gave her an amulet to be tied around the Badshah's arm. She came into the Badshah's chambers to meet him. He was in high fever and in his delirium he said, 'Begum, you are looking so beautiful. I am reminded of Mumtaz Begum today.'

'What happened then?'

'There were a few khojas and maids around. One of the maids, on hearing the Badshah's words, shouted, "Ya Allah!" The Badshah came into his senses and asked, "Dear, is that you?" Jahanara held her father's hand and tied the amulet given by the aulia. She sat there with him holding his hand till it was past midnight. Tears continued to flow down her cheeks.'

Aurangzeb did not react but stood at the window looking outside. Danishmand Khan and Asad Khan waited for further instructions. There was no doubt in Aurangzeb's mind about Danishmand Khan's intelligence and Asad Khan's truthfulness. He had been hearing a lot of rumours about the relationship between his elder sister and his father. At times he was tempted to believe them. He looked up and saw Danishmand Khan had tears in his eyes. He asked, 'Danishmand Khan? What is the matter?'

Danishmand Khan knelt on the floor and, holding the edge of Aurangzeb's flowing robe to his forehead said, 'Huzoor-e-Ala, Mohammad Paigambar spent his entire lifetime trying to find the ultimate truth. An ordinary man cannot find that. I request you not to pursue the matter further. The Badshah at Agra is old and on his deathbed. Let bygones be bygones. He will have to face Allah in his court. Who are we to pronounce our verdict? I suggest you to go to Agra and plead for his mercy. It will be a peaceful end to his life.'

Aurangzeb could sense the sincerity and turmoil in Danishmand Khan's voice. Oftentimes, while reading the Quran, a pang of guilt would trouble him. He would be tempted to rush to Agra and fall at his father's feet shouting, 'Abba Jaan, you are free! Do what you wish. Punish me whichever way you feel suitable.' But the evanescent thought would vanish in as quickly as it had came and Aurangzeb would be back to his old self. For a moment he was tempted by the sincere request made by Danishmand Khan. 'Danishmand Khan, I put my faith in Allah. I shall do whatever He guides me to do.'

The fingers moved the beads and the lips chanted the kalmas. The meeting was over.

༺ ༻

A sudden shower had washed the streets clean. It was Aurangzeb's birthday and the durbar, to be held in the late afternoon, was filled with officials waiting to congratulate their Badshah.

It had been a Mughal tradition followed for generations now. The Diwan-e-Aam, the durbar for the common man, had been thrown open and thousands thronged to wish their emperor. The sardars vied with each other to gift camels, elephants and horses, not to mention precious gems and jewellery. The lesser ranked sardars were given expensive clothes as gifts by the emperor. It was an occasion to bestow titles and honours on select officials. The ground facing the Red Fort was brimming with crowds. It seemed the entire world's wealth had descended on to the fort.

The Khaas durbar followed the Aam one once the Badshah seated himself on the Peacock Throne. The officials and the Shahzadas had gathered in the huge marble courtyard. As per protocol, the Shahzadas were the first ones to offer their gifts followed by other officials in order of hierarchy. The Rajputs followed the Mughal sardars. When Raja Jai Singh came forward Aurangzeb asked, 'So what has Raja Jai Singh brought on this happy occasion?'

Raja Jai Singh uncovered the trays his servants were carrying to show them filled with glittering diamonds. The emperor touched the tray as a sign of acceptance and the trays were taken away.

Aurangzeb was in a happy mood. He said, 'We are pleased. We would like the Rajput sardar to carry out an important task on our behalf.'

Raja Jai Singh bowed once more. 'Hazrat Salamat needs only to command. We Rajputs are always ready to carry out your orders.'

'You are aware that the only thorn in our vast empire is the Maratha sardar who surreptitouly attacks our forts and territories and runs away to hide like a mountain rat. I believe you can tackle him. Make him agree to our demands or else punish him appropriately; I leave it to you. Are you ready to take on this responsibility?'

Raja Jai Singh replied, 'Beshak! You need not be worried about a petty rebel zamindar. I will take him to task.'

Aurangzeb offered him the traditional tray with betel leaves. Picking up of a paan signified that Raja Jai Singh had committed to the task. Aurangzeb exclaimed, 'Shabbash!' Turning towards Jaffar Khan he added, 'I am bestowing Raja Jai Singh with the title of Mirza Raja. He is equal in hierarchy to the Shahzada. I am increasing his mansab to seven thousand foot soldiers.' He added, 'You will have Raja Jai Rai Singh Sisodia, Raja Sujan Singh Bundela and your sons, Kirat Singh and Ram Singh, apart from Narsingh Gaur and Puranmal Bundela for your support. You may have to face Adil Shah there. I am thus ordering Sardar Diler Khan and Daud Khan to accompany you. Mirza Raja, I shall be waiting for the good news on your return from the campaign.'

The people in attendance were taken by surprise to see an ordinary mansabdar being felicitated by the emperor. The fact that he had been bestowed such a huge responsibility was a matter of awe and jealousy for most. They could never guess correctly what the emperor would do next.

The officials were in for another surprise. Before getting up Aurangzeb asked, looking at the Wazir, 'What else do you think we should do for Mirza Raja Jai Singh?'

'The Mughal tradition says we have to give a return gift. Now that you ask, may I suggest we need to accord him with more honour?'

'I agree.'

Aurangzeb indicated to the guards standing next to him. They helped him remove the heavily embroidered satin robe he was wearing and put it in a large tray. As Mirza Raja received the tray, Aurangzeb said, 'Mirza Raja, I am handing over this royal robe to you. It is up to you to keep the Mughal reputation intact.'

It was beyond Mirza Raja Jai Singh's wildest dreams that he would be felicitated in such a manner. Jaffar Khan picked up the robe and draped it around Mirza Raja's shoulders.

The felicitation ceremony was the talk of the durbar. Raja Jaswant Singh, standing in the fourth row along with other ordinary mansabdars, left the durbar with a bitter taste in his mouth. He knew he had been deliberately ignored by the Badshah.

꧁ ꧂

It was after a long gap that Aurangzeb found time to visit Nawab Bai. She welcomed him with the traditional Hindu custom of putting a tilak on his forehead. Wiping it away with his palm he said, 'Begum, how many times have I told you I don't like these customs.'

'I know. But I wish you will allow me some liberties within these four walls.'

'You can be so adamant! Having married me you are part of my religion now. You need to do away with these kafir customs. Yet, you choose to ignore my wish.'

'If I didn't care, would I be wearing clothes as per the Islamic tradition? I know Huzoor does not love me any more. You may insult me, shout at me, even taunt me by marrying the young Udaipuri begum. But I will continue to pray for your good health and long life.'

'Begum, it is unfortunate we are not able to understand each other. I came in as you sent messages four times during the day. Now, if you are through with your customary rites, I will take leave. There is a lot of work pending.'

'Please sit down for a while. It has been four months since Hazrat's birthday. I hadn't seen you since then.'

'I know the cause of your sorrow. I married Udaipuri and now I have gifted the Kohinoor diamond to her. You need not be jealous. I have sent you a sum of two lakh rupiyas and have increased your personal jagir by the same amount. What's there to complain?'

Aurangzeb was in a hurry. He never felt comfortable in Nawab Bai's mahal. Yet, he did not want to be rude. He was aware of the way Roshanara had insulted her during his illness. But he was unable to fathom the cause of her sadness now.

'Huzoor, I am not talking of the diamond you have gifted Udaipuri begum. It was something else about which I have repeatedly asked you.'

'What are you referring to?'

'My son Sultan too is a Shahzada. On the occasion of your birthday, you released some diehard criminals. But Huzoor seems to have forgotten my son Sultan who sits behind the tall walls of the Gwalior prison and for whom this woman's heart aches.'

'How many times have I told you? The emperor can pardon

many sins but not treachery. Sultan committed a heinous crime by challenging the throne. That can never be pardoned.'

'Huzoor, don't you have any consideration for his age?'

'A Shahzada's age cannot be taken into account. The fact that he is Shahzada is good enough. It is said that the true enemies of a Badshah are his sons themselves.'

'Huzoor, your father Shah Jahan Badshah …'

'Enough! If you have something to say regarding your son, please speak. Let us not discuss politics here. You have no business to interfere in those matters.'

'I wish to see him once.'

Aurangzeb looked at Nawab Bai. He could sense her desperation. It had been ten years since he had ascended the throne. He had thrown his eldest son Muhammad Sultan into prison as he had dared to fight against him. Both he and Nawab Bai had not seen him since then. Nawab Bai had got tired of sending requests through various officials. It was quite natural that Nawab Bai would hope that he would accede to her request for the release of her son on the happy occasion of his birthday.

'I am his mother. I don't want anything else. Please let me see him once.'

'It is not possible. I need to go now. I have other tasks pending.'

He turned to leave when Nawab Bai said, 'I have another request in that case. If you cannot release my son, put me there along with him. I will be able to see him each day and my soul will not be tortured.'

'Begum, are you out of your mind?'

'How can I be in my senses when my son has been cruelly taken away from me and thrown into a dungeon?'

'An insane mind has no logic. Whatever said and done, you are my begum. The protocol does not allow that.'

'Huzoor, it is surprising that the same protocol allows you to keep your son behind bars for ten years.'

'I cannot release him from prison; nor can I allow you to visit him.

I have a way out: I will send the royal painter to get his latest portrait. You will at least be able to see how he looks now.'

Nawab Bai began to sob. She said, tears flowing down her cheeks, 'Huzoor, you did not agree to any of my wishes. But your suggestion will allow me to see his face. Please don't delay sending the painter. My heart aches to see him. I will soothe my heart by hugging the painting.'

'Begum, I will do as you say, but frankly, I am unable to understand your pain.'

'And I don't understand by what thread Allah has woven the fabric of your heart.'

'It is the entanglement of those threads which confounds me. *La ilahi ilillah …*'

⁂

The huge marble statue of an elephant at the grand entrance of the Red Fort was being pounded by sheets of rain. It had been pouring heavily in the capital. Chandni Chowk was drowning in rainwater while the moat around the fort was full, the extra water flowing down into the Yamuna.

Despite the inclement weather, the Diwan-e-Khaas was in full swing. The officials had arrived in their covered palanquins. As soon as the officials had taken their place, Alamgir Badshah made his entrance as the announcer read out his complete official name with the titles.

Jaffar Khan, the prime minister, presented a set of papers. 'Zille Subhani, we have some very good news.'

Aurangzeb gestured with his hand, giving him permission to speak.

'Huzoor, the Mughal forces in the Deccan under the able leadership of Mirza Raja Jai Singh have managed to get the Maratha sardar Shiva Bhosale to surrender.'

Aurangzeb's fingers, busy telling his rosary beads, stopped for a brief moment.

Jaffar Khan continued, 'Shiva Bhosale is now pleading for his life. Mirza Raja has managed to capture all his forts including the strategically located Purandar Fort.'

'Who is the messenger?'

'Mirza Raja has sent his message through his confidant Durgadas Rathore.'

Durgadas Rathore, a young man in his early twenties, stepped forward and saluted on hearing his name.

'Alampanah, we have been blessed by Allah the merciful. Ala Hazrat's troops took no time in capturing Shiva's forts. Very soon Shiva surrendered in the presence of Diler Khan and Mirza Raja. He has agreed to give up all his forts and wealth.'

'Very good.' Aurangzeb's words did not reveal any emotion. 'Wazir, we need to ensure the veracity of the news. I have heard similar stories from Shaista Khan earlier.'

'I have verified it to be true. Not only that, the other news is that our royal forces are marching on towards Bijapur having captured Phaltan and Mangalwedha near Sholapur. We are expecting Adil Shah to surrender soon.'

'Anyway, we will hear the good news when it occurs. At the moment I am pleased that Mirza Raja Jai Singh has performed his duty well. This Maratha zamindar had been a nuisance ever since I took charge of the Deccan. What gift do you suggest we should give this messenger of good news?'

'I recommend a gift of a hundred gold coins, Ala Hazrat.'

'Is that all? I must say you lack imagination.'

Durgadas Rathore, stood quietly with his hands behind his back. Proudly puffing his chest he said, 'Huzoor-e-Ala, what better gift can I expect than your words of appreciation? If Huzoor so wishes to gift me, I will request him to wait till I present the Maratha sardar in your court.' Realizing that he may have spoken out of turn, he quickly put his head down and waited for further instructions.

A faint smile played on Aurangzeb's lips. 'Wazir, let Durgadas know that he has royal patronage now. I am bestowing a mansab of a hundred troops and appointing him as an ustad for my younger Shahzada Akbar. Durgadas will be responsible for teaching the Shahzada the art of sword fighting, usage of guns and other weapons.'

The officials in attendance raised their hands in air shouting, 'Karamat! Shahi karamat!'

⊰⊱ ⊰⊱

Ram Singh, with fifteen horsemen, reached Jaffar Khan's haveli. An old guard came running hurriedly seeing Mirza Raja's son at the doorstep. He welcomed him. 'Please make yourself comfortable. I had no prior intimation. I shall inform Khan Sahab immediately.'

Ram Singh was a fair, handsome man in his mid-thirties. The tips of his moustache were twirled upwards in the Rajput fashion. Within minutes, the old guard came out and escorted him into the living room, where the old Wazir sat enjoying a hookah. 'Please come in! Welcome, welcome! Please take a seat.'

Ram Singh sat down on his knees. He glanced for a brief moment at Jaffar Khan's bloodshot eyes; his penchant for alcohol was well known in Delhi's circles. 'I apologize for coming in unannounced. I can come later, if you are busy.'

'I see! You are hesitating seeing me drunk, isn't it? It is an old habit.'

'Khan Sahab, I thought Ala Hazrat had banned consumption of such things.'

'That is true! Islam does not permit drinking alcohol, it seems!' He chuckled to himself. Caressing his long beard he said, 'Ala Hazrat is an aulia at heart; he is a fakir in the robes of an emperor. Allah has given us many things to enjoy but some people do not know how to. That is their fate and the irony!'

'Khan Sahab, I am surprised to hear this from you.'

'You are still very young, Rajaji. Don't worry! I am in my senses. Tell me, what brought you here?'

'You are aware that Mirza Raja has managed to capture Shiva Bhosale. He plans to present him in the Mughal court here.'

'Yes, I am aware! Where is the confusion then?'

'Mirza Raja feels that Shiva should not be chained and presented to the Emperor as an ordinary criminal. He has his own following and prestige amongst the Marathas. He wants to appeal to the Badshah to receive him with due respect and endow a mansab to get him under Mughal patronage.'

'What! You want him to be honoured in the Mughal court? A rebel, who has attacked and looted the Mughal territories? I don't think Mirza Raja should propose this.'

'Mirza Raja has thought about it a lot. Shivaji may think he is invincible in the mountains but once he sees the Mughal might he would not foster any dreams of challenging it. Once he is honoured, he will become a loyal servant of the empire.'

'I trust Mirza Raja's judgement. He has my full support.'

'Your assurance will be of great help. I shall ask Mirza Raja to get Shivaji here with the assurance that he will be received with honour in the Mughal court. We will leave the rest to the blessings of the Lord Eklingji.'

৩৫ ৯৯

It was past midnight, but Aurangzeb had not finished his work. He had been busy reading some important papers. As a routine, his last official work involved meeting his spies. After his evening prayers, he would go to Udaipuri begum's mahal for dinner. Udaipuri begum's maids had already enquired twice and Anwar had sent them back saying that the emperor was busy.

Aurangzeb sat in his room lost in his thoughts. The moonlight streamed through the satin curtains at the window but he was not in a mood to enjoy the beautiful night. He paced up and down for a while and sat down again with a sigh. He read the paper at hand once more.

Anwar, keeping guard outside, had noticed his master's behaviour and surmised that the news at hand was not pleasant. It had rarely happened that his Lord had missed the evening prayers. Quite evidently, the news was disturbing. After a long time, Aurangzeb stepped out of his room and asked Anwar to pour water on his hands to prepare for his prayers.

He read the namaz for a long time. Anwar, dozing at the door, would get up every now and peep in to find him engrossed in the prayers.

It was almost dawn when Aurangzeb closed the Quran. The first rays of the sun could be seen on the eastern horizon. He offered his regular morning prayers and then got up.

Anwar could not resist. He asked, 'Huzoor, the whole night you were ...'

'I was reading the Quran the whole night. Please send word for Shahzada Muazzam to meet me.' Shahzada Muazzam had been recalled to Delhi when Mirza Raja Jai Singh had left for the campaign against Shivaji.

Muazzam entered his room and bent in salaam.

'Shahzada, I have a very urgent but delicate job for you.'

'Please command me. I am willing to stake my life for it.'

'Shahzada, a wise man uses the least words possible. You have a habit of speaking unnecessarily.'

'I apologize.' Muazzam bent and kissed the edge of Aurangzeb's robe. 'Please pardon me.'

'Enough! You are speaking too much again. Listen to what I have to say.'

Muazzam was too scared to say anything lest the Badshah got upset.

Aurangzeb looked at his son. He said, 'You are aware that your grandfather, my father, is under house arrest at the Agra Fort. I am told he is on his deathbed now. He won't last more than a few weeks.'

Muazzam managed a glance at his father. He was not sure why his father was revealing the information in bits and pieces. He was not sure of the task he had spoken about. He thought it was best to keep quiet with a sorrowful face.

Aurangzeb sprung a question, taking the Shahzada by surprise: 'So what do you make of it?'

Muazzam thought it prudent to speak the truth. He said, a little hesitantly, 'Zille Subhani, it is sad news.'

'*Shabbash!* I am happy you spoke your mind!' Aurangzeb said. 'I was worried you may say something just to please me. I can entrust you with the job now. I want you to go to Agra. Meet the Badshah personally and give my salaam. I need you to make an appeal to him.'

He continued, 'Now, listen carefully. When I arrested him, he was the emperor of Hindustan. He had never imagined that his son would put him under house arrest. He is upset with me. I want you to plead on my behalf and ask him for forgiveness. Tell him I won't be at peace unless he gives in writing that he has forgiven my misdeeds.'

'Ala Hazrat ...'

'I know, Shahzada. I know what you want to say. You will say I committed no crime hence there is no question of asking for pardon. If the Badshah feels that I have committed a crime, it is my duty as a Shahzada to ask for pardon in his last days. Such a delicate task can be undertaken by none other than you. My elder sister, your aunt Jahanara Begum, is there with my father serving him at his deathbed. Request her to plead on my behalf in case your words fail to impress him. Once you send me the message that he has pardoned me, I will personally come to place my head at his feet. Now, carry on!'

Muazzam saluted thrice and left.

Jaffar Khan was restless. Shahzada Muazzam had left for Agra the previous day. He was waiting in the Diwan-e-Khaas when the guard announced the arrival of the Badshah. The satin screen was removed to reveal the emperor sitting on his throne. A glance at the Wazir and Aurangzeb knew something was amiss. He asked, 'Wazir, is everything fine?'

'Khudawant, Zille Subhani, Jahanpanah, this old man has the misfortune of bringing disturbing news to you. I heard from a messenger a little while ago: Badshah Shah Jahan is no more.'

The court was stunned into pin-drop silence. Even the guards dared not move. Aurangzeb did not react. He fingered his rosary for a few moments and then, getting up, left the durbar without uttering a word.

Within an hour, the news had spread across all corners of the city. Delhi was enveloped in a cloak of sadness while the key officials made arrangements to leave for Agra.

A royal boat stood on the banks of the Yamuna. Aurangzeb, with a few select men in tow, left for Agra the next day. The emperor of

Hindustan was on his way, travelling over the grey waters, to get a last glimpse of his father.

ᕋᕬ ᕫᕬ

A clear reflection of the lovely marble mausoleum, the Taj Mahal, shimmered on the surface of the Yamuna. The shamianas, erected on the sandy banks, fluttered in the sharp wind. The mild sun did not have the strength to provide warmth in the cold winter morning. Aurangzeb sat near Shah Jahan's grave offering his prayers. The grave had been built next to that of Mumtaz Mahal's. Shah Jahan's grave was damp and cold, the soil still fresh. The three key officials, Danishmand Khan, Jaffar Khan and Asad Khan, stood nearby while Anwar Khoja maintained a respectable distance.

Aurangzeb prayed for more than an hour. Then on his knees, he read from the Quran in his deep, sonorous voice. Bowing down at the graves of his parents, he prayed again. After a while, he walked out of the main hall.

Aurangzeb looked at the verses from the Quran engraved in black on the white surface of the Taj Mahal's walls. The tall minarets seemed to be kissing the clouds. He said, 'Danishmand, everything ends with death, isn't it?'

Danishmand Khan was in tears. He said, 'Huzoor, anyone who comes into this world has to go. The law applies to all; whether a Shahenshah or an ordinary ryot.'

Aurangzeb walked down the steps. Anwar was waiting with his sandals at the base while the palanquin bearers got ready. Turning to look at the Taj Mahal once more he said, 'I don't want the palanquin. Let us walk on the sand. I wonder how long our footsteps will remain imprinted here.'

As soon as Aurangzeb reached the shamiana, Shamim came forward saying, 'Huzoor-e-Ala, the elder Begum Sahiba is waiting for you.'

Aurangzeb entered the women's quarters. His elder sister Jahanara Begum was dressed in white. As she adjusted the dupatta on her head the solitaire in her finger shone in the light of the lamps. Aurangzeb was meeting his sister after nearly ten years and memories of the past flooded his mind. He recalled the time he had come rushing to see her when he'd heard she had got singed in a freak accident, her dupatta having caught fire. She had looked so innocent, so beautiful then! Now, as she stood before him, having gone through the vicissitudes of life, with dark circles under her eyes, he realized she was a pale shadow of her earlier self. Yet, the sharp acquiline nose, the quivering lips and the deep blue eyes still spoke of her famed Iranian beauty.

Sister and brother stood watching each other. Jahanara began, 'I request Shahenshah Alamgir Badshah to accept this lowly maid's salaam.'

Aurangzeb was jolted back from the past into the present. Holding her hands he looked into her eyes and said, in a hurt tone, 'Begum Sahiba!'

Jahanara removed her hands from Aurangzeb's grip saying, 'Huzoor may pardon me if I have erred.'

Sitting down, Aurangzeb said, 'Badi Begum Sahiba, in this shamiana, when we are next to the Taj Mahal, I wish you don't address me as Huzoor or Shahenshah.'

'As you command.'

'Begum Sahiba, I am Muhi-ud-Din Aurangzeb, your younger brother. You have a right to punish me. You are now in Abba Jaan's place. Punish me if you wish; but don't hurt me with your words.'

No one spoke for a while. A maid came in carrying a beautifully decorated wooden box and placed it on the carpet. Jahanara pointed towards the box. 'Aurangzeb, this box was given by Abba Jaan in his last days to be handed over to you.'

The maid opened the lid. The box was filled to the brim with precious gems.

'These are exquisite gems which have traditionally been handed over to the next of kin from Shahenshah Akbar's time. Two days before his death he asked me to hand them over to you.'

Aurangzeb stared at the box for a while and then asked, 'Begum

Sahiba, you were with him in his last days. Has he not given anything else for me?'

'What can be more precious than these gems?'

'I had sent Shahzada Muazzam to meet you and Abba Jaan but it was too late. By the time he reached Agra, Abba Jaan was no more. How often I have prayed for his pardon!'

'Aurangzeb, an hour before he died Abba Jaan pardoned all your sins. I was present alongwith the kazi. He put an impression of his palm as a seal of approval. The letter is below the jewels. He had no rancour in his last moments. He had forgiven all your crimes. He died a peaceful man.'

Aurangzeb removed the jewels to find a piece of paper below. He read the note eagerly and said, 'Begum Sahiba, you have taken away a huge load off my chest. I can live the rest of my life in peace knowing Abba Jaan has pardoned me. What has happened cannot be changed. Tell me what you want and I shall arrange for it.'

Jahanara could not hold herself back and tears flowed down her cheeks.

'Begum Sahiba!' Aurangzeb exclaimed. 'Abba Jaan has pardoned me. Please remove any doubts of your safety. You are my responsibility now. I am giving you my word as the emperor of Hindustan.'

Jahanara tried to wipe her tears but they continued to flow. 'Aurangzeb, I believe your political enmity with Abba Jaan ended with his death. He was, after all, the Badshah of Hindustan for nearly thirty years. I was under the mistaken belief that he would be accorded a royal funeral, befitting his earlier status, when his body was being taken to the Taj Mahal. I know it is too late to rake up the issue. His funeral was attended by a mere handful of people. I dreamt of a royal procession with the amirs and the Mughal sardars in tow. I imagined gold coins being showered on the crowds of people who had come to get a last glimpse of their favourite Badshah. Aurangzeb, I had expected the enmity to end with his death. He could have been treated with the respect he deserved.'

'Do you think I really intended to insult him?'

'But you did not do anything to ensure he got the royal honours.'

'I know that time cannot be reversed. Abba Jaan has pardoned me. Will you not do so?'

Aurangzeb did not get a reply to his question. He left disappointed.

✦✦✦

Noor Manzil in Agra was identified as Jahanara's new residence. Aurangzeb personally ensured that she was comfortably housed there.

One Friday afternoon, Aurangzeb visited Jahanara, along with his key officials Abdul Wahab, Danishmand Khan and Asad Khan. Jahanara received them sitting behind the screen along with Dara's daughter, Jahanzeb. After the initial formalities Aurangzeb came to the purpose of his visit: 'I am keen to get Shahzada Azam's nikah done now.'

'He is of the right age. But have you found a suitable bride for him?'

'She is sitting beside you!'

'Hai Allah!' Jahanara blurted out excitedly. Kissing Jahanzeb on her cheeks she said, 'I must start preparations right away. I am going to have a lot of work on her trousseau.'

'Begum, I hope she is not angry with us any more.'

'Leave that to me. Now that we are talking of marriage, there is something else I wish to talk about.' She continued, after a pause, 'I am told you had ascended the throne with a lot of pomp and show. It has never happened that a son occupies the throne when the father is still alive. I will repeat what I said: the Badshah needs to formally ascend the throne only on death of his father. I wish you carry out the coronation ceremony with all the pomp and glamour at Agra. Let the world know that Hindustan has a new Badshah now.'

Aurangzeb looked askance at Danishmand Khan.

Danishmand Khan was his confidant and advisor. He said, 'I cannot agree with Begum Sahiba more. When you declared yourself the emperor, it was the need of the hour. It is important to let the world know that you are the true emperor of Hindustan. From Iran to the firangi traders in Hindustan – they all should know that Hazrat

Alamgir is now the emperor. I would subscribe to the view of a formal coronation ceremony.'

Asad Khan nodded in agreement.

Aurangzeb ignored the comments. Showing least interest in the suggestions he continued, 'Begum Sahiba, I shall wait for your message once you have convinced Dara's daughter for the marriage.'

Within a matter of two days, a *shahi firman* was issued shifting the capital from Delhi. Agra regained its lost glory in no time. The only topic of discussion in the bazaars was the forthcoming coronation ceremony.

৵ৎ ৎ৵

Agra Fort had awakened to a new life, quickly dispelling the pall of gloom that had enveloped it since the death of Badshah Shah Jahan. There was a kind of urgency felt in the lanes and bazaars of the city, preparing itself for the royal occasion. The amirs outdid each other in sprucing up their havelis. Some nobles, in fact, razed their old havelis to ground and built new ones.

Agra city police chief Siddhi Fulad Khan and the fort keeper Radandaz Khan did not get a moment of respite. They were bombarded with orders from all quarters. There was no budget constraint and money from the royal coffers flowed easily.

Fulad Khan received instructions from the zenankhana that a tula ceremony should be carried out during the coronation. It was a royal practice to weigh the emperor in gold. The begums in the zenankhana would provide the required gold coins and jewellery, and the collection was to be used for constructing serais, roads, riverside ghats, etc.

The king of Persia sent his emissary with expensive gifts while the firangi traders around Dhaka displayed their eagerness to honour the emperor. Emissaries from all across Asia including Kabul and Kandahar were expected to arrive. The English and the Portuguese representatives and priests waited patiently for an audience with the emperor.

Bakshi Muhammad Amin Khan issued a *shahi firman* as per the

Badshah's instructions: Mirza Raja Jai Singh's repeated requests had been taken into account and Shiva Bhosale was to be presented before the emperor honourably.

Jaffar Khan expressed his fear when he met the Badshah in private that evening. 'I am a little worried, Alampanah. I don't need to remind Hazrat that Shiva Bhosale is a dangerous fellow. You must be aware of the ghastly death Bijapur's Afzal Khan met at the hands of this Maratha sardar. I am worried of his intentions.'

Aurangzeb's lips parted in a smile. He said, 'Wazir, I am surprised you worry about a puny Maratha rebel sardar. I have issued instructions that he should be treated with the same respect accorded to a Shahzada of the Mughal Empire. He has been given one lakh rupiyas from the Deccan treasury for his expenses. You will understand my intentions at the appropriate time. I have asked Ghazi Baig to escort him all the way to Agra. He will ensure his safety. He has been asked to keep an eye on Shiva day and night. Do you get my point now?'

Jaffar Khan was amazed at Aurangzeb's foresight. He said admiringly, 'Ala Hazrat, I may be old but you have shown me wisdom! On one hand you ask the thanedars to take care of Shiva and on the other you ensure that Ghazi Baig does not leave him for even a minute. Now I know why Allah made you the Badshah of Hindustan.'

Aurangzeb hardly heard Jaffar Khan's words. He was busy moving the beads in his rosary.

◦◦◦

Agra was brimming with guests as emissaries thronged to celebrate the event. It was a hot summer day and the gardens in the havelis of noblemen were being sprinkled with rose water many times a day. The fact that the coronation ceremony was being held on Aurangzeb's fiftieth birthday added to the glamour of the celebrations.

Ram Singh was struggling to find his way through the crowds. He was worried of reaching late for the durbar. The main ceremony was being held in the Diwan-e-Aam of the Agra Fort.

The red walls of the Agra fort radiated the summer heat. The

Diwan-e-Aam was overflowing with the Mughal officials and other noblemen. Raja Jaswant Singh was present, having been recently honoured by the Badshah. Each of the officials present was dressed in their finery.

Large Irani carpets were spread across while dark green satin and velvet curtains hung on the sides of a large shamiana erected especially for the officials. The dome, made of real gold, was visible from a long distance as it glittered in the hot sun. At the appropriate hour, the mullahs and the kazis announced the arrival of the Badshah. A large screen was removed to reveal Alamgir Badshah sitting on the Peacock Throne. Those in attendance raised their hands up in the sky and shouted in unison, 'Subhan Allah! Subhan Allah! Allah o Akbar.'

The trumpeters began and were quickly followed by those standing on the ramparts. Very soon, a chain reaction followed and trumpets sounded across the entire city announcing to the people at large that the Mughal emperor had ascended the throne. The sound of the trumpets and the cheering of the sardars continued for nearly half an hour. The crowd fell silent when the gurzbardar raised his hand holding a golden staff. It was a magical moment. There was a pin-drop silence in the hall. Each one could hear the other person's breath.

The Peacock Throne on which Aurangzeb sat was a grandiose affair. The seat, rectangular in shape, was nearly six feet long and four feet wide. It stood on four gold-encased legs above which rose twelve columns decorated with bands of pearls. Two large emerald peacocks on either side added to the allure. It was a sight to behold. The Mughal emperor sat wearing a traditional kimosh, the cap worn by emperors. The kimosh was decorated with the classic Mughal crescent encrusted with diamond.

Aurangzeb's eyes scanned those in attendance. The sardars stood with heads bowed. Aurangzeb raised his right hand signalling the durbar to begin. His sons Muazaam, Azam and Akbar stood nearby, theirs being the first right to greet the emperor.

Muazzam stepped forward and bent low touching his palm thrice to his forehead. He kissed the edge of Aurangzeb's flowing robe.

The servants came forward and placed twenty trays, covered with embroidered cloth laden with precious gems and jewels. Muazzam uncovered the trays one by one. A nod from Aurangzeb indicated his acceptance. After the trays were displayed, Muazzam gestured towards the entrance of the Diwan-e-Aam. At it stood an elephant bedecked in jewels. It was a gift to the emperor from Muazzam. He bowed once more before presenting a tray containing a thousand gold coins.

It was the turn of Azam and Akbar to present their gifts to the Badshah. Akbar, despite his young age, followed all the protocol required in the royal durbar. This was followed by Jaffar Khan, Asad Khan and other officials. The top noblemen presented their gifts in person while for those below a certain rank, had their names read out by the gurzbardar.

On a special request from Jaffar Khan the emperor personally received the gifts from the emissaries who had come from abroad. He took special interest while receiving the gift from the king of Persia while others had to contend with a mere nod or a smile.

The fiftieth birthday celebrations in the Diwan-e-Aam continued for nearly three hours.

⋘❧ ❧⋙

Normally the durbar at the Diwan-e-Khaas with select officials would follow that of the Diwan-e-Aam. The tula ceremony of weighing the Badshah in gold coins and jewellery was held on the marble floors of the zenankhana. Due to the presence of women, only select sardars like Jaffar Khan, Shaista Khan and such were invited. Danishmand Khan supervised the ceremony. The chains holding the two sides of the gold-plated weighing balance were decorated with pearls. The women from stood in one corner, satin curtains separating them from the gaze of the men.

En route to the ceremony, Asad Khan whispered to Jaffar Khan: 'Raja Jai Singh has just reached the fort along with the Maratha sardar.'

'It is too late. Ask Ram Singh to present Shiva in the Diwan-e-Khaas now.'

Asad Khan nodded and immediately passed on instructions to a khoja standing nearby.

Meanwhile, the staff bearer announced the Badshah's arrival in a high-pitched voice. Danishmand Khan, taking Aurangzeb's hand, led him to the weighing balance and made him sit comfortably on one of the scales.

Danishmand Khan recited from the Quran and then, with a bow, asked for the permission to begin.

The khojas stood in attendance holding trays containing gold coins, jewellery and other items for the ceremony. Danishmand Khan, picked up the items one at a time and announced the names of the women from the zenankhana before dropping them on the other scale. The first name to be announced, in order of seniority, was that of Nawab Bai followed by Udaipuri begum, the daughters Zebunissa and Zeenat and finally Jahanara begum. The side on which Aurangzeb sat lifted slowly and stopped once the weight of gold matched that of the emperor's.

A loud applause from the women followed. Aurangzeb was about to get up when Danishmand Khan said, 'Huzoor, the ceremony is not over yet.'

'Not over yet?'

'I have a request. The begums and the shahzadis have something to offer you on this day. Please allow them to present what is most dear to them.'

'If that be the case, I have no objection. I would most welcome it.'

The first one to come out was Zeenat. She carried a small book in her hand, wrapped in a red cloth. Aurangzeb looked at her with curiosity.

'Badshah Salamat, this is the holy book of Quran which I have copied in my own hand.'

'Waah! I am impressed.'

Zeenat bowed and stepped back.

The next one to come out was Zebunissa. Walking with silent steps on the thick Persian rug, she stood before her father and bowing down, presented him a book, similar to the one Zeenat had given earlier.

'Is that too a Quran handwritten by you?'

'No, Zille Subhani. It is a book of my poetry.'

'I know your interests are not the same as your sister's.'

'I hope Ala Hazrat will like it.'

'Yes. Any word in praise of Allah is to my liking.'

Zebunissa bowed and stepped back.

It was Nawab Bai's turn now. She adjusted her dupatta bringing it over her face as she stepped forward decked in jewellery from head to toe. It was the first time she was facing the Badshah with many close relatives in attendance. She was a Kashmiri Hindu by birth and none of the relatives present were hers. For a moment she forgot the reason she had come forward. She then noticed Muazzam amongst those present, the only face she recognized. Seeing her carrying a small packet in her hand Aurangzeb looked quizzically at Danishmand Khan and asked, 'Won't my Begum Sahiba tell me what she wishes to present?'

'It is a small wooden box, Huzoor.'

'What does it contain?'

'The elder begum has presented a box of sindoor to you,' Danishmand clarified.

'Sindoor?'

'It is a Hindu ritual; she prays for you to live up to a hundred years.'

A trace of irritation flashed across Aurangzeb's face but he quickly recovered. Sighing deeply, he accepted the gift reluctantly. The next one to follow was Udaipuri. Aurangzeb was curious to see what his latest begum would present. Decked in her finery, she looked every inch the renowned beauty. She carried a long-necked pitcher, decorated with precious gems. She bowed slightly before putting the pitcher on a low stool.

Danishmand Khan smiled. 'Begum Sahiba has presented her favourite Shiraz wine.'

Aurangzeb did not appreciate the gesture one bit but continued to smile saying, 'Begum Sahiba, I am aware of your favourite wine but it would have been appropriate not to have displayed that in public.'

Those in attendance sensed a tense moment ahead. Danishmand Khan thought it wise to keep quiet. Udaipuri fluttered her eyelids but words did not escape her lips. Aurangzeb looked at Danishmand Khan and said, 'I am curious to see what Jahanara Begum Sahiba has for me. Please ask her to step forward.'

Jahanara spoke from behind the curtain. 'Huzoor, I need not step forward. I can present my gift sitting here itself.'

Aurangzeb waited for her to continue.

'Huzoor may consider my silence as my most precious gift.'

'I am not able to understand. Can you elaborate?'

Jahanara repeated, 'Shahenshah! I believe my silence is the best gift I can give you.'

'I accept it,' Aurangzeb said.

Aurangzeb stepped down from the weighing scale. The trumpets announced the end of the ceremony.

◦◉ ◉◦

The last ceremony was to be held at the Diwan-e-Khaas, meant for selected mansabdars. The general expectation was that those in attendance would be showered with royal largesse. It was a day of celebrations and the attendees had raised their hopes high in anticipation. Some expected a higher category of mansab, while others were looking forward to a cash reward. Yet others were looking forward to being felicitated in public. Those not allowed inside spent their time waiting outside in the sprawling lawns.

Asad Khan sudenly left the gathering with two gurzbardars and two armed soldiers. The men around looked at them surprised to see them walking in the direction opposite to that of the crowd.

Soon the news that Asad Khan was to present Shivaji in the durbar spread. Men in the streets craned their necks to get a glimpse of the man who had dared thumb his nose at the Mughal Sultanate and had had the courage to loot Surat. Ram Singh, Shivaji and his son Sambhaji waited at the entrance. They spotted Asad Khan from a distance and one of the sardars, Mukhlis Khan, rushed forward to receive him. He pointed towards Shivaji saying, 'Please meet Shivaji. Raja Jai Singh has sent him from the Deccan for a personal meeting with the Badshah.'

Asad Khan looked at Shivaji. He was relatively short but his stature hardly seemed diminished. Asad Khan hugged Shivaji and said, 'Mukhlis Khan, it was good that you introduced Shivaji Raja to us as the man from the Deccan. Else, with the kind of personality he has, I would have assumed he was a Mughal sardar.'

Shivaji was busy observing the crowds. Asad Khan said, 'The next durbar is in the Diwan-e-Khaas. We need to move quickly.'

The gurzbardars, holding their maces, cleared the path as Shivaji and his escorts moved ahead. They walked at a rapid pace. The narrow entrance to the special durbar was being guarded by four soldiers, their naked swords resting on their shoulders. The emperor had already taken his seat and the durbar was on.

Asad Khan and the entourage along with Shivaji walked with silent steps and reached a place from where they would be directly visible to the emperor. Asad Khan bowed and said, 'I am here to present Shivaji Bhosale and his son on behalf of Mirza Raja Jai Singh.'

Aurangzeb focused his gaze on the visitors. Shivaji returned his stare without blinking. For a moment it seemed they were assessing each other. Aurangzeb, used to seeing people wilt in his presence, was surprised to see Shivaji returning his stare fearlessly.

Aurangzeb indicated to the mace bearer to allow them inside the private enclosure. Shivaji and Sambhaji stepped in and bent thrice in salaam. Two Rajput men, accompanying them, stepped forward with trays in hand. Shivaji took out a pouch containing five thousand coins and put it in a tray for the traditional aarti. As a token of courtesy he presented another tray containing a thousand gold coins. Sambhaji followed suit. With their right palms touching their forehead, they saluted again as they stepped back.

Aurangzeb was intently observing the two. Seeing him look at Sambhaji with curiosity, Jaffar Khan clarified, 'He is Sambhaji, Shivaji Bhosale's son.'

Shivaji and Sambhaji walked backwards, careful not to show their backs to the emperor. Walking back nearly twenty steps, they stood in line with other officials.

Scanning his eyes over the rows of mansabdars standing nearby, Shivaji was startled to see Shaista Khan. He had briefly encountered the Badshah's uncle when he had attacked his haveli at Pune. Seeing Shaista Khan curl his fists at him, Shivaji was convinced that it was indeed the now famous subedar of Bengal. He also deduced that the person standing behind, adjusting his Rajput-styled turban must be Raja Jaswant Singh. Shivaji recalled the way he had made life miserable for Raja Jaswant Singh's troops during the attack of Kondana.

Shivaji was not able to see the Badshsah from where he stood but he surmised that the emperor was now honouring the mansabdars. Those who had received the royal blessings returned with their chests swelled with pride. Other mansabdars, standing around, whispered words of appreciation.

Shivaji heard his name being called out by the court attendants. Shivaji and Sambhaji were granted a mansab of five thousand soldiers each. Ram Singh was overjoyed and whispered in his ears, 'Raja Sahab, you are a mansabdar now!'

Shivaji was least impressed with Ram Singh's joy and asked, his voice deliberately loud, 'Ram Singh, who is that Rajput sardar standing there?'

'He is Maharaj Jaswant Singh. I request you to keep your voice low.'

Shivaji ignored his request. 'Is that the way I am treated here? My ordinary soldiers routed Jaswant Singh's troops. And we both get a mansab of five thousand. Is that a way to treat Shivaji Bhosale?'

'Raja Sahab, we will discuss this later. I urge you to remain silent in the durbar.'

'No! That is not possible. I cannot tolerate this insult. I will never accept this,' Shivaji shouted.

The officials turned around to find a fuming Shivaji. They sniggered a little at his apparent discomfort. Shivaji, unable to tolerate the insults, went and stood at the end of the durbar hall.

On hearing the commotion Jaffar Khan, craned his neck: 'Ram Singh, what is the problem?'

Ram Singh's face was red with embarrassment. 'Not to worry, Huzoor. Shivaji Bhosale is not familiar with the protocol followed in the royal durbar. He is not well. It seems the heat here has taken a toll on his health.'

'Is that so?' Aurangzeb asked. It was evident he was not convinced.

'That is all, Ala Hazrat. He is a little upset.'

'About what?'

'About the fact that he was awarded a mansab of five thousand men only.'

'Ram Singh, tell him that we intend to honour him much more. Ask him to have patience. Get him to me when he is feeling better.'

Ram Singh bowed once. Turning towards Shivaji he said, 'Raja Sahab, the Badshah would like to honour you. Please accept these royal clothes as a token of his appreciation. His intention is not to insult you.'

'If this is the way one is treated in Mughal court, I would not have taken the trouble to travel hundreds of miles. Ram Singh, you are aware of my prestige in the Deccan. Badshahs like Adil Shah and Qutub Khan vie for my friendship. The firangis are trying their best to be in my good books. I had come here to meet your Badshah as an equal. I had not come here to bear these insults.'

'Raja Sahab …,' Mukhlis Khan tried.

'Khamosh! I don't want to listen any more. I am convinced it was a deliberate attempt by the Badshah to insult me in front of those present. I don't accept these royal clothes. I distribute such clothes amongst my men in my court each day.'

Asad Khan stepped forward. 'Shivaji Raja, please be careful with your words. Don't forget you are in the Mughal emperor's court.'

'You don't need to remind me. I would rather die than accept such insults camouflaged as honours!'

Shivaji walked a few steps and sat down. His body was shaking with anger.

Jaffar Khan heard the Badshah's voice. 'The zamindar from the Deccan is excused. He has permission to leave the durbar. Let him present himself in court when orders to the effect are issued.'

The event in the Diwan-e-Khaas was a fodder for the gossip. Those present had never witnessed such a scene. It was a topic of discussion for many evenings in the bazaars.

ഏ ഇ

The whole city had celebrated the coronation with a lot of fanfare. But the very next day Aurangzeb was back to his regular work in the Diwan-e-Aam giving orders, meting out punishments, looking into minor complaints, and everyday activities of the court.

Aurangzeb noticed Ram Singh waiting for an audience. He looked in his direction and told Jaffar Khan, 'Ask Ram Singh whether he has passed on my message to Shiva.'

'He apologizes and says it was because of his unfamiliarity with Mughal court practices.'

Aurangzeb waved his right hand dismissing the point. 'If he wants to apologize, why is he not in court today?'

'Huzoor, he has fallen ill. He has asked for permission to see you the moment his fever subsides.'

'I shall pray for his health then.'

The maulvis in the court raised their hands up and murmured, 'Karamat, karamat.' They could not believe their ears hearing the Badshah praying for a kafir's health.

As soon as the murmur stopped Aurangzeb asked, 'What about Shiva's farzand; his young son? What's his name?'

'Sambhaji.'

'Sambhaji! Why has he not come to the court?'

'He is a young boy and could not leave his father alone.'

'Ram Singh, ask him to present himself in court this evening.'

Ram Singh saluted and stepped back.

ഏ ഇ

Zebunissa had decorated her quarters especially for her Abba Jaan's visit. Thick Persian rugs covered the floor while curtains strung with pearls hung from the windows. Zebunissa had painted scenes from Sheikh Sa'di's *Gulistan* and *Bostan,* the collection of poems. The shahzadis of the zenankhana were experts in making perfumes from flower extracts since the time of Noor Jahan. The fragrance of the perfumes pervaded the rooms. A fountain gurgling with rose water added to the comfort of the interiors.

Zebunissa sat on the edge of the fountain listening to a maid humming one of her ghazals when another maid announced the arrival of Zeenat.

Zebunissa got up to receive her sister. They were only five or six years apart but it was difficult to tell which of them was older. Both were exquisite beauties, having got their looks from their Iranian mother.

Zeenat rushed towards her elder sister: 'Apa, I have some interesting news for you. A Maratha sardar called Shiva Bhosale apparently insulted Abba Jaan! The surprising part is Abba Jaan was not at all angry. Everyone present there were stunned seeing his reaction, or rather lack of it.'

'Oh! So it was the sardar from the Deccan who created the commotion in the durbar.'

'Apa, I realized I had seen him earlier when he bowed in salute before Abba Jaan.'

'What?'

'It was when I was supervising the construction of the sarais and reached Muluk Chan's sarai. I saw a crowd there when Amin Khan came running. He said they had a visitor from the Deccan by the name of Shiva Bhosale and that he had sent his regards. I looked in his direction. He had a young son with him who, seeing me, saluted. A sudden gust of wind uncovered my hijab for a brief moment. Shiva immediately turned his face the other way. I was impressed with his manners.'

Zebunissa was silent. Zeenat continued. 'I was surprised to see the same person behave so differently in Abba Jaan's court. He seemed so well mannered.'

Zebunissa got up and, picking up a painting from a corner, she asked, 'Is this the same person?'

'The face does look very familiar though the person I met was a little older and had a much longer beard.'

'It is Shiva Bhosale then! You may not remember; I had painted this many years ago. Abba Jaan had not approved of it. We were in Aurangabad then. There were a lot of complaints about this rebel. If he is the same person, I am a little concerned.'

'Why should it concern you? After all, he is just a small zamindar.'

'That is true, but ...' Zebunissa checked herself.

She gently picked up Shivaji's portrait. Propping it against a wall, she observed the same intently. She looked at her sister and said, 'Zeenat, don't mention your encounter with Shivaji to anyone. You know Abba Jaan's anger. He does not like anyone from the zenankhana overstepping the boundaries of protocol set by him.'

Zeenat was silent though she was not convinced about her elder sister's reaction. Zebunissa's mind was in turmoil. She sat there looking at the painting for a long time.

༄ ৯

Aurangzeb was in office when, after looking into a few general matters, he turned towards Ram Singh and asked, 'How is Shiva Bhosale's health now?'

'He is fine but still quite weak.'

'Is he taking the special rose water I sent across?'

'Yes. That has helped a lot but it will take another week before he is able to present himself. Huzoor ...' Ram Singh hesitated.

'What is it?'

'Shivaji's son Sambhaji is here to pay his respects.'

'Please present him.'

Ram Singh lead Sambhaji inside. Sambhaji bent low and saluted. His black eyes looked at Aurangzeb fearlessly. For a moment

Aurangzeb's fingers on his rosary stopped as he looked at the young boy. He looked at Jaffar Khan and asked, 'Wazir, ask Sambhaji whether he is willing to work under the Mughal Sultanate as a mansabdar.'

'Huzoor, Sambhaji is very young but his father has given his word on his behalf. It is safe to assume he will be honoured to work.'

'But I would want him to learn some basic courtesies before I grant him any title.'

Jaffar Khan looked up once at Sambhaji and then at Aurangzeb.

Sambhaji looked straight at the emperor.

Aurangzeb continued, 'Tell him that it would do a lot of good to him if he learnt not to look into the emperor's eyes but rather keep his head lowered.'

Sambhaji lowered his gaze.

'Shabbash!' Aurangzeb muttered. 'Tell Sambhaji we are pleased with his behaviour. He has the regal posture of a Shahzada. A mansab of five thousand soldiers will suit his personality. Please present him with the royal clothes.'

Ram Singh took a tray from the servants and dressed Sambhaji in a mansabdar's clothes. He placed a Mughal turban on his head, a satin cloak around his shoulders and a pearl necklace around his neck. A bejewelled dagger, stuck in his cummerbund, completed the attire.

Aurangzeb looked at his newly appointed mansabdar with pride and affection.

Sambhaji bent in an elaborate salaam. Aurangzeb was amused: 'Bahut khoob! Sambha, I am confident you will maintain the prestige of the mansabdar's title.'

Sambhaji was unable to follow most of what Aurangzeb spoke in Persian. He was escorted by Ram Singh back to the rear of the court and made to stand along with other officials, the panch-hazari mansabdars.

Aurangzeb continued with the official work at the durbar. Whenever he glanced in the direction of Sambhaji, he met his stare. Ram Singh's coaching had not had much effect. Seeing the young boy's self-confidence and lack of fear, Aurangzeb smiled indulgently.

The anger in the zenankhana was palpable. All the begums had come together and were gesticulating angrily when Aurangzeb walked in.

Amongst those present were Shaista Khan's begum, Jahanara Begum, Asad Khan's begum and a few other relatives. Shaista Khan's begum's cheeks were flushed with anger when she began: 'We are all here to hear how you are going to punish someone who has treated you with such disrespect.'

Aurangzeb looked at the women in assembly. Jahanara, taking the liberty asked, 'Bhai Jaan, how can you afford to keep quiet when you have been insulted in your court?'

Shaista Khan's begum added: 'This Maratha sardar attacked your uncle by daring to enter the zenankhana and cutting off his fingers. He killed my son. He has walked into our territory now, but instead of punishing him, you have been allowing him to cock a snook at you in your court.'

'Punishments are not meted out in the zenankhana. It has to be done in the court. There are rules that an emperor has to follow. He cannot act on his own whims and fancies,' said Aurangzeb.

'I am aware of that. I assumed you don't need to consult anyone when the throne has been insulted. I wonder what is stopping you,' Shaista Khan's begum said.

'Begum Sahiba, I need to consult my advisors before I take any action.'

'That is what is irking us,' Shaista Khan's begum erupted. 'If Ala Hazrat cannot take action we will have to go ahead and do something. We too have khojas and kotwals under our command. A mere nod from us is enough for them to come forward and behead the man who dared insult Shaista Khan and kill his son.'

'Begum Sahiba, please think of the consequences.'

'Bhai Jaan, it is you who needs to think,' Jahanara interrupted. 'He looted Surat. He did not think twice before burning the city down and killing innocent people. Such a kafir is now in your clutches. He needs to be punished.'

'I will wait for two days. Else …' Shaista Khan's begum paused for a moment. 'Else, my khojas and the Tartar women will raid his haveli and finish off the job. Only then will there be justice.'

'Begum Sahiba, please have patience.'

'I have been patient all this time. You cannot imagine the insults I have had to bear when people sniggered seeing Khan Sahab's condition. I need a final decision today.'

Aurangzeb understood the anger amongst the begums. He knew they were capable of taking things in their own hands. And Shivaji, with a mere hundred odd soldiers protecting him, would have no chance if the begum's men were to raid his residence. Shaista Khan's begum was like a coiled cobra waiting to strike. Jahanara was looking for a chance to avenge the looting of Surat. Aurangzeb, as usual, did not allow his emotions to surface and contemplated the situation.

The beads of his rosary moved slowly.

৵ৎ৹ ৹৹৵

The job of guarding the royal quarters inside the Agra Fort was entrusted to different mansabdars each day; at times Rajput sardars and oftentimes Mughal sardars were given the prestigious task. It was an honour to be awarded the job as it showed the trust of the emperor. Amongst the Rajputs, Mirza Raja Jai Singh and Maharaja Jaswant Singh had been given the job. It was four days after the coronation ceremony that Ram Singh was asked to take charge.

Ram Singh, after ensuring that the guards had been duly instructed, was about to leave when he got a message from the zenankhana requesting his urgent presence. He was surprised as he had never visited the royal quarters beyond what were the normal permissible boundaries. The message mentioned that Shahzadi Zebunissa Begum was waiting for him. Ram Singh stepped inside the main door. The khojas, naked swords in hand, stood in a line guarding the path next to the daroga's office. He crossed a few courtyards and reached the inner quarters. Ram Singh could see armed Tartar women standing guard as he walked escorted by a maid.

They reached a spacious verandah, one side of which was shielded with screens. The verandah was covered with soft rugs but there was no place to sit. Mughal protocol demanded that the person on the other side stand with his head bowed when speaking to the begums or shahzadis.

A soft female voice from the other side asked, 'Kunwarji, are your men guarding the royal quarters tonight?'

Ram Singh was about to respond when another voice from behind the screen repeated the question. 'Kunwarji, Shahzadi Zebunissa Sahiba asks whether your men are guarding the royal quarters tonight.'

'Yes, Shahzadi Sahiba. Badshah Salamat has given this poor soul the honour to do so.'

'Kunwarji, I have called you to discuss a delicate matter.'

'Please command me.'

'I cannot command. I have to ask you something. Is Shivaji Raja of the Deccan being hosted near your quarters?'

'Yes.'

'Kunwarji, Begum Shaista Khan, Begum Asad Khan and my aunt Jahanara Begum Sahiba amongst other begums have complained against Shivaji to Abba Jaan.'

'But Shahzadi …'

'Let me continue: Shivaji Raja is in danger.'

'Shahzadi, it was only after assurance from the Badshah that Mirza Raja managed to convince Shivaji to come here.'

'I am not denying that. But I cannot guarantee his safety. You need to warn Shivaji.'

'We have taken all the usual precautions.'

'That may not be enough. I am told Shivaji is to be shifted to Rad-andaz Khan's place tonight. Maybe …'

That got Ram Singh thinking and he asked, 'What could be the reason?'

'I don't know. I don't understand politics. The only thing I am sure of is that Shivaji's life is in danger. You have been entrusted with the task of protecting him. I thought I should warn you.'

'But Shahzadi, what can this Rajput do if the orders have been given by Badshah Salamat himself?'

'Tell me, did Muhammad Amin Khan not visit Shivaji when he came into Agra?'

Ram Singh, surprised that the begum was aware of the meeting, looked up. Quickly realizing that it was against protocol, he looked down and said, 'Please don't ask me to answer difficult questions.'

'I won't put you in a spot,' the voice from behind the screen said. 'Suffice to say that Muhammad Amin Khan and Shaista Khan do not see eye to eye.'

The voice was silent. All Ram Singh could hear was the fluttering of a few caged birds. The maid's voice behind the screen said, 'Shahzadi informs that if Kunwarji has nothing else to say, he may excuse himself.'

Ram Singh asked hesitatingly, 'Shahzadi Sahiba, if I may …?'

'Please.' The maid replied, 'Shahzadi Sahiba has given permission to ask.'

'I am curious as to why Shahzadi Sahiba would take so much of interest in Shivaji Raja.'

There was no response to his question. Ram Singh waited with bated breath. The maid replied, 'Shahzadi Sahiba does not intend to answer the question at this moment.'

However, Shahzadi's delicate voice said, 'Kunwarji, I am bored of seeing men in the Badshah's durbar going around with their heads bowed. It was music to my ears to hear of someone walking with a straight spine and having the courage to look the Badshah in the eye.'

'Shahzadi Sahiba, it would the end of me if Badshah were to hear this.'

'Don't worry on that count. If matters come to head, I will be the one who will bear the punishment and not you.'

Ram Singh heard a deep sigh from behind the screen. 'Kunwarji, it had happened once before. I was deeply impressed with a naked fakir who had the courage to face Abba Jaan without any fear. My heart ached to meet this person who was man enough to challenge the emperor. But the next day I heard that he was beheaded. It hurts me till date. Now another person has shown such courage. I wish my heart's desire is fulfilled. Kunwarji, do you need any more explanation?'

Ram Singh's forehead glistened with sweat. His entire body trembled with a mixture of fear and strange emotions. He fumbled to find the right words and said, 'Shahzadi Sahiba, this servant of yours does not know what to say. I shall try my level best to follow your orders.'

৵৹ ৶৹

The Diwan-e-Aam was in full attendance. The common theme being discussed these days, whether in the havelis of the officials or in private meetings, was the way Shiva Bhosale had behaved. Speculation on the Badshah's action was rife.

Amin Khan stepped forward : 'Shiva has a special request for you, Huzoor.'

Aurangzeb smiled. 'It seems Shiva has no other job than send requests. I would like to know whether the jagirdars of Bijapur have any job.'

Amin Khan smiled briefly and said, 'Ala Hazrat, Shiva is overwhelmed by the beauty and grandeur of the Mughal capital. The very mention of Huzoor sends shivers down his spine.'

'I am familiar with all his old tricks now. Please let me know if he has any particular request.'

'Ala Hazrat, all his forts are under your control. He requests that the forts are returned ...'

'The forts are under our control not due to his generosity. They have been captured by Mirza Raja rightfully when Shiva Bhosale surrendered. What does Shiva want?'

'He is willing to pay a sum of two crore rupiyas if the forts are returned to him. On top of it, he is willing to let his son Sambhaji serve in the Mughal court.'

'Is that so? He expects me to believe him? He will be back to his old habits once we return the forts to him.'

'Shiva is willing to swear by his loyalty to the Mughal throne.'

'What else is he willing to do?'

'He is willing to support any campaign in the Deccan in support of the Mughal Empire. He says he is willing to lay down his life for the Mughal flag.'

Aurangzeb, despite his casual demeanour, listened intently to Amin Khan. He said, 'Let him know I am pleased to know his intention of working for the Mughal Empire.'

'As you command, Huzoor. I request Badshah Salamat to give his views on the first proposal.'

'What proposal?'

'The proposal to return the forts against a sum of two crore rupiyas. After all, those are merely ordinary hill forts.'

'Ordinary? Ask Ram Singh what efforts he had to make and how many lives were sacrificed to capture them. Shiva is under the impression that we will be willing to return the forts easily.'

'Shiva has one more proposal in case this is not acceptable to the Badshah.'

'Please tell me.'

'Shiva is willing to hand over the rest of fifteen-odd forts under his command.'

'That is very good! He should immediately put this into action and wait for further instructions from me.'

'Shiva has requested that he be asked to go back to the Deccan to be able to fulfil his promise.'

'Where is the need for him to go?'

'He would like to personally visit each fort and hand it over to the mansabdars concerned.'

'That can be done sitting here as well. Let him issue release orders. Our men will take charge once they have the orders.'

'Shiva is worried that his sardars will not give much credence to his orders in writing.'

'I think he needs to stay here to understand how to run a kingdom. I don't trust that he will hand over the fort once he leaves this place. Does he have any other requests?'

'Yes, Huzoor. He has one last request.'

'What is it?'

'If Badshah Salamat does not believe him, he requests that he be permitted to attend the court and present himself here.'

'We shall consider his request at the appropriate juncture.' He turned towards Jaffar Khan and said, 'Ask Siddhi Fulad Khan to guard the external boundary of Shivaji's residence with five thousand soldiers. Let Ram Singh's men continue to guard inside. Let Shiva relax in this well-guarded place till we decide to meet him. He is free to give charity and donate alms to the fakirs, aulias and whosoever he wishes. I am sure his good deeds to the poor and downtrodden will give him some wisdom.'

ᨺᕲ ᕲᨺ

The capital city was drenched with torrential rains. Dark clouds made a permanent cover over Agra. Streams of water from the streets flowed into the Yamuna which was already in a spate. The reddish brown waters of the Yamuna clashed against the embankments threatening to overflow into the city. It was a miserable monsoon for the poor and homeless.

Shivaji, encamped in the accommodation provided by Ram Singh, continued to send requests every alternate day through Ram Singh, Amin Khan, Jaffar Khan and Fulad Khan but it had had no effect. His patience was being tested. Months passed by. The rains abated and the city was granted bouts of intermittent sunshine.

Sambhaji was in attendance for the evening durbar at the Diwan-e-Aam. His regular attendance had reduced his earlier childlike curiosity and he had learnt a few manners of the court as he attended the durbar each day with Ram Singh. He fidgeted a little, getting bored by the official discussions but he knew that he could not leave till the durbar was dismissed.

He looked around to find Shahzada Akbar missing. Sambhaji missed his presence. He had heard that he was down with fever and had been advised rest.

Aurangzeb instructed Ram Singh, 'Shahzada is not well. He will get bored sitting alone in his haveli. I suggest you visit him along with Sambha. Let him give Akbar company for a couple of hours after which you can take him back to Shiva's haveli.'

Ram Singh and Sambhaji left the durbar. The mahouts waited in the courtyard adjoining the main gate. The moment they were atop the elephants, they moved in the direction of Akbar's haveli. Fifty-odd soldiers followed them.

The people on the streets were a little surprised to see the procession moving in the direction of Akbar's haveli. The moment they reached the haveli, the guards guided the soldiers to wait on one side while allowing the elephants to enter through the huge gates. Instructions to receive the visitors had reached in advance.

Durgadas Rathore ran down the steps to receive the guests. He saluted and escorted them into the haveli.

It was a mixed reaction from the amaldars, ustads and other servants as Ram Singh walked in to the inner quarters. The maids and other ladies looked curiously at Sambhaji as he walked alongside Ram Singh.

They entered a large room. Akbar sat on a large four-poster bed wearing loose silk pyjamas and a kurta. A Pashmina shawl was draped around his shoulders. He asked the hakeem to step out. A pair of khojas and a maid continued to stand near his bed.

Ram Singh bowed in a low salute. Sambhaji followed suit, smiling at the Shahzada.

'Kunwarji, is this Shivaji Raja's son?' Akbar asked looking at Sambhaji.

'Yes, he is, Shahzada Sahab. Please don't exert yourself by speaking.'

Akbar chuckled. 'You too are speaking like the hakeem. I am quite fine really. A mere mention that I am feeling feverish made the hakeem overreact and feed me all kinds of medicines. The message of my illness was sent across to Abba Jaan and to Badi Begum in the zenankhana. I was forced to take bed rest.'

'Rest will do you good, I am sure,' Ram Singh added.

'Anyway, my illness vanished the moment I was told of your visit. Why don't you introduce me to Shivaji's son? What is his name? And, by the way, why are you still standing? Please make yourself comfortable. I will feel good only if you take a seat.'

Ram Singh and Sambhaji sat on a low divan placed nearby. Akbar looked at Sambhaji, 'What is your name?'

Sambhaji met Akbar's eyes saying, 'I am called Shambhu Raja.'

'Kunwarji, I am not able to follow his tongue. Does he not know Farsi?'

'He can speak in Hindavi though.'

'That is fine. Let me start; Shambhuji, do you like Agra?'

'Yes. It is very nice.'

'What did you like? The River Yamuna, the Taj Mahal on the banks of it, or the exquisite buildings around?'

'We have much larger buildings in the south.'

'Really? What kind?'

'We have tall mountains. On top of those mountains we have forts kissing the skies. One of the forts is so tall that we can see the clouds below us.'

'Kunwarji, is that true?'

'I haven't been there. But I think it's true from what Mirza Raja mentions in his letters.'

At that moment one of the khojas walked in hurriedly. 'Shahzadi Zeenat Begum Sahiba is coming in. Your time is up.'

Ram Singh and Durgadas got up hurriedly. Zeenat came in minutes after their departure. She kissed Akbar's forehead and said, 'Allah is great. I was worried about you. I was told you are not well. I rushed to see you.'

'Begum Sahiba, you are getting worried unnecessarily.'

Zeenat turned to see Sambhaji standing and asked, 'Isn't he the son of that sardar from the Deccan?'

'Yes. His name is Shambhuji Raja. It is quite surprising,' Akbar said, getting down from the bed, 'He does not know Arabic and Turkish. I have to speak to him in Hindavi.'

'Shahzada, do you like your new friend?'

'He is so good-looking, Begum Sahiba. I have a request; can you ask Abba Jaan to allow him to stay with me here in the haveli for a couple of days?'

'*Tauba, tauba!*'

'What is so strange about it? You can tell Abba Jaan that I will get well soon if he stays here.'

'Didn't you just say that you are quite well?'

'But there is nothing wrong in telling Abba Jaan that I am not; if it helps Shambhu Raja to stay here!'

Zeenat smiled. Sambhaji too could not help smiling at Akbar's logic. The three of them sat for a long time chatting in the haveli. Anyone passing by would have assumed they had known each other for years.

ஒஓ ஓஒ

The rose gardens were in full bloom in the royal palaces. Rose plants, specially ordered from Ispahan, Kabul and Kandahar, had blossomed much to the delight of Zebunissa who spent hours in the garden. She enjoyed watching the rose petals float gently on the water at the fountain. At times baskets of roses would be sent across to Jahanara Begum's house. Other officials, on receiving a basket of flowers from the royal palace, would talk of it with pride for days on end.

One afternoon Zebunissa was walking in the gardens after her evening prayers, when her maid Saloni came in. Her smile suggested she had something to tell. Zebunissa asked, 'What is the matter Saloni? You seem to be quite amused.'

'The news is such. You know Jaffar Khan Sahab's eldest begum Farzana?'

'What about her?'

'You are aware that she had made a formal complaint to the Badshah regarding Shiva sometime back? That time they had threatened to take action if they found Ala Hazrat not fulfilling his promise. Apparently angered at the lack of response from the Badshah, she sent fifty of her soldiers to Ram Singh's house two days ago. Their intention was to attack Shiva but they encountered Fulad Khan's men outside, who had to fire just two rounds of ammunition in the air for the begum's men to run away.'

Zebunissa let out a deep sigh of relief. Saloni continued, 'Farzana Begum learnt a good lesson. No one likes her in any case.'

'Why do you say that? I thought she was a pious lady who spends her time reading the Quran.'

'That may be true now. Once upon a time she was quite known for her extramarital activities.'

'Is that so?'

'The fact that she stayed in Shah Jahan Badshah's zenankhana as his begum is a well-known fact.'

Zebunissa was enjoying the gossip. She chided her gently saying, 'Don't you girls have anything else to discuss?'

'Begum Sahiba, you are in your own world with your poetry and music. You don't know what's going on in the world around.'

'Now what?'

'A few maids from the elder Shahzadi's mahal got married and left the zenankhana.'

'Is that so? How did they do that?'

'One of the maids acted ill. When the firangi hakeem, who had come to the zenankhana for some other work, was asked to inspect her pulse, she took his palms and put them on her breasts.'

'You have a habit of saying ridiculous things.'

'The maid requested the hakeem to tell the daroga that her illness could be cured only if she were to get married. A bag of gold coins was delivered to the hakeem in lieu of his services.'

'What happened then?'

'He advised that the maid needs to get married to get over her illness. As expected, a few more maids fell ill in quick succession with the same ailment and left the zenankhana. It was only then the daroga realized the ploy. The hakeem was banned from entering the zenankhana forever.'

Zebunissa listened to Saloni with her hand resting on her chin. 'Saloni, if you do an errand for me I will personally ensure you get the Badshah's permission to get married.'

'What is the task?'

'It is a delicate one. You remember the Maratha sardar under the custody of Ram Singh? I am told he sends boxes of sweets and other gifts to be distributed amongst the poor, the dervishes and the aulias. In fact he sends gifts to the other sardars too.'

'Yes, I am told he does that for his good health.'

'When the empty boxes are being returned, I want you to slip in one of the boxes I give you. Can you get that job done?'

'Hai Allah! And what do you plan to put inside the empty box?'

'That is none of your business. Can you see the garden full of rose blooms? Assume for a moment I am sending him roses.'

'Shahzadi Sahiba, Fulad Khan is a very suspicious character.'

'I have faith in your abilities. These rosy cheeks, the liquid eyes and the arched eyebrows; what more arsenal do you need? Passing on a simple box amongst the lot is an easy job for you.'

'But Shahzadi Sahiba ...'

'No buts. In case you are in trouble, remember I do carry a certain clout.'

᠙᠑᠑᠊

Aurangzeb received two messages from Mirza Raja Jai Singh. In the first he clarified that he had not given any assurance beyond those that were discussed in the treaty of Purandar. He urged the Badshah to treat Shivaji with respect and not to keep him in custody but rather send him back to the Deccan. The other message asked the Badshah to hold Shivaji back and not allow him to return under any circumstance. The message warned that if Shivaji's commander Netaji Palkar were to surmise that Shivaji was being kept in custody he was likely to take back the support given to the Mughals. It was a confusing set of messages that Aurangzeb received.

Aurangzeb was wizened with age and had learnt the tricks of the trade. He was not likely to fall for the various pleas and urges that Shivaji had been making from time to time.

Fulad Khan's soldiers continued to guard Shivaji's quarters. Shivaji sent a strange request asking for the removal of Ram Singh's guards. Aurangzeb declined the same replying he trusted Ram Singh as much as anyone else.

Shivaji sent another request in a few days: his men were sitting in Agra idle increasing the cost of feeding them. His request was to allow them to proceed to the Deccan. Shivaji was sending confusing signals asking for his forts to be returned to him and on other occasions suggesting he may as well move to Kashi and spend the rest of his days there at the feet of the Lord.

Ram Singh presented an odd request. He had given a personal guarantee that Shivaji would not try and run away. Ram Singh had now requested that his personal guarantee be withdrawn. Jaffar Khan was surprised. He knew Shivaji was safe till Ram Singh's men continued to guard from the inside. Removing them was exposing Shivaji to Fulad Khan's men. Yet, Ram Singh had asked his men and his personal guarantee to be withdrawn. Aurangzeb agreed to his request and soon Ram Singh withdrew his men. He was no longer bound by his personal guarantee for Shivaji.

Jaffar Khan and many other sardars were totally confused with Shivaji's requests. The only person in Agra who was not falling for the confusion being created by Shivaji was Shahenshah Alamgir Aurangzeb.

৵৹ ৹৵

The city police kotwal, Siddhi Fulad Khan, met Aurangzeb in his private discussion room. Aurangzeb had just finished taking the report from the spies who reported each evening.

In the mild light of the burning candles in Aurangzeb's quarters, Fulad Khan's dark, burly face looked frightening. Fulad Khan, as always, briefed Aurangzeb on each and every detail whether it was the movement of important officials inside the city, or visitors entering the city, or the distance Shivaji's men had covered since leaving Agra on the way back to the Deccan, or the number of horses and men left behind and anything else that was deemed important. This was routine. After the briefing, Aurangzeb glanced at the door when the guard at the clock tower announced the hour. 'It is time for my namaz. If there is nothing else, you may leave.'

Fulad Khan hesitated as he wiped his sweaty brow with the sleeve of his robe.

'Do you have anything else to say?' Aurangzebe asked testily.

'It is an ordinary matter, but I thought it wise to present it; it is also somewhat delicate.'

'Please make it quick. I need to go for my namaz.'

'Jahanpanah, Shiva is sending boxes of sweets to the fakirs at the masjid and to the amirs and other officials in the city.'

'Fulad Khan, you are in charge there. If you feel you need to inspect the boxes, please do so.'

'It was with that in mind I decided to inspect the incoming boxes ...' Fulad Khan said nervously.

'Fulad Khan, I know you are a loyal servant of the throne. But if you don't speak your mind, I will be forced to appoint someone else in your place.'

'Tauba! Tauba! Zille Subhani! Please pardon me. It is a delicate matter and I was trying to find the right words.'

'Please continue ...'

'It happened last evening,' Fulad Khan said, licking his lips. 'I decided to check the empty boxes being returned. I was shocked to find one of them filled with roses!'

'Roses?' Aurangzeb raised his eyebrows in surprise. 'I thought the Marathas were an uncultured lot. It seems their stay in Agra has taught them to appreciate the finer things in life. It is good to know that.'

'Ala Hazrat, I need to apologize for what I am going to say now. They were no ordinary roses. They were from the royal gardens.'

'How can you say that?'

'I found out that Shahzadi Zebunissa Begum Sahiba had sent the roses for Shiva.'

In the silence that followed, Fulad Khan's breathing and the moving of the beads of Aurangzeb's rosary sounded loud. Aurangzeb watched the sand clock as he thought of an appropriate response.

Anwar Khoja peeped into the room as it was past Aurangzeb's regular time for his evening prayers. A mild breeze from a narrow window moved the flames creating eerie shadows on the walls. Without turning to look at Fulad Khan, Aurangzeb issued his orders.

'Fulad Khan, you are no more authorized to inspect the baskets. This is a personal matter and I shall look into it. Please present your request tomorrow at the Diwan-e-Khaas.'

Fulad Khan wanted to see Aurangzeb's expressions but he was disappointed as Aurangzeb did not turn towards him. All Fulad Khan could see was Aurangzeb's back as he exited the private room and proceeded for his prayers.

ॐ ॐ

The waters of the Yamuna had receded exposing the sandy banks near the walls of the Agra Fort. Citizens, used to partaking of their food only after a glimpse of their Badshah, cheered as they could stand there and see him. As per his routine, Aurangzeb started sitting at the window each morning for an hour or two, allowing his subjects to have a glimpse of their emperor.

Aurangzeb turned towards the zenankhana instead of moving towards the Diwan-e-Aam. Anwar sent word for Zebunissa who came in adjusting her dupatta on her head. The small bells in her anklets made a soft, tinkling sound.

Aurangzeb looked at his daughter, now nearing her thirties. He realized how beautiful she was as she stood with her head bent low. He indicated with a wave of his hand for her to sit. Zebunissa adjusted her long flowing skirt and sat down taking care to fold her legs and not expose them. She asked, 'Abba Jaan wanted to see me?'

'How are you spending your time in the zenankhana these days?'

Zebunissa had not expected her father to enquire about the way she spent her time. She knew it was not a simple direct question. She answered, a little cagily, 'Hazrat, I spend my time the way other ladies do.'

'That's not true. Both the royal begums have things to occupy them. Nawab Bai has her children while I entertain Udaipuri whenever I get time. But you, on the other hand, are all alone.'

'Why do you say that? I have my sister Zeenat. And then there is Akbar. Even Azam miya comes here once in a while. Time just flies.'

'You are quite cunning.'

'Did I say something wrong?'

'No. But you did not talk about your poetry.'

'I thought it was wise not to mention it; you don't like it.'

'Do I then assume that things that I don't like don't happen here?'

Zebunissa's kohl-lined eyes fluttered. Her pink cheeks lost their colour.

Aurangzeb continued, 'You did not answer my question, dear.'

'Abba Jaan, I don't know what you want to know. How can I answer?'

Aurangzeb smiled. 'Dear, I have survived so long thanks to my suspicious nature. In the language of your poetry, there will be thorns when there are flowers. You must have seen the roses in the royal gardens.'

'Yes, Abba Jaan. They have bloomed well in the gardens here too.'

'Why didn't you send a few of them to me?'

'I did not know you liked roses. I would have sent them otherwise.'

'Did you know that Shiva would like the roses from the royal gardens?'

Zebunissa looked up sharply at Aurangzeb's calm face. Her throat went dry. She blurted, 'Abba Jaan, you knew! I have committed a blunder. Please pardon me.' Getting up, she kissed the edge of Aurangzeb's flowing robe. Teardrops rolled down her cheeks. Aurangzeb observed his daughter's emotions for a while. He said, 'Dear, what I heard is true! You have violated the decorum laid down for the Mughal zenankhana. I don't need to tell you about my begums. But I expected my shahzadis to know their father's wishes well.'

'I made a mistake, Abba Jaan.'

'I am surprised at your actions. You have sent flowers to a man who has had the temerity to insult the throne.'

'Abba Jaan, I made a mistake. Please pardon me.'

'Did you two meet anywhere before?'

She shook her head.

Aurangzeb let out a deep sigh saying, 'I wonder why you would send flowers to a person whom you have never met and who has not sent anything in return.'

Zebunissa did not reply. Tears continued to flow down.

'I am waiting for your answer, dear.'

'Abba Jaan, I made one mistake. Don't ask me to commit one more.'

'I don't understand.'

'By answering your question.'

'Then you have to be prepared for the eventuality.'

Zebunissa was silent. Aurangzeb too was silent for a while. He knew in his heart that his daughter had not transgressed her boundaries. But there was certain decorum, a set of rules which were expected to be followed in the zenankhana. Punishing her publicly would lead to gossip and ridicule. Aurangzeb's mind was working hard to find a solution that would ensure the punishment was just and at the same time not inconvenient to him. Zebunissa, seeing her father silent, surmised that he was deeply hurt. She said, 'Abba Jaan, I had been taught since childhood that if I can't give you happiness I should have at least ensured that I don't give you grief. I have failed.'

Aurangzeb, lost in his thoughts, replied, 'If I don't punish you for your wrongdoing I would be failing in my duty.'

'I am willing to accept whatever punishment you give me.'

'Dear, I will not punish you. I will punish Shiva Bhosale. Fidai Khan's haveli is getting ready in another two days. It has a huge basement. I shall issue instructions to shift Shiva to the basement.'

'Abba Jaan, Shivaji is your prisoner. You can punish him whichever way you want. You haven't told me what punishment I have to bear.'

'Dear, I have enough understanding of the human mind to know why things happened the way they did. Shiva would not come out of Fidai Khan's basement alive. That's the punishment for you.'

'Abba Jaan, Abba Jaan!' Covering her face with her hands, Zebunissa burst out sobbing.

৵৹ৎ ৡৡ৵

The festival of Janmashtami was celebrated by the Rajputs, Bundels and other Hindu officials with pomp and show. Ram Singh had personally supervised the decoration of the Krishna temple in the city. He had invited many of the Muslim sardars when the prasad was being distributed, but only Amin Khan made a brief appearance. The bhajans and kirtans continued all night.

It was a Friday two days later and an official holiday for the durbar. Aurangzeb sat with Abdul Wahab and other religious leaders to dispense religious orders. He liked to issue orders as per the shariyat on Friday. The lists for distributing alms to the fakirs were made while orders were issued for punishing certain officials who had not followed the religious rites. Abdul Wahab glanced at the others in attendance and said, 'Huzoor, as a true follower of Islam, we are all very happy that you ascended the throne in place of that hypocrite Dara Shikoh. But some imposters are getting emboldened enough to raise their heads right here in Agra.'

Aurangzeb had placed a copy of the holy book for each person in a rihal, a wooden stand. He wanted to use this meeting to read the Quran together but the kazi had started an altogether different topic, much to his irritation. Abdul Wahab was much older to the Badshah and knew how to get his point across. He continued, 'Huzoor, the hypocrites are getting bolder since the arrival of that Bhosale.'

Aurangzeb was surprised hearing Shivaji's name. He said, 'Shiva is under custody. What kind of help can he provide to these kafirs?'

'Jahanpanah, the Hindus celebrated a festival recently. There is a large temple in Mathura. There are smaller temples of the same deity here in Agra. Apparently, the Hindus took out a large procession.'

The other maulvis nodded in agreement. 'Yes, that is right. We too heard of a large procession and the celebrations in the temple. It is sad that this is happening right under your nose in your capital city.'

Aurangzeb ignored the taunt and asked, 'Kazi Sahab, what is this celebration about?'

'They have a god called Shrikishen. The Hindus celebrated his birthday.'

'It must be happening each year then?'

'Yes. We request Ala Hazrat to take some action.'

One of the old maulvis said, 'The Hindus have been pampered rotten by Dara Shikoh. He gifted a gold balustrade at the temple at Mathura.'

'What is the celebration all about?'

'Huzoor, it is like a child being born in a household. The kafirs put the deity in a crib and decorate the same with flowers.'

One of the other maulvis added, 'Zille Subha, I was told that Shiva had managed to send across exquisite roses for the celebration. They were a sight to behold.'

Aurangzeb glanced at the maulvi who was busy recounting the evening of celebrations. He let out a deep sigh. Abdul Wahab was not the one to give up easily. He said, 'Ala Hazrat needs to take some action immediately. The golden balustrade at the temple at Mathura needs to be broken down at the earliest.'

'I agree with you. I shall give orders regarding all the temples in Hindustan at the appropriate time. I don't want to issue orders right away for the existing temples. But I will think of an action plan for the temples that have been constructed since I took over the throne.'

Those present nodded their heads in approval. The kazi smiled victoriously at his colleagues. He said, 'Ala Hazrat, you are a living representative of the Almighty. We are confident Islam will continue to shine as long as you are our emperor. We request Huzoor to read the Quran with us. Let us clear the stale air that the kafir celebration has created.'

৩৫ ৩৫

The Diwan-e-Aam was in progress and the matters for the day were nearly over when a mace bearer, ignoring the decorum, pushed his way through the crowd and stood in front of Jaffar Khan. After a salute he whispered into his ears. Jaffar Khan could not believe what he had just heard. He looked across the crowd of officials where Ram Singh stood. At an indication from Jaffar Khan, the mace bearer went to Ram Singh and then escorted him across the hall to stand in front of the Badshah.

Seeing Ram Singh bow in a low salute Aurangzeb asked, 'What is it you want to present to the court now?'

Ram Singh's voice was barely audible. 'Jahanpanah, Parwar Digaar, Zille Subhani! It is a calamity!'

'What happened?'

'Shiva Bhosale has managed to escape and run away!'

Ram Singh's words shattered the silence of the court. A faint murmur spread across the hall.

'What!'

Aurangzeb's cold stare pierced Ram Singh's heart. After a moment he turned towards Jaffar Khan and said, 'It is time for my prayers now. I will meet you in the Diwan-e-Khaas. Meanwhile, get all the information from Ram Singh.'

On cue, the brocade curtains near the throne fell indicating the end of the durbar. Aurangzeb walked down the corridors lost in thought.

৩৫ ৩৫

The silence in the Diwan-e-Khaas was unusual but expected after the news of Shivaji's escape. No one dared face the Badshah.

'Wazir, have you got the details of Shiva's escape?'

Jaffar Khan was nervous. He looked at the mansabdars once before saying, 'Jahanpanah, Shiva was supposedly ill. He had not moved out of his room for two days. Fulad Khan's men were guarding as usual.'

'I asked you about his escape. Please come to the point.'

'I apologize, Huzoor. As per plan Shiva was to be moved to Fidai Khan's haveli. When Fulad Khan's men went to inform Shiva they were told that he was ill and had not slept the whole night. He had just fallen asleep and requested that he be not disturbed for a while. After a couple of hours Shiva's men left the haveli to get some medicine. Time passed. Fulad Khan's men, seeing no movement inside the haveli, went in to inspect. To their surprise they found the room empty. Shiva had disappeared.'

Jaffar Khan wiped the sweat from his forehead. His nervousness was evident. Aurangzeb asked, 'Are any of Shiva's men around?'

'No, Jahanpanah. Most of them had been despatched to the Deccan earlier and the ones remaining had left the haveli on some pretext or other.'

'How did Shiva disappear then?'

'It is beyond our comprehension, Huzoor. We are clueless.'

Fulad Khan stood in one corner fearing the worst. His face was contorted with a mixture of fear and helplessness. All those present were curious to hear what punishment the Badshah would pronounce. Aurangzeb's voice rang across the durbar, 'You were supposed to be guarding with five thousand men, artillery, cannons and everthing else needed, isn't it?'

'That is correct, Alampanah.'

'And yet Shiva managed to run away?'

'I am unable to fathom it, Huzoor. We have been trying to enquire around the city but have found no clue yet.'

'It does not work when Agra's police chief says this. You were given an important task and you have failed in it. And to top it all, you have no idea how the prisoner escaped!'

'Ala Hazrat, it seems he has vanished in thin air. The walls of the prison have swallowed him. I give you my word; I shall find him and present him in your court.'

Aurangzeb ingored his rant much to the amusement of those present. The police chief continued, 'But Huzoor, may I say that he was as much under Ram Singh's supervision as under mine. He had taken a personal guarantee. I urge Hazrat to question Ram Singh.'

Aurangzeb did not expect his kotwal to pass on the blame to Ram Singh.

'Jaffar Khan, please tell the kotwal that he is here to implement orders and not dispense advice. Let him know that he need not enter the durbar till he is able to catch the criminal and present him here.'

The next moment two guards surrounded Fulad Khan. With his head bent low, Fulad Khan walked out of the durbar.

Aurangzeb turned to Ram Singh. 'Kunwar Ram Singh, please state your views.'

'Ala Hazrat, ever since Fulad Khan had taken charge, I had removed my men.'

'Did you not give a personal guarantee in writing that Shiva would not resort to any mischief?'

'Huzoor, I thought my guarantee was no longer valid since the guard duty was handed over to Fulad Khan.'

'Oh, it seems anticipating Shiva's escape you had very cunningly removed your men!'

'Ala Hazrat, the Rajputs have served this throne with utmost loyalty for generations. I cannot even dream of dishonesty. If I had had the slightest clue of his plans to escape I would have warned you.'

'Jaffar Khan, I want you to get to the bottom of this. You are authorized to arrest anyone you feel had a hand in Shiva's escape. I want all the routes towards the Deccan, Bengal and Lahore manned. Tell the subedars to get me Shiva, alive or dead. Anyone not following orders will be dealt with severely.'

'As you command, Hazrat.'

'And one more thing: inform Mirza Raja Jai Singh that Shiva has run away without my permission. He should capture him and present him in this court. Ask him to arrest Shiva's general Netaji Palkar.'

Fidai Khan was present in the court. He was ordered, 'Check all the havelis and see if Shiva's men are hiding anywhere. I want to know the exact details of his escape within two days.'

Aurangzeb looked at Ram Singh. 'Kunwar, you are banned from the court till Shiva's whereabouts are known. I will announce further punishment later.'

Fulad Khan and others searched everywhere for Shivaji Raja. It was a golden chance to prove one's loyalty and earn royal patronage. Ram Singh's men went up to Dholpur while Jaffar Khan's men searched all the serais and temples including mosques all the way up to Varanasi. Hundreds of fakirs and sanyasis were hauled up for questioning. Carriages of merchants loaded with goods were checked.

Days passed by. Jaffar Khan would report each evening on the progress, or lack of it. It had been ten days but they had not made any headway.

Amin Khan's men had combed the area right up to the banks of the Narmada. They were at their wits' end. They knew that Shivaji would return to the Deccan but they had not found any clue indicating his hiding place.

It was a month now since Shivaji's escape. Aurangzeb had expressed his irritation at the lack of progress. All kinds of rumours regarding Shivaji would surface each day. Someone would claim to have spotted him in guise of a sanyasi somewhere while someone else would say he had stayed a night in a temple in some other location. On careful inspection all such information turned out to be false. Rumours continued to do their rounds.

As time passed by, the intensity of the search reduced. There were pressing matters at hand that Aurangzeb could ill afford to ignore. He had promised the maulvis to take some action in favour of Islam. The pressing ambition was to capture the sultanates of Bijapur and Golconda so that the borders of the Mughal Empire could touch the shores of the ocean.

While Aurangzeb was planning his next move, one of his spies got the news that Shivaji had managed to reach one of his forts. The spy also mentioned that Shivaji's son Sambhaji had apparently died on the way back to Pune. Aurangzeb did not realize it then that it was Shivaji's way of spreading rumour to mislead him.

The mansabdars on the other hand continued to brag about how their men were relentlessly trying to track Shivaji. Aurangzeb, having known the reality, was least interested in hearing the false stories.

༄ ༄

Any major event in Agra had repercussions from Kabul to Kanyakumari but the waters of the Yamuna flowed in a steady stream unmindful of them. Life went on as usual. Intermittent disappointments were soon forgotten and time blunted the sharpness created by disputes, doubts or squabbles.

The zenankhana was back to its normal routine of song, dance, poetry recitation and the liberal flow of wine. Newer arrivals from Iran, Turkey and Arabia added to the glamour of the zenankhana.

The capital, having moved temporarily to Agra for the Badshah's birthday celebrations, now prepared to move back to Delhi coinciding with the onset of the winters. The road to Delhi was lined with thousands of camels, bullock carts and hundreds of elephants, all engaged in the shifting.

The royal palace at the Red Fort and the havelis of the amirs in the city sprung back to life with a fresh coat of paint. The bazaars in Chandni Chowk were flush with newly arrived goods. Emissaries from different countries made a beeline to the durbar.

The call of the muezzin from Jama Masjid once again penetrated the skies. Amongst the celebrations in Agra some bitter events stood out like thorns, but soon a chain of happy events at Delhi made those memories of a distant past.

Udaipuri begum gave birth to a male child. Ignoring the usual protocol, Aurangzeb celebrated the birth with pomp and show. He was christened Kambaksh – the one who fulfils desires. The celebrations continued with exchange of gifts and was accompanied as usual by song and dance. This was followed by Aurangzeb's second son Shahzada Azam's marriage to Dara's daughter Jahanzeb Banu. The bride and bridegroom had celebrations suiting their impeccable lineage. The next few months saw a string of dinners and lunches hosted in honour of the newly-weds while the exchange of gifts and return gifts followed suit. The mullahs, maulvis, kazis, fakirs and the dervishes received liberal alms from the Badshah. The common man had not seen such a large-hearted Mughal emperor in a long time.

It was in the midst of such happy events that Shivaji's emissary landed at Aurangzeb's durbar. The Badshah pardoned all his sins. Shivaji, an insurgent and a mutineer in the eyes of the Badshah, and though unofficially referred to as Raja by many, was now accorded the formal title of a 'Raja'. Aurangzeb gave his consent for the treaty of Purandar which Mirza Raja had penned. Aurangzeb believed he would be able to get what he wanted through love and trust rather than force.

Mirza Raja Jai Singh, en route to the north after having led an unsuccessful campaign against Bijapur, died in mysterious circumstances at Burhanpur. Not many mansabdars mourned his death but it was a personal loss to Ram Singh. Aurangzeb bestowed upon him the jagir of his late father and asked him to continue looking after it.

In the midst of all this, the gold balustrade from the Mathura temple had been removed without a fuss. Jaffar Khan was of the belief that no one had noticed its absence. It was a Friday evening and Aurangzeb, atop an elephant and wearing a simple cotton dress, was on his way to the Jama Masjid. Chandni Chowk was filled with Hindus celebrating a festival. Drums and trumpets could be heard everywhere. The Hindus were busy singing bhajans as Aurangzeb's elephant marched slowly towards the mosque.

Aurangzeb's armed soldiers cleared the path when suddenly two men, naked swords in hand, jumped at him from the crowd. Letting out an expletive, one of them attacked the elephant, his sword delivering a hard blow on its trunk, while the other one jumped at Aurangzeb's howdah but was able to reach only up to the base of the seat. The soldiers, taken by surprise, realized what had happened only when Anwar Khoja screamed for help. The cavalry men, riding astride the royal elephant, did not wait for instructions from Aurangzeb and within minutes, hacked the attackers to pieces.

The mahout gently removed the sword stuck in the elephant's trunk. Blood spurted like a fountain drenching the mahout's clothes. He heard the words, 'Let the elephant move towards the masjid. Don't stop anywhere.'

The elephant trumpeted in pain but the mahout managed to steer it to reach the mosque gates. Aurangzeb got down and walked towards the mosque unruffled. He read the namaz for a long time and then returned to the palace on another elephant.

୬ଓ ୨୬

The news of the attack on Aurangzeb spread like wildfire, and soon hordes of people gathered on the sandy banks of the Yamuna to have a glimpse of their emperor. Amirs and other officials rushed to the palace. The rumours on the streets echoed in the hallways of the palace. A few people had witnessed the incident first-hand. What happened was known to all but no one knew the exact reason behind it. It was fertile ground for all kinds of rumours to erupt.

The zenankhana was buzzing with anxious anticipation having heard the news from the khojas. Udaipuri begum rushed to Begum Jahanara's quarters with her three-year-old Shahzada Kambaksh and within moments they were followed by Nawab Bai, Zebunissa and Zeenat.

Seeing her aunt Jahanara, Zeenat could not restrain her tears. 'Aunt, I feel it is the end of the world.'

Jahanara consoled her: 'Dear, thanks to Allah's mercy Badshah is safe. All we can do is pray.'

'Aunt, we were hoping to get some more details from you,' Zebunissa said. 'We don't feel like praying till we get more news. We need to know who attacked Abba Jaan and why.'

Jahanara knew the begums and shahzadis had come in hoping to get more details. She assured them saying, 'I will do my best to get to the bottom of this.'

At that moment one of Udaipuri begum's maids came and whispered something in her ears.

Zeenat said, 'If you know something, why don't you spell it out?'

'I am told the attackers were Rajputs,' she replied casting a suspicious glance at Nawab Bai.

Nawab Bai, unable to take the indirect taunt, blurted: 'The religion of the killers is not important. What is important is to find out the reason behind their actions.'

'Isn't it evident?' Udaipuri begum asked. 'Ever since the Badshah has ascended the throne the Rajputs and the other Hindus are jealous of him and they have their support here in the zenankhana too,' she added, pointing her finger straight at Nawab Bai.

Nawab Bai, sitting with her head down, was deeply hurt: 'It would be good if Badshah's favourite begum were to speak straight rather than using such insidious words and making indirect allegations.'

Udaipuri was not in a mood to stop. It was a rare occasion when the begums were together. Normally the gossip would be passed on through the khojas and the maids. She had got a chance to confront Nawab Bai in person. She was not going to lose such a golden opportunity. She said, pointing at her young son, 'The elder begum is jealous ever since I gave birth to the Shahzada. She may wear a burkha but at heart she remains a kafir. She is unable to tolerate the fact that Kambaksh could be the true successor to the Mughal throne. The elder Shahzada is languishing in prison, while everyone knows what the other one is doing in the Deccan.'

Jahanara held Udaipuri's hand saying, 'Enough! Nawab Bai's Shahzada is the eldest son of my brother. Why should she be worried?'

Ignoring Jahanara, Udaipuri continued, 'I knew you would say that, but the fact is Kambaksh was born after the Badshah ascended the throne. It does not matter how many are born to him before he was made the real Badshah.'

'Udaipuri! You are crossing your limits. The attack on my Bhai Jaan has no connection with Nawab Bai. Yes! It is possible a Hindu may have attacked him but the punishment for the offender will be decided by my brother. We should not sit here and pass judgement.'

Zebunissa and Zeenat did not wait for further comments and walked out of the quarters.

ஃஃ ஃஃ

The enquiry began the next day at the durbar. There was an outrage in the city. Hundreds of people had gathered at the banks of the river. The city police chief and his men tried their best to manage the crowds who were shouting slogans like 'Alamgir! Zinda Pir.'

It disturbed Aurangzeb to know that the crowds had elevated him to the position of a Paigambar. He ordered the soldiers to pacify the people and disperse them. It was only then the matters in the court could be taken up.

The court was in full attendance. Everyone stood with worried faces. Jaffar Khan presented the facts based on the investigation done by the city police chief. The attackers were from Mathura. The local faujdar there, Abdul Nabi, had been able to recognize their faces.

'I would like to personally hear it from Abdul Nabi,' Aurangzeb said.

'Huzoor, you had issued orders to remove the gold balustrade from the temple at Mathura. But the local people were dead against it stating that it was erected under the supervision of Dara Shikoh with funds from the royal treasury. I had tried my best but there have been violent protests against it.'

An old maulvi stood up from the crowd. 'Zille Subhani, it is not surprising that the Hindus are protesting against a minor order issued by you. Man loses his sense of wisdom when death hovers overhead. Huzoor, I am sure, will take the right decision but I would like to state that the number of people urging others to revolt against the throne has increased. Huzoor needs to deal with an iron hand.'

Jaffar Khan noticed that Aurangzeb had not appreciated the unsolicited advice given by the old maluvi. He said, 'Mullaji, please be quiet and let the faujdar speak. You may give your advice if asked to.'

The maulvi was offended at the snub and said, raising his hand, 'If Huzoor himself says so then …'

He heard the deep-throated voice of the Badshah, 'The wazir has advised rightly. It is not right to interrupt the faujdar.'

The faujdar continued: 'I called the rich merchants in Mathura to make the people understand that I was just following the *shahi firman*. I suggested that they should build a wooden balustrade instead. While many were agreeable to my suggestion, one man in the crowd shouted slogans against the Badshah. I was told that this man was responsible for provoking people to not pay their taxes.'

'What is the name of this fellow?'

'Uddhav bairagi.'

'Seems like an ordinary fakir.'

'Yes, Ala Hazrat. He is one of those fakirs who smear their bodies with ash. I got the man arrested. The other Hindus realized that it made sense to listen to my suggestion and got the wooden balustrade made.'

'I am unable to understand the connection between the incident at Mathura and what happened here.'

'I made a mistake of not capturing that bairagi's two disciples then. They were the two attackers.'

The Rajput sardars and other Hindus were restless hearing Abdul Nabi. Puranmal Bundela stepped forward and said, 'Huzoor, I would like to say something.'

'Please speak. I would like to listen to anyone who has something to say before I announce my verdict.'

'I am sure Badshah Salamat has not heard such a one-sided story till date,' Puranmal said.

Aurangzeb arched his eyebrows questioningly at Puranmal. 'Puranmal, are you saying the faujdar is making a false statement?'

'Hazrat, I am not saying that. But I don't believe he made efforts to pacify the people at Mathura the way he says. It is my own ancestors who had built the temple at Mathura. We believe in guarding it with our lives. The Jats, Bundels or the Raputs consider the temple more precious than their own lives.'

'But Puranmal,' Aurangzeb interrupted. 'The question is of a mere balustrade. The faujdar did not mention anything else.'

'That is his cunningness. He knows we are willing to lay down our lives for the Mughal throne. Had he requested us we would have helped him to implement the *shahi firman*. We would have deposited the equivalent amount of gold in the royal treasury.'

Aurangzeb did not reply. Instead he looked at Jaffar Khan. Jaffar Khan was well versed in the matters of the court and said, 'Puranmalji, the world knows the mercy which our Badshah shows. He has the same love for all people whether Hindu, Muslim or Christians. What we are discussing today is only for those who attacked the Badshah yesterday. Puranmal Bundela is an old ally of the throne. I hope he is not suggesting that the attack was justified due to the balustrade being removed forcilbly.'

Touching his palms to his cheeks Puranmal said, '*Tauba, tauba!* I cannot even dream of saying that. The Bundels have been loyal to the throne since the time of Shahenshah Akbar. Forget the balustrade; we will not go against a *shahi firman* which asks us to destroy the temple.'

'Puranmal Bundela, I urge you to consider your words before speaking in this court. Hundreds of mansabdars have seen me dispensing justice and I hope they have learnt something there.' Turning towards Abdul Wahab, Aurangazeb said, 'You have heard both the sides. What is your advice?'

'The Mughal emperor is a representative of Muhammad Paigambar himself. Any person attacking him deserves to be punished to death.'

'Even if the attackers were Musalmans?' Aurangzeb asked.

Abdul Wahab was taken aback at the unexpected question. Recovering quickly he said, 'As the Mughal emperor represents the Paigambar, any attacker has to be treated the same way. It is a well-known fact that Muhammed Paigambar did fight battles with other Musalmans.'

'It is fine then. I agree with the advice given by Abdul Wahab. The two attackers have already met their fate. The only one left is Uddhav bairagi. The leader deserves the same fate as his followers. I am ordering Abdul Nabi to implement my orders within seven days and report to the durbar.'

꧁ ꧂

The orders given by the Badshah had repurcussions in the zenankhana as well. The maids and khojas were busy poisoning the minds of the begums about the possible successor to the Badshah. There were speculative debates on who would have been the possible successor had the Badshah not survived the attack. Shamim listened to each side without giving her opinion.

Aurangzeb had just returned to his quarters one evening when he got an urgent message from Udaipuri begum requesting his presence. He turned towards Udaipuri's palace, the rooms of which were decorated in anticipation of his visit. Knowing his preference, she had strategically placed a copy of the Quran on a sandalwood rihal.

Udaipuri, dressed in all her finery, touched her palm to her forehead in salute and welcomed the Badshah saying, 'Please pardon me for asking you to take time out of your busy routine.'

Aurangzeb put his hands around her waist and said, 'Dear, I am sure all this fuss is for demanding something special. What is it?' He lifted her chin and looking into her eyes continued, 'Don't think I will get swayed away by these mesmerizing eyes.'

'I know you can't be trapped.'

'*Tauba, tauba!* Begum Sahiba, I am already in your captivity.'

'I have served Hazrat long enough not to get fooled by such sweet words. I want your promise before I speak my mind.'

Aurangzeb placed his palms on Udaipuri's and said, 'I give you my word. Tell me what you want.'

Udaipuri, lifting her head from Aurangzeb's chest said coyly, 'All the Shahzadas here have been given a subah to manage, except my son Kambaksh.'

Aurangzeb was taken aback by Udaipuri's demand. Keeping a straight face he said, 'Begum, he is far too young right now. Let him grow up a little and you would be surprised at the kind of responsibilities I give him.'

'Those are things of the future. You call the Rajput begum a kafir, yet you have given her Shahzada the subah of the Deccan. Recently the Irani begum's Shahzada got married and was given the charge of Gujarat. But Huzoor has not bothered to give my son anything.'

'Is that so?' Aurangzeb asked as he locked his lips on her in a deep passionate kiss. 'When you have the subah of my heart what is the use of other subahs made of mere bricks and stones?'

'You won't understand the heart of a woman. I remember you had mentioned Kambaksh's birth had proved auspicious for you. But you don't want to back your words with real action,' Udaipuri said in mock anger.

Aurangzeb could not resist seeing her cheeks turn a deeper shade of pink. 'Begum, managing a subah is no joke. Kambaksh is still very young. Once he is capable I can give him a lot of other responsibilities.'

'Talking of capabalities,' Udaipuri said, moving a little away from Aurangzeb, 'I have seen the kind of work Irani begum's Shahzada Akbar has shown till date!'

'Begum! Akbar has been given the task of managing Ajmer. He is sixteen now.'

Aurangzeb hugged her tightly and showerd her cheeks, forehead and neck with kisses. 'Begum, my dear! You know you are my dearest here in the zenankhana. I named your son Kambaksh as he fulfilled my dreams. I feel it is Allah's gift to me.'

'Then I wish you give him a subah and show your gratitude to Allah.'

Aurangzeb played with the crescent shaped diamond hairpin for a while. 'Begum, managing a territory means being in court to handle things. The officials may well manage the daily affairs but Kambaksh should be available whenever needed.'

'Then in that case why don't you give him the subah of Delhi? I can manage his affairs from behind the screen.'

Aurangzeb closed his eyes in contemplation. He caressed her body as he thought of the consequences of such a decision. He knew it was a trying moment. Seeing him hesitate, Udaipuri said, 'It seems Hazrat is not in a mood to hand over Delhi.'

Aurangzeb let out a deep sigh. He looked around to check if the khojas were out of earshot and said keeping his voice as low as possible, 'Begum, traditionally the subah of Delhi is reserved for the successor to the throne.'

'Then in that case it is a right decision. After all, it is Kambaksh who is going to succeed Hazrat, isn't it?'

'Begum, you don't understand! It is fine to speak of these things within the four walls, but it would be disastrous if this were to be heard by anyone outside this room. My eldest Shahzada may be in prison but his younger siblings Muazzam and Azam are around. Even Akbar is elder to Kambaksh. Announcing Kambaksh as my successor would be akin to welcoming a bloodbath here.'

Udaipuri lifted her head resting on his chest. Her voice was emotional and she could hardly speak coherently. 'I don't know what Hazrat has in mind. I am after all a mere maid, a concubine who came into your life. I don't have the pedigree of the Irani or the Rajput begums. I know their Shahzadas would get preference over my son. I was a fool to dream of my son being your successor. It is my mistake.'

Tears flowed down Udaipuri's face. Aurangzeb was mesmerized seeing her beauty heightened by her tears. Her cheeks were flushed and she looked vulnerable. Hugging her he wiped her eyes and said, 'Begum, you know my weakness. You are the only one who makes me happy. I cannot afford to make you unhappy and lose the place of solace in this entire zenankhana. I promise you; I give you my word.'

'Really? Will Kambaksh be given the subah of Delhi?'

'Yes. But listen to me. I have seen many ups and downs in the last thirty years. I have ruled with a naked shamsher in hand all the time. You must be careful.'

'I will listen to whatever you say.'

Ignoring her words Aurangzeb continued, 'I know the consequences of my actions are going to be disastrous.'

Udaipuri hardly heard his words, lost in dreams of managing Delhi through Kambaksh. It was too tempting a thought.

It was dawn when Aurangzeb got up and left Udaipuri's quarters. He met Shamim on the way and instructed her, 'Change all the khojas and maids in Udaipuri's palace. Post them elsewhere. Fine them fifty rupiyas each.'

The amirs and other officials were at ease ever since the capital had moved to Delhi. Shahzada Muazzam was managing the Deccan with the help of Diler Khan. Only the sultanates of Bijapur and Golconda were left to be annexed. The threat of an attack from the Shah of Iran was a distant memory now. Hindustan was enjoying a period of peace.

The officials, used to a life of luxury since the time of Jehangir, were enjoying their stay at Delhi, always finding reasons to throw a party or celebrate a festival. Aurangzeb was blessed with a grandson within two years of Azam's marriage. Muazzam had had two sons a couple of years back. But the birth of Azam's son in the Irani Begum's lineage was a cause for celebration. The city witnessed celebrations for a week with the beggars and fakirs receiving alms.

Jaffar Khan, nearly eighty now, celebrated the birth of a son after a gap of many years. The haveli celebrated the event with a lot of fanfare. Carpets were laid out right up to the Red Fort to welcome the Badshah along with a select few officials.

Aurangzeb came in an open palanquin and was welcomed by the ladies from the zenankhana with their veils thrown back. As soon as he took his seat, a group of dancers began their performance.

The first dance was by a group of concubines ordered specially from Iran. This was followed by a qawwali recital. The coy gestures of the singers sent the officials into raptures. Wines ordered from Kabul flowed generously.

Jaffar Khan escorted Aurangzeb to the dining area where food was laid out in gold trays. Aurangzeb sat down as Jaffar Khan personally fanned him. On Jaffar Khan's request, Aurangzeb blessed the trays by touching them with his right hand. The trays were then taken away by the khojas to serve the other officials in attendance. After partaking a few morsels, Aurangzeb indicated the end of his meal by picking up a couple of almonds from another tray.

Surprised, Jaffar Khan asked, 'Hazrat, you have finished early? These items were made under strict supervision of my begum.'

'Jaffar Khan, I had my fill enjoying the dance and seeing the officials get drunk on the imported wines.'

'I would consider myself lucky if Huzoor has enjoyed the dance.'

'Jaffar Khan, I am happy that you have sired a son at this age. I also enjoyed seeing the beautiful women dance, but I am surprised to see the men being offered alcohol in my presence. Seeing the officials drinking wine in front of my kazi, who is supposed to ensure such practices are not followed, is quite a shock to me.'

'Ala Hazrat, the mohtasib and the kazi themselves have given permission for such things in Delhi. They are as per your orders.'

Aurangzeb put the almonds back in the tray and looked at Jaffar Khan. 'Wazir, you must be mistaken. My orders are to ban alcohol and singing by prostitues across the sultanate. The job of the mohtasibs is to ensure that the orders are followed.'

'Jahanpanah, the orders for the subah of Delhi are different.'

'Who has issued these?'

'The subedar of Delhi.'

For a moment Aurangzeb's brow furrowed. 'Oh! Shahzada Kambaksh.'

'And Begum Sahiba.'

Aurangzeb was clearly disappointed to know that Udaipuri begum was using her authority to do things against his wishes. But he did not allow the disappointment to reflect on his face. Instead, he smiled and said, 'In that case, they are not breaking any rules. I may not like dancing or touching alcohol but that does not make them guilty of having a glass of wine. I am done with my meal. I am eager to see your newborn son.'

The servants stepped forward to remove the plates.

The Badshah was accorded the privilege of naming newborns. It had been a tradition since Akbar's time. Aurangzeb stood in an open courtyard while the other officials stood at a respectable distance. A khoja brought Jaffar Khan's son. Jaffar Khan's eldest son Namdar Khan stood nearby. Aurangzeb glanced at Namdar Khan and then at the infant. Aurangzeb noticed that there was hardly any similarity between the two. As usual, he did not allow his thoughts to reflect on his face. He said, 'Jaffar Khan, the young Wazir is really handsome.'

'It is Allah's grace,' Jaffar Khan said, raising his hands. 'We are eager to hear his name.'

'I am naming this son Abdul Hasan.' Those in attendance shouted, 'Karamat, karamat!'

As Aurangzeb returned to his palace, a thought continued to disturb him – Jaffar Khan's eldest son Namdar Khan was the spitting image of his elder brother Dara Shikoh.

People in Delhi had a habit of gossiping about things which did not concern them.

❧❦❧

The news from the Deccan was disturbing. Since the time of Shahenshah Akbar, the Mughal Empire had strived to touch the shores of the seas but had not succeeded. Aurangzeb had harboured the ambition since the time he was deputed to the Deccan as a subedar. It was not possible to achieve his ambition till the Nizam was defeated. He had now entrusted the task on Shahzada Muazzam and Diler Khan but the news Aurangzeb received was not encouraging.

Diler Khan, instead of defeating the forces of Golconda and Bijapur, was finding excuses to delay while the Shahzada seemed content expanding his zenankhana and enjoying the luxuries of life. To top it all, both Muazzam and Diler Khan were sending secret messages putting the other person down.

Aurangzeb had had a treaty with Shivaji and had bestowed the title of Raja on him. But that had resulted in temporary peace. Aurangzeb had the niggling feeling that Muazzam was in fact secretly in pact with Shivaji.

Aurangzeb waited for another year but his restlessness increased. He then despatched Muazzam's mother Nawab Bai with a strong message for Muazzam to take his duties seriously. His trusted Sardar Hoshdar Khan, who accompanied Nawab Bai, was told to give clear instructions to Muazzam along with a threat that if he failed he would have to face dire consequences.

Shaista Khan, having failed in the Deccan, had proved his worth in Bengal enriching the royal treasury with crores of rupiyas. The only thorn in the otherwise shining Mughal Empire was that of the two sultanates in the Deccan.

A bad news in the form of Jaffar Khan's death reached Aurangzeb. Luckily Aurangzeb's aunt's husband Asad Khan was a capable successor and was immediately nominated as the Wazir in place of Jaffar Khan. But the season of bad news had not ended.

Aurangzeb had given Shivaji a lakh rupiyas for his visit to Agra. Shivaji had subsequently been instructed to recover the amount through his jagir and send it back to the royal treasury. The subedar had managed to get the amount from Shivaji but subsequently Shivaji and his men had started looting the Mughal-occupied territories. Aurangzeb kept a blind eye for a while but the news of Shivaji's second attack on Surat made him sit up and take notice.

Aurangzeb spoke his mind that evening in the durbar at the Diwan-e-Khaas. 'We have till date worked in a manner not to disturb the peace of the country. But there is a limit to my patience. After all, Allah has put me on this throne to do my duties. I have no option to call for jehad now. Adil Shah of Bijapur and Qutub Khan of Golconda are using Shivaji to attack us. We will have to find another way to tackle them. We had pardoned them till date but we cannot tolerate their sins any more.

For days following the Badshah's pronouncements, people in the streets spoke of Shivaji's attack on Surat; a few describing the event factually while many exaggerating the same.

✦✦✦

Nawab Bai's visit to make Muazzam mend his ways had had little effect on his behaviour and she returned after staying there for a year. Aurangzeb sent Mahabat Khan, who had done a good job in Gujarat, to the Deccan under the pretext of giving support to Muazzam. As per Mughal tradition the Shahzadas were married when they turned fifteen. Akbar was of marriageable age now and Jahanara and Zebunissa, on the lookout for a suitable alliance, finally found a match leading to a month-long celebrations after the marriage. Thus distracted, Aurangzeb's tense mind relaxed for a while.

But the news of the Mughal forces getting routed by the Marathas near Saler was disturbing. Aurangzeb realized the Marathas were taking advantage of the fact that the Deccan was not being managed well. He decided to take matters in his own hands. Incidentally, his milk brother Bahadur Khan was in Delhi and Aurangzeb decided to confer with him.

When they met, Aurangzeb proposed, 'Bahadur Khan, I want you to lead the campaign in the Deccan. Set up your camp on the banks of the Bheema near Pedgaon. I don't think one can manage sitting in Aurangabad. You can attack the Marathas or the Bijapur territory whenever you get an opportunity.'

Bahadur Khan was a few years older than Aurangzeb. But despite his not so robust health, the opportunity to lead an independent campaign spurred him. 'I am aware of the situation there. I have a request. I need to get the same free hand given to Mirza Raja Jai Singh. I will be happy if the Shahzada and Diler Khan don't interfere while I am there.'

Aurangzeb smiled. 'Bahadur Khan, this was the same assurance Shaista Khan had been given when he had left for the campaign. I had to then transfer my uncle to Bengal. Mirza Raja had managed to get things under control for a while but that too did not last long.'

'I would prefer to speak less and let my deeds do the talking.'

Aurangzeb smiled again. He was aware of the exploits of his milk brother. He said, 'Bahadur Khan, you have to fight the enemy in the battlefield as well as in his durbar.'

After a while when Bahadur Khan turned to leave, he heard his name being called again. Aurangzeb said, 'I forgot to tell you something. It has been many years now, but I don't forget things easily.'

Bahadur Khan was at a loss. He muttered, 'I would be obliged if you can clarify. I don't understand what you are referring to.'

'I also don't forget insults,' Aurangzeb continued, ignoring him. 'Bahadur Khan, often the criminal makes a mistake of assuming he will never be caught. But Allah is omnipresent. He ensures justice is delivered in the end.'

Bahadur Khan's face turned red. He knew what Aurangzeb was referring to. His beard shook with fear. Unable to face Aurangzeb's stern gaze, he looked down at the floor.

The words he heard next felt like hot lead being poured into his ears. 'I have two reasons to send you on this campaign. You had committed a crime by entering my zenankhana. If you succeed in this campaign, your sins will be pardoned. If you fail, don't dare to show your face in Delhi again. I shall make arrangements for your burial there itself. Bahadur Khan, *Khuda hafeez!*'

๛ ๛

The month of Ramzan began and Aurangzeb spent all his time in namaz and distributing alms to the poor.

A few days after Eid, Aurangzeb was in conference with Siddhi Fulad Khan in his private chambers. After the meeting he walked over to his palace where Akbar, along with his sisters, was waiting to seek his blessings before leaving to take charge of Ajmer as subedar. Akbar's intention was to take the emperor's blessings, give him his gifts and then take leave as soon as possible.

The signs of marriage celebrations had not yet been completely washed away. Akbar's hands showed faint traces of the henna decoration. The warm embrace, the nights and days spent drunk in wine were still visible on his face. Akbar, wearing a loose silk dress, saluted as Aurangzeb entered the room. Aurangzeb was fond of his two sons Akbar and Azam. He had a soft corner for the sixteen-year-old Akbar who had lost his mother at childbirth.

Without openly expressing his happiness at seeing Akbar, he said, 'Shezada, I am told you are ready to depart for Ajmer.'

'Yes, Abba Jaan. I came here to seek your blessings before I do so.'

Aurangzeb knew Akbar had not yet faced the hardships of the world. 'I am there to guide you whenever you need me. But a Mughal Shahzada should use his own mind and wisdom. In war and in durbar, events don't come announced. I will help you if I am around, else you have to use your own wit.'

Akbar nodded in confirmation. Aurangzeb smiled and continued, 'You are young. Youth has a propensity to attract the evil. You need to protect yourself from such.'

Akbar looked up a little surprised. He wondered whether the news of his sexual exploits in the zenankhana and, before his marriage, with the concubines and maids, had reached his father. Zebunissa had warned him that he should agree to whatever his father says and not argue. He thus nodded and said, 'I shall always be looking for your guidance. I shall not eat unless I read your message each day.'

'Wonderful! I am pleased, Akbar miya.' With a knowing smile he turned towards Zebunissa and Zeenat saying, 'It seems you have coached your brother well.'

Zeenat's face turned pale. She thought it was a snide remark and said, 'Abba Jaan, when someone like you representing the Paigambar himself is there to guide Akbar, what guidance can we provide?'

Aurangzeb looked at his daughters. Zebunissa was now in her mid-thirties but her beauty was untarnished. Her cheeks were flushed with anger and had turned pink. He said, addressing both of them, 'A Badshah rarely gets a chance to speak his mind in court. I want to say a few things to Akbar miya here; I am sure it will help him.'

Akbar seemed visibly relaxed. 'Your words are always a guidance to me.'

'Just wait for a while. You will soon realize what I want to convey.'

A huge silk curtain hung in one corner. Aurangzeb stood gazing at the curtain for a while. Both the daughters and Akbar were curious to see what lay behind the curtain. On cue from Aurangzeb, a khoja escorted kotwal Fulad Khan into the room. He saluted elaborately almost touching the floor with his hand. No words were exchanged but Fulad Khan knew the Badshah's instructions.

With a flourish he pulled down the curtain in one stroke. The shahzadis and Akbar gasped in surprise to see Aurangzeb's eldest son Muhammad Sultan sitting on a small stool. Akbar had never seen his stepbrother before. Zeenat and Zebunissa recognized him immediately. The broad forehead, the sharp nose and the long limbs; he resembled Aurangzeb a lot. He was a bag of bones, his blank eyes staring into nothingness. White strands of hair in his beard showed early ageing. He seemed weak and fragile and was barely able to sit straight on the stool.

Zebunissa and Zeenat covered their mouths in surprise. It was a shock beyond their wildest imagination. Akbar was confused. He was unable to understand the reason for his father to introduce him to his stepbrother when he was about to leave for Ajmer. He asked, 'Abba Jaan, my elder brother seems to be in a bad shape.'

'Ask him why he has landed in such a situation.'

Akbar looked askance.

'He made the mistake of taking up arms against me. He thought he could defeat me if he joined the enemy camp.'

Muhammad Sultan muttered a few incoherent words. Aurangzeb glanced at Fulad Khan and he went over to help Sultan to stand up. Taking the support of two khojas, Sultan stood up gingerly, his legs shaking. He barely had the energy to stand, yet his ankles were tied in chains on one end and to his wrist on the other. The metallic sound of the links rubbings against each other sent a shiver down the spines of those present.

'Abba Jaan! It is a torture to see the Shahzada in such a pitiable state. Whatever his crime, the punishment seems too harsh,' Zebunissa shouted in agony.

Aurangzeb, unperturbed at the reaction, said addressing Akbar, 'Take a good look. You are going to manage Ajmer independently. It is in the heartland of the Rajputs. Bear this in mind: As long as you work for me loyally, you have nothing to fear. I am here to shield your mistakes and to protect you at all costs. But I hope you learn a lesson seeing your brother here. Banish the thought of a revolt, however tempting it may sound. Don't get swayed by words other than those of Allah's. You may take leave now.'

The servants came in with a traditional tray for Akbar's farewell when everyone turned to hear loud commotion at the door. The khojas bowed in salute as Nawab Bai rushed into the room, without bothering to ask for permission shouting, 'Hazrat, Hazrat!'

She turned to see her son, chained and helpless, staring vacantly at her. Hugging him, she showered kisses on his face. 'My dear, my dear!' She could not stop caressing him as tears flowed down her cheeks.

The mother and son were seeing each other after years. All she had had these years was an oil painting of his. She had finally got to see her son, hug him, touch him and caress him. Aurangzeb allowed a few moments to pass. Zebunissa and Zeenat, touched by the agony of a mother waiting for a long-lost son, could not hold back their tears. It was a heart-rending scene as Nawab Bai continued to hug and caress her frail son. Aurangzeb said, his voice sans any emotions, 'Begum, what kind of an emotional display is this? Don't you follow any protocol, rushing in here without permission?'

Nawab Bai howled, 'Shahenshah! I have followed decorum for many years. You may give me whatever punishment you deem fit. Put me in chains for the rest of my life, but release my son. Place your hand on the holy book and promise me.'

At an indication from Aurangzeb four heavily built Tartar women walked and pulled Nawab Bai away from her son. As they dragged her out of the room her pleas rented the air, 'Sultan, Sultan! My dear child! Why did you take birth in this cursed Mughal family?'

Her screams subsided after a while. Fulad Khan dropped the curtain hiding the uncomfortable sight of the helpless Sultan.

Sighing deeply Aurangzeb addressed Akbar, 'Shahzada, in a way it is good that you witnessed this. A hundred words of mine would not be able to convey what you just saw. You can take leave now. Remember! You are there to represent the Mughal Empire.'

⋘⋙

Aurangzeb got up from the window at the palace overlooking the banks of the Yamuna where, as usual, thousands had gathered for a glimpse of their favourite emperor. Getting up, he walked back to his quarters with Kazi Abdul Wahab and Wazir Asad Khan. There was still time for the durbar at the Diwan-e-Aam to start and Aurangzeb indicated to the two men to sit. He said, 'I wonder why the Mughal Badshah should show his face to the ryots each day.'

'Huzoor, the people are emotional,' the kazi clarified; caressing his flowing beard. 'Many Hindus, I am told, do not partake of even a drop of water till they have had a glimpse of your face.'

'That is precisely what I wanted to say,' Aurangzeb said. 'It is a kafir tradition. Darshan is a Hindu concept. It was started by Din-e-Elahi Akbar Badshah to please the kafirs. It is one of the reason the Hindus do not see any need to embrace Islam.'

'But Huzoor, such traditions had allowed the Mughals to rule the country without any resistance,' Asad Khan said.

'I agree with you, Wazir. And that is sole reason I have allowed this practice to continue. But I was not made the emperor to just create a large empire. Allah wants me to show people the right way of Islam and punish those who do not follow it.'

'You are absolutely right, Jahanpanah,' the kazi concurred as usual, eager to please the Badshah. 'I hope you have heard the news of the recent event at Mathura.'

'Why, what happened?'

'The faujdar at Mathura has been murdered.'

Aurangzeb was taken aback hearing the news. Mathura's police chief Abdul Nabi was a close confidant of his. He had recently issued orders to raze the temple to ground.

'Veer Singh Bundela had managed to build the temple taking out money from the royal treasury through deceit. The orders to raze the temple were issued sometime back. But look at the end result,' the kazi added. 'The people there do not care about the royal orders.'

'But I had sent Rad-andaz Khan there with his men.'

'That is true, Jahanpanah. But the rebels intercepted them before they reached Mathura and hundreds of Mughal soldiers were killed.'

'Who is behind all this, Wazir?'

'A Jat called Gokul.'

'I see! Asad Khan, I am hearing many such cases of rebellious these days. Earlier it was restricted to the Deccan but it is worrying to hear of such incidents from places like Mathura, so close to the capital city. Give orders to Rad-andaz Khan to arrest the traitors and present them here. Ask Hasan Ali Khan and Bhagalpur's Sheikh Raziuddin to help him. We need to eliminate these troubles from the roots.'

Turning towards the kazi he said, 'Kazi Sahab, I am discontinuing the practice of sitting at the window. Let the drummers announce this in the city today. Find out all the kafir practices which are being followed in our official duties. All temples that have come up since the time I took charge should be razed to the ground. We need to start implementing the main purpose for which our ancestors came into this country – to spread the word of Islam. Those who come in the way will be beheaded and their bodies will be fed to the wolves.'

⚜

Years passed by. Thousands of *firmans* were being issued and the subedars, eager to please the Badshah were implementing them with vigour. In the wake of pursuing the orders many old temples along with the new ones were destroyed. The poor and the meek converted to Islam partly out of fear and partially out of greed. The Badshah received all kinds of figures on the number of people who had adopted the religion of the Mughals.

The Marathas in the south were getting bolder and had demanded a share of the revenue from Surat. One day news from Narnaul reached the durbar. Rad-andaz Khan personally came over to the durbar to meet Aurangzeb. He said, 'Huzoor, I have some disturbing news. There has been an uprising at Narnaul and our entire contingent wiped out.'

'Rad-andaz Khan, are you out of your mind? An entire contingent gets wiped out so close to Delhi and we have no inkling of it? Who are these people?'

'They shave their heads and are called Satnami sadhus or Mundis.'

'How many were they?'

'Not many; around five or six thousand of them.'

'That's it? And they killed the entire Mughal contingent stationed there? Rad-andaz Khan, I would not have been surprised had you stayed back in your zenankhana wearing women's clothes than have the courage to inform me.'

'*Tauba, tauba!* Huzoor, I agree this servant of yours has erred but I urge you to hear the entire story.'

'Say whatever you have to; quickly!'

'The sadhus have a lady amongst them. Some say she is a representation of the Goddess Kali herself.'

'Do you believe in this nonsense?'

'I didn't, Huzoor, till I heard of her powers to create kafirs out of nothing. Our daring soldiers would have barely beheaded a kafir when another hundred would spring from nowhere. What can one do against such powers? We had despatched our top sardars to Narnaul. They witnessed these with their own eyes, unbelievable as it may sound,' Rad-andaz Khan continued.

'Rad-andaz Khan, I am ashamed to hear that our mansabdars are being beaten up by an old woman and are scared of such hocus-pocus.'

'Huzoor …'

'Enough! I don't want to hear any more of this nonsensical talk. I am tempted to stop reading the holy book sitting here in Delhi and move out into the heartland of Hindustan, a naked shamsher in my hand. I am going to lead the forces to Narnaul myself. I would like to see the power of the magic you talk of.'

Within four days the trumpets announced the march of the emperor out of the fort. Aurangzeb, riding atop an elephant, moved with a contingent of elephants, camels and ten thousand soldiers.

Four or five miles before Narnaul, the mansabdars met Aurangzeb, their faces clearly showing mortal fear. They pleaded, 'Huzoor, we request you not to face the old woman. No one is able to stand her magical powers.'

Ignoring their pleas, Aurangzeb got off his elephant and sat astride an Arabian steed. He nudged the horse to reach the head of the marching contingent. Each of the mansabdars was carrying a green flag. He wrote a couplet from the Quran on to each of the flags and then raising his hand shouted, 'We are Allah's men. We have been sent here to spread his word. Your flags have the holy word written on them. There is nothing to fear now. Victory is yours. Attack! And present me the heads of the enemies!'

Kazi Abdul Wahad too was astride a horse. He shouted, 'Alamgir, Zinda Pir!' The troops repeated, 'Alamgir, Zinda Pir!' and then with shouts of 'Din, din!' they rushed towards the town of Narnaul.

Aurangzeb peered through his binoculars. It was getting hot but he refused an umbrella offered by one of the khojas. He could see the dust flying in the distance. The distant shouts and screams were audible from where he stood.

It was afternoon when Rad-andaz Khan, badly wounded, presented himself bowing down with his right hand still holding the sword.

'Badshah Salamat has won. We have managed to rout the enemy.'

'What about the magical powers?'

'The powers had no effect in Badshah's presence. Our brave soldiers have beheaded all the Satnami sadhus.'

The shouts of 'Alamgir, Zinda Pir!' were heard. The trumpets sounded the end of the battle and victory for the Mughal emperor as the caravan lumbered its way back to the capital.

It was late evening when the Badshah, having finished his prayers, met the officials in the Diwan-e-Khaas. They had barely finished congratulating each other when news of a fresh uprising dampened the victory.

A new leader had emerged in the north who had been spreading word against the emperor. He was urging the people to take up arms against the Mughal forces and had managed to gather a large army of volunteers. The men were creating havoc in the province of Punjab and the Kashmir Valley.

'Who are these people?' Aurangzeb asked, as usual not losing his composure.

Asad Khan answered, 'They call themselves Sikhs.'

'And who is their leader?'

'He is called Tegh Bahadur.'

'I see! It seems my efforts in spreading Allah's words are not enough. I will have to strive more. Send a word to the subedar at Lahore asking him to capture this Sikh guru Tegh Bahadur and present him in my court.'

৯৫ ৯৯

The news of the Kashi Vishwanath temple at Varanasi being razed to the ground spread like wildfire. The Rajputs, Jats, Bundels and other Hindu sardars were deeply hurt. While they did not openly protest, it was impossible for them to carry out their duties in such a condition.

One evening, on getting the information of the arrival of Raja Jaswant Singh from the Deccan, the Rajput sardars Raja Ram Singh, Puranmal Bundela and a few other sardars rushed to receive him. After the initial enquiries, Ram Singh came to the moot point.

'Maharaj, you must have heard of the news.'

'The destruction of Kashi Vishwanath has hurt the sentiments of all the Hindus,' Puranmal said in a pensive mood.

'I am unable to understand why the Badshah behaves so ruthlessly these days. Frankly it is we Rajput sardars who are running the principalities and not the Mughal mansabdars. Yet the Badshah does not leave any opportunity to hurt us. He has no respect for our emotions.' Ram Singh's words were filled with sadness.

Ram Singh was right. The maulvis and mullahs were using their proximity to the Badshah to get *firmans* issued as and when they wished. The recent massacre of the Satnami sadhus, the arrest of Gokul Jat and the *firman* to capture Tegh Bahadur were all in the same vein.

Earlier Kazi Abdul Wahab justified his actions saying they were directed against only those Hindus who had supported Dara Shikoh and had not wanted Aurangzeb to ascend the throne. But years had passed by and the local officials misued the powers given to them to harass the common people. Any complaint reaching the court was decided only after consultation with the maulvis present. The Hindu sardars in the court were flooded with complaints from all over. They were at their wits' end trying to pacify the ever-increasing angst amongst the people.

'Maharaj, you need to request the Badshah to show some restraint,' Ram Singh pleaded. 'You are married to the Badshah's sister. She has access to the Mughal zenankhana. I request you to use her good offices to get the Badshah's ears. We need to find a way for the complaints to reach him.'

'As I said,' Jaswant Singh clarified, 'I am not sure what effect these efforts will have but I will try. I have spent my entire life serving the Mughals. I have seen their power rise by the day. If you think of the reign from Shahenshah Akbar's time till date, you will realize that it makes sense to keep one's mouth shut. When a huge wave rises in the ocean, the person who ducks survives. Those who try to raise their heads are thrown away. We need to tread carefully.'

Ram Singh was not convinced with Jaswant Singh's reasoning. He said, looking around to ensure there was no one within earshot, 'Maharaj, pardon me for being blunt.'

'Please go on, Rajaji. You are like my son. I may have had my differences with your father Mirza Raja but that ended with his death. Please speak your mind.'

'Maharaj, it is precisely for the reason you mentioned that the Rajputs and other Hindus have been loyal to the Mughal throne. It is a fact that more Rajput sacrifices have been made compared to that of Arab or Mughal sardars.'

'Ram Singhji, it seems you have started thinking of these things since recent times. I have not heard you or Mirza Raja say so earlier.'

'I cannot compare myself to Mirza Raja. I am nobody compared to him. But I remember having spent many months with Shivaji Raja when he was in custody at Agra. He would be at pains to explain this to me.'

'What were Shivaji Raja's views?'

Ram Singh knew Maharaj Jaswant Singh did not give much

weightage to Shivaji's views but he replied, 'His view was that the Badshah understands the language of competency.'

'You believe we are competent to challenge the Badshah?'

'I would not have, earlier. But since listening to Shivaji and hearing of the events in the Deccan I am confident that we can challenge the superiority of the Mughal Empire. I don't say victory is easy but it is possible. If all of us decide to come together, it is definitely possible.'

'Ram Singhji, it is your youth which is making you say this. I have been around long enough to know that it is not possible to defeat the Badshah. You would be rudely mistaken if you believe you can have your way.'

Puranmal Bundela was not convinced and added, 'But Maharaj, bad times are on us in any case. I too think that we should find a permanent solution for this.'

'You are aware of the way I was routed when I decided to fight against the Badshah. It was an insult too difficult to bear and I returned to Jodhpur only to be spurned by my own queen. I was forced to take refuge and beg for pardon from Badshah Aurangzeb who sent me to the Deccan. Unfortunately, I did not see success there. Having seen such defeats, I don't have the courage to take up arms against the Mughal might.'

'Please tell us what we should do. Our people are not happy when we support the Mughal army. We are not sure what future beholds for Guru Tegh Bahadur. I cannot forget that the Sikhs too had sacrificed their lives for the Mughal Empire in Assam.'

Despite earnest appeal, they were unable to convince Jaswant Singh. He said in conclusion, 'Let me confer with the Maharana of Udaipur. He is the only Rajput who has not surrendered to the Mughals. I will seek his opinion and then decide what we should do.'

⚬⚬ ⚬⚬

Aurangzeb's ability lay in acting quickly. On getting information from his spies, he immediately deputed Jaswant Singh to Jamrood in Afghanistan to fight against the Afghans. He demoted Ram Singh reducing his mansab and sent him to Assam while Puranmal Bundela was despatched to Dhaka. In one stroke he had managed to nip the Rajput threat in its infancy.

Shahzada Muhammad Sultan died in his Salimgadh Fort prison. The Sikh guru Tegh Bahadur was beheaded in full public view at Chandni Chowk. It was Aurangzeb's way of teaching the Sikhs a lesson.

There was no real threat to the Mughal Sultante right from Kabul up to Dhaka. The only irritant was Shivaji who continued to challenge the Mughal might. Bahadur Khan, deputed at Pedgaon, was fighting the Marathas. The news that reached Delhi was not encouraging: the Marathas were gaining ground.

But these events did not deter Aurangzeb from his daily activities. He would read his prayers five times a day without fail. Fridays were meant for dispensing justice while mansabs were reduced or increased for sardars based on their performance. The capital city followed the traditional month of mourning after the death of Shahzada Muhammad Sultan.

The other shahzadas, away from the capital for years together, found an excuse to return home. Muazzam from the south, Azam from Gujarat and Akbar from Rajputana made their way to Delhi to mourn the death of their eldest brother. Aurangzeb could not express his displeasure openly and the princes stayed back for months on end spending time in debauchery.

One Friday evening Aurangzeb received news from his spies on the activities at Shahzada Muazzam's haveli. On hearing the same Aurangzeb dressed in a simple kurta and trousers, wrapped a shawl around his shoulders, and with a couple of khojas and twenty-odd soldiers, left the fort with a sword in hand. The men on guard were taken by surprise. They were not used to seeing the emperor leave the fort with a handful of men and that too without any advance notice.

Galloping across the streets of Delhi, the group reached Muazzam's haveli. Ignoring the salutes of the guards, Aurangzeb dismounted and entered the haveli. He asked a servant to inform Muazzam and then, without waiting for a reply, entered his personal quarters.

The sight which greeted Aurangzeb surprised him. Muazzam sat on the floor of his room reading from a Quran placed on a low stool while a mullah sat on the opposite end reading it aloud.

Seeing Aurangzeb at the door, they both got up hurriedly. The Shahzada bent thrice in a low salaam and requested Aurangzeb to seat himself. He said, 'Hazrat has come into my haveli without any prior warning. I am keen to know the reason for the same.'

Aurangzeb adjusted his shawl on his shoulders saying, 'You may feel the need for the Badshah to inform you in advance but Muhi-ud-din Aurangzeb does not feel so.'

Aurangzeb looked around the room. Except for lovely silk drapes and beautiful paintings hanging on the walls, the room was quite sparse. He stared at a carpet hanging in a corner. Muazzam said, 'I apologize for the lack of cleanliness in this room. The servants must have hung the carpet to dry. They had no idea of your visit.'

Aurangzeb smiled. 'Shahzada, I am pleased to see that you too are following the rules laid down in our holy books.'

'I am still confused not knowing the purpose of your sudden unannounced visit.'

'Today is Friday, the holy day. You know the importance I give to this day. I wish my sons follow my example. Some people, who are jealous of you, misinformed me that you are whiling away your time in merriment and dance. I thus came in to check it out for myself.'

'*Tauba, tauba,*' Muazzam said, slapping his own cheeks. 'Zille Subhani, I hope you believe me that I spend all my time reading the Quran. And, knowing your dislike for dance, I have banished the dancers from this haveli.'

'*Waah!* I am really pleased. You have exceeded my expectations. By the way, who is this mullah helping you to read the Quran?'

Muazzam, proud of his father's praise for him, said, 'Hazrat, he is a very learned mullah. Not only does he know the Quran word by word, he is also a very good astrologer.'

'Is that so?' Aurangzeb asked, looking intently at the mullah. 'No doubt he has to be very learned if he is teaching the Shahzada. I would like to ask him a few questions, if you don't mind.'

'But of course, Hazrat. We are all your servants.'

'I have nothing to ask you regarding the Quran, Mullahji. I am sure you know it like the back of your hand.'

The mullah bent down, his flowing beard touching the floor and said, 'Yes, Jahanpanah. This old man has learnt a little.'

'I am keen to ask you regarding astrology.'

'I shall try my best to clarify.'

'This Shahzada standing here; I want to know if he is likely to revolt against me anytime.'

Muazzam, deeply hurt at the question, interjected, 'Abba Jaan! The mullah need not answer the question. I will answer – I shall never even dream of revolting against you.'

'Shahzada, the question is regarding the future. The mullah is capable of answering the question, not you.'

The mullah cleared his throat and said, 'Alampanah, it is sad but true that the Shahzada will revolt against you.'

Ignoring Aurangzeb's presence Muazzam shouted, 'Mullahji, are you out of your mind? I hope you are not drunk.'

Aurangzeb, unperturbed at the mullah's prophecy said, 'Please don't get upset Shahzada. Let the mullah speak his mind.' Looking into Shahzada's eyes he said, 'I am happy that the mullah has told the truth without fear.'

'Alampanah, it is not true. It cannot be. Please ignore whatever he has said.'

'I thought Shahzada will be happy hearing my predictions,' the mullah said.

'What?' Muazzam shouted. Before he could react further, Aurangzeb raised his right hand shutting him up.

Seeing the Badshah's support, the mullah continued, 'Hazrat Salamat, I don't think you have got the entire meaning of my prediction. I would like to clarify.'

He continued, 'Shahenshah Alamgir Badshah is a true devotee of the Paigambar. When I said revolt, I did not mean a revolt against the throne.'

'Please clarify. I am unable to follow you.'

'What I meant was that the Shahzada would revolt against the religious practices. If Hazrat reads the Quran once, he will read it twice a day. He will spend so much money for supporting the pilgrimage to Mecca that it will anger you. He would distribute alms to the poor and needy. In all aspects of religion he will outshine you. This is what I predict for him in future.'

It was a great relief for Muazzam to hear the mullah clarify. After a while, Aurangzeb, while walking down the steps of the haveli said, 'Shahzada, I was not sure if the men who surround you are religious or not. But I know that they are quite clever.'

Instead of returning to the Red Fort, Aurangzeb turned towards the Jama Masjid for his evening prayers. He prayed, 'Allah, let my children have bad habits but give them the wisdom of Shahzada Muazzam.'

ೲ ೲ

The princes had assembled in Aurangzeb's private quarters before leaving for their respective provinces. He shouted 'Takhliya' to ensure complete privacy. Aurangzeb looked at the assembled shahzadas. The youngest of them, Kambaksh, twelve years of age now and managing the territory of Delhi, sat a little closer to him than others signifying himself as Aurangzeb's favourite. Looking around to ensure that there was no one within earshot Aurangzeb said, caressing his beard, 'I thought it was an appropriate moment to talk about certain things before you leave for your respective territories.'

Azam said, 'All we know is how to follow your commands, Hazrat.'

Aurangzeb was aware of Azam's daredevil attitude. Ignoring his comment he continued, 'This may be true for all matters related to the territories. I am here to talk about something different.'

'We are always eager to hear Abba Jaan's words,' Akbar said.

'You must be aware by now of the circumstances under which I ascended the throne at Delhi,' Aurangzeb said, his voice taking on a serious note. None of the Shahzadas responded waiting for him to continue. 'I killed Dara Shikoh and put Badshah Shah Jahan in jail.'

'I am told you received such instructions from the Allah,' Akbar said.

'You came to power on your own strength. What is wrong with that?' Azam asked rhetorically, puffing his chest. Muazzam, listening to his brothers, was silent. He continued looking down at the carpet, his hands behind his back.

'I am not asking for your opinion on whether what I did was right or not. What I want to ask is whether or not you want to occupy the throne. Don't you feel it is high time you took charge?'

The question was unexpected and the shahzadas glanced up at Aurangzeb, surprised. The only one unperturbed was the young Kambaksh. He replied, 'Yes, why not? I am eager to take charge. That is why I insisted on getting the subah of Delhi.'

The others relaxed a bit hearing Kambaksh's response. They assumed their father wanted their frank opinion. Aurangzeb said, 'No doubt all would like to ascend the throne but only one can. I want to know from all of you: Who do you think is most eligible? Shahzada Muazzam is the eldest. Let me ask him first.'

'Shahenshah has answered the question himself.'

'I would like to hear it from you.'

'I wish the Shahenshah a long life. But if he ever considers retiring from the throne to spend the rest of his life in the service of Allah, I would, as the eldest of the shahzadas, be willing to take charge. I thus consider myself the most eligible to take your seat.'

Aurangzeb, moving the beads of his rosary, observed the others who were silent. He said, 'Let me ask my second Shahzada Azam for his view.'

'I would like to clarify something before I answer,' Azam said. 'I hope Abba Jaan does not intend to create a rift amongst us brothers by asking each one of us for his opinion.'

Aurangzeb was perturbed for a brief moment. Regaining his composure he said, 'Azam, I wish to precisely avoid such a situation. I would consider myself blessed if, while I am alive, I don't have to see the death of any of my sons.'

Azam realized his blunt question had not been taken well, and he looked down saying, 'I apologize. Please pardon me.'

'It is not a question of mistakes. I like your direct approach. Anyway, tell me what you feel.'

'I will, if you promise not to get angry with me.'

'Go on ...'

'I don't know why my elder brother believes he is the rightful heir,' he said, throwing a snide glance at Muazzam. 'The person proclaiming the throne should check his antecedents. I have impeccable antecedents both from my mother as well as my father. I am thus the most eligible.'

Aurangzeb let a rare smile flicker across. He turned towards Akbar who said, 'My birth has proven lucky for the Badshah. He has won numerous victories since my birth and I feel it is my right to claim the throne.'

'So what do you have to say?' Aurangzeb turned to Kambaksh.

'All my three brothers aspire to be the emperor but they forget a simple fact; one needs to be born to the Badshah. I am the only one who was born after you ascended the throne. I am thus the most eligible.'

Pointing his forefinger heavenwards, as if receiving the blessings from the angels, Aurangzeb muttered, 'Ameen.'

Getting up from his seat, Aurangzeb hugged all his four sons and said, 'I am happy that you spoke the truth without fearing anything. Whatever Allah wishes will finally happen. Devote your life in the service of Allah and you will get what you want. The one who serves with most devotion will be rewarded. But remember, your victory is still years away. An astrologer has predicted that I will live to be a hundred and twenty-five! You have a lot of time to serve Allah.'

He hugged the shahzadas once more and then bid them farewell.

ംഉ ഉം

The day began with good news. The messengers had travelled almost non-stop to deliver the news. Bahadur Khan had not been able to make any difference and Aurangzeb had put Shahzada Muazzam back in charge along with the support of Diler Khan. The turning point came when Sambhaji, sulking over differences with Shivaji, had joined forces with the Mughals. The messengers got news of Sambhaji having camped with Diler Khan in the cantonment.

Aurangzeb got up and prayed, thanking Allah for his blessings. Aurangzeb had spent a lot of time conferring with Muazzam before his departure and the plan to create a rift amongst the Marathas seemed to have borne fruit. It was now an easy task for the Mughals to rule over the Deccan.

Another piece of good news followed. Jaswant Singh, fighting against the Afghans at Kabul, had died there unable to bear the cold in the dry, dusty and mountainous terrain of Afghanistan. This opened doors for Aurangzeb to take over Rajputana completely. Jaswant Singh had died childless and his territory of Jodhpur, independent since Emperor Akbar's time, could now be annexed to the Mughal Sultanate. It was possible to defeat the Raja at Udaipur too. Allah seemed merciful.

Within a few days, the news of Jaswant Singh's death was officially announced in the court. Aurangzeb deputed Bahadur Khan along with key officials to Jodhpur. Aurangzeb conferred with Wazir Asad Khan, Shaista Khan and Shahzada Akbar to chart further course of action.

But for Aurangzeb, good news was not to last for long. Within two months' of Bahadur Khan's departure to Jodhpur, Aurangzeb heard that Jaswant Singh's two queens had delivered a baby boy each at Lahore. One of them had survived and was christened Ajit Singh. He had been nominated as Jaswant Singh's heir and the troops were marching back towards Jodhpur with their newly crowned king. Realizing that he was likely to lose his hold on the territory, Aurangzeb declared that Ajit Singh's birth was a concocted story and that he was not Jaswant Singh's heir. He despatched Durgadas Rathore to escort both the queens and Ajit Singh to the durbar in Delhi.

The key officials conferred with Aurangzeb in the private discussion chambers. There was a dire need for funds. Launching a campaign against the Rajputs was going to be a drain on the treasury. The affairs at the Deccan were rapidly depleting the treasury at Daulatabad while the territory of Kabul did not contribute anything worthwhile. Finally, the decision to extract taxes from people for their protection was taken. Within a month the *shahi fatwah* was announced. The dreaded Jizyah tax, banned a hundred years ago since the time of Emperor Akbar, was reimposed. Money was not going to be a problem now.

The Rajput, Bundels and other Jat troops participating in the campaign were exempt from paying the tax while everyone else was subjected to amounts as per the individual's ability. The rich merchants were penalized heavily. Officials carried out a census of sorts to ascertain the amounts to be paid by various individuals. The festival of Holi was not celebrated across Delhi that year. People, afraid of being questioned on the roads, avoided going out. Thousands of offenders were put behind bars. The same scenes were being repeated in different territories across the sultanate.

❦

Aurangzeb was restless suspecting nearly everyone of plotting against him. Good news, instead of creating an atmosphere of happiness, would be lost with some other worrisome news by that evening. Jahanara had tried reasoning with Aurangzeb against the Jizyah tax. But Aurangzeb, convinced that it was the duty of the emperor to turn the people at large towards Islam and that he was merely following the wishes of the Paigambar, was unable to see Jahanara's logic.

Asad Khan at times attempted to explain the atrocities being carried out by the officials under the garb of tax collection. But he too was unable to make headway with the emperor.

Aurangzeb sat in his room, praying to Allah. He murmured his prayers, explaining each and every step he had taken and asking Allah for directions. After praying for a long time, he got up and stood near the window. Before he had taken charge of the throne, there were no signs of Islam except for the minarets of the Jama Masjid. Now he could see the skyline dotted with tall minarets competing with each other. Fakirs and aulias could sit in the masjids and discuss and debate the holy books. Aurangzeb spoke aloud to himself, 'Nothing has been achieved yet. There are so many enemies to capture. Allah, my lord! I have turned sixty now. You need to help me achieve my dreams. It is on your faith that I am hoping to spread the word of Islam to the far corners of the world.'

Tears gathered in his eyes. He steadied himself holding the edge of the window frame when he felt he was losing balance. He muttered, 'Ya Khuda! Let my body not lose its strength. I need the energy to carry out your task.' As he looked out of the window he got the shock of his life. One of the minarets, which he had been adminring a few moments back, seemed to have broken into half. He sat down on the carpet muttering, 'Am I losing my balance? Are my eyes deceiving me? How can a holy minaret break into half? Maybe I am losing my eyesight now.'

At that moment Anwar Khoja came in and said, 'Huzoor, the city has been hit by a massive earthquake.'

'Don't be silly. I did not feel anything yet.'

'Huzoor, but the shocks were felt everywhere, including the zenankhana. Many buildings have fallen down. One of the minarets of the Jama Masjid has fallen.'

Looking out of the window Aurangzeb mused, 'So it wasn't my eyes deceiving me. I was witnessing the earthquake. I still have the same strength as before. Parwar Digaar, I know you want me to complete your task. You have given me the zeal now to make it happen.'

When Aurangzeb attended the durbar a few hours later, only a handful of officials had been able to make their way through the city ravaged by the earthquake. Amin Khan requested an audience saying, 'Huzoor, the people at large believe that Allah is displeased at the tax being imposed on the common man. They say Allah showed his wrath by shaking the core of the earth.'

Aurangzeb laughed out loud, 'The people are fools to think so. I have spent my lifetime trying to make them wise. It is true the earthquake took place but the reasons are entirely different. Amin Khan, the earth is shaking with joy. The heavens too have shown their gratitude with the rains. Natural disasters have happened for generations. One should use one's wisdom rather than attribute our actions for their causes.'

A few of the older maulvis nodded in acknowledgement.

ฬ๑ ๑ฬ

It was easy to talk about the natural events but many other events continued to confound the officials. Durgadas reached Delhi with Jaswant Singh's queens and the young prince. They were kept under house arrest despite the protestations from Durgadas and other Rajputs. Aurangzeb, having suffered Shivaji's escape many years back, did not want to take any chances and ensured that the security was fool-proof.

The general feeling amongst the people was that Jodhpur would soon be in the Mughal fold followed by Udaipur, thus paving the way for the Mughal flag to be planted across Rajputana.

Durgadas Rathore and the queens were not the ones to sit twiddling their thumbs and one day, Aurangzeb got the message of their daring escape. The Mughal forces chased them but by evening Aurangzeb was informed that the Rajputs had not only managed to thwart the Mughal attack but had escaped towards Jodhpur unharmed.

Aurangzeb erupted, 'Were my soldiers sleeping while this happened?'

'Alampanah, you may see for yourself; the road is littered with hundreds of devoted soldiers who tried to stop them.'

The capital witnessed the festival of Holi in a different form. The streets were splattered red with the blood of the Mughal soldiers. Aurangzeb knew Durgadas Rathore had managed to fool the soldiers guarding the queens.

Aurangzeb recovered from the initial shock. 'It seems Allah wants me to take the shamsher in my hand and teach a lesson to the ones challenging the Mughal might. I am issuing orders right away. We know the Rathores and the Sisodias do not see eye to eye. Take advantage of this and attack them at the same time. I would like to see how long the might of the Rathores can last. I will lead the attack from Marwar. Ask Shahzada Akbar and his faujdar Tahawwur Khan to be ready. Let the other shahzadas know that jehad has been called. We will attack Rajputana simultaneously.'

Unlike other days, the curtain did not fall signifying the end of the durbar. Aurangzeb decided to offer his prayers in the court in honour of the jehad declared against the Rajputs.

ᴔᴅᴇ ᴑᴇᴧ

The call for jehad saw action at an unprecedented level.

The activities, held up for a month due to incessant rains, began as soon as the monsoons receded. The royal forces streamed out of the fort with shouts of 'Din, din'. The soldiers numbered more than a hundred thousand. The elephants, with their slow march, were still exiting Delhi when the soldiers had reached the tenth mile.

The caravans consisted of the zenankhana, hundreds of elephants, a few thousand camels, and a hundred thousand bullock carts carrying rations and other items. The long chain of caravans stretched beyond the line of sight. The soldiers, excited by the call of jehad, now and then shouted 'Alamgir, Zinda Pir'.

Jahanara, old and weak with age, had decided to stay back though she would accompany them for a while. The waves of soldiers and the caravans laboured their way towards Ajmer.

As the Badshah passed the lanes and streets of Delhi, women threw back their veils revealing their faces, as they joyously showered flower petals in honour of the emperor who had taken up arms for the cause of Islam.

Aurangzeb turned to have a last look at the capital as his elephant crossed the borders. *Delhi! The symbol of Mughal power for generations! The city known for its beautiful buildings!* He was leaving the city to fulfil his final ambition in life.

For a moment Aurangzeb's emotions took charge of him. He took a longing look at the tall minarets of the Jama Masjid piercing the skies above. Then turning his back, he took a deep breath as he watched the armies of his loyal men surging ahead. The carts, carrying the heavy cannons, creaked as they lumbered on.

The jehad had finally begun.

They soon reached their evening camp. The cantonment had been set up at a rapid pace. The green flag of the Mughals fluttering atop a hundred-foot-tall pole and lit with lanterns was visible for miles around.

◦◦◦◦

They were to begin their march the next morning. After conferring with the commanders for a while, Aurangzeb came into the zenankhana where his sister Jahanara waited for him. She was to return to Delhi while her brother carried out the jehad he had chosen for himself.

Jahanara was about to stand up seeing Aurangzeb enter when he said, 'Begum Sahiba, you have followed protocol for years now. You are not getting any younger. You are excused from such rules henceforth.' Settling down beside her he continued, 'The Paigambar says we should start the journey by distributing alms. I want to begin by excusing you of any royal duties henceforth. You are free to do what comes to your mind. You are not bound by any official protocol or decorum starting now.'

Touching her right hand to her forehead, she acknowledged Aurangzeb's gift and said, 'Aurangzeb, I have seen you work at close quarters and oftentimes criticized your decisions too. I apologize for them. I hope Allah showers victory on you.'

'Begum Sahiba, my faith will lead me to victory. I will feel I have finished my task the day I am able to plant the Mughal flag on the shores of the ocean.'

Jahanara could not mask her displeasure. 'You are the Shahenshah of Hindustan and are free to do what comes to your mind. But I am concerned about your two shahzadis and your loving begum. They have never stayed in such harsh conditions of war.'

'Begum, Allah takes care of the poorest of the poor. What is there to worry?'

Jahanara could not hold back her tears. Aurangzeb said, 'Begum Sahiba, I get restless seeing tears in your eyes. I want you to bid farewell to your brother with a smiling face.'

'Aurangzeb, I cannot help it. I have spent all my life worrying about the family. I am concerned about Zebunissa and Zeenat.'

'Why?'

'Aurangzeb, now that you have excused me of any protocol, I can voice my innermost thoughts.'

'Begum Sahiba, please speak your mind. You are not only elder but also wiser than I am.'

'Aurangzeb, you talk of the religion of Islam but you seem to be forgetting the religion of man.'

'I believe there is nothing more superior than Islam.'

'Don't you realize your two daughters have spent their youth rotting in the close confines of the zenankhana?'

'Begum Sahiba!'

'Let me speak, Aurangzeb. I spent my entire life in the zenankhana. My sister Roshanara's life too withered likewise. I see the lavish lifestyles the begums enjoy but I wonder why it never occurs to you that you are committing a crime by not allowing your daughters to get married and enjoy a complete life.

'Begum Sahiba, where will I find a suitable alliance for my shahzadis?'

'Aurangzeb, a man can never find an answer if he choses to blindfold his eyes with ignorance.'

'I have never wavered from the path of Islam. I have been loyal to it.'

'Aurangzeb, you can't take only what suits you and not bother with things that are difficult. Tell me, did Muhammad Paigambar not get his daughters married? I wonder what stops you from doing so.'

'Begum Sahiba!'

'If my words disturb you, I will keep quiet. I want to tell you one thing though; you are making a huge mistake making your daughters spend their life in the zenankhana. You are also insulting the religion you base your life on.'

'What you say may be true but there are other considerations. If I interpret everything in Islam to my convenience I will fall into my own trap.'

'That is your problem, Aurangzeb. You do interpret it to your convenience. I don't want this farewell to end in bitterness. Forget what I said as an old, bitter woman's rant. I wish you well. This sister of yours would be waiting eagerly to hear the trumpets signalling your victory. I may not be able to rush out and welcome you or bless you, but my thoughts will always be with you. Aurangzeb, it is time for your namaz now. I take my leave. May Allah take care of you.'

Aurangzeb had no words. He kept looking at his sister and then murmured, 'Khuda hafeez.'

Jahanara left with silent footsteps.

⚬◎ ◎⚬

Emotions took a back seat once the jehad was announced. The next halt was at Ajmer near a lake adjacent to Khwaja Moinuddin's shrine. The month of Ramzan began but the rules of jehad being different, Aurangzeb could not afford to halt his activities and continued his daily briefings with Akbar reported each morning and evening.

Ajmer's faujdar Tahawwur Khan, familiar with the Rajputana territory, was given charge of the campaign against Jodhpur.

Within two months Tahawwur Khan reached Jodhpur defeating small principalities on the way. He captured Jodhpur without much resistance and destroyed many temples in search of the royal treasure. They soon reached Udaipur and ransacked the Lake Palace there. The looting of temples yielded unbelievable treasures.

The early victories gave a moral boost to the Mughal forces who firmly believed that they had the blessings of Moinuddin Chisti, the Sufi saint. Ajit Singh's mother, Jaswant Singh's wife, was the Udaipur maharaja's sister. The Mughal soldiers combed the entire territory, looking into all possible hiding places but were unable to find the young prince Ajit Singh or Durgadas Rathore, who was supposedly taking care of him. But the success in the campaign was overwhelming and the minor fact that the heir to Jaswant Singh's throne was untraceable was overlooked.

Aurangzeb deputed Akbar to camp at Chittor and asked to capture the maharaja at Udaipur. The capture of Rajputana would fulfil a dream unfulfilled since Shahenshah Akbar's time. Aurangzeb, in order to encourage Shahzada Akbar, stayed at his camp for a few days before returning to Ajmer.

Muazzam and Azam had responded to the call of jehad and had promised to proceed with their respective troops. Aurangzeb, having tasted early success, did not see their presence of much value.

Aurangzeb sat in conference with his key officials in a meeting room behind the shrine when Asad Khan arrived with an urgent message. Hearing the news Aurangzeb's face fell. He said, 'I am told Shiva Bhosale attacked Jalna and damaged the shrine of Jan Muhammad Dervish there. Allah will never pardon someone defiling the shrine of a pious man like Jan Muhammad. Shiva's son Sambha is with us now. We have Shiva's right hand. We need to teach him a lesson.'

Amin Khan responded, 'I am told Diler Khan has managed to convince Sambhaji to take up arms against his father. Luck seems to be favouring Badshah Salamat; we will soon see the Maharana of Mewar surrender and it won't be long before we attach Shiva's territory to our Deccan subah.'

'Amin Khan, I believe in ambition being backed by action. Ask Diler Khan to take Sambha's help to capture Shiva's forts. His strength is in his forts. The moment we have them, we can get him too.'

'As you command,' Amin Khan said, bending low.

Bahadur Khan, having returned from the Deccan red-faced with defeat, managed to restore royal favours by succeeding in the campaigns with Tahawwur Khan. On the other hand, the news from the Deccan was not good; Sambhaji had run away from Diler Khan's cantonment and rejoined his father. Jan Muhammad Dervish's curse had not worked. Aurangzeb, tasting defeat after a long time, spent time alone in the dargah reading his prayers.

༄෴ ෴

The entire monsoon was spent reinforcing the outposts in Marwar and Mewar. On getting news of the Maharana hiding in the Aravalli mountains, Aurangzeb asked Akbar to surround the hills. He had a contingent of twelve thousand Kazakh soldiers to help him.

The campaign resumed at the end of the rainy season. Except for a few scattered incidents the Rajputs were almost invisible. They would spring a surprise attack and then vanish into the mountains. Shahzada Akbar, camped in the Chittor Fort along with his zenankhana, directed the troops searching for the Maharana.

Finally, it seemed, Khwaja Moinnudin, having seen the devotion of his devotee, blessed Aurangzeb with good news.

Aurangzeb, though camping at Ajmer, had his sights trained on the Deccan all the time. He received the good news of Shivaji's untimely death. A major thorn has been finally removed. Aurangzeb attributed Shivaji's death to the curse of Jan Muhammad Dervish.

The victory of the jehad finally seemed within greachBut hope and despair were inseperable twins for him. He thus restrained himself to not get overjoyed.

Tahawwur Khan suffered a major defeat at the hands of the Rajputs who had managed to capture the Mughal cannons and other ammunition. The Rajputs continued to spring surprise attacks catching the Mughal soldiers off guard.

Aurangzeb received the news that Shahzada Akbar, afraid to get into a direct conflict, was hiding in Chittor Fort. All he did was issue orders from his safe confines and, not surprisingly, most of the orders were not followed. Aurangzeb was livid. He had not expected such behaviour from Akbar and sent him a strongly worded letter stating that he was ashamed to have sired such a pusillanimous son. The very next day Shahzada Akbar's zenankhana narrowly escaped an attack by the Rajputs thanks to the timely intervention of Tahawwur Khan and his thousand-odd soldiers.

The Rajputs, buoyed by their initial successes, were now emboldened and started attacking vigorously. The Mughal troops found themselves trapped in narrow valleys and fell easy prey to the charging Rajputs. The scenario changed rapidly. Sensing a major loss, Aurangzeb sent another severe message to Akbar and ordered him to get into the battle personally. He hoped such a threat would make Akbar get into real action.

Tahawwur Khan was given the task of capturing Durgadas Rathore and the Maharana of Udaipur without any delay.

⋘ ❦ ⋙

Cold winds blew relentlessly in the Rajasthan desert. Durgadas Rathore and his men continued their attack on the Mughal troops.

Aurangzeb received an urgent request for a meeting with Shahabuddin Khan, who had travelled more than sixty miles to meet him.

Despite the cold he was sweating and said, without preamble, as soon as he entered, 'Huzoor, there has been a great calamity.'

He paused for a moment before saying, 'Hazrat, I don't know how to put it; Shahzada Akbar has joined the Rajputs.'

Shahabuddin was curious to see Aurangzeb's reaction but all he could see was a calm face. Not getting any response from the Badshah, he continued, 'Hazrat, we never expected that. We were busy fighting when we received the message that he had defected to the enemy camp.'

'Is there anything else?'

'I dare not speak further, Huzoor.'

'Please. I am waiting.'

'Shahzada has declared himself the Badshah of Hindustan. He has sent a *firman* stating the removal of Ala Hazrat from the throne.'

Shahabuddin took out a crumpled piece of paper and handed it to Aurangzeb. He glanced at it for a brief moment and kept it on a desk nearby.

'Ala Hazrat, we need to take action against the Shahzada immediately. It seems he plans to attack the royal cantonment here.'

'You may leave now. I shall pronounce my judgement regarding Shahzada's actions in the durbar tomorrow.'

⋙⋘

The news of Akbar's revolt spread across the city of Ajmer the next day. Taking the help of four ulemas, who had interpreted the religious texts to Akbar's advantage and proclaimed Aurangzeb as having no right to the throne, Akbar had declared himself the emperor. A *shahi firman* in his name reached Asad Khan. *'You are not bound to carry out any commands on behalf of Aurangzeb. Akbar has removed Aurangzeb from the throne due to his unjust and oppressive policies. Tahawwur Khan has been named the new Wazir with the title of Amirul Umra. If you join Akbar's forces, you too will be treated with dignity.'*

For many of the old soldiers it was a repeat of what had happened nearly twenty-five years ago when Aurangzeb had claimed his stake to the throne defeating his brother.

The durbar was in full attendance that day. All the officials present in Ajmer were eager to hear Aurangzeb. They were shocked to hear that commanders like Tahawwur Khan, loyal to the throne, had defected. One of the officials in attendance, Inayat Khan, had married his daughter to Tahawwur Khan. He faced a barrage of questions for which he had no answers.

The murmurs subsided when Asad Khan entered the hall. He was followed by Amin Khan. The Badshah entered a few moments later. No one dared look up as his penetrating stare bore into the audience.

Asad Khan read out Akbar's message. Everyone eagerly waited to see Aurangzeb's reaction. Turning towards Fulad Khan he asked, 'How many troops do we have in the cantonment right now?'

Fulad Khan hesitantly answered, 'Nearly one thousand, Huzoor.'

Turning towards Asad Khan he asked, 'How many troops has Akbar managed to assemble?'

'I am told he has nearly twenty thousand Mughal troops.'

'And the Rajputs?'

'Nearly fifty thousand.'

The mention of such a large contingent supporting Akbar did not disconcert Aurangzeb. He continued to move the beads of his rosary as he asked, 'I wonder what is holding Akbar back from attacking Ajmer. We have a mere thousand people to protect us. The rest is the zenankhana and the maids and servants. He can easily capture us if he wishes to.'

Asad Khan licked his lips nervously. 'Huzoor, this won't happen. Allah will not allow the Shahzada to take the wrong path. I will not be surprised if he comes begging for your pardon.'

'I am surprised that you have learnt nothing after being in my company for so many years. The Badshah's first enemy is his Shahzada. I don't believe in false hopes. Send urgent messages to the other two Shahzadas to leave for Ajmer with their troops immediately.'

Asad Khan nodded. Fulad Khan said, 'Hazrat, it will take time for those two to reach. In the meanwhile, I will create a moat around the city within two days. I will place cannons at strategic points on the hills and ensure that all roads leading to Ajmer are guarded. Shahzada Akbar will not be able to attack without warning.'

'Fulad Khan, I am not one to sit protected in a guarded tower. I ascended the throne with a shamsher in my hands. I have picked up the sword again for jehad. It seems we will have to fight our own son instead of the enemy. So be it. We will march out tomorrow at first light. We will be the first to attack.'

'But Huzoor, we have such a small army,' Asad Khan said.

Raising his hand to interrupt Asad Khan, Aurangzeb said, 'If I have followed the path of Islam rightfully for the past many years, Allah will grant me the strength of fifty thousand soldiers. What else do we need when we have His support?'

Those in attendance shouted, 'Ameen, Ameen.'

◦৹৹ ৹৹৹

Inayat Khan, waiting outside the tent, was ushered in by the guards. The moment he entered, he fell at the feet of Aurangzeb crying.

'Huzoor, you may cut my head off if you wish. I am ashamed that my own son-in-law has committed this treachery.'

Aurangzeb asked, 'Is is true that Tahawwur Khan's begum and children are in town?'

'Yes, Jahanpanah. My daughter and her children are residing in my house.'

'Inayat Khan, listen to me carefully. Send a letter to Tahawwur Khan stating he should come and present himself in my court without any delay. If he does not do so, his daughter will be raped by the slaves in the town square and the children's legs and arms will be cut off.'

'Ji, Huzoor. I shall send the note immediately.'

Inayat Khan bent to salute and was about to leave when Aurangzeb added, 'And mind you! If you try any tricks, your begum and children will suffer the same fate. Carry out my instructions as I have told you to.'

৵৹ ৹৵

As planned, Aurangzeb left Ajmer the next morning with a thousand soldiers and a handful of sardars. Asad Khan was asked to look after the zenankhana and other administration.

The cannons were light and carried on camel back. Most of the troops and ammunition were with Akbar. Aurangzeb marching with a small contingent reached the same place where a couple of decades back he had encountered his elder brother Dara. History has a way of repeating itself. The spies informed him that Akbar stood just ten miles away with his troops waiting for his father.

The sixty-five-year-old Badshah stood in the battlefield, as rains lashed heavily. Astride his horse, he gave instructions to the men, patting one on the back, urging someone else in the name of Islam and calling out the sardars by their first names.

Aurangzeb received the encouraging news that Hamiduddin Khan was reaching soon with a contingent of sixteen thousand soldiers from Delhi while Muazzam, marching at rapid pace, was expected to reach by nightfall. Their combined strength was expected to reach forty thousand.

That evening, Tahawwur Khan presented himself in his tent. The guard announcing his arrival said, 'I asked him to hand over his sword and dagger to me before entering the tent but he shouted back saying he is not a criminal and refused to do so.'

Asad Khan warned Aurangzeb saying, 'Huzoor, he may have ill intentions. Do not allow him to enter armed.'

Aurangzeb, incensed at the audacious behaviour of Tahawwur Khan shouted, 'Let him enter if he dares to.'

The guard, seeing Aurangzeb throw his rosary away, unsheathed his sword in one swift motion. The next moment it landed on Tahawwur Khan's chest.

The sword clanged against Tahawwur Khan's armour but did not harm him. Realizing that he was under attack, he ran to save his life but tripped and fell at the tent's guy ropes. He was overpowered before he could get up. Blood-curdling screams pierced the night sky. The silence that followed was enough for those in the tent to know the outcome.

Inayat Khan bowed before Aurangzeb and said, 'I wish I had got the chance to punish my son-in-law for daring to revolt against you.'

Aurangzeb silently moved the beads of his rosary again.

'Shahenshah, some of the mansabdars from Akbar's camp are here to meet you. It seems Akbar is reconsidering his decision now.'

'It is good news but we should not forget the fact that we are in Rajputana and that Akbar has a huge force with him. I had appointed Durgadas with a lot of faith but he turned out to have kafir's blood in him. We have Muazzam's support and Hamiduddin Khan too is joining us shortly. We will decide the next course of action tomorrow. Muazzam will lead the attack.'

⊷⊶

The next morning the cantonment woke to find everything silent; there was no clarion call for action. Something unexpected had happened the previous night.

Akbar's camp in the far distance was sans any activity and soon the trumpets at Aurangzeb's cantonment announced victory. The soldiers, surprised at the turn of events, eventually came to know the details.

Apparently a letter sent by Aurangzeb to his Shahzada had been intercepted by the Rajputs. Durgadas Rathore, believing that the father and son were actually working together to trap the Rajputs, left the camp overnight without infoming Akbar. Most of Akbar's troops had already rejoined Aurangzeb's cantonment leaving Akbar with a handful of men.

Seeing his troops vanish before his own eyes, Akbar, fearing his life, fled to the mountains.

Aurangzeb's cantonment wore a festive look. He had managed victory without firing a single shot. His ploy of sending a fake letter so that it would be intercepted by the Rajputs before it reached Akbar had worked. Shahzada Muazzam was bestowed the honorific of Shah Aliza while Asad Khan got a larger mansab to manage. Gifts were distributed amongst the other officials. The court resounded with shouts of 'Alamgir! Zinda Pir!' as he sat on his throne. No one had a doubt that Allah was with the Shahenshah.

The four ulemas, who had advised Akbar to proclaim himself emperor were presented in court. Aurangzeb ordered them to be whipped in the public square. Each of them received a hundred lashes. Others, who were directly involved with the revolt, were thrown into dungeons or punished by having their limbs cut off.

Aurangzeb got the news that Akbar, in the meantime, had been hiding in the mountains moving from one place to another to prevent getting caught.

Nawab Bai was honoured, much to her happiness, because her son Muazzam had provided timely help to Aurangzeb. As soon as Nawab Bai left, Aurangzeb called for Shamim and said, 'Shahzadi Zebunissa played a key role in instigating Shahzada Akbar against me. She had sent a letter asking for Sambhaji's support. I am ordering her to be imprisoned in the Salimgarh Fort. All her privileges too are revoked from this instant.'

The next morning Aurangzeb spent time praying at the shrine of Khwaja Moinuddin. The cool air of the hall was pervaded with a pleasant smell from the incense sticks burning in one corner. Aurangzeb prayed to the saint: 'Ya Allah, Parwar Digaar! I left Delhi to fight against the kafirs but you made me declare a jehad against my own son. I will do whatever you make me do. The Shahzada has taken refuge with the Marathas. I will now have to march on to the Deccan to rout both the enemies together. I shall do whatever it takes to spread your word and to remove the darkness from people's minds. I pray that you give me the strength to carry out your work.'

Aurangzeb rested his forehead on the floor for a long time.

BOOK THREE

Aurangzeb's camp, set up on the flatland near Aurangabad, spread from the banks of River Seena to the base of the mountains. Tents, temporary cottages, shamianas, elephant and camel stables were spread over the wide expanse. The royal tent area, or the Gulalbar, distinguishing itself from other tents with the red tent clothing, was set up a little higher than the rest of the cantonment, at a gentle slope on the mountain side. The tents hosting the zenankhana stood adjacent. The royal insignia, atop a tall pole nearby, fluttered in the wind and was visible from far away. A lovely masjid was erected for the Badshah to offer his namaz.

Aurangzeb was informed of an urgent request from Zeenat Begum for a meeting. He waited in his tent for the Shahzadi to arrive. She seemed a little pale, and a careful observer could have noticed the fine ageing lines on her face. She was in her early forties now.

Zeenat stepped forward and kissing Aurangzeb's hand said, 'Abba Jaan, there is good news.'

'What is it, dear? I haven't heard single good news since I stepped into the Deccan. Please tell me.'

'Shahzada has sent a letter.'

'Who? That rogue Akbar?'

Zeenat's face fell hearing her father's harsh words. 'Abba Jaan, if you say such things about your son, what will the people say?'

'Dear, the people have already said what they had to. He showed his true character when he revolted against his father and joined hands with the kafirs. My keeping quiet will not change that.'

'Abba Jaan, he is young and immature.'

'Dear, at his age I was dreaming of managing the subah of the Deccan. I was working hard to earn it. But now, thanks to my wayward son, I am forced to get back into the ravines here at my advanced age.'

'Akbar is willing to come here to Aurangabad to meet you if you promise to pardon him.'

'Really?' Aurangzeb raised his eyebrows. 'Let me see the letter.'

Reading the letter he sighed deeply. 'Zeenat, you have spent your life in the zenankhana and are not familiar with the politics of the world outside. The letter reeks of a ploy. My sardars have trapped him and, in order to avoid arrest, he is now putting forth the proposal to surrender and ask for pardon.'

'It may be true but what is the harm in allowing him to meet you?'

'You don't understand politics. I have given strict instructions to capture him – dead or alive. If the sardars come to know of my correspondence with him, they would be demotivated.'

'Abba Jaan,' Zeenat said, her eyes wide with disbelief. 'I cannot imagine you could give such an order. You can't be that harsh on him!'

'He did not stop at his revolt. Knowing fully well of my hatred towards these Marathas, he has joined them and urges them to fight against me. My men have been toiling here for the past five or six years. At my age I should have been in the Jama Masjid offering my prayers but I am forced to sit here in the open, bearing these cold winds, in pursuit of a rogue Shahzada who has had the temerity to challenge his father. There is no crime which he has not committed.'

Zeenat made a last-ditch attempt saying, 'Abba Jaan, I urge you to have a large heart and pardon him just this time.'

'It is impossible. You may let him know that if he decides to come here with his hands tied I may meet him.'

'I will do as you say, Abba Jaan. I am pleased you are agreeing for this at least.' She added a little coyly, 'Abba Jaan, shahzada has sent two lovely Arabian steeds for you as gift. Would you like to see them?'

Aurangzeb was not happy at her request. Making a face he said, 'No, dear. I cannot accept any gift from Akbar now. Till he is brought here as a prisoner, I cannot even meet him.'

'Abba Jaan, how will he believe me if you don't accept his gift? He won't come here fearing the worst.'

'Let me tell you something; the day you are born to a Shahenshah you are to forget fear. The Shahenshah has to look after the crown and not trust his own sons. Dear, it is time for my namaz now. Akbar's father could not drill any sense into him. I hope his sister's efforts are not wasted.'

ഷൈ ഈ

Aurangzeb could not concentrate on his prayers that day. It had been happening more often these days. He returned to his private quarters instead of his durbar. The shoulders, of late, had drooped and more strands of grey flecked his beard. The skin on the back of the palm was loose and wrinkled.

He knelt on the carpet and opened the book of Quran but soon realized that his eyes had moved but he had not registered anything. His mind was elsewhere. He knew each line of the Quran by heart and would get emotional reading them. Aurangzeb realized the words were having no effect on him.

Sighing deeply, he picked up his rosary. The copy of the Quran which he held had been written by him in his own hand. On the borders he had repeated the words 'There is only one God and his representative is Paigambar. There is no one else who represents Him.' He read the words again to no effect. It had been five years since he had left Delhi to relocate to the Deccan. He sometimes wondered whether the officials sniggered at him behind his back.

He had been in the prime of his youth when Muhammad Sultan had revolted against him. He had developed a kind of cautious detachment since childhood. He had thus been able to see his death without getting affected.

'I left Delhi when the call for jehad was raised,' Aurangzeb mused. 'Jahanara Begum had tried to tell me something but I had not agreed. It was a bad omen to hear of Jahanara Begum's death the moment I left for the Deccan. Whatever said and done she was my sister. Did she have a premonition of her death? Who knows? I had great hopes of Akbar. He was a little immature but I had never expected him to revolt. I thought Azam was capable of it but not Akbar, but I was proven wrong. What was more shocking was to see the number of people who stood by Akbar. I had never imagined people like Bahadur Khan, my milk brother, to help him to escape from my clutches. He had managed to escape each thana by a whisker. It was all pre-planned, undoubtedly, and I was forced to cross the Narmada in his pursuit. That night when I stayed at Burhanpur, the explosion of the ammunition stored in the basement was not a mere accident. It was Allah's way of warning me. I reached Daulatabad, the city which reminds me of the days of romance in my youth. I am seventy now but I was in my thirties then. Hira's embrace was heaven to me. I stayed back in Daulatabad reminiscing the old days. I was in tears hearing from my khojas that the hillock on which I used to roam around freely with Hira is now called *Majnu ka tila*, the hill of the romantics. I personally went to check whether the lamp was being lit daily near Hira's grave and had fainted seeing the burning lamp. My loyal servants had carried me into my room without making a fuss and letting no one know about it. I was lucky to have been blessed by Sheikh Zainuddin when I had prayed at his shrine at Khuldabad. My khoja told me I was drenched in sweat, kneeling at the grave of the saint. I had a vision of Paigambar. He had pointed me to another grave, a vacant one. I could see myself lying there. I saw Hazrat Paigambar personally giving a helping hand in my burial. I was unconscious after that for nearly two days. I had managed to somehow not let my mansabdars know of this incident. I had left Daulatabad in a hurry after that. Now my destiny is being written by my own Shahzada. I will not stop till I see the Mughal flag fluttering on the shores of the ocean. My mansabdars are not loyal, my Shahzadas fight amongst each other and the zenankhana is not very happy with me. I can see all that but I am helpless. I have to walk the path of my duty as Allah does not permit me to stop working despite my old age.'

Aurangzeb opened his eyes and, caressing his face with his palms, got up and walked towards his durbar.

Seeing Anwar he said: 'Give the message to Zeenat that the

Arabian steeds sent by Akbar as a gift may be sent across to the dargah at Khuldabad. I shall give further instructions later.'

‌‌ಀಀ

The campaign in the south began with renewed vigour. Aurangzeb had transferred the old officials, used to a life of luxury, to faraway postings and had promoted new mansabdars in their place.

One day a piece of good news reached Aurangzeb. A few sardars, on whose strength Sambhaji was fighting against the Mughals, defected and joined Itikad Khan's camp. The sardars, Kanhoji Dakhani, Jagdevrao Dakhani, Arjoji and Acholji were presented before Aurangzeb.

The sardars saluted thrice as soon as they entered the durbar. Aurangzeb asked, looking at Jagdevrao, 'What is the main reason for you to leave Sambhaji?'

'Alampanah, we are tired of Sambhaji's style of functioning. He is ready to punish the slightest of mistakes. We tried our best to explain to him that our fight against the Mughal might was futile but he is adamant. We had no option but to leave him and take refuge under you.'

'*Waah!* If all the sardars think likewise, it won't be long before we capture the rest of the territory.'

Looking at Asad Khan he said, 'I am awarding each of these sardars a mansab of two thousand soldiers and a cash reward of five thousand rupiyas.'

The sardars received the honours, bowing, when Aurangzeb said, 'Please remember, if you try deceiving me, you will be in great trouble.'

Kanhoji Dakhani said, 'We are willing to swear with the water of the Ganga in our palms. We will take up whatever responsibility you give us.'

'Remember! Our aim is not to loot the enemy and run away into the mountains. If you are hoping to do that, you may as well return to your raja.'

Arjoji, caressing his luxuriant moustache replied, 'Shahenshah, Zille Subhani, we are willing to prove our loyalty. Tell us what we need to do for that. Once we have sworn in loyalty, we Marathas never waver in our duties.'

Aurangzeb was tempted to give a fitting reply but checked himself. He said, 'Your loyalties will be tested soon. I will consider you loyal if you produce Sambha here in chains.'

'*Beshak*! We will do our best.'

That night, in Aurangzeb's secret meeting chamber, Hamiduddin Khan presented another of Sambhaji's confidants. He was an old man, bent with age, wearing a Mughal-style turban and a loose-fitting overcoat and pyjamas. Hamiduddin Khan introduced him, 'He is Mullah Haider. He was Shiva Bhosale's principal advisor for all legal matters.'

'I don't understand. You are a Musalman yet you serve under the kafirs?'

'Huzoor, I intend to leave the Marathas now.'

'I am willing to hear you if you apologize for working under the kafirs.'

The kazi looked directly into Aurangzeb's eyes and said, 'Shahenshah, I worked under Shivaji Raja while he was alive. I never felt he was a kafir. But things have changed now. I am getting old and would like to spend the rest of my life in the service of Islam.'

'It is good to hear that you have chosen the right path in the last years of your life. I will give you a year's time; a probation of sorts. If I am convinced of your loyalty, we will see what we can do with you.'

Hamiduddin Khan added in the kazi's favour, 'Huzoor, he has great insights into the way the Marathas work. He also knows their territory like the back of his hand. He will be very useful in our campaign.'

'Hamiduddin Khan, I don't plan my campaigns based on support from enemy camps. But if you so strongly recommend him, I have a few questions for him.'

Sitting atop a high chair, he asked, 'My men have been scouting the ravines and the mountains for the past five years. Even the hard rains do not deter them. What then is the reason for not being able to get Sambha?'

The kazi looked at the floor and muttered incoherently. Aurangzeb asked again, 'Mullah Haider, I want a straight answer. This is a test; if you try to fool me, your dead body will leave this camp.'

The kazi was shaken to the core. He had not expected such a direct warning. He said, his voice sounding helpless, 'I will tell whatever I know.'

'Place your hand on the Quran before you speak.'

Placing his hand on the holy book the kazi said, 'Any amount of efforts will never get you Sambha.'

'Why? Is he a devil incarnate who cannot be seen or caught?'

'That is not the point. But as long as the Sultans of Bijapur and Golconda are there to support him with men and ammunition, you cannot touch him.'

'Many of his sardars have defected. I am told the ryots too are unhappy with his policies.'

'That may be true. But he took charge just a few years back. Shivaji Raja had created a strong team. I request you not to assess Sambha's strength based on the few sardars who have joined you. And about the ryots; the millions of Hindus here in this mountainous region consider Shivaji their god and are willing to pardon many of Sambha's sins.'

'I will give you a task to carry out. Will you do it?'

'Whatever you command, Huzoor.'

'I want you to correspond with all the Musalmans who are still loyal to Sambha. Get them on our side. Ask them to leave Sambha's camp and join us in the jehad.'

∾ର ଓଵ

Aurangzeb had received news of Nawab Bai's ill health but was unable to attend to it for nearly a week. When he finally visited her, she looked frail. Shahzada Muazzam stood on one side with his children while his two begums stood on the other.

Holding Nawab Bai's hand, Aurangzeb said, 'Begum, you look very ill.'

Nawab Bai did not answer; instead looked at Aurangzeb, her eyes filled with tears. A khoja got a low stool on which Aurangzeb sat and said, 'Begum, you take everything to heart. That is why you do not recover soon. You should feel good seeing your son, their begums and their children here.'

'Seeing them reminds me of my eldest son.'

Remembering Muhammad Sultan, Nawab Bai burst into sobs. Aurangzeb turned his face away unable to tolerate the emotional outburst. Aurangzeb had avoided meeting her because she always talked of Sultan. But he had no choice now. He said, 'Begum, it seems you don't wish to stay in the cantonment. If you wish I shall make arrangements to move you to Delhi.'

'Hazrat, please don't mind me speaking bluntly. I find that despite my presence here my Shahzada has not been given any special responsibilities. I worry what his fate will be if I were to move away.'

'Begum, your constant presence and pampering is not good for the Shahzada. I had sent him on a mission to Konkan but he returned empty-handed.'

'I am aware,' Nawab Bai said, weakly. 'You had sent Murad Khan along with him. His failings are being pinned on to my Shahzada.'

Aurangzeb glared at Muazzam who avoided his eyes. He said, 'Begum, he is my Shahzada too but what can I do if he does not follow orders diligently? Quite obviously, I get annoyed and it hurts you when I do so.'

'I was hoping you would believe in the loyalty shown by Muazzam when that Irani begum's Shahzada revolted against you.'

'Begum, I treat all my Shahzadas equally, whether he be from the Rajput begum or the Irani begum.'

'But Hazrat, isn't it a fact that the revolt was led by the Irani begum's son?'

'Have you forgotten the ill deeds of your eldest?'

'He did not revolt. It was your so-called confidant Mir Jumla who enticed him into it.'

When she said this no one spoke for a while; Muazzam fixed his gaze on the floor. Then he said, 'Abba Jaan, Begum Sahiba wants to request something.'

Aurangzeb's eyes bored into Nawab Bai and then turned back to Muazzam: 'I am waiting to hear what she has to say.'

Nawab Bai said, 'Hazrat, I am not sure how long I will live. I wish you to send my Shahzada on an independent campaign. I am sure he will fare well and come back with honours.'

Aurangzeb knew it was Muazzam speaking through his mother. It tired him to no end knowing that the zenankhana was a fertile ground for all kinds of gossip to flower. He said, 'I will see to it that the Shahzada gets an independent responsibility. If he wins, he will prove his right to take charge of the throne and if he loses ...'

Nawab Bai interrupted, 'He won't. I am sure of it.'

Aurangzeb found it difficult to look at Nawab Bai's sunken cheeks, dull eyes and pale skin.

⋙◍◍⋘

The news of Aurangzeb's visit to Nawab Bai's quarters reached Udaipuri. She was agitated hearing what had transpired there. After mulling over it for a couple of days, she went to meet Zeenat.

Seeing Udaipuri's long face Zeenat asked, 'Begum Sahiba, what's the matter?'

'I am told Ala Hazrat visited the Rajput begum recently. I know all her tricks,' Udaipuri said.

'Begum Sahiba, should you not be a little careful before using such harsh words?'

'Haven't you heard? She has managed to convince the Shahenshah to send her son on an independent campaign. I am told her Shahzada is going to prove his superiority in such a campaign and gain the Badshah's confidence.'

'Begum Sahiba, Abba Jaan loves each and everyone in the family. I am sure he will shower you with benefits at the appropriate time.'

'The time is now. He did not shift to the Deccan for pleasure. I am told he has discussed big plans in the durbar.'

'It is not good to spy on the discussions in the durbar.'

'If only your sister Zebunissa had her ears on the discussions in the durbar. She would not have suffered such a fate.'

Zeenat flinched at the memory of what had transpired with her sister.

'Shahzada Muazzam is being sent on a campaign but my Shahzada Kambaksh has not been given any important task yet. He continues to sit in Delhi,' Udaipuri continued.

'You should be happy. Isn't it good that Kambaksh is away from the battlefield?'

'Shahzadi, do you think I am naive? Muazzam and Azam, thanks to their campaigns, are in the news all the time and are known to all the sardars, whereas Kambaksh is becoming a non-entity.'

'But he was independently managing the subah of Delhi for a while.'

'I want you to request the Shahenshah to give Kambaksh an independent assignment. I am confident of his capabilities and supported by the right sardars, I am sure he will come out triumphant.'

Zeenat suppressed a smile: 'I will do as you say but may I suggest something? Instead of sending him on an independent mission he will learn a lot more if he were to go with my brother Azam. He will not only get the necessary experience but also earn my Abba Jaan's favours.'

'Go with Azam?' Udaipuri nearly screamed. 'I don't want to make that mistake. I don't want him to get ideas of revolt from Azam.'

Zeenat was hurt hearing Udaipuri, and tears gathered in her eyes. She said, 'I will do as you say Begum Sahiba but I request you not to hurt me further with such insinuations.'

৯৫ ৯৯

The cantonment at Ahmednagar, spread over nearly ten miles, was busy with preparations for the campaign. Temporary workshops were set up to mould cannons while traders from different countries came in to display their Arabian and Iranian horses. English and Dutch merchants showcased their guns and ammunition. Mir Atish, in charge of ammunition, tested the cannons. The cantonment buzzed with activity.

The Mughal Army was busy recruiting men from the hills who had a deep understanding of the mountain tracks and the forts in them. The Maratha sardars, who had recently defected to the Mughals, helped in these recruitments.

The idea of recruiting locals had been proposed by Ruhullah Khan and Asad Khan. Curious to assess these half-naked locals willing to enlist on a meagre salary, the Badshah expressed his desire to inspect the newly recruited troops personally.

The Maratha sardars, along with their new recruits, stood for inspection a few miles from the royal tent. Seeing the Badshah arrive, the dark-skinned locals threw their spears and swords on the ground and saluted him. There were nearly two thousand in number. After the inspection, the Badshah returning to his tent asked Ruhullah Khan, 'I hope these new recruits are willing to work with complete loyalty?'

Jagdevrao, hearing Aurangzeb, stepped forward. 'Ala Hazrat need not worry. These Deccani soldiers are known for their loyalty.'

'Are you taking complete onus?'

'Ji, Huzoor.'

'It is fine then.' Turning towards his commander he said, 'You may start their daily wages from today. But warn them – the slightest doubt about their loyalty, and heads will roll.'

On his return to the Gulalbar tent, Aurangzeb stopped to inspect the cannons and other ammunition. He turned his horse towards the local kotwali responsible for general law and order. The men, seeing the Badshah come in unannounced, rushed to receive him.

'Huzoor, we have captured a few men from Pedgaon. We will present them in the durbar tomorrow morning.'

'Tell me the details right away. I don't believe in postponing things.'

'Bahadur Khan's troops encountered a few enemy soldiers as they were crossing the river. After a brief skirmish, in which our people killed a few of them, the rest surrendered. There are around a hundred of them, currently being held captive in our makeshift prison here.'

'Were they carrying any important documents?'

'We found a letter written in the Hindavi script. I have translated it into Farsi for your perusal.'

'Get the letter to my camp after the evening prayers. I will discuss then.'

Asad Khan and the kotwal reached Aurangzeb's tent that evening. The letter was from Golconda's Badshah to Sambhaji. To support Sikandar Adil Shah's fight against the Mughals, the Golconda Badshah Abdul Hasan was willing to send twenty thousand of his men as well as extend all the monetary support needed. The Goldonda Badshah, through his letter, urged Sambhaji to support Bijapur. The letter also mentioned that the Mughals were a common enemy and Aurangzeb was cunning enough to decimate each of them separately if they did not stick together.

Aurangzeb was lost in thought for a while. Then he issued his order: 'Ask Bahadur Khan to take these captured men back to Pedgaon. Behead them and hang their heads at the entrance of the nearby villages. Warn the public that anyone opposing the Mughals will be considered an enemy and meet the same fate. If they do not follow the orders their villages will be burnt down. Ask Bahadur Khan to implement this within the next two weeks.'

The kotwal left immediately. Aurangzeb turned towards Asad Khan saying, 'It seems Sambha is being guided by Shahzada Akbar. Mullah Haider's advice was right; we cannot do anything to Akbar as long as Sambha has the support of the Badshahs of Golconda and Bijapur.'

Asad Khan nodded in agreement. It was late evening when the meeting was over.

᪥᪤᪥

Zeenat got the opportunity she had been waiting for. Thursday mornings were assigned by the Badshah for resolving problems at the zenankhana. Shamim, responsible for the daily activities, was just finishing up with the Badshah when Zeenat walked in and said 'Takhliya'. She wanted complete privacy.

Shamim walked away leaving them alone.

'What is it, dear?'

'Abba Jaan, I am told you have given specific tasks to Shahzada Muazzam and Azam.'

'That is true. After all, how long can I manage alone? I am getting old; it is time they bore most of the responsibilities.'

'Abba Jaan, you haven't given any independent task to Kambaksh yet. Why so?'

Aurangzeb sat up straight on hearing Kambaksh's name. He looked at Zeenat, who knelt beside him, her head bent low. Glancing at the guards standing out of earshot he said, 'It seems the Begum Sahiba has complained to you.'

Zeenat, quick to deny this, said, '*Tauba, tauba!*'

'Dear, I have spent my whole life reading people's minds. Anyway, it is up to you to shield her. What were you saying about Kambaksh?'

'Abba Jaan, Kambaksh is now an adult. He is a married man and I feel he should be given a chance to go on an independent campaign and prove his merit.'

'And also ensure that he is in the fray were there to be a fight for the throne, isn't it?'

Zeenat glanced up to look at Aurangzeb in surprise. Looking down again she said, 'I just voiced my thoughts, but if Abba Jaan wants to interpret things differently, I will not speak further.'

'Can you elaborate?'

'You keep one Shahzada close to your chest while you push the other one away; and the third one is sent on a campaign far beyond his capabilities.'

'Zeenat dear, it seems you won't be satisfied unless I speak my mind. I cannot forget the fact that the biggest enemy of the emperor are his own sons, but I am unable to fathom the deep affection and love I have for Udaipuri begum and her son Kambaksh. I can send my other sons on any assignment without hesitation but I feel uncomfortable putting Kambaksh's life at any risk. I know I need to make him tough but I cannot live without seeing his face now and then. I was told men have a special soft corner for children born in their later ages but I never expected such a strong emotional connect as I have with Kambaksh.'

'Abba Jaan, should I assume you love us less?'

'Dear, I spoke from my heart. I don't think you should interpret it literally. One has to be a father to understand what it takes to run a huge empire like this at an old age, when the body is growing weak each day.'

Zeenat could not believe her ears. She remembered the stories told by the maids about her father's debaucheries in Hira Bai's palace. This was the first time her father had opened his heart to her.

'Dear, I know you have proposed this on behalf of my begum. Let her rest assured I will be assigning an important task to Kambaksh at an appropriate time. I would have appreciated had my begum spoken herself. But then, I cannot read everyone's minds, can I?'

Zeenat was happy to hear her father's words. Touching her palm to her forehead she was about to get up when Aurangzeb continued, 'Zeenat, I have seen you making requests on behalf of others. You are the only one who has never asked anything for your own sake. Don't you have anything to ask for?'

Zeenat continued looking down at the carpet. 'Abba Jaan, what is the point in asking for something I won't get?'

'Zeenat, I don't understand. What is it that you asked for and I refused?'

'Abba Jaan ….'

'Don't hesitate, dear. I won't force you though. If I can fulfil your wish I will do so!'

Zeenat had tears in her eyes. She turned her head avoiding her father's gaze and said, 'What is the point in asking for it now? When the fruit was ripe, it was a pleasure to see the admirers. Now that the fruit has fallen down, there is no fun any more. I have nothing to ask.'

Aurangzeb knew what Zeenat was referring to. He said, his voice low and almost apologetic, 'Dear, you don't ask for anything despite my persuasion. You speak in riddles. I will give you something; I hope you don't refuse.'

'Abba Jaan, I consider whatever you give as a gift from Allah himself. How can I refuse?'

'Spoken like my daughter! I am nominating you the head of the zenankhana from today.'

'Abba Jaan, what about Begum Sahiba?'

'Leave that to me. I need someone I can trust to manage the zenankhana. I was not worried when Jahanara was alive. Now you must take on the job. I will not be interfering in any matters whatsoever. No one can question your decisions. You have complete authority over all the things here. Does that make you happy?'

Forcing a smile, Zeenat said, 'Yes, Abba Jaan. I am very happy.'

જી જી

For nearly two months messages were exchanged back and forth between Aurangzeb and the Badshahs of Bijapur and Golconda. The Mughals had asked for permission to march across Bijapur territory to attack the Marathas. Not only did the Bijapurkars refuse permission, they demanded a refund of the annual levies paid earlier to the Mughals. It was clear that the Bijapur Badshah Sikandar Adil Shah had been emboldened by support from elsewhere.

Aurangzeb issued immediate orders to capture some of the strategic outposts under the Bijapur territory. He instructed Shahzada Azam to attack and capture the capital city of Bijapur. The monsoons were about to begin but Aurangzeb did not want to waste any time and sent an urgent message for Azam. The Mughal troops, camped on the bank of the River Bheema near Pedgaon, moved into the Bijapur territory.

Azam, despite a direct order from Aurangzeb, was dilly-dallying. Aurangzeb, after waiting for a week, instructed Asad Khan, 'I want Azam to march forward within a fortnight. Ensure that foodgrains and ammunition are sent across towards Solapur. Let Azam know that I have asked his zenankhana to be shifted to the cantonment here.'

Asad Khan was in a quandary. It was a Mughal tradition to allow respective Shahzadas to look into their personal matters. Thinking that Aurangzeb may have overlooked this aspect he suggested, 'Hazrat Salamat, would it not be advisable to let matters be decided by the Shahzada himself?'

'That was the case till now. But henceforth I intend to take charge of these matters too. Asad Khan, had you advised me to ask Shahzada Akbar to leave his zenankhana behind in Ajmer then, we would not have been spending our old age in this mountainous terrain of the Deccan today.'

'Huzoor, I had not expected Shahzada Akbar to do what he did even in my wildest dreams.'

'The occupant of the throne has to assume that each and every person is out there to attack him. I made a mistake at Ajmer and I don't want to repeat it.'

'I shall convey your message to Shahzada Azam but I feel we need not distrust him.'

Aurangzeb's gaze bore through Asad Khan. He had worked as a commander-in-chief and prime minister in his durbar. Aurangzeb knew that Asad Khan was one of his closest confidants. His words surprised him. He said, 'Your job is to be on the alert at all times. I agree, Shahzada Azam may not be like Akbar. But you must not forget that one of his begums is Dara Shikoh's daughter. It may have been years since Dara Shikoh lost his life but I cannot believe that his daughter would have forgiven me completely. To top it all, his second begum is Sikandar Adil Shah's sister. Asad Khan, tell me, is it wise to allow the zenankhana to accompany the Shahzada? Don't you think expecting a revolt is quite natural?'

Asad Khan was Aurangzeb's aunt's husband. He genuinely believed Aurangzeb was over reacting and that the mistrust was not justified. He said, 'You have to trust the Shahzada if you want him to succeed.'

'Asad Khan, do you think I am going to rest in peace after entrusting Shahzada with the responsibility? I plan to monitor the activities and movements of each of the sardars. If need be, I will personally march across to the city of Bijapur.'

ඦඬ ඬඦ

It was less than a month ago that Azam, travelling across Dharwad, Gokak and Koppal along with nearly forty thousand troops, had learnt of the advance party led by Ruhullah Khan and Kasim Khan having reached the borders of Bijapur city. Aurangzeb had not expected his men to reach the city without resistance. The city seemed within grasp now.

But things were not as favourable as they seemed. Aurangzeb received news that Azam and his men, progressing rapidly into the Bijapur territory, were attacked fiercely near the banks of the Tungabhadra by Bijapur's Sardar Sarja Khan. His target was to intercept carriages carrying foodgrains. Ruhullah Khan and Kasim Khan, on the verge of taking over the city, were asked by the shahzada to hold their attack.

Aurangzeb, hearing the report presented by Asad Khan, asked, 'What's the reason for shahzada to give such orders?'

'Shahzada wanted to capture the city himself and prove that he is more capable than Shahzada Muazzam.'

'His childish acts are a deterrent to the campaign's ultimate aim. Does he think Sarja Khan and other sardars will keep quiet while he moves his troops from Tungabhadra towards Bijapur?'

Aurangzeb was impatient and unhappy with the delays. He said, 'I don't like to sit here and make plans on paper. I have not come here to the Deccan to spend the rest of my life. We need to teach the Bijapurkars a lesson before we attack the Marathas. Shahzada Azam's casual attitude has cost us a lot. I cannot be sitting here far away in Ahmednagar. I think we need to move the cantonment near Solapur, closer to Bijapur. That way I can keep an eye on both sides.'

'Hazrat, if the Marathas come to know that we have camped at Solapur, Sambhaji will be encouraged to provide all the necessary help to Akbar. Right now Akbar knows we are in a position of strength. The moment we move out of Ahmednagar, the Marathas will intensify their efforts.'

'I have seen to it that Akbar will not do anything of that sort.'

'Huzoor, Shahzada Akbar is camping in the Konkan region with the hopes of getting Sambhaji's help. He knows our presence here in Ahmednagar prevents him from moving up north. The moment we move, it will be a clear path for him.'

'Asad Khan, my son is a novice when it comes to politics. He revolted against me in a fit of emotion. Very soon he realized he has no support anywhere. I am told he is surviving in a village in the mountainous terrain of Konkan in an ordinary hut with just a hundred odd men provided by that treacherous Durgadas.'

'Hazrat, what surprises me is that the Shahzada has not admitted his guilt and has not presented himself here in your cantonment. He is still hoping to get a chance to attack you with Sambha's help.'

'Asad Khan, my spies are not sitting idle. They have managed to put the thought in Sambha's mind that Shahzada Akbar and Durgadas have been sent by us to actually capture Sambha. Hence, Sambha is never going to give him any help, nor will he allow Akbar to leave the territory. Akbar has dug his own grave. He thought he can declare himself a king having captured a mere two or three forts. We will move our camp to Solapur. We shall tackle the enemy in our own manner. Just wait and see, the kind of things you will witness in the Deccan.'

'I am sure nothing is impossible for Hazrat once he makes up his mind. We can tackle the Marathas once we take care of Bijapur.'

'That is precisely my plan. Send an advance party right away and send messages to all the subahs across Hindustan that we are shifting base to Solapur.'

The cantonment stayed at Solapur through the rainy season. The vast expanse of the cantonment, spread across a wide flat plain, could be seen from miles away. The royal Gulalbar, hosting the emperor and his zenankhana, resembled palaces from afar and were no less in comforts for the facilities they provided.

The rains that year had been scanty while the fields had been barren for nearly four years. The ryots had run away. The movement of the troops across the territory had had its toll on the common man. It was now threatening the existence of the cantonment itself as foodgrains and essential supplies were critical for a long-term stay. Aurangzeb deputed Firoz Jung to arrange for the supplies, and soon, thousands of bullock carts, laden with grains, cereals and other supplies landed at Shahzada Azam's cantonment. The troops had renewed confidence in their efforts now.

The Badshah of Golconda had sent a huge force under the command of Ambaji Pandit in support of the Bijapur Badshah while Sambhaji had sent ten thousand of his men led by Hambir Rao.

Aurangzeb got into action immediately and despatched Kasim Khan to intercept Hambir Rao while Shahzada Muazzam was given the task of confronting Ambaji Pandit. This had led to a significant reduction in the forces engaged in the attack on Bijapur, but Aurangzeb was not worried. His trusted men were busy with their work inside Adil Shah's palace.

One afternoon, when Aurangzeb had just returned from his prayers, ten ulemas from Bijapur, representing Adil Shah, came into Aurangzeb's cantonment. They waited patiently while Aurangzeb, his eyes closed in meditation, finished his prayers. Opening his eyes after a while and putting his rosary aside he asked, 'I wonder why your Lord has remembered me today?' The sarcasm was evident.

One of the ulemas said, 'Shahenshah, you are a true follower of Islam and it is thanks to your efforts that Islam can raise its head proudly across the world.'

'If you have come all the way to say this, please inform your Lord, who calls himself Badshah, that we don't have time for such useless prattle.'

'Alampanah, we mean it. It was a red-letter day for Islam when Shahenshah Ghazi Alamgir Badshah took charge of the throne at Delhi.'

'I wonder what the ulemas are waiting for. Why don't you advise Sikandar Adil Shah wisely?'

'We have come with a request from him.'

'Oh, it seems wisdom has dawned on you. Anyway, please state your request.'

'Shahenshah had come to the Deccan with the intent to rout the Marathas. But you have focused your energies on Bijapur. Our Badshah is deeply hurt because of that. He is a believer of Islam too and he never expected his elder brother to have ambitions to annex his territories. He is unable to understand the reason.'

'Is that so? I knew that Sikandar Adil Shah is young, but I wonder if his advisors like Sarja Khan and wise ulemas like you are able to understand that.'

'We are not able to follow you, Shahenshah.'

'Let me make it clear: you ulemas are responsible for interpreting the word of Islam. You are aware that we have been putting all our efforts for the past five years to take over the Marathas but never has Sikandar Adil Shah come forward to offer his help. Now, with the noose around his neck, you remember Islam and come here to remind me of brotherhood? You must be naive to imagine that such words can fool me.'

'Ala Hazrat, but we are brothers by religion!'

'I think the jolts you have received are not enough to wake you up yet. You did not even allow our troops to pass through your territory. On top of it, you gave your discreet support to Sambha. Shiva was a mere sardar in your territory but he managed to raise a large kingdom under your very nose. You have the nerve to come and propose brotherhood and talk of Islam? Tell your Sikandar that Ghazi Aurangzeb has come into the Deccan to teach everyone what real Islam is. Tell him, Aurangzeb intends to march into Bijapur and teach him how to read the Quran and how to manage a territory under the sharia laws.'

'Shahenshah Aurangzeb has been misinformed. We have never supported the Marathas.'

'I would be the happiest if that were true. I would have believed you too. But you forget that I have known you since I was a Shahzada here many years back. And I have been running this campaign for the past five years now. It does not require much intelligence to know who is supporting the Marathas.'

'If I may ask ... what proof does the Shahenshah have for his allegations?'

'I need not go as far back as Shiva. Do you notice who has come forward to help you? It is the kafirs Ambaji Pandit from Golconda and Hambir Rao from the Marathas. If Adil Shah were to be a true Musalman, the Sultan of Golconda would have rushed personally to help. Not a single Musalman sardar came forward. The kafirs know that the moment we capture your territory, they would be the next to be swallowed by the Mughal Army.'

The ulemas knew they had no defence. They were in a bind. They had left Bijapur confident that they would be able to convince Aurangzeb by appealing to his faith in Islam. One of the elderly ulemas, who had been listening to the conversation with rapt attention, stepped forward. 'Shahenshah, people like Sambha do not deserve the attention you are giving them. You have taken the trouble to come all the way from Delhi. Instead, had you given an indication to our Badshah, we would have shown him his place. Sambha, his father Shiva; they are mere mountain rats. Shahenshah need not worry about them.'

The false praise was more than what Aurangzeb could tolerate. He was livid : 'You call them mountain rats? The rat called Sambha has the temerity to loot Surat and Burhanpur and destroy mosques in the wake. Complaints have reached Delhi that our people cannot pray as many mosques have been forced to close down. We had sent umpteen messages to you but you chose to ignore them. All you did was find ways to enjoy luxuries in the name of Islam. You never bothered if Sambha was nibbling away at your territories. I had no choice but to pick up my sword to protect the mosques in the Deccan.'

'I request you to have a little patience. Entrust us the job and we shall do it,' the ulema persisted.

'Tell Sikandar Adil Shah that I don't have the patience now. I have taken up the task under orders from Allah. I shall not rest till the flag of Islam flutters across the Deccan. If Sikandar Adil Shah is keen to help us, let him come walking into our camp and I shall explain to him his duties. You may leave now.'

The ulemas, having come with a lot of hope, were forced to return dejected.

⚬⚬ 𝇍 ⚬⚬

Months passed by. Aurangzeb continued his supervision over the Deccan with an eagle eye. Qutub Khan, forced to vacate Hyderabad under pressure from Shahzada Muazzam, had taken shelter in the Golconda fort. The Bijapurkars were unlikely to receive any support from that front. But another disturbing news reached Aurangzeb's camp. A large contingent of the Marathas had managed to reach Bijapur city. They had been personally welcomed by Adil Shah. Aurangzeb had had enough of sending *firmans* from his durbar. He decided to get into the action himself. That evening he announced, 'I suspect our mansabdars and Shahzada are not doing their best and I need to step in. Let me see how long Sikandar Adil Shah can last.'

Within a fortnight Aurangzeb's huge army camped at Rasoolpur, a couple of miles before Bijapur. Azam and his men were given the task of attacking one part of the fort where Adil Shah's famous Malik-e-Maidan cannon was hosted. The attacks continued unabated.

Aurangzeb took a round of the city the moment his camp was set up. His keen eyes spotted two weak areas of the fortified city and ordered his men to start firing cannons there. The city was protected by a wide and deep moat all around and filled with water, making a full-scale attack impossible. Aurangzeb ordered his men to fill the moat with mud.

Shahzada Azam was worried that he may be reprimanded for not having taken any concrete action till then. Aurangzeb called for Shahzada Muazzam to confer when Azam said, 'Ala Hazrat, it is quite a daunting task to fill the moat completely. And it will involve thousands of men.'

Muazzam seized the moment saying, 'If Shahenshah entrusts me, I shall see that the task is done to satisfaction.'

'*Shabbash!*' Aurangzeb said, getting a chance to divide the task between the two. 'Muazzam will look at the moat while Azam will focus all energies on bombarding the Landa Kasab tower and the Mangal Darwaza which we have identified as weak points.'

Within a week Muazzam, as promised, filled the moat and the troops were ready to climb the fort walls. But a shower of bullets and arrows prevented them each time they tried. In the process they were losing a lot of men. The only way they could climb was with the support of accurate shelling of the cannons on to the ramparts of the fort.

Aurangzeb moved from Rasoolpur and camped himself a mere two hundred yards from where the action was. This was a tremendous boost of morale to the Mughal forces. The soldiers created a tunnel right up to the base of the fort. Aurangzeb personally inspected the same at night and then ordered the explosives to be placed appropriately. The shelling of the cannons, the continuous attack of the foot soldiers and the vice-like grip on the moat was taking a toll on the soldiers inside the fort. They were fighting a losing battle and each day their strength was depleting.

Aurangzeb' presence, a morale booster to the Mughal troops, sent shivers down Adil Shah's soldiers. At the same time Aurangzeb had deployed his men in the city to send appropriate messages to Adil Shah.

The Bijapur residents were fully aware that the Mughal forces, who had been camping for nearly a year, would be most difficult to contain once they breached the walls of the fort. They would not stop from looting, burning and destroying everything in their wake, not to talk of the threat to the ladies. The message was clear: if you want to protect whatever is left, put up a flag of friendship on the Landa Kasab tower and the Mughal forces would stop shelling. The sardars were told that they had one last chance to surrender and save their lives.

The sardars realized they had no choice. Aurangzeb's mighty Mughal Army would crush them in no time. It was suicidal to think of repulsing the Mughal attack.

It was a Friday, when Aurangzeb having returned from his namaz, got the message of Adil Shah's intention to surrender; and that too without any preconditions! Adil Shah had sent a message that the doors to the fort would open in another two days and he would walk down to Aurangzeb's camp.

The task had been finally achieved. That evening Aurangzeb prayed for a long time thanking Allah for the turn of events.

✦✦✦

The cantonment at Rasoolpur was especially decorated to receive the Badshah of Bijapur. Aurangzeb's Gulalbar camp, the green Mughal flag atop fluttering in the mild wind, was ready to receive the royal prisoner. The excitement was palpable across the camp. It had been an ambition since Emperor Akbar's time to annex the territory of Bijapur but had eluded the Mughals each time. The mansabdars were eager to see Aurangzeb's prized catch.

Aurangzeb deputed Rao Dalpat Bundela to escort Adil Shah to the camp. It was a deliberate message to all the Mughal mansabdars: if you try to extend your help to the kafirs, you will be treated like dirt.

Dalpat Bundela entered Adil Shah's palace. Adil Shah, seeing a mere low-ranking sardar sent as his escort, was unable to hide his disappointment. He turned in the direction of his sardars but they continued to look down. Adil Shah could hear the sobs emitting from behind the vetiver screens. It was time for him to go. He closed his eyes for a moment and then, head bent low, nodded once accepting the *firman* sent by Aurangzeb.

The amaldars stood up as Adil Shah walked down towards the door. Refusing the palanquin, he walked towards Aurangzeb's camp. The teary-eyed residents of Bijapur had gathered on the streets. Their Badshah, whom they could not dare to look into the eyes, was walking down the streets as a mere prisoner.

The durbar hall was full as the crowd waited eagerly to see Adil Shah. As soon as the group reached the entrance, Mir Bakshi Ruhullah Khan and other seniors came to receive him.

Adil Shah bent down thrice in an elaborate salute. He stood up and touched his hand to the forehead in salaam once more. Bending down he touched Aurangzeb's long overflowing coat and kissed the egde. He then stood up, his spine straight. The young Badshah, in his royal clothes and sporting the royal insignia on his turban, was an impressive sight. Asad Khan quickly wiped off his tears which had gathered at the edge of his eyes.

Wazir Asad Khan announced, reiterating for effect and for the benefit of those present, 'Bijapur's Sikandar Adil Shah has surrendered himself to Hindustan's Shahenshah Ghazi Alamgir Badshah and has handed over his territory completely.'

In response Aurangzeb raised his right hand, acknowledging the announcement. He smiled at the young Badshah and said, in a low voice which was audible only to those in the front rows, 'You have acted wisely and Allah will be merciful. You may rest assured that we will continue to show our mercy.'

On cue, Asad Khan escorted the young Badshah to take a seat next to Aurangzeb's grandson Muizuddin, who sat near Aurangzeb's dais. Sikandar Adil Shah was handed over the royal clothes as a sign of his welcome. Asad Khan helped him to remove his erstwhile insignia and replaced it with the Mughal kimosh, the prestigious cap worn by the Mughals.

Sikandar's new title, that of Umrao, was announced in the durbar and he was granted a salary of one lakh rupiyas each year. The Bijapur sardars were incorporated into the Mughal army at appropriate levels, who reciprocated with lavish gifts to Aurangzeb.

It was the end of Adil Shah's rule. His turban, and the gems glittering in it, remained unnoticed as it lay in a tray on the side.

⚬ঙ ঙ⚬

After a gap of two days, Aurangzeb, sitting in an open carriage, decided to take a round of Bijapur. The booming cannons had already announced his arrival. The crowds, who had heard of the Shahenshah of Hindustan, had gathered out of curiosity to see him in person, while the Mughal soldiers did their best to clear the path as Aurangzeb's carriage moved forward slowly.

It was a near-cloudless sky, the rains having ended a few weeks back. Aurangzeb dipped his hand into the trays of gold and silver coins carried by the slaves as they walked alongside the carriage and shower them on to the onlookers. After an inspection of the fort, the procession moved towards Jama Masjid, where a crowd of fakirs and dervishes had gathered. Receiving a shower of coins, the fakirs blessed Aurangzeb as he walked up the stairs of the mosque. That evening, he prayed and thanked Allah for the victory.

After the prayers at Jama Masjid, Aurangzeb visited Adil Shah's durbar and sat on his throne for a while, when he was honoured and presented with gifts by the mansabdars and local businessmen.

Aurangzeb visited the palace and was curious to see a wall in one of the halls painted with various scenes from the Mahabharata, showing Krishna playing with the gopis. He asked Danishmand Khan, 'What do you make of these?'

'Now I know why Sikandar lost.' Danishmand said, smiling.

A particular painting attracted Aurangzeb's attention. The gopis were shown standing nude in the water, while their clothes hung on a tree nearby. Krishna, playing his flute, stood nearby enjoying the helplessness of the women as they cajoled him to return their clothes. Aurangzeb said, 'Danishmand, you read my thoughts correctly. These paintings tell me the extent to which Sikandar Adil Shah was attached to the kafirs. One does not need an astrologer to predict that being in company of kafirs would lead you to hell.'

'Shahenshah, I was alluding to something else.'

Aurangzeb looked at Danishmand Khan for him to continue. 'I was suggesting that it was not surprising for Sikandar Adil Shah to lose if he too was indulging in such sports.'

Aurangzeb did not agree with Danishmand Khan's interpretation. Showing his disagreement he said, 'It is the audacity and arrogance of a man to think he can recreate the world by painting such scenes. We need to bow down before Allah.'

'Shahenshah, but aren't there paintings of all the Mughal emperors in the Red Fort?'

'They are as per Islam's rules. There is no restriction on creating portraits as per Islamic law. It is the other paintings which I am against.'

Ruhullah Khan stood nearby. Aurangzeb, turning to him, said, 'Get your men to scrub the walls clean and then paint them afresh. I want verses from the Quran to be painted on these walls. I suggest we convert this palace into a school which will teach Quran to children.'

Aurangzeb stepped out of the palace to inspect the famed Malik-e-Maidan cannon. It was a magnificient cannon, long and impressive. Aurangzeb commented, 'If one could win wars with cannons alone, my head of ammunition would have been the commander. Carve out the message of our victory on the cannon. Let the generations later know that no power can stand in the way of Ghazi Alamgir Badshah's victory.'

৵৹৫ ৯৹৶

It was time for the camp to move from Bijapur and return to Solapur. Sikandar's accommodation had been made in a special tent in the Gulalbar area.

Golconda's Badshah Abul Hasan Qutub Khan had sent his emissary to meet Aurangzeb. Guilty of not having paid their yearly dues for many years in a row, the Badshah of Golconda had sent a plea not to disturb the peace in his territory and had promised to pay the arrears.

Aurangzeb, irritated at the request, raised his eyebrows enquiringly. 'I am aware of the arrogance with which your Badshah has avoided paying the dues. Now, seeing the way the Bijapur sultan has been defeated, it seems your Badshah is extending a hand of reconciliation.'

'Huzoor-e-Ala,' the emissary tried, his head bent low. 'The only crime we have committed is having delayed the payment. We request you to show some laxity.'

'Do you think the Shahenshah has come all the way from Delhi to collect the dues? I can as well entrust the task on to any of my Shahzadas.'

'Our Badshah is unable to fathom your anger towards him. What crime has he committed?'

'You have seen the fate of the Bijapur Badshah for having supported Sambha. Qutub Khan has committed a crime of far bigger proportions. I am told he received Shiva Bhosale in court and honoured him.'

'Shiva Bhosale is Adil Shah's zamindar. It was our duty to honour him when he came visiting.'

'Please tell your sultan that I am not a child who can be told such tales. If your sultan is afraid of such kafirs it might be better that I take charge of his territory at the earliest. I am told that Qutub Khan had honoured Shiva adorning his horse with a necklace of pearls. If these are the kind of acts he indulges in, we will have to intervene immediately.'

Aurangzeb's voice boomed again. 'I believe he has nominated two Brahmin diwans to supervise the affairs of the state. All they do is get drunk and spend time in the company of nautch girls. I cannot tolerate such debauchery.'

'I believe there is some misunderstanding, Ala Hazrat.'

'I am tired of your lies and lame excuses. It is a known fact that Qutub Khan spends all his time fiddling with the sarangi while more than twenty thousand concubines are doing roaring business in the city of Hyderabad. Hundreds of barrels of wine are being consumed each day. If this is his idea of running his sultanate let him know that we have a tent for him ready in the Gulalbar and that he can give company to Sikandar Adil Shah for the rest of his life.'

The emissary had no words. He realized it was wiser to keep quiet than argue with the Shahenshah.

Asad Khan took the opportunity to let the emissary know of Aurangzeb's wish: if he wanted to win Aurangzeb's trust, he was to instruct Qutub Khan to behead the two Brahmin diwans and present their heads at the earliest.

The emissary, coming to a conculsion that the sultanate was safe for the time being, was overjoyed. He promised to get the Shahenshah's wish fulfilled and excused himself.

ஃஒ ஒஃ

The news of Aurangzeb moving his camp from Solapur to Gulbarga under the pretext of visiting the old dargah there was enough to send shivers down Qutub Khan's spine. Aurangzeb had, as always, not spelt out his plans clearly but the officials, having seen his ways of working, knew that there was more to it than what met the eye.

Qutub Khan's was quick to react and beheaded the two diwans the moment Aurangzeb arrived at Gulbarga. In order to pacify Aurangzeb further, he sent out gifts to all senior officials in Aurangzeb's court. His sole intention was to prevent Aurangzeb from turning his gaze towards Hyderabad.

Firoz Jung, having left earlier with a contingent of troops, captured the fort at Yadgir and the moment Aurangzeb got the news, he moved towards Hyderabad.

Within a week, Aurangzeb got the message that Qutub Khan had locked himself in the safe confines of the Golconda Fort. Aurangzeb wasted no time in surrounding the fort. He positioned the cannons at various places and his spies briefed him of the possible weak points for attack.

That evening, while returning to his camp, Firoz Jung said, 'Shahenshah need not have taken the trouble. I would have captured Qutub Khan and presented him within a week.'

'I trust you, Firoz Jung, and that is the reason I have given you all the key tasks. I was hoping that my Shahzadas would have pleased me by defeating each of the sultanates but you have seen their attitude. I had to personally intervene to get the Bijapur sultanate under our command. It seems I have to take charge here too. The Shahzadas have been complacent and lazy, enjoying the compliments sent in by Qutub Khan. I don't believe they can focus their minds on winning this battle.'

The rays of the dying sun fell on Aurangzeb's face. Firoz Jung could clearly see he was disappointed. He turned his gaze away but Aurangzeb was quick to recognize his discomfort. He asked, 'It seems you are not convined with what I am saying. You may speak your mind.'

'Shahenshah, I cannot deny what you are saying. It is true that the Shahzadas are responsible for the delays.'

Aurangzeb did not say anything further. He instructed Asad Khan that evening. 'Ensure that all people coming out of the fort should be checked thoroughly. Also note down details of all people who visit the fort from our camp.'

'Does Ala Hazrat suspect anyone in particular?' Asad Khan asked.

'Yes. The very fact that the Mughal sultanate and its Shahenshah have to camp in the Deccan for seven years and manage just one victory is a clear indication that the mansabdars are not doing their job.'

'The Mughal troops are a formidable force in the battlefield but not when it comes to wearing the enemy out by surrounding the fort; they do not have the adequate experience.'

'It's all in the mind. One can conquer mountains if there is a will, else even a hillock can look insurmountable. I want you to send select men from your cavalry to guard both the Shahzadas' tents.'

'Huzoor, won't the Shahzadas take it as an affront? They have their own troops too. I fear there should not be any skirmish.'

'Order their toops on a mission elsewhere. Send our men on the pretext of guarding the Shahzadas. Asad Khan, I am not getting any younger. I want to complete my tasks at the earliest and not waste any more time.'

Asad Khan glanced at Aurangzeb's slightly bent body. He had seen the Shahenshah either immersed in reading the holy book or in continuous campaigns for the past many years. He was unable to understand the urgency behind Aurangzeb's actions.

৵৩ ৩৶

The task of surrounding the fort was in full swing. Asad Khan and Firoz Jung, after their evening round, reported to Aurangzeb. Seeing their worried faces, Aurangzeb asked, 'What is the matter?'

'Huzoor, it seems Qutub Khan is trying to corrupt some of our officials as we suspected. But the matter seems to be deeper than that. We have been able to get some letters written by Qutub Khan.'

Aurangzeb looked at a bag containing a few letters. Reading them carefully, he put them aside and let out a deep sigh.

'I could be indifferent and turn a blind eye to their debauchery for a while but it is unfortunate to know that they have tried to win over Qutub Khan's friendship and stab us in the back.'

'I request the Shahenshah not to get unduly worried on this count. You may question the shahzadas once we take over the fort,' Firoz Jung suggested.

Fiddling with the letters in hand for a while, Aurangzeb contemplated. 'If these letters are to be believed, I will have to look into the matter right away. Tell me are you sure that these were written by Muazzam?'

'I can present you a witness, Huzoor, if you so wish.'

Aurangzeb nodded in acknowledgement and soon, Asad Khan returned with Hamida Banu, responsible for the upkeep of Muazzam's zenankhana. She had been appointed by Aurangzeb personally and ensured that all information regarding the zenankhana was conveyed regulary to him. Aurangzeb asked, 'Tell me, what is happening in Shahzada's zenankhana?'

'You had instructed me not to supply any stationery when the shahzada is alone with his begum in the zenankhana but, for the past three days, he insists on me sending in writing materials. I have no choice but to acquiesce as he threatens me with dire consequences if I do not heed his command.'

'Anything else?'

'I was given a strange order last evening: the zenankhana tents are a little away from the Shahzada's tent. He ordered that a few of the tents be moved closer to his.'

'Any reason for the same?'

'I did not dare to ask him, Alampanah.'

Firoz Jung, on Hamida Banu's departure, got up excitedly saying, 'I am sure Ala Hazrat must be convinced now. Shahzada has promised Qutub Khan that he would convince the Shahenshah to pardon him and return the sultanate. He had also promised that if he were unable to convince the Shahenshah he would come over to the Golconda Fort with his zenankhana and join Qutub Khan's forces.'

Seeing no reaction from Aurangzeb, Asad Khan commented, 'It would be a tragedy if this were to happen. Huzoor, there is something else which I wanted to say.'

Aurangzeb's mind was in turmoil. He had had a niggling doubt for the past few days but now the evidence was irrefutable. Azam had shown some loyalty when he had been given the task of surrounding Bijapur, but Muazzam had failed here. Aurangzeb had got tired of Muazzam's two-faced behaviour. Muazzam enjoyed all the luxuries in life but pretended to be a devout follower of Islam whenever Aurangzeb had enquired. To top it all, Muazzam's offer to Qutub Khan to move to the Golconda Fort with his zenankhana was difficult for Aurangzeb to accept.

'What is it? I don't want to hear anything unless you have concrete evidence,' he said. His voice did not betray the inner turmoil.

'I have all the evidence, Ala Hazrat. It was his begum, Noor Nissa, who had personally gone to meet Qutub Khan. I am convinced that she is responsible for poisoning Muazzam's mind.'

'I am really at a loss to understand the reason for Muazzam's treachery. What doesn't he have here that prompts him to join hands with Qutub Khan? I don't think he is planning on rebelling against me to get the throne at Delhi the way his brother Akbar tried.'

'Huzoor, you are right but there can be an aspiration for something other than the throne at Delhi.'

'For example?'

'It seems he is aspiring to take an independent charge of the Deccan. Qutub Khan has promised to put him in charge of the entire

Deccan once Shahenshah returns to Delhi. It was with this greed that Begum Noor Nissa took the risk to meet him at the fort.'

Aurangzeb knew that Asad Khan was not lying. He said, 'Ambition is a funny thing. It compels one to risk one's own reputation at times. I was myself very ambitious when I punished Muhammad Sultan. I had no choice but to punish Akbar. Frankly, Asad Khan, it hurts me to be so harsh.'

It was probably for the first time that Asad Khan had heard such words of confession from Aurangzeb. He had never seen the Shahenshah so dejected. He tried, 'I suggest we let the Shahzada go off with a strong warning. Please do not give much weightage to his transgression.'

Aurangzeb had probably blurted out his words in a rare moment of helplessness. He was his own self the next moment and said, 'I may have agreed to your suggestion but my spies have something different to tell. They say that Muazzam has not rested making a pact with Qutub Khan but has invited the kafir Sambha to join in too and has requested him to send across his Maratha forces for Qutub Khan's support.'

Aurangzeb threw away the letters he was holding in disgust and said, 'I cannot believe it! Here I am, toiling day and night to capture the sultanates and finish off the kafir menace once and for all, and the Shahzada, on the other hand, has the gall to join hands with Samba. It is beyond my tolerance. I cannot pardon such acts.'

Hearing the watchman announce the hour, he got up and said, turning to Asad Khan, 'I cannot do anything against Allah's wishes. I want Muazzam and his four sons in the Diwan-e-Khaas tomorrow morning. I will decide their fate then.'

Aurangzeb left the room with a heavy heart. Muazzam's treachery had been a huge blow. Putting his hand on Anwar Khoja's shoulders for support, he walked back slowly towards his quarters.

❧ ❧

Shahzada Muazzam presented himself in the Diwan-e-Khaas the next morning. His four sons, with a small dagger each in their cummerbund, were in their formal attire. They assumed they had been summoned to discuss some matters related to the seige of Golconda.

Aurangzeb, sitting on his throne, glanced at Muazzam. The piercing eyes spoke a lot and Muazzam was unable to return the gaze. Aurangzeb, turning towards Muazzam's eldest son Muizuddin, said, 'Dear, I wish to hand over the subah of Hyderabad to you once we defeat Qutub Khan.'

'Hazrat Salamat, this ordinary servant of yours is honoured by your magnanimity.'

'But first we have to capture the fort.' A quick glance at Asad Khan was a cue for him to stand up and say, 'Shahzada Muazzam, Zille Subhani has some very important and delicate orders to be conveyed which cannot be read out in the court. Please step into the adjoining tent alongwith the children. I shall read out the orders there.'

Muazzam retreated form the Diwan-e-Khaas and the children followed suit. The moment they reached the tent, Muazzam asked, impatient to know the reason for such secrecy, 'What are the orders which you were told not to read out there?'

Asad Khan, avoiding Muazzam's gaze, said, 'Shahzada, I may be the Wazir but at the end I am a mere servant of the throne. You are Hazrat's Shahzada after all and I beg your pardon in case I am to inadvertently say something unpleasant.'

Muazzam was confused. Asad Khan, stressing on each word, said slowly, 'Shahzada, I have to inform you that you and your four sons are under arrest.'

Muizuddin, putting his hand on the dagger at his cummerbund shouted, 'Arrest? What are you blabbering? And why are we being arrested?'

The soldiers, waiting outside, stepped in when Muizuddin screamed, 'Abba Jaan, Abba Jaan! Allow me to take on these soldiers. We are four of us. We cannot allow you to be insulted like this.'

Muazzam was upset but had the sense to maintain his composure and said, 'Muizuddin! Hold your horses and don't dare to touch your dagger. Our Shahenshah is the representative of Allah himself. His words are like those of the Quran.'

'Abba Jaan! Why are we being arrested? Is this what loyalty gets us?'

'*Khamosh!* Enough of it now.' Turning to Asad Khan he said, 'Wazir, I would like to know specifically what the Shahenshah's orders are.'

Asad Khan's face turned ashen. He had not expected Muazzam to be so composed. Licking his lips nervously he said, 'It is with great regret that I inform you that you and your sons are under arrest. I ask you to put your weapons down and stand in one corner. The Badshah himself will decide the next steps.'

Muazzam promptly unsheathed his sword and put it down on the floor. Unbuckling his cummerbund he removed his dagger. The sons followed suit and then the five of them stood in one corner waiting nervously for Aurangzeb's arrival. Asad Khan stepped out of the tent and into the durbar. He whispered in Aurangzeb's ears, 'Your orders have been followed.'

Hearing the words, Aurangzeb got up abruptly and, without waiting for the curtain to fall, stepped out of the tent and walked with brisk steps towards the zenankhana.

Zeenat sat in her room reading the Quran and, seeing her father step in, got up hurriedly to receive him. 'Abba Jaan, I did not have any information about your visit.'

Aurangzeb, avoiding her eyes, said, 'Zeenat dear, I am sure Allah would never pardon me. I am confused; I don't know if I am doing the right thing.'

It was Zeenat's turn to be confused. She had never seen her father in such an emotional state. Holding his hand she guided him to the bed and then, sitting down on the floor, asked, 'Abba Jaan, what happened at the durbar?'

'Dear, I was forced to uproot the very plants which I have been watering with my blood and sweat for the past forty years.'

Aurangzeb's lips were quivering with emotions. It was a disturbing sight for Zeenat. She said, 'Abba Jaan! You don't seem to be at ease. Why don't you rest for a while? Shall I send in Udaipuri begum?'

'It is of no use dear. My sorrow cannot be assuaged by anyone else.'

Zeenat looked at her father. She waited for him to continue.

'I had the unfortunate task of giving an order to arrest Muazzam and his sons.'

'What!'

'Yes, dear. I know it is impossible for you to believe me. I had never imagined that fate would play such a cruel hand with me. Heavens cannot wash away this black spot. A man expects his sons to become his support in old age but when the very sons turn traitors, it is a black day in the man's life. The elder one turned traitor and the second one is running away from everyone hiding in mountain caves, and now Muazzam was planning to join the enemy camp. I am the unfortunate father who had to order the arrest of Zebunissa too. I don't know where and when this will end.' Aurangzeb, his hands lifted high in the air, prayed aloud, 'Ya Khuda! Please show a way to this lost soul. I do not know where to go. Please hold me in your hands and take me to my destination.'

Aurangzeb, spent emotionally, was quiet for a long time. Rosary in hand, he looked far away, his eyes vacant and expressionless. Zeenat left the tent without making any sound. She knew her father would prefer to be alone.

৵৩ ৩৵

The next morning, Aurangzeb was back to his old self. No one, seeing him, would have imagined the emotional state he had been the previous evening.

Having arrested Muazzam, Aurangzeb did not want to take chances and ordered the arrest of many of Muazzam's key sardars, one of them being Safshikan Khan, the man in charge of the cannons. Aurangzeb had now taken complete charge and left for Firoz Jung's camp with Azam.

Azam, worried that his father may get hurt in the milieu, suggested that he return to the safety of the cantonment, but Aurangzeb was adamant. He had decided to inspect the progress first-hand and continued his march till they reached a few hundred yards from the scene of the main attack. Asad Khan said, 'Huzoor, it is not advisable to progress beyond this. We may come under enemy fire from the ramparts of the fort.'

'Wazir, there is nothing to fear for someone whose heart is filled with love for Allah. I shall proceed further. You and Shahzada Azam may take charge on the other side. I will see you in the evening at the camp.'

Asad Khan had no choice but to obey. The troops, engaged in the attack, were surprised to see their Shahenshah in the midst of the battle. At that moment, a cannonball from the fort landed close to the palanquin. A splinter suddenly sliced away a hand of one of the palanquin bearers. Aurangzeb, unperturbed by the attack, ordered his soldiers to intensify targeting a particular area on the fort. Shells were landing all around and soldiers, wounded in the ensuing gunfire, were seen crying in pain but Aurangzeb continued his inspection without flinching once.

He reached the place where Firoz Jung and his men had created a tunnel. He sent a message to the cantonment that he intended to stay back in the tunnel that night.

Before anyone could react, Aurangzeb had entered the tunnel bending a little as it opened into a large cave-like structure which was enough to seat eight or ten people. Within an hour, Asad Khan and Ruhullah Khan came in. The sound of the cannons had reduced as the night progressed, though intermittent gunfire could be heard.

Aurangzeb said, looking at Azam, 'Shahzada, I have done a thorough inspection of their defence and I feel we have managed to breach the wall at one place. What we need is a bunch of brave men who are willing to enter in the darkness of the night.'

Ruhullah Khan knew that Aurangzeb's presence had been a tremendous boost of morale for the troops. He said, 'Ala Hazrat, the troops are now fighting with renewed vigour after seeing you right here in the midst of them. I suggest you rest for a while in your camp.'

'I am going to rest only when Qutub Khan surrenders. I intend to stay here till then. If your men cannot do the job, I will get a few men and enter myself.'

Firoz Jung was quick to react. 'My men would never back out of such an opportunity, and you may rest assured that we will do the job tonight.'

'It is decided then. Your men will enter at midnight and by dawn, when the sun is about to rise and when I get up for my prayers, I should get the news of our victory. Tonight is a night of challenge for my sardars. If they fail, I will have to carry out the task myself.'

It was a little past midnight when Firoz Jung, along with fifty odd select soldiers, managed to climb over the walls at the point where they had breached, and reached the main door to the fort. The guards there, taken aback at the unexpected attack, were slaughtered in no time. With shouts of 'Din, Din', Azam and Ruhullah Khan's men, waiting outside for the doors to open, entered the fort as soon as the doors were thrown open.

It had been months since the siege had been laid and Qutub Khan's men, confident that they will eventually win and unprepared for a sudden attack, were taken in by complete surprise. It was a bloody massacre as Firoz Jung rushed towards the main palace. Azam had stayed back guarding the main doors.

Ruhullah Khan stopped in his tracks at the doors of the main palace. He could hear music! Qutub Khan was seated on a platform, while nearly fifty-odd dancers danced on a carpet spread out in the middle of the hall. The Badshah, drunk and puffing away on his hookah, was immersed in the dance when he glanced up on seeing the men enter the hall. The dancers shrieked in terror nearing the soldiers with naked swords in their hands but Qutub Khan, stuttering in his drunken state, said, 'There is no need to stop the music and dance. These are the few precious moments of life and I want to fill them with beauty. Let the dance continue.'

The lead dancer took a hesitant step forward while the singers struggled to find their voice.

Firoz Jung, disgusted at seeing Qutub Khan's state, rushed forward and snatched away his hookah. Pulling him down from his seat he screamed at him, 'Abul Hasan, you are now a prisoner of Shahenshah Ghazi Alamgir Badshah Aurangzeb.'

Qutub Khan simply smiled in response saying, 'I knew that this was to happen one day. I had, in fact, been waiting for it. As you say, I am a prisoner now. But I want to ask for a favour, if you may permit.'

'It depends on what it is.'

Smiling again, Qutub Khan said, 'I know it is difficult for you to believe me, but if you can release me, for just a minute, the world would not collapse.'

'Fine,' Firoz Jung said, releasing his grip from Qutub Khan's wrist.

Qutub Khan walked towards the lead dancer who was quivering in fear. He took out a pearl necklace from around his neck and threw it in her direction saying, 'I would at least be not blamed of having enjoyed these luxuries free of cost.' Turning towards Firoz Jung he said, 'I am ready now. You may tie me or put me in chains, as you wish.'

Azam, waiting at the doors of the fort, let the trumpeters announce their victory as Firoz Jung led Qutub Khan out of the fort. He glanced at the sky to see the thin crescent of the moon rising in the sky.

৵৹ড়ৣ৹

Adil Shah and Qutub Khan were prized posessions for Aurangzeb in his camp. Their immense wealth, now part of his empire, was a cause for celebration each evening in the cantonment. Aurangzeb, for a change, had let go of his habit of cautious spending and had turned a blind eye to the dancers, concubines and singers entertaining the troops while wine from Iran and Istanbul flowed freely. Aurangzeb nominated his key officials at places of importance in the newly acquired territories. Some were gifted elephants while the lucky ones were presented with Arabian steeds.

It was in the midst of such celebrations that Aurangzeb got the news of Shahzada Akbar having fled to Iran. The only thorn in the mighty Mughal Empire continued to be Sambhaji, who ruled the

Konkan region. The Mughal forces were sure that once they defeated the Marathas, they would be the undisputed rulers of the entire subcontinent.

Despite the celebrations all around, Nawab Bai's tent was immersed in sorrow. The hakeems treating her were worried as her health was deteriorating rapidly. Aurangzeb came in with Zeenat the moment he found time. He knew Nawab Bai's health had been getting worse ever since she had heard of the arrest of Shahzada Muazzam and his sons. Seeing the hakeems, he raised his eyebrows in question when they said, 'She is unconscious.'

'How is the fever?'

'We are at a loss. We have tried many medicines.'

'Call for the chief hakeem. Let him have a look.'

The hakeem present did not answer but looked down at the floor. Aurangzeb asked, 'What is the matter?'

'Huzoor, Begum Sahiba is in her last stages now.'

Aurangzeb rushed towards her bed. Nawab Bai, shrivelled and worn out, was hardly visible amidst the heap of sheets and pillows. He could barely recognize her withered face as she laboured to breathe. The maid standing near the bed said, 'She has had this high fever for the past two days and has been complaining of pain in her shoulders. The royal hakeem inspected her this morning.'

Aurangzeb stood near her bed for a while without saying anything. He then turned to leave, one hand on Zeenat's shoulders. He knew the cause of Nawab Bai's sorrow and ill health, but he had no solution for it. Zeenat asked her father to stay back when Shamim barged in hurriedly and, after a quick salute, said, 'Hazrat, Asad Khan is waiting for you outside with a very urgent message.'

Aurangzeb stepped out to see Asad Khan's worried face. 'Hazrat, we never expected such a calamity. It has been a dampener to the celebrations around.'

'What happened?'

'Firoz Jung is down with high fever and so are many other soldiers and cavalrymen. The symptoms are the same; there is a high fever for two days and a lump develops in the armpit. By the second day the man is dead. We are unable to understand this strange malady.'

Aurangzeb was stunned hearing of the situation. He was aware of many soldiers falling ill and had heard murmurs in the ranks about Allah's wrath on the Mughal forces for having taken over two Islamic sultanates. Aurangzeb was doubly disturbed as Firoz Jung was the key sardar who had led the attacks on both Golconda and Bijapur.

Aurangzeb thought for a while and said, 'Let us wait for a week and then, if the epidemic does not stop, we will move the cantonment to the banks of the Bheema near Pedgaon.'

As planned, the camp moved after a week. In the meanwhile Aurangzeb had to witness another tragedy; that of Nawab Bai succumbing to her fever.

◈◈◈◈

The two sultanates were now under the Mughal rule and it was only the Marathas who needed to be conquered. Realizing that Sambhaji might, in the event of being surrounded, escape northwards, Aurangzeb ordered the cantonment to move towards Nasik.

By the time the rains ended they had camped a few miles near Pandharpur. The weather was pleasant, just before the winters. The troops had been rewarded lavishly and had recovered from the bout of fever. On Asad Khan's request they rested for a week before setting up the cantonment on the banks of the Bheema.

One day, while Aurangzeb was looking into regular matters, Shaista Khan from Bengal sent in some disturbing news. The English had reportedly looted the Mughal post on the banks of the Hooghly. Aurangzeb, irritated at the daring shown by the English traders, shouted, 'Send an urgent message to Shaista Khan to drown their ships in the Hooghly. Also, send in a word to Matbar Khan at Kalyan: he should give a week's time to the English stationed at Mumbai to pay for the damages incurred at Hooghly; else we would drown their ships anchored at the Mumbai harbour. They would also be forbidden from carrying out their merchant activities on our soil.'

Asad Khan tried, 'Jahanpanah, would it be fair to punish the English traders at Mumbai for the attack on the Hooghly?'

Aurangzeb raised his voice saying, 'I had made a mistake of showing restraint when the enemy had looted Surat. It is thanks to that mistake that I am forced to spend my time in this age in the company of cannons. I am not going to repeat my mistake with the English.'

'Shahenshah, these men are traders. Their representatives present themselves in our court from time to time with expensive gifts.'

'Let that be, I don't care. Keep in mind that when an enemy bends down to touch your feet showing servility, he may be thinking of pulling your legs to make you fall.'

Asad Khan was silent realizing that the emperor had made up his mind.

Aurangzeb glanced at Ruhullah Khan standing nearby and noticed his tired face. He assumed he must be battle-weary, having constantly been on the move for the past two months. He said, 'It seems Ruhullah Khan is tired and needs some time to recoup. I suggest a week's off.'

Ruhullah Khan replied, 'I may be a little tired but I am pained hearing some bad news.'

'What is it?'

'Hazrat, you had mentioned that the tall spires of the hundreds of temples around the banks of the river were sticking out like sore thumbs and I had been asked to inspect them thoroughly. I witnessed a strange thing during one such inspection of a large temple at Pandharpur.'

'I hope you managed to destroy the idol there.'

'The strange thing was that there was no idol in the sanctum sanctorum.'

Aurangzeb, not one to believe such stories, challenged him. 'Why would such an old temple be sans the idol?'

'Huzoor, the fact is that the kafirs these days are taking away their idols in anticipation of a raid and the temple getting destroyed.'

The comment put a smile on Aurangzeb's lips. 'I am glad to hear that, Ruhullah Khan. It's music to my ears that the kafirs are really worried now. They would not agree that their gods are not rushing to help them in their bad times. On the contrary their gods are running away from us.'

The mullahs and maulvis, ever ready to praise Aurangzeb, raised their hands in air shouting, 'Alamgir, Zinda Pir!' Ruhullah Khan waited for the moment to pass and continued, 'I could not find the idol there but Ala Hazrat, I found something much more dangerous; two of Sambha's men were hiding there!'

Aurangzeb raised his eyebrows in surprise and said, 'That is precisely the reason for my orders to destroy these temples. They have become a safe haven for the kafirs to hide. You have done a good job. What did these two fellows have to say?'

'They had been sent to get information regarding our cantonment.'

'What exactly were they looking for?'

'The total strength here, the kind of weapons we have, the number of people guarding the Gulalbar tents and so on and so forth; quite detailed information.'

Aurangzeb was more amused than surprised. Caressing his beard, he said, 'So the Marathas are now planning to raid our cantonment, it seems. We managed to get the two sultanates to their knees. If the Marathas have not learnt their lessons yet, even Allah cannot save them.'

Asad Khan commented, 'When Aurangzeb Badshah has come to fulfil the task as ordered by Allah, one cannot expect the kafirs to get some divine help.'

Ignoring his comment Aurangzeb continued, 'What else were the spies looking for?'

'I got a letter written by Sambha.'

'Letter? Whom was it addressed to?' Aurangzeb asked, unable to mask his curiosity.

Ruhullah Khan did not answer immediately. Instead he looked at Asad Khan for support. He was aware that Zeenat sat on the other side of the screen, listening to the conversation. Glancing in the direction for a brief moment he said, in a beseeching tone, 'I request Hazrat not to question me further in the durbar.'

'Why so?'

'It is a delicate matter. I am willing to answer your questions in private.'

Aurangzeb shook his head, 'No. I don't have much time, and there is no need for secrecy. You may tell whatever you have found right here.'

Ruhullah Khan took out a letter from his pocket reluctantly and handed it over to Asad Khan, who handed the same to Aurangzeb; saying, 'The letter is in the Hindavi language. There is a Farsi translation alongwith.'

'Is it addressed to me?' Aurangzeb asked.

Asad Khan, tilting his head in the direction of the screen said, 'No, Ala Hazrat. Sambha has addressed the letter to Begum Sahiba.'

Aurangzeb did not react but continued to hold the letter in his hand. His eyes bored into Asad Khan's trying to read his mind. The officials in attendance waited with bated breath; not sure how the Badshah would react now. Aurangzeb looked at Ruhullah Khan once and then, sighing deeply, dismissed the durbar.

Zeenat had reached the zenankhana in anticipation of the confrontation. Asad Khan followed Aurangzeb and stood in one corner while Zeenat, her veil flowing down to her chest, stood with her head bowed. Aurangzeb, chucking the letter in the direction of Asad Khan, said, 'It would be a sin to even read this letter written by a kafir. Please tell me the summary of the contents.'

Asad Khan picked up the letter and then, glancing at Zeenat once, said, 'I would request Begum Sahiba to be allowed to leave.'

'No. She is the one to whom it has been addressed. Let her be present to answer my questions.'

Asad Khan read out the contents: 'Your brother Shahzada Akbar had told me about you before he left Hindustan. He had not replied to the letter you had sent but had instead asked me to convey his reply. It is as follows: Badshah Salamat is not a Badshah just for the Musalmans. Hindustan consists of people from different religions and he is supposed to represent all of them. He has achieved the purpose for which he came to the Deccan. I hope he has the wisdom to return to Hindustan. I have managed to escape from his clutches but if the Badshah continues his adamant pursuits, he will not be able to escape from my clutches and return to Hindustan. He will then have to find a place for his burial right here in the Deccan itself.'

Aurangzeb listened intently but did not say a word. Instead, he closed his eyes and prayed. After a few moments of silence he asked, looking at Zeenat, 'Do you have to say anything?'

Zeenat was at a loss for words. 'I am no one to advise Hazrat. Sambha is just a child; I urge you to ignore him.'

Aurangzeb, keeping his rosary down on a table, shouted, 'Child? This "child" has been troubling us for the past ten years and you call him a child? Asad Khan, I have a plan. Where are the Maratha spies you caught the other day in Pandharpur?'

'They are imprisoned in the camp. I was planning to issue orders to behead them once you reply to this letter.'

'No. On the contrary I plan to honour them.'

Asad Khan was taken aback. He asked, a little hesitatingly, 'I am unable to follow you, Huzoor.'

'You will, Asad Khan. Treat them courteously and send them back with honour. Give a diamond pendant to be presented to Sambha.'

It was beyond Asad Khan's understanding and all he could do was look at Aurangzeb wide-eyed, saying, 'Ji, Huzoor.'

Aurangzeb continued, 'Listen carefully now; write to Sambha saying that the Shahenshah has read the letter addressed to the Shahzadi. Let him also know that I have found a place for my burial and have announced it to the world. But Sambha should note that we have defeated the two sultanates in the Deccan and if he does not mend his ways, it would be an unfortunate situation that there would not even be a piece of his body left for the people to bury. Sambha is advised to wear this diamond pendant and I pray that it gives him wisdom. *Ameen!*'

ஐஒ ஒஐ

The durbar was in full attendance and the topic of discussion was the Marathas. The Maratha kingdom was part of the erstwhile Bijapur sultanate and Aurangzeb selected Sheikh Nizam and Sarja Khan from Bijapur to lead the discussion. He had named them Mukarrab Khan and Rustam Khan giving them a mansab of five thousand men. Apart from these, the Maratha sardars Kanhoji, Arjoji and Achloji were in attendance to give their opinion. Aurangzeb asked Mukarrab Khan, 'How long do you think we need before we can defeat the Marathas?'

'Alampanah, what chance do the Marathas have when the two powerful sultanates could not withstand the Mughal might? The strength of the Marathas is in their forts. I suggest we take their forts to bring them to their knees.'

Rustam Khan interrupted, 'Alampanah, if I may ...'

'Please speak up, Rustam Khan.'

'It would take years for us to capture the forts. They are all in treacherous mountain terrain and it is impossible for us to reach them during the monsoons. By the time we make plans and reach the forts, it would be rainy season again. It is for the same reason the Bijapur sultanate could not capture them. The terrain there is their biggest ally.'

'I agree that we should not waste our time trying to capture the forts,' Asad Khan said.

'I could not agree more,' Mukarrab Khan said. 'It would take years to capture a fort like Salher Mahuli, but Ala Hazrat was able to get the fort by bribing the fort keeper there. We can try similar tactics now.'

'I would like to hear the opinion of the Maratha sardars,' Aurangzeb said.

Kanhoji responded saying, 'Rustam Khan's suggestion is quite valid. I too would not suggest wasting time trying to capture the Maratha forts.'

Aurangzeb did not respond immediately and continued moving the beads in his rosary. Mukarrab Khan and Sarja Khan waited expectantly, eager to know the Badshah's mind.

Aurangzeb, looking at his Wazir said, 'Asad Khan, I think we should focus our energies on capturing Sambha rather than his forts. But I wonder if Sambha would run away and hide in one of the forts, in which case we may have no option but to surround it. We have the experience of surrounding Bijapur and Golconda.'

Jagdevrao said, 'I have a suggestion, Jahanpanah. I don't think Sambhaji would hide in one of the forts.'

'Why do you say that?'

'We know the Marathi Raja Sambhaji as well as we knew his father Shivaji Raja. Earlier when Mirza Raja had marched upon the Deccan, Shivaji Raja did not hide in the forts but preferred to confront the Mughal Army. Likewise, Sambhaji too would dare to challenge the Mughals.'

'That is quite surprising! It makes our job easy.'

Aurangzeb was smiling at the prospect of meeting Sambha in a battlefield and said, 'Bravado makes a man careless and he loses because of his arrogance. Are you sure Sambha would not hide?'

'Yes, Jahanpanah. If you were to challenge him for a battle, I am sure he would accept it.'

'That would be an opportunity Allah would hand us on a platter.'

'Jahanpanah, Jagdevrao's suggestion is quite sound. It seems Sambha is itching to confront us in a battle.'

'It is decided then,' Aurangzeb said, looking at Azam. 'Shahzada, you have managed two victories for us here. Your begum, my favourite Jahanzeb Banu, too has contributed significantly to the victory. I want you to take responsibility for the final act in the Deccan. You will be supported by these able sardars here. Defeat the Marathas and capture that rascal Sambha.'

Azam, getting up, touched his palm to his forehead in salaam and said, 'I am honoured that you have entrusted me with this task. I request your permission to grant me a week's time to prepare.'

'I am fine with that. I shall pray for your success this evening.'

***

Aurangzeb, past his seventies now, sat in his shamiana waiting for Azam before his departure. Oftentimes, his finger would tremble while he moved the beads in his rosary and, of late, he had complained of knee pain while sitting down for long to read his prayers.

While he was counting victories on the battlefield, memories of the past would disturb him. Though he continued to rule with an iron hand, taking tough and often merciless decisions, his concentration in prayers would be interrupted by thoughts of his zenankhana, which he badly missed. At times, the aching memories would not allow him to continue further and he would pray fervently for the strength to return.

Zeenat, aware of his father's condition, would try her best to engage him but would fail more than succeed.

Aurangzeb at times would pour his heart out to her.

His cantonment, having moved from Pandharpur, was now spread alongside the banks of the Neera. On Fridays, Aurangzeb met many of the maulvis and mullahs. Kazi Haider, nominated as the main kazi, presented two aulias for a meeting. One was from Sheikh Zainuddin's dargah at Khuldabad while the other one from Syed Gesudaraz dargah at Gulbarga. Aurangzeb asked the kazi from Sheikh Zainuddin's dargah, 'I hope the dargah of my guru is being looked after well.'

'Things are as per orders given by Hazrat.'

'And what about my grave?'

'Tauba! Tauba! Hazrat, I pray Allah gives you a long life. Please do not torture us by using such words.'

'Why, miya? I too am a mortal and someday I have to put my body in the grave, isn't it? I want to ensure that the preparations are in place when the day arrives.'

The aulia from Gulbarga caressed his long-flowing white beard and said, 'I entreat the Hazrat not to be bothered of his grave so early. He has a lot of time ahead to spread the message of Islam across the world.'

'I know that. The mind may be willing but the body is getting old, and I know I shall not stop till I have the last ounce of energy in me. Rest is Hazrat Paigambar's wish.'

After a while, he dismissed the visitors and turned to enter into his private tent for his prayers. He had barely sat down when he heard Anwar come in. No one would dare to enter when Aurangzeb was busy with his prayers but Anwar was allowed such transgressions. 'I beg your pardon for my intrusion, but there is an important message for you in the private meeting room.'

'Anwar, are you not aware of today being Jumma?'

'Please pardon me, Hazrat, but this seemed important. Shahzada Azam has sent a very urgent message with someone called Khanduji.'

Getting up with a sigh Aurangzeb said, 'I hope this kafir messenger has something good to say.'

He entered the private chambers to see a Maratha soldier, who salaamed thrice bending down up to his waist on seeing Aurangzeb. Looking down at the floor he said, 'I travelled overnight for an urgent message from Shahzada Azam.'

'Hurry up! What is the message?'

'Mukarrab Khan has managed to capture Sambhaji Raja. He is on his way to your camp, Huzoor.'

Aurangzeb, not able to believe the good news, closed his eyes for a moment before saying, 'Has Shahzada sent anything as a token of his good news?'

The messenger took out a pouch tied to his waist. Without touching it Aurangzeb said, 'Take out whatever is inside and show me.'

The messenger untied the small pouch to reveal a shining large diamond; the one Aurangzeb had presented Jahanzeb Banu. Aurangzeb immediately called for Anwar and said, 'Anwar, this messenger has brought some very good news. Take him to the daroga and ask him to give five hundred rupiyas as his reward.'

Anwar escorted the messenger out leaving Aurangzeb alone. For a long time Aurangzeb, holding the diamond in his palm, stood there with his eyes closed. His prayers seemed to have been answered.

*

In celebration of the arrest of Sambhaji, the town of Akluj was renamed as Asadnagar. The celebrations were beyond anybody's imagination. The Mughal Badshah had left Delhi for jehad and now the task had been fulfilled. The most elusive of the enemy had finally been captured. The mansabdars and other officials could not have enough of the victory celebrations.

The cantonment moved back to the banks of the Bheema near Pedgaon where Bahadur Khan had set up a beautiful camp. The picturesque town, where the river took a wide turn, had been decorated for the arrival of the victorious emperor. The streets were tree-lined and water from the river was carried all the way to the innumerable havelis where fountains spluttered giving a cool ambience. Small canals ran across the length and breadth of the town; a relief in the hot summers. The ample water supply had also created gardens and public baths at many places. Aurangzeb's haveli was designed in a fashion to allow him to see the wide expanse of the river and the plains beyond while sitting at his throne in the durbar hall. Pedgaon was rechristened as Bahadurgadh.

The durbar hall, overflowing with officials of all ranks, eagerly awaited the arrival of their Badshah. The celebrations had been on for days now and many mansabdars were now dreaming of a trouble-free life, sans enemy, full of enjoyment and relaxation in the days ahead. The days of troubles seemed over, once and for all. All they could foresee in the future was a life of fun and frolic.

Hamiduddin Khan, hearing of Sambhaji and ten other prisoners having reached the outskirts of the town, rushed out to receive Mukarrab Khan and his son, who had shown great courage. As per Aurangzeb's instructions they were to be honoured with special clothes and jewellery and escorted to the royal palace seated atop royal elephants. The instructions were to make the prisoners ride on camels with Sambhaji wearing a wooden cap meant for ordinary clerks.

The curtain was raised the moment Aurangzeb stepped on to the dais and sat on his throne. Aurangzeb glanced in the direction of the river to see Mukarrab Khan and Ikhlas Khan proudly riding an elephant followed by Sambha and other prisoners trussed and tied up on camelback. Aurangzeb watched Mukarrab Khan get off the elephant two hundred yards from the durbar. He ordered the Wazir: 'Please escort Mukarrab Khan personally to the court alongwith the prisoners.'

'Jo Irshad,' Asad Khan replied.

The curiosity of those present in the court had reached its peak. There was an expectant hush as Mukarrab Khan and Ikhlas Khan stepped in. Ruhullah Khan honoured them with trays full of gold coins. Aurangzeb, after the ceremony of honouring those who had performed the critical task of capturing the enemy was over, said, 'I will see only two of the prisoners now: Sambha and his Wazir Kalusha. Present them before me.'

The guards, holding Sambhaji and Kalusha, tied with thick iron chains at their ankles and wrists, dragged them into the court. The men were a sight to behold: their hair dishevelled, their mouth gagged with a black cloth, their clothes tattered. The chains rattled as those in the court waited with bated breath to see their emperor's reaction.

Despite everything, the thirty-two-year-old Sambhaji's face shone as before. The small beard on his chin quivered a little as he looked at Aurangzeb with bloodshot eyes. Seeing his condition a scream erupted from behind the screens, from where the ladies watched the spectacle. It was obvious whose voice it was, and Aurangzeb, irritated at the interruption, threw an angry glance in the direction of the screen.

For a moment, Aurangzeb closed his eyes. He remembered the young, innocent face of Sambhaji in his court nearly twenty or twenty-two years back. He remembered how the eyes had been enamoured seeing the Mughal display of wealth.

He recalled how he had honoured the young lad and how Shiva had presented him in the court. He had never imagined that the young boy would one day trouble him and make him spend years in the hot Deccan sun. But that was what probably Allah had in mind for him, Aurangzeb mused.

The thought of Allah made Aurangzeb turn his face westwards. Getting off his throne he prayed to Allah. Aurangzeb's face was turned away from those present and it was only Anwar who noticed that his eyes were moist as he prayed.

Sitting back on his throne Aurangzeb looked at Kalusha, the short, stocky Kanauji Brahmin who sported a thick walrus moustache and a ponytail.

Asad Khan replied, sensing Aurangzeb's questioning stare, 'Huzoor, he is Sambhaji's Wazir Kalusha.'

'Is he not familiar with the Mughal customs?'

'Mukarrab Khan and Ikhlas Khan have told both the prisoners to bow before the emperor, but it seems the Brahmin Wazir is not able to understand him. He is mumbling something constantly.'

'There is a tent next to Adil Shah's accommodation in the Gulalbar area. Let the prisoners be kept there.'

As soon as the orders were passed, the prisoners were escorted out of the durbar.

৵৻৶ ৶৻৽

The next day Aurangzeb offered his prayers at Bahadurgadh's Jama Masjid and thanked Allah for all the success he had received. He further prayed that he may continue to get Allah's benevolence for his future campaigns.

After spending a couple of hours at the masjid, he returned to the camp visiting Abul Hasan's tent on the way. The royal prisoner from Golconda was housed there. Resting his hand on Hamiduddin Khan's shoulders for support, he entered the tent much to the surprise of Abul Hasan, who had been resting with his two begums. He could barely recognize the Shahenshah who was dressed in a simple white kurta and pyjama.

Abul Hasan hurriedly got up and bending down in salaam requested Aurangzeb to sit down but ignoring the same Aurangzeb said, 'I hope the Badshah of Golconda is happy in his palace here.'

It was a taunt which did not go waste; the pain was clearly visible on Abul Hasan's face who said, 'I am as fine as I was in my Golconda Fort.'

'Abul Hasan,' Aurangzeb said, his voice a bit loud, 'I hope you realize the punishment Allah metes out when one does not follow his orders.'

'I am not sure how Allah punishes, but I know now how others punish under his name.'

'Abul Hasan, I hope you realize that had you followed the tenets of Islam and not allowed kafir Brahmins the royal patronage and given Shiva Bhosale the kind of support you gave, you would not have been in such a situation.'

'Shahenshah, I am aware that this Abul Hasan, before he became a Badshah, was once an ordinary man. That is what my Abba Jaan has taught me from the holy books. A man's poverty or wealth is in the hands of Allah. What is in our hands is to be human and show humanity. That power was with me in the fort there and in your camp here.'

'If you believe Allah would come to your rescue if you use such high-flowing words, you are totally mistaken.'

'I have no such hopes, Shahenshah. I know Allah is not content with me but I will happily accept the troubles as I accepted the good times when he favoured me. I have not studied the religious books as you have. But Allah has given me enough humanity to live the rest of my life in happiness. And I am sure Allah would not forget me.'

'Abul Hasan, I was under the impression that you would be ashamed of your deeds. Let me recount them in case you wonder what I am referring to: the kafir, whom you felicitated in your court, Sambha, is my prisoner now. You are guilty of not just hugging the kafirs in friendship but even adopting some of their customs. I have removed such un-Islamic rituals from their roots once and for all.'

'We are not in Allah's good books now, but at least in our final years we are blessed that we are being punished by a true servant of Islam. Shahenshah, what an irony! I am the lucky one whose needs are being taken care of by the emperor of Hindustan while you are the unlucky one who has to look after an ordinary criminal who once befriended kafirs and did not follow the tenets of Islam.'

It was a snub difficult for Aurangzeb to bear any further. Turning his back to Abul Hasan he called Hamiduddin Khan and said, 'I thought Abul Hasan would have some wisdom left in him. Khuda has already deserted him, but his servant too has no choice now. Ask the jailor at Bahadurgadh to chain him at his ankles and let him suffer for the rest of his life watching the sky from the cells at Khuldabad prison. Hopefully, he will remember some of the lessons he learnt while reading the holy book and it will make him wiser.'

Aurangzeb left Abul Hasan's camp and climbed into the palanquin without taking the help of anyone. None of those present could realize that he had been deeply disturbed by Abul Hasan's defiance. He knew that he may have captured Abul Hasan but he could never conquer his heart.

ഛരുള

The next day Aurangzeb conferred with Hamiduddin Khan, the camp commander, and his Wazir Asad Khan regarding the royal prisoners.

The discussion centred around Sambha. Asad Khan was of the view that he too should be held prisoner in the Gulalbar camp, alongside the two other erstwhile Badshahs.

'I agree with the Wazir,' Hamiduddin Khan agreed. 'Sambha and Sikandar Khan, erstwhile jagirdar and his Badshah, staying imprisoned together would send the right message to the world.'

Aurangzeb did not react immediately. Mulling over it for a while he said, 'We have to keep in mind that Sambha's territory is not the same as the other Badshah's. We haven't got hold of his territory yet.'

'Our soldiers would do so soon.'

'I would be the happiest if that were to happen,' Aurangzeb said, caressing his beard. 'Till then we need to keep an eye on Sambha. His father, after escaping from Agra, had made a mockery of the Mughal Empire and thumbed a nose at us.'

Hamiduddin Khan said, 'We have the king in custody and we shall soon get his kingdom. I am unable to follow you when you say we need to make use of him.'

'When I had come to the Deccan I had assumed that the Marathas were united and would offer a unified resistance. But we were able to defeat them thanks to many of their sardars who defected. If their sardars can join us, there is no reason to assume that our sardars cannot join them. We need to get the true picture from our prisoners.'

'Ala Hazrat, what you say cannot be true! Our amirs and mansabdars are loyal to the throne and there is no reason for them to join the enemy.'

'Hamiduddin Khan, I know the human mind and how it can behave for its personal gains. I remember when Shiva was in our custody and how he had almost reached Shahzada Muazzam. Later, he managed to get Shahzada Akbar to his side. If my own Shahzadas can betray me where is the doubt about the mansabdars?'

Asad Khan agreed, but with a subtle hint. 'You are right, Huzoor. After all, there are many Rajputs, Jats and Bundels amongst our sardars.

Aurangzeb smiled. 'You are truly a Wazir, Asad Khan. Distrust may be seen as a negative trait for many, but for those who are in politics it is essential that one learns not to trust anyone. I want you to pry the information from Sambha and get the names of our people who are secretly supporting him.'

'Huzoor, I really doubt, seeing the attitude of our prisoners, whether we will be able to get what we want.'

Aurangzeb was not convinced. He looked out of the tent speaking to himself, 'A man will be willing to share anything once he knows his life is in danger. I am yet to meet a man who will not trade information for his own life.'

Aurangzeb continued, 'There is one more thing; we managed to lay our hands on the treasures of Golconda and Bijapur quite easily, but we are yet to find out where the Marathas have hidden their loot. It has to be in one of the forts. If we are able to get the names of the mansabdars who have betrayed us and also the place where he has hidden the treasures we may consider some pardon for Sambha.'

Asad Khan said, 'Huzoor, give me a week's time for me to present the details before you.'

Aurangzeb shook his head saying, 'I cannot wait for a week. Hamiduddin, let me know by evening tomorrow whether Sambha is willing to consider this or not. I will decide the next course of action then.'

It was pitch-dark by the time Asad Khan and Hamiduddin left Aurangzeb's tent. The hooting of owls near the riverbanks created an eerie atmosphere while the intensity of the darkness around was contrasted by the small light of the burning mashaals stuck on various poles along the way.

৵৹৹ ৹৹৵

The murmur began since afternoon and the rumours gathered force by evening. Some of the officials present in the court concluded that the Badshah was mighty upset with Sambha and may order his eyes to be gouged out. They felt it was a lesson for anyone who dared to stand up and look into the emperor's eyes.

It was past midnight. Except for a solitary call of the guard or the sound of a soldier on horseback, the camp was sleeping peacefully. One could hear the water flow in the river in the distance.

Zeenat stepped out of her tent and, accepting the salutes of the guards, made her way to Aurangzeb's tent. Anwar, on guard as usual, got up hurriedly seeing the Shahzadi near the tent.

'Please inform Hazrat Salamat,' she said, and then, without waiting for more than a few moments, stepped into the tent. Aurangzeb sat on the floor reading from the Quran. He turned hearing Zeenat's footsteps. Anwar picked up the holy book and kept it on a table. Despite the cold breeze outside, Aurangzeb had draped himself in a simple shawl. Adjusting his shawl on his shoulders he asked, 'Zeenat dear, you haven't slept yet?'

'You too are awake, Abba Jaan.'

'That is my routine. I get a chance to read the holy book only after the official duties are done with. I read till I see the morning star shining on the horizon. What brings you here?'

'Abba Jaan, I came here to discuss a delicate matter which you may not approve of. It is regarding the Maratha raja who is in imprisoned in your Gulalbar tent.'

'Zeenat, what is that you want to discuss regarding him?'

'I feel your punishment is far too strict,' Zeenat said, coming to the point straight away. 'I heard of it this evening and was upset. Abba Jaan, he is under your custody and is helpless. Why such a drastic measure?'

'Oh! So you have come here to plead for him.'

'You may interpret it that way, but I was shaken to the core hearing of the punishment. His only fault is that he revolted against the Mughal Empire.'

'You think it is a minor offence?

'Abba Jaan, isn't it true that the Badshahs of Bijapur and Golconda were giving him clandestine support?'

'It is a fact, no doubt.'

'Then, do you believe that those Badshahs would help Sambha if he were ill-treating the Musalmams in his territory?'

'Are you saying that the maulvis and kazis who have informed me are lying?'

'Abba Jaan, I cannot say that but I would surely not believe them unless I check it out for my own. There can be many reasons for them to make such false complaints.'

Aurangzeb was amused to see an emotional Zeenat whose cheeks had turned crimson. Smiling indulgently at her, he said, 'Shahzadi Sahiba, I hope I don't have to learn how to run my empire at this age from you!'

Zeenat was clearly disappointed. She was silent for a few moments before she appealed, 'Abba Jaan, can you not punish him in some other way?'

'What do you have in mind?'

'Abba Jaan, you love your religion and you talk of spreading the religion to all corners of this land. Isn't that true?'

'No doubt about it. All my actions too are as per the tenets of Islam.'

'Don't you think it is a golden opportunity for you to convert this kafir king to our religion? Won't that be a feather in your cap?'

'Dear, I remember you advising me against converting all the kafirs in the Deccan. Isn't it ironical that you are now asking me to convert their king?'

'I am suggesting this to save Sambha from a disastrous fate. Making him a Musalman is a far lesser punishment.'

'You believe he would agree to it?'

'I will convince him, Abba Jaan.'

'I think it is not going to be easy for you. Remember, he is Shiva's son and a proud king to boot. I know he is an intelligent fellow. He knows that we are going to keep Sikandar Khan and Abul Hasan in custody for the rest of their lives. In such a case, Sambha would choose death over conversion.'

'Are you planning to keep him in your custody forever?'

'It was a grave mistake to have allowed his father to escape. If I let him go now, I may end up spending the rest of my old age roaming in the hills and valleys of the Deccan. But I am not able to understand one thing.' Aurangzeb stopped mid-sentence to see Zeenat's reaction. Seeing her father's adamance, she was a pale shadow of her earlier self. Aurangzeb looked at her for a few moments before asking, 'Tell me dear, why are you so concerned about Sambha?'

'Abba Jaan, I knew you would ask me this.'

'I am waiting for your reply.'

'Abba Jaan, I had met Sambha once when he was young. It was in Agra; when Shahzada Akbar was indisposed due to fever. He must have been younger to Shahzada by just a year, and a thought crossed my mind – if I had a younger brother he would have been like Sambha.'

'Zeenat, it is not right to compare a Shahzada with a kafir.'

'Please pardon me Abba Jaan but even the other day, on seeing

Sambha in chains in your court, I was reminded of his young face in Agra and a strange emotion pierced my heart.'

'I know that. I had heard your gasp from behind the screens and it was very annoying to say the least. Listen to me carefully, there is no place for emotions in politics. The one sitting on the throne has to steel his mind and heart. You have seen me when it came to Akbar or Muazzam. Nor was it different for Zebunissa. I had no choice.'

'Abba Jaan,' Zeenat said in a voice quivering with emotions. 'If this is the sacrifice one has to pay to sit on the throne, why take all the trouble to be there?'

Aurangzeb curled his fists before replying, 'It is destiny, dear. It is not in one's hands.'

'How do you say that?'

'Haven't you spent your entire life in the zenankhana alone? Was it not destined having been born as a Shahzadi?'

'But Abba Jaan, you had a choice not to sit on the throne.'

'I had no choice when it came to being Badshah Shah Jahan's son.'

'Why, Dara Shikoh too was a Shahzada for that matter.'

'It was my fate that he was my elder brother. There are not many things which a man can control. He is a puppet in the hands of the divine power which decides his life. Someone is born into a royal family while someone else a beggar. You may not understand all this, but what I say is true. Despite my love for you I cannot reconsider the decision regarding Sambha's punishment. Each one of us, be it a Shahenshah or a slave, has to accept what fate has in store. It is getting late now. *Khuda hafeez.*'

Zeenat was in tears now. She pleaded, 'Abba Jaan, I had come with a lot of hope.'

Aurangzeb said, avoiding Zeenat's face, 'Dear, it is human nature to live with hope but not all of them are fulfilled. It takes years to understand this. Maybe you too would understand what I did when you are older.'

It was with a heavy heart that Zeenat left Aurangzeb's quarters putting her hand on her maid's shoulders for support when she found Yasmin running towards her. She seemed to be pointing in the direction of the camp shouting, 'Begum Sahiba, Begum Sahiba!'

At that moment heart-rending screams pierced the silence of the night. Zeenat clasped her ears with her palm to shut the noise. What she dreaded was finally happening.

෴ ෴

Aurangzeb moved the cantonment from Bahadurgadh within a fortnight to a place near Tulapur on the banks of the Bheema. Aurangzeb wanted to be as close as possible to Gulshanabad, what was later also known as Nasik. The soldiers, having enjoyed a rest at Bahadurgadh, were back to a tented accommodation at the new camp.

The Gulalbar, as always, stood out amongst the thousands of tents, its golden canopy visible for miles across. Ruhullah Khan had appointed the senior Maratha sardars like Shirke and Mohite in important positions while Achloji and Arjoji were inducted into lower ranks.

One afternoon Shirke and Mohite presented themselves in Aurangzeb's court and after the usual protocol of paying their homage in the form of gifts waited for the Badshah's orders. Aurangzeb said, 'Shirke, I am going to give you an important task soon.'

'Alampanah,' Shikre said, 'We are here at your command. We did the impossible by capturing Sambhaji. I am told you tried your level best to drive some sense into his adamant head, but finally fate had something else in store for him and he had to suffer a horrible death. Finally, your biggest enemy is out of the way.'

Aurangzeb glanced at those present in the court before saying, 'Shirke, Mohite, we managed to capture Sambha but I am told his younger brother is out there trying to gather support against us.'

'That's correct,' Mohite nodded. 'Jahanpanah, Sambhaji's younger brother Rajaram declared himself the king after Sambhaji's death.'

'Mohite, I am glad that you did not hide this information.'

'Hazrat, the Maratha loyalty is unquestionable to the hand that feeds him.'

'Is it true that Sambha had only one brother?'

'Yes.'

'What about his family?'

'They are all in Raigadh.'

'How is the fort?'

'It can't stand for long against the might of the Mughal Empire,' Shirke tried to impress, puffing out his chest.

Aurangzeb was quick to realize that Shirke was exaggerating and displeasure was evident on his face when he said, 'I am tired of such exaggerations. Come to the point; can the fort be captured easily?'

'Well, the fort is a little difficult to capture, Shahenshah.'

Turning to Asad Khan he asked, 'How long have our troops surrounded the fort?'

'It has been a few months now. But we believe that if we get the right information we can manage to get in and take over.'

Aurangzeb turned to Shirke and said, 'Shirke, I will fulfil your desires soon. Let the entire Maratha territory come under our control. We will then allot the jagirs to the deserving Maratha sardars but you have to put in some efforts till then.'

'We shall not shy away from any work, Huzoor.'

'Shabbash! Send your informants towards Raigadh. Let them find out the weak spots and inform Itikad Khan accordingly.'

'I shall look into it right away.'

'And one more thing; send me someone who can get into the fort and defuse their ammunition and find a way to open the doors at the right time. They should also disable all the cannons up there.'

'As you command, Huzoor,' Shirke said, saluting once again.

The Maratha sardars were eager to get the Shahenshah's goodwill. They stood expectantly while Aurangzeb contemplated, his fingers moving the beads of the rosary as usual. After an uncomfortable silence he asked Asad Khan, 'Has Kalusha's son prepared a model of the Raigadh Fort?'

'Yes, Huzoor. It was on this condition that his life was spared. We are ready to present it to you whenever you say so.'

Aurangzeb raised his hand. 'There is no need to. Let it be first seen by our Maratha sardars here. If they find it a good replica I will have a look at it and decide the next steps. Shirke, Mohite, I hope you have a good knowledge of the fort.'

'Yes, Alampanah. We have been there since the time it was being built and have complete knowledge of all its defences. We will explain the various strategic points once we have the model.'

Acholji and Arjoji were listening to the conversation and were hopeful that they too would get prominent mansabs as promised by the Badshah. Finding an opportunity to speak Acholji said, 'Jahanpanah, Shikre and Mohite have been inducted into your camp recently but we have been with you since the time your camp was at Ahmednagar. We too are keen that we get the mansabs we have been promised.'

Aurangzeb's cold stare was enough to silence Acholji. He asked in a sharp voice, 'I am told you are related to Shiva. Is that so?'

'Despite that we have shown complete loyalty to you and are willing to lay down our lives. Please command what we must do.'

'I am told one of Shiva's queens is in the Raigadh Fort. But I don't remember you mentioning it. Shirke, what is the queen's name?'

Shirke, proudly puffing out his chest till then, was suddenly at a loss for words. He was willing to share all the information regarding Rajaram, Sambhaji and their families, but the reference to Shivaji's wife put him in a dilemma. His face turned pale. Aurangzeb waited for a while to see his reaction and then said, 'If you don't want to tell us, it is fine. We shall get our spies to find out.'

'I will give the details,' Acholji said, stepping forward. 'I am related to Shivaji Raja and I have all the information.'

'*Shabbash!* Tell me, how many of Shiva's queens are still alive and who amongst them is in Raigadh?'

'Alampanah, only one of his queens is alive and her name is Sakvar Bai. I am told she is in Raigadh.'

'I see,' Aurangzeb said. 'You have given me an important piece of information.'

Aurangzeb's keen eyes noticed the fact that Shirke looked stricken. He asked, 'Shirke, what is it? Why are you so upset?'

'Alamgir Badshah is a true representative of the Paigambar himself. The Maratha raja had to lose his life due to unfortunate circumstances. You cannot be blamed for it. It is quite likely that you will capture Raigadh and Sambhaji's brother as well as his family. But we request you to grant pardon to Sakvar Bai.'

'Why do you ask for her to be pardoned?'

'It is not that she would ask for it, but we wish you don't hurt her. She is a mother to all; from the smallest of the ryots to the prime minister Peshwa. We request that you do not arrest her but rather send her away to her father's place with honour. Not only will you win a political victory but you will get the blessings of millions of poor ryots who will consider you their god.'

Aurangzeb contemplated Shirke's request. He said, 'I shall consider your request, Shirke. Continue your good work and you shall be rewarded suitably.'

ରେ ର

It was late evening when Aurangzeb was invited to inspect a model of the Raigadh Fort. Kazakh soldiers, specially meant for guarding the emperor, stood watch outside the tent. There were a few Maratha sardars amongst those present. Bahramand Khan, being aware that it was the first time the Badshah was going to be physically so close to the Marathas while he inspected the model, ensured that he was alert and tried keeping the distance between them and the Shahenshah as much as possible.

The model was nearly ten-foot square and was an exact replica of the fort. Small flags marked the positions of Itikad Khan's troops who surrounded the fort. After a long inspection Aurangzeb asked, 'Asad Khan, it seems Shiva has selected a fort quite impregnable. What do you say?'

'No doubt, Huzoor. The way Itikad Khan described the fort, it does seem a tall order to take it.'

'We will not give up so easily,' he said turning to Mahadji Nimbalkar. 'What exactly is the meaning of this being Shiva's capital? The palaces and other havelis seem quite small.'

'It was this very fort where Shivaji got himself coronated.'

'Coronated?'

'*Ji*, Huzoor. The Brahmins performed the coronation ceremony and Shivaji dedicated the kingdom to his people.'

The very mention of the priests made Aurangzeb curl his fists. Raising his eyebrows he said, 'These Bammans are dangerous fellows. Abul Hasan of Golconda too fell for their sweet words and forgot his duties towards Islam. By the way, Mahadji, you haven't shown me where Shiva has hidden his treasure in the fort.'

Mahadji stepped forward and pointing to a small building said, 'Here. This is the place where the royal treasures are kept.'

Looking down at the model once again Aurangzeb asked Shirke, 'I am curious to know the things they treasure the most. Something which makes them truly believe in the Maratha Empire.'

Shirke nodded his head saying, 'There is one thing for sure; the gold throne on which Shivaji was coronated.'

'Gold throne? How big is it? Bigger than the royal Mughal one?'

Shirke said, 'This slave of yours has not had the pleasure of seeing the Takht-e-Taus, Alampanah, but I am told it weighs a few tons.'

'What else?'

'People pray to the throne and to the Bhawani sword placed on it.'

Aurangzeb realized the impact Shivaji had had on the ryots. He was being worshipped after his death. He closed his eyes for a moment and muttered, 'This Shiva has managed to really befool his people.'

Mohite, not wanting to be left behind, added, 'You are right, Ala Hazrat. Even the golden legs and the symbol of fish on the throne are revered by the common folks as objects of worship.'

'Men who call themselves rulers need such symbols of power,' Aurangzeb said. Turning towards Mukarrab Khan he added, 'Khan Sahab, you and your son Ikhlas Khan, keep the pressure on from the side of Panhala so that others cannot come in defence of Raigadh. Asad Khan, I want you to take ten thousand troops and join forces with your son. Let the cannons continue their bombardment. I want the cannons to breach the bunds of the lake that supplies water to these forts. I am told Sambha treated his sardars with contempt. I am sure they will themselves open up the gates of the fort and welcome the Mughal troops inside.'

Asad Khan did not openly oppose Aurangzeb's plan but added gently, 'Zille Subhani, Shirke and Nimbalkar tell me that there are at least a hundred forts in this mountainous terrain. Should we not look for a better way to capture them?'

An exasperated Aurangzeb raised his hands up saying, 'I am sure Allah will take care of us. It is for his sake we are doing all this. Join me in praying for his blessings. We need them.'

They stepped out of the tent. A special tent in the Gulalbar area was designated for his prayers, its floor covered with simple mats.

They stepped into the tent while Anwar stood guard at the entrance. They could hear some disturbance outside but Aurangzeb focused on his prayers. Asad Khan raised his eyebrows questioningly at Anwar who, seeing Aurangzeb in prayer, did not respond. At that moment shouts of 'Catch them! Kill them!' were heard. Aurangzeb got up with a start when Anwar entered the tent and reported, 'Huzoor, some unknown men tried entering the Gulalbar area and were captured.'

'Oh, is that all?' Aurangzeb said, sighed deeply, and went back to his prayers. Asad Khan could not focus on his prayers and continued looking out every now and then. The sounds coming from a distance were distracting him. After a while, there was a loud crashing noise and the commotion reduced considerably.

Stepping out of the tent, Aurangzeb raised his hand telling his palanquin bearers to stay put and instead walked down towards the tents. Bahramand Khan came running in with a naked sword in his hand, blood dripping from it. Aurangzeb looked at the sword without reacting and asked, 'What is the situation?'

'Huzoor, we were taken in by surprise. The enemy dared to enter the cantonment.'

'Who were they?'

'The Marathas. Shirke and Mohite could recognize them.'

'How many?'

'We could not estimate correctly because of the darkness but I estimate around a thousand.'

It was clear that Aurangzeb was not convinced, but he did not comment. He walked off further when Mukarrab Khan ran up to him, saluted and said, 'Victory to Shahenshah. We managed to kill many of them.'

'It is a matter of shame that the enemy dares enter our camp despite our having experienced sardars like you around.'

Khan did not respond and did not dare to look into Aurangzeb's eyes. Aurangzeb surveyed the area. Dead bodies of Mughal and Maratha soldiers lay around everywhere. Many were injured. The tent in which he had inspected the model of the Raigadh Fort, had been razed to the ground, the model smashed to bits.

His keen eyes noticed that the gold-coated dome atop the tent was missing. He walked back to his quarters without saying a word.

ෙ෧ ඓ

For the next two months Hamiduddin Khan's men raided the villages near Koregaon creating turmoil. The only information Hamiduddin Khan had been able to gather about the surprise attack was that the Marathas had managed to slip in through the heavy security in disguise, and the only thing he was able to find out was that the two men were named Santa and Dhana.

In retaliation nearly a hundred-odd villagers from the surrounding villages were rounded up and the next morning their decapitated heads were seen hanging at the entrance of the villages. It was a stern warning to anyone daring to support the Marathas.

An all-out attack had now been declared. Asad Khan took a large contingent to support Itikad Khan who was camping at the base of Raigadh. Mukarrab Khan and Ikhlas Khan, the father–son duo, were holding ground at Panhala while Shahzada Azam made a march into Maratha territory with the massive Mughal Army behind him.

One day Bahramand Khan presented himself at Aurangzeb's

court with the request, 'The qiledar of Panhala has requested the Shahenshah to meet his sister, who has come in as his representative. If you permit, I will usher her in.'

Aurangzeb was surprised at the request and asked, 'Why does the qiledar's sister want to meet me?'

'She has a message from him. If the Shahenshah makes him a jagirdar, he is willing to hand over the fort to Mukarrab Khan.'

Aurangzeb was silent for a while. He looked at the seats, normally occupied by the Maratha sardars but who were all out on various duties, whether at Raigadh, Panhala or Sinhagadh. Aurangzeb, as usual, had ensured that the sardars had left their families behind in the cantonment.

He looked at Bahramand Khan and said, 'Let her meet Zeenat.'

The qiledar's sister was dressed in typical Maharashtrian fashion, in a nine-yard-long saree, a large bindi on her forehead, her neck and arms adorned with gold jewellery. She did not seem afraid and asked her maids to stand outside as she entered the tent while Yasmeen escorted her in.

Zeenat sat relaxing against a pillow. She indicated to her visitor to seat herself. The qildear's sister sat down adjusting her shawl around her shoulders.

'Ala Hazrat asked me to meet you, Begum Sahiba.'

'I am aware of it,' Zeenat replied, a little curtly.

Adjusting the saree on her head she said, 'The Mughals will never be able to capture Panhalgadh. My brother is willing to give up the fort if he is promised his jagir around Panhalgadh.' She waited for Zeenat to respond.

'Why should the jagir be given to him?'

'It belonged to him before Sambhaji Raja took it away forcefully and made him work under him.'

Zeenat observed the Maratha lady as she spoke. She was probably younger to her by ten or fifteen years. A huge diamond shone in her nose ring matching the jewellery on her arms and around the neck. She said, 'Let me tell you something you don't know. Before announcing

Sambhaji's punishment, Abba Jaan had asked the exact location of the treasury and the names of people who had betrayed the Shahenshah.'

'It was a simple question.'

'But the fact is your raja did not answer Abba Jaan. He preferred to die a horrible death.'

'He deserved it.'

Zeenat got up with a start. Turning her back on the lady she addressed Yasmeen: 'Tell the lady that the meeting is over. The shrieks of Sambhaji's horrible death are yet to be silenced and his blood is yet to dry; despite that the lady is here to negotiate for her own selfish reasons. I don't want to see the face of such a person.'

The lady in question was not one to give up easily. She managed to get an audience with Aurangzeb by requesting Danishmand Khan to intervene.

After listening to her, Aurangzeb said, 'I am willing to sign an agreement giving the jagir to your brother but we want him to promise Mukarrab Khan that the fort will be handed over.'

'I am like your sister. I hope you trust me.'

Aurangzeb could not help but smile. He said, 'Bai, you have shown your trust in us by visiting us. Please continue to do so. Mukarrab Khan is a close confidant of mine. He is the one who captured Sambha and is well versed in the affairs of the Deccan.'

'Should I assume that you will fulfil your promise of giving us our jagir once we sign the treaty of handing over the fort?'

Aurangzeb was visibly disappointed and looking at the Wazir standing nearby said, 'Let the lady know that I could not have been more explicit.'

'I had come here with a lot of hopes, Jahanpanah. I will be happy if I leave your camp with some gesture of kindness from your side.'

Aurangzeb looked at the lady standing in front of him with her head bowed. He was quite impressed with her courage. The very fact that she demanded some gesture from Aurangzeb was in itself quite unexpected.

He called for the daroga of the zenankhana and said, 'As a token of our goodwill present her a silk shawl, some jewellery and money.' Turning to the lady he said, 'Bai, I have never treated a kafir with such dignity. I am doing so as I am impressed by your boldness. Please coordinate with Mukarrab Khan for further action now.'

It was fifteen days since the incident. Aurangzeb was eagerly waiting for Panhalgadh to be handed over to the Mughals, but one day he received shocking news. Mukarrab Khan and his son had been routed and more than seven hundred Mughal lives lost. Both Mukarrab Khan and Ikhlas Khan had been severely wounded but somehow managed to find shelter in Kolhapur.

On enquiry he found that the Maratha sardar was called Santa. He recalled it was the same sardar who had dared to attack the cantonment a few months ago. It was not difficult for Aurangzeb to surmise that the Marathas were taking revenge!

He closed his eyes for a moment and nodded to himself. Turning to Danishmand Khan he said, 'It has been repeated ad nauseam that how many times a fly may attack a flame, it will finally get burnt. But I am unable to understand the Marathas completely,' he added.

Danishmand Khan said, 'These Marathas are mountain dwellers and do not understand Mughal customs. They do not realize that what can be solved by dialogue need not escalate into battle. They are the ones who will finally lose.'

'Their behaviour is inexplicable. On one hand they take revenge for the way we punished Sambha and on the other, some of their sardars are looking for jagirs. We need to encourage more of such sardars to surrender. We need to send a stern message to people like Santa. Danishmand Khan, I want you to personally go and meet Mukarrab Khan along with the firangi hakeem Sebastian. Please carry royal clothes and some jewellery as a token of my regard. You need to boost the morale of the soldiers. Let the world know that I care for those who are willing to shed their blood for me.'

⋘☙❧⋙

The rains had ended and the signs of early winter were all around. It was a Friday and time for Aurangzeb's afternoon prayers when Bahramand Khan stepped into Aurangzeb's tent with good news.

'Badshah Salamat, Itikad Khan has finally managed to breach Raigadh and capture it.'

Aurangzeb did not react immediately. Instead, he looked at Bahramand Khan and asked, 'Did he manage to enter or were the doors opened for him?'

'I could not get the details but I do know that Itikad Khan has managed to take charge, and Ala Hazrat's flag is now planted on the fort.'

'I am happy to hear that we have managed to capture their capital. Let me know the details; I wish to reward anyone who has shown valour and courage in this important achievement.'

Within a week the details were presented before Aurangzeb. Itikad Khan, supported by his father Asad Khan, had been bombarding the fort for months and had been finally rewarded when one of the sardars had opened the doors of the fort on the temptation of being given an ample reward and a jagir of his own. Greed worked where hard work had failed! Itikad Khan had captured Sambhaji's wife and children. He had also found innumerable treasures including Shivaji's throne at Raigadh.

Aurangzeb, on hearing the details, announced, 'Asad Khan shall escort Sambhaji's family with honour to the camp here. Both Asad Khan and Itikad Khan shall present themselves here with all the treasures captured at the fort. They will be suitably rewarded.'

A large durbar was held within a few days of the capture of Raigadh. Itikad Khan was given the honorific of Zulfikar Khan while Asad Khan was awarded the title of Umdat-ul-mulk. They both were rewarded with the finest of elephants, hundreds of Arab horses and ten thousand gold coins each. Other sardars, who had shown exemplary courage, were rewarded with gold coins and given positions of higher responsibility.

The cantonment at Koregaon rejoiced for nearly a week celebrating the capture of the Maratha capital. Aurangzeb sat in his room carefully going through the list of prisoners captured at Raigadh. A name in the list made him stop and ponder for a long while. Amongst the names was that of Sakvar Bai, Shivaji's wife! Her name triggered a thousand thoughts in his mind.

⋄⋈ ⋈⋄

The capture of Raigadh had been a critical point in the Deccan campaign. There was hardly any merit in looking at other forts, having got Raigadh. Aurangzeb was being shown the treasures captured at the fort. Nearly twenty khojas came in holding Shivaji's golden throne and placed it in the centre of the tent. Looking at the throne Aurangzeb asked, 'Is that the throne Shiva Bhosale sat on?'

'That is what we have been told, Ala Hazrat. It had been concealed under an ordinary cloth and kept in a corner. We found it thanks to the information we had gathered beforehand.'

Zulfikar Khan showed him a sword, its handle encrusted with jewels and said, 'Hazrat Salamat, this is Shiva Bhosale's sword.'

Aurangzeb held the sword in his hand and inspected it carefully. Observing the handle he said, 'It seems to be a firangi sword.'

Aurangzeb sat on his throne and then looking at Zulfikar Khan said, 'I have gone through the list of prisoners. I have a few questions. I was told that Shiva had another son. I don't see his name in the list.'

Asad Khan looked at Zulfikar Khan who said, 'Huzoor, we were told that he was inside the fort when we surrounded it but, apparently, he managed to slip away before we could start the bombardment of the shells.'

'Where do you think he could have gone?'

'He managed to escape from Panhalgadh and slipped into Karnataka.'

Aurangzeb thought for a while, moving the beads in his rosary. He said, 'I am told Shiva's brother manages a small territory near Thanjavur. I need you to send some cavalry which can race fast and intercept him.' Putting his rosary aside he said, 'I expected two more names in the list. Shahzada Akbar escaped into Iran sometime back but I was told that he had left behind a son and a daughter.'

'Ala Hazrat, we too were expecting to find them there, but when we enquired we were told that they are with the Rajput Durgadas. It is unfortunate that I did not get an opportunity to capture them.'

'Let us do what is possible and be content with it,' Aurangzeb muttered to himself.

Asad Khan said, 'Huzoor-e-Ala, may I share the general feeling amongst most of the sardars?'

'What is it?'

'They believe you are representative of Hazrat Paigambar himself. You have managed victory where everyone else failed. The beauty of the north beckons them. The soldiers are tired of having spent more than ten years living a life in tents and are desperate to go back to Hindustan. We have captured the Deccan and the Mughal flag flies high till the shores of the ocean. They have a request to return to Hindustan now.'

'Your suggestion is quite valid. We have captured the Deccan now and all the territories have been annexed to the Mughal Empire. But I would like to make a round of the captured territories and then make plans for our return.'

৵৹ৎ ৯৹৵

The plans to return to the capital were gaining ground in Aurangzeb's mind. He ordered Danishmand Khan to supervise the movement of much of the heavy equipment to Aurangabad. Discussing the details of the movement one day Danishmand Khan said, 'Badshah Salamat has been generous in handing over titles to many mansabdars. Many have been recipients of his largesse, whether jewellery, money, gifts or titles. But it seems one person has been ignored all through.'

Aurangzeb looked at Danishmand Khan. He could guess whom he was referring to. Yet he said, 'If there is someone I have missed out it would mean he was undeserving.'

'Huzoor, your largesse is akin to the rain falling from the sky. It may fall on tigers and sometimes on deer too. The giver should not bother about the recipient.'

Aurangzeb's face, wrinkled with age, contorted when he spoke. His hands were trembling a little as he said, 'I have never understood your poetic language. I have given as per my wisdom and understanding, but if I have missed out someone deserving, please tell me so.'

'I have taken this liberty as I was sure you would hear me out. I wanted to bring to your notice that amongst the cannons, royal treasury and many prisoners, which we are moving to Aurangabad, we have Shahzada Muazzam too.'

'Yes, I know that. He is a prisoner in our camp.'

'Hazrat Salamat, he may be a prisoner but he is still a Shahzada.'

'All the more reason for my displeasure. He has not shown his inclination to learn and take on the responsibility of being a real Shahzada.'

'Huzoor, he has spent many years in custody now. He had come to the Deccan as a subedar and had participated in a lot of battles and campaigns; some successful and some not. I don't deny that he committed a crime but that was many years ago. I am now entrusted with the task of taking him back to Aurangabad, where he had taken charge as the subedar of the Deccan once upon a time. Hazrat, the entire Hindustan is now under Mughal rule. You have, over many happy occasions, pardoned hardened criminals. I appeal to you to look at Shahzada Muazzam compassionately too.'

Aurangzeb was silent for a while. He said, 'I am unable to understand the change in me but I am not as hard-hearted as I used to be. I will consider your request. Let Shahzada Muazzam continue staying here. Don't take him along with the other prisoners.'

'Huzoor, are you likely to pardon him soon?'

Aurangzeb and Danishmand Khan were in the midst of their discussion when Asad Khan came in looking crestfallen. He held a letter which he handed over to Aurangzeb saying, 'Hazrat, we had managed to capture all the Maratha forts sans one when we got the news that Rustam Khan from Bijapur, who had been spearheading the campaign, has been captured by the Marathas.'

Aurangzeb glanced at the letter and sighed deeply, 'Rustam Khan is one of our finest sardars and has conducted many successful campaigns. It is a matter of concern if he has been caught by the Marathas. Who is the leader who captured Rustam Khan?'

'His name is Santa!'

Aurangzeb raised his eyebrows. The irritation on hearing Santa's name was evident. 'Santa! That name seems to be making rounds these days.'

'Huzoor, he had twenty-five thousand cavalrymen with him.'

'We need to punish that upstart.'

'Badshah Salamat, the troubles don't end here. The Marathas have demanded a ransom of five lakh rupiyas to release Rustam Khan. His two wives and two sons conveyed this message to us today. The Marathas have warned that if the ransom is not paid within a week, they will behead Rustam. There is one more thing ...'

'Tell me.'

'I am unable to speak, Huzoor. These Marathas are uncouth and have no respect for anything and are an uncultured lot.'

'I am prepared to listen to anything. Please speak.'

'They have threatened to throw Rustam's head on to the Burhanpur mosque if we don't pay the ransom in time. *Tauba, tauba!* Alampanah, what kind of people are these Marathas? They don't care for any sentiments.'

Danishmand Khan was sitting quietly listening to the conversation. Aurangzeb's glance at him was the cue for him to speak. He said, 'Huzoor, if we expect the enemy to behave in a particular fashion, we too have to reciprocate.'

'What do you mean?' Aurangzeb blurted out.

'The way we tortured and killed their king, their demand for a mere five lakh to release Rustam is quite gentlemanly, I would say.'

'Khan Sahab, Zille Subhani is the emperor and a true servant of Hazrat Paigambar. We cannot tolerate such insults from the uncouth Marathas.'

Danishmand Khan did not reply. Aurangzeb said, 'Let the shifting of equipment and other things to Aurangabad be on hold for a while. I was planning to visit Bijapur soon but now I will march on to the city at the earliest. Please assemble the best of our sardars and ask them to charge into the Maratha territory. We have captured most of their forts. Now direct the cannons to their villages. Burn any village if you see even the minutest of resistance. These are my orders. It seems Allah wants us to continue our jehad. Parwar Digaar, I accede to your wishes.'

'Jehad! Jehad!' Aurangzeb uttered.

⚬◦೧ ୭ୡ◦⚬

The cantonment had been set up on the banks of the Neera. Aurangzeb, having despatched most of the army to capture the remaining forts and territory from the Marathas was a bit free to look into other matters. He had handed over the charge of looking after some of the select prisoners to Zeenat. He stepped into Zeenat's tent to meet them when Zeenat said, 'Abba Jaan, I have a request.'

'What is it, dear?'

'One of the prisoners is Shiva Bhosale's begum. As per Maratha tradition it would be improper for her to show her face to you. You may excuse her.'

'What is her name?'

'Sakvar Bai.'

'Let her be excused. Present the others.'

'There is one more lady.'

'Who is she?' Aurangzeb asked, a little impatient.

'Sambha's begum.'

'Sambha's wife? How old is she?'

'Around twenty-five or so.'

'She is much younger than you, dear. She cannot be excused then. Let her be present.'

'Abba Jaan, Sambha's begum has put a condition that she will not mind meeting you if you treat her like your daughter.'

'You heard me; I am sure she would not mind.'

A young boy stepped in at that moment. Aurangzeb looked intently at him for a few seconds and exclaimed, 'He looks just like his father! I recall Sambha had come along with Shiva to Agra and must have been of the same age as his son now.'

Zeenat, touching the young boy said, 'He is Badshah Salamat. Please bow to him.' The young boy immediately did an elaborate salaam.

Aurangzeb asked, 'What is your name?'

'Shiva.'

'What?'

'Yes, Abba Jaan. He has been named after his grandfather.'

'Well, I hope he has not inherited the rogue genes of his grandfather.'

'This is Sambha's begum,' she added, pointing in the direction of a young woman.

'She seems so young! What is her name?'

'Yesubai,' Zeenat said.

'Zeenat dear, please explain to her in Hindavi language whatever I say.'

'Yes, Abba Jaan.'

'Tell them that they will be allowed to stay in the Gulalbar tents if they promise not to create any sort of problems. They will not be troubled at all here and will be housed in a tent next to that of the Shahzadi. Their servants and their maids too will be housed nearby and they will have all the freedom to move about in the area. If they try to leave the camp and establish any contact with the rebel Marathas however, we will have to curtail their freedom.'

Zeenat explained the same in the Hindavi language. Aurangzeb continued, 'If the prisoners want to say something they may go ahead.'

Yesubai, hearing Zeeant's translation pulled her saree pallu further down her forehead and said, 'Badshah Salamat is like my father to me. I promise that my son and I will not do anything which is against protocol.'

Aurangzeb replied in Hindavi, 'Bai, I heard you, but I have learnt over the years that there is a lot of gap between words and actions. You have been a kafir till date and while you may honour me by calling me your father, your actions are going to be strictly monitored. Shiva's other son is still going around creating mischief. I hope you keep in mind the manner in which your husband met his end before you even think of establishing contact with Rajaram.'

Aurangzeb could distinctly hear a sob from behind the screen. The mention of Sambhaji's torturous death was enough to open old wounds. Zeenat, in order to distract Aurangzeb's attention said, 'I am going to keep Sambha's young son near my tent. I suppose Abba Jaan may not like him being addressed as Shiva. May I ask Abba Jaan to suggest a different name for him?'

'That is a good idea! Shiva was a rogue. He has troubled me a lot and his son Sambha made matters worse. We need to bury the memories for ever. Shiva was a thief. Let us call Sambha's son Shahu. From today he will be addressed as Shahu,' declared Auranzgeb.

Yesubai said, in a voice loud enough for Aurangzeb to hear, 'Father, the Maratha territory belongs to my father-in-law and my husband. My husband's brother is forcibly trying to usurp the throne. So the question of keeping in touch with him does not arise. In fact, I have a request to make.'

'Dear, please tell me.'

'If Huzoor were to defeat Rajaram and hand over the kingdom to us, we shall be indebted forever.'

Aurangzeb smiled and said, 'I know Shahu is the real heir to the throne. We shall then honour him by calling him Shahu Raja. We shall award him a mansab of seven thousand. Shahu Raja, did you understand what Ammi Jaan just said?'

'Yes, Jahanpanah,' Shahu Raja said, on cue from Zeenat.

'It is decided then. We shall catch your uncle and hand over the territory to you. You need to help us in this mission.'

'I am in the service of Badshah Salamat. I may be young but I am sure you will not find me lacking when it comes to valour in the battlefield.'

Aurangzeb could not help but smile. He said, caressing his beard, '*Bahut khub! Bahut khub!* Shahu Raja, I am impressed with your words. But I wonder whether it is your grandfather's emotions which are behind your words.'

Turning towards Zeenat, Aurangzeb said, 'I think we need to focus on his education. I suggest we get the best of the pundits from the Deccan and let Shahu Raja and his two brothers get the best education possible.' Then remembering something he added, 'And yes, we have Shiva's begum under our custody. I will allow her to get her best maids and servants for her comfort. She should not get the feeling that they are under the arrest of the Mughals. Shiva may have been an enemy, but let the world know that I have nothing against his begum.'

Zeenat escorted Yesubai and Shahu out of the tent. For the good work done, Aurangzeb presented her a jewel-encrusted tray for serving betel leaves.

༄ঌ ঌ৯

On getting the news that Rajaram was in the fort at Jinji, Aurangzeb made a different plan to rout the Marathas. He planned to break the Maratha territory into two, pushing his army in between the Sahyadris on one side and towards Jinji on the other. In order to be closer to the place of action, he moved the camp from the banks of the Neera to Bijapur. Top sardars like Kasim Khan, Alimardan Khan, Bahramand Khan and Zulfikar Khan were nominated for the attack at Jinji.

There were victories but many setbacks too. While the Mughal Army was able to overrun minor forts, they were being troubled consistently by Santaji Ghorpade and Dhanaji Jadhav, who were experts in mountain warfare, and attacked the Mughals in surprise raids, charging through inaccessible forests and vanishing before the Mughals could retaliate. Aurangzeb spent enormous manpower and money to get the main roads in shape. He also created roads along the banks of many rivers so that elephants and huge carriages could move with ease. It took nearly two years for these to get into shape.

༄ঌ ঌ৯

Udaipuri's consistent efforts finally reaped dividends.

Till date, Shahzada Kambaksh had been given various responsibilities, but in reality they were all for the name's sake. His men, stationed far and wide, would fulfil the tasks given, leaving

Kambaksh with literally no direct responsibility. Shahzada Muazzam, having earned Aurangzeb's ire, was under house arrest while Akbar had escaped into Iran. It was only Azam who had been given some real tasks and he had spared no efforts to fulfil them. His son Bedar Bakht too was helping him in his job. The fact that he had played an important role in the fall of Bijapur and Golconda was another reason for Udaipuri's discomfort. She was worried that if things were to take a different turn tomorrow, Kambaksh would be seen as incompetent, having spent all his life in the camp. The fact that Azam was unhappy at Kambaksh's spending all his time with the Shahenshah had been brought to Aurangzeb's notice by his spies. Azam had expressed his fears to some of the sardars that Kambaksh might poison the Shahenshah's mind against him. Aurangzeb thought it was wise to send Kambaksh out on a campaign for a while. It would also help to reduce Azam's unnecessary anxiety.

Having sent Kambaksh on a campaign, Aurangzeb gave detailed instructions to Asad Khan to ensure that the Shahzada was safe and was asked to keep a close watch and not allow any harm to come to him.

Azam, waiting for an opportune moment, requested a meeting with the Shahenshah. He had been managing the subah of Hyderabad ever since it had been annexed to the Mughal Empire. Azam was in his mid-forties now. His face had tanned having spent many years in the hot sun of the Deccan, where he had been camping for nearly ten years.

Before leaving on a different assignment he wanted to meet the Badshah. One day, he decided to pay a visit to his sister Zeenat.

Aurangzeb was in Zeenat's quarters at that time and, on seeing Azam enter, he said, 'There! Your brother has come to visit you, Zeenat.'

Zeenat asked, 'Where would he get time when Abba Jaan sends him on one campaign after another?'

Azam, ignoring the jibe said, 'I came in to enquire if Begum Sahiba liked the jewellery I sent from Hyderabad.'

Zeenat said, 'Shahzada, I loved the jewellery you sent. I am happy that, albeit late, you did remember me and sent diamonds from the Golconda mines for me.'

Aurangzeb said, 'That reminds me; you had been here all the while in the camp, but I forgot to mention. It was regarding the mangoes you sent from Hyderabad.' He continued, reminiscing the past, 'I recall a similar instance when I had sent mangoes from Junnar, knowing that Badshah Shah Jahan loved them. But unfortunately he was very upset.'

'Upset? Why was he upset?'

'Due to intense summer heat, many of the mangoes had ripened earlier and got spoilt. My men had selected the best of the lot and presented a small basket to the Badshah, who felt insulted seeing such a small quantity. My brother Dara provoked his anger by falsely stating that I had deliberately sent only a handful. You are lucky I don't think like that!'

Azam, referring to Kambaksh without taking his name said, 'You are right! There is no one here at the moment to instigate you against me.'

Aurangzeb threw a sharp glance at Azam saying, 'Keep in mind I don't get influenced so easily by anyone.'

'Please pardon me, Abba Jaan. I should not have said that.'

Aurangzeb let out a deep sigh of relief and then turning to Zeenat said, 'Dear, old age is the worst thing which can happen to a man. One feels loss of control over many things. The mind starts playing tricks on one. I hope the Shahzada has patience and believes that Allah, and not mortals like us, is the one who makes things happen.'

Azam asked, 'Should that stop a person from trying, Abba Jaan?'

'You will be able to understand that only when you turn seventy.'

'Abba Jaan, I am unable to understand you.'

'Had everything been under man's control, I would not have lost any campaign.'

'Please command me, Abba Jaan. Which campaign should I go on?'

'I will, at an appropriate time. In the meanwhile, I suggest drop your habit of suspecting others.'

‿ᘓ ᘐ‿

Zeenat finished her morning prayers. Putting the Quran aside, she lightly brushed her palms over her face. The daroga, waiting outside, announced the arrival of Yesubai.

Yesubai entered the hall and sat a little distance away, adjusting her shawl on her shoulders.

'Not there. Please come and sit next to me,' Zeenat said, patting a cushion near her.

Yesubai was a bit confused. She was trying to ascertain the reason for the meeting. Zeenat's request to sit next to her added to the confusion.

'I need to speak to you in private,' Zeenat clarified.

As Yesubai sat down, Zeenat asked, 'Bai, I hope you have no trouble in the camp.'

Yesubai said, 'When the Begum Sahiba is taking personal interest, where is the question of any trouble?'

'What about Shivaji Raja's Begum Sahiba? Is she fine?'

Yesubai sighed, 'She is fine, I suppose.'

Realizing that Yesubai wanted to say something further Zeenat asked, 'You may be frank with me. Does she have any complaints?'

'As a rule, she does not believe in partaking of food till she has finished her Monday pooja at the Shiva temple.'

Zeenat did not respond. Noticing her silence Yesubai continued, 'She is keen to get a Shiva temple built here inside the Gulalbar camp. I know it is not possible and hence I was reluctant to say so.'

'You are right; it is quite impossible. You know my Abba Jaan's views on other religions. I really doubt he will permit building a temple here but you may tell her that I will try my best.'

For a while both of them were silent. Zeenat was uncomfortable discussing the reason for which she had called Yesubai.

Taking the lead Yesubai asked, 'You called me here to discuss something. What is it?'

Zeenat picked up a small wooden box placed on the side and putting her hand on Yesubai's shoulder said, 'Abba Jaan wanted to hand this over to you.'

'Anything which the Shahenshah gives will be of great value, I am sure.'

Zeenat rubbed Yesubai's back affectionately saying, 'It is a very precious thing. Abba Jaan wanted you to have it.'

Zeenat opened the box to reveal an emerald necklace, with a large pendant at the centre. Yesubai had to glance at it for a brief moment to realize what it was. Her lips quievered and she said, her voice choking with emotion, 'It is the necklace worn by my Swami!'

'It was lying in the royal treasury till now. Abba Jaan wants you to have it.'

Yesubai's tears fell down her cheeks. She pleaded, 'Why are you playing with my emotions?'

'I am aware of your sorrows, Bai. Abba Jaan is merciful and wants you to accept this gift. I am sure he will reward you more once you take this.' Zeenat knew her words sounded hollow.

'Shahzadi Sahiba, I beg your pardon, but if you were really aware of my sorrows, you would have requested the Shahenshah not to reopen wounds which have barely healed. You know what a husband means to a Hindu wife. I would have rather accepted death than being tortured in this fashion.'

Zeenat sighed deeply, 'Each person tackles his or her sorrow in their own ways. You do not know the kind of effort I took to prevent Abba Jaan from preventing the tragedy but it was of no use.'

Yesubai knew Zeenat was telling the truth. She could not control herself and hugged her tightly as sobs wracked her body. 'Begum Sahiba, I was told he suffered miserably at the end. Is that true?'

'What is the point in knowing the truth now?'

'Is it true that he was tortured beyond imagination?'

'Bai, I plead you to let it go.'

'Begum Sahiba, you are like a mother to me. Tell me, were you able to see him in the end? How was he? What did he say? Did he remember me or my son?'

Zeenat patted her back saying, 'Bai, I had met Sambhaji earlier too.'

'Really?' Yesubai asked, wiping her tears with the back of her palm. 'When was that? What did he say? Where did you see him?'

'It was many years ago. I am not sure if you were married to him then but he was of the same age as Shahu Raja is today. He had come visiting Shahzada Akbar who was ill. That was the first time I saw him. I met him a few times when he was under arrest. But those painful memories of his end are torturous and I plead you not to ask me to recall them. The very thought of his end makes me shiver. After hearing about the way he died, I feel lucky that I never married. If my husband had been subjected to such an unbelievably torturous end I would have been unable to live.'

Yesubai wiped her eyes and said, 'Begum Sahiba, if only one could ask for one's death. But God is not that compassionate, else He would not have allowed me to live even for a moment more.'

Saying so, she hugged Zeenat again. For a long time, her sobs wracked her body while her tears drenched Zeenat's shoulder.

The emerald necklace lay forgotten on the carpet below.

੧ଓ ଓ੧

The camp shuttled between Bijapur and Galgal twice over a period of two years. The campaign against the Marathas had not been very successful. At Jinji, Zulfikar Khan was unable to make any headway despite support from his father Asad Khan and Shahzada Kambaksh. On the other hand, Santaji and Dhanaji would raid the Mughal Army wherever they found a weak spot. Aurangzeb, fed up of hearing the exploits of the two Maratha sardars, sent Kasim Khan, Khanajad Khan and others to support the attack at Jinji.

Maratha troops were finding ways to win back the forts they had earlier lost to the Mughals. Rajgadh, Torna and Panhala went back to the Marathas. Aurangzeb had realized that it was futile to try and capture the hill forts. He had focused all his attention on Jinji with the intention of capturing Rajaram. He believed his mission against the Marathas would end once he captured him. Rajaram had promised his sardars that they would be made jagirdars of any territory which they manage to repossess from the Mughals. Aurangzeb too, not wanting to be left behind, was showering all kinds of gifts and honours on his men. He had managed to get the treasuries from Kabul in the west to Dhaka in the east to supply him money for his campaign. He was confident that monetary power would finally lead to success.

It was Aurangzeb's seventy-seventh birthday. He decided to celebrate it sans any pomp having sent messages to his sardars in advance not to get any gifts. He spent most of the day in prayer. That afternoon he decided to visit Udaipuri begum. It was a rare occasion as he hardly met the begum, now in her mid-forties, these days.

Age showed on her face but she continued to lead a lavish lifestyle, her tent filled with various bottles of perfumes, wines from Shiraz and Istanbul, and rose petals strewn all over the floor. Despite being told of Aurangzeb's visit, she did not move the wine bottles away.

Aurangzeb entered the tent, looked displeased, but did not comment.

Aurangzeb was tired. He was wearing a simple white dress, a pearl necklace being the only ornament on him. Looking at Udaipuri begum he said, 'Today is my birthday. I have come to ask what gift you would like to have from me.'

Udaipuri was happy that Kambaksh had been sent on an important mission at Jinji. She would send him letters asking him to behave as a future Badshah. Little was she aware that each of her letters was read out to Aurangzeb before being sent to Kambaksh. He asked, feigning ignorance of her state of mind, 'I hope you are happy these days, begum.'

'Ji, Huzoor. I have nothing to complain about.'

'Then what would you like to have from me? Tell me and I shall order for it.'

Udaipuri, with her finger on her cheek, looked at Aurangzeb and said, 'If you so insist ... But I am sure Huzoor will not be very happy with my request.'

'Ask. If it is possible, I will surely fulfil it.'

'Huzoor, we have been staying in the army cantonment for nearly fifteen years now.'

'That is right. We have called for a jehad. One does not count years when such an act is called for.'

'You may not; but I do. I don't think it suits your health to stay here any further. I suggest you hand over the responsibilities to Kambaksh.'

'Kambaksh has been given the important task of arresting the rogue Maratha king. Once we capture him we have no reason to stay here any more.'

'You had said the same thing before capturing Sambha. You captured him, put him to death, captured his family, and yet the campaign is far from over. This is that I ask from you: hand over the task to Kambaksh and return to Delhi.'

'Why? What is it that you don't have here?'

'Nothing, really, but a camp is a camp, after all. I remember Huzoor meeting me for the first time in the gardens of Shalimar with the chinar trees in the background. I remember the lovely havelis, the beautiful buildings of Agra and Delhi and the huge domes piercing the sky; there are many things I miss. I pray to Allah that I would get a chance to see them again. My eyes are tired of seeing this dry and desolate Deccan. I entreat Huzoor to return and spend the rest of his life in a heaven on earth like Shalimar Bagh.'

Aurangzeb did not react immediately but continued to move the beads in his rosary. Finally he said, 'Begum, this servant of Khuda has no time for himself ever since he proclaimed jehad. Gardens, palaces, havelis and such are not for me. I am entitled to the tents, the shamianas, the weapons, the cannons and my soldiers. That is what Allah has given me. I cannot afford to ignore his gifts.'

Udaipuri was clearly disappointed. She said, 'The Badshah of Hindustan comes into my tent, asks for my wish and then finds excuses to not honour them. Isn't that strange?'

'It is not,' Aurangzeb replied. 'What is strange is that my begum has not yet realized my true mission and the passion with which I am pursuing this jehad. If my own begum is unable to fathom it, how can I expect my sardars and the common soldier to?'

'Do I then assume that you have not granted me my wish?'

'I hate to see my begum disappointed but you must understand,' he said, sighing deeply. 'I am fighting a jehad on two fronts. One is with the kafirs and the other with my own self. I know I cannot return to Hindustan but at the same time, I don't like the fact that my family is suffering unnecessarily on that account. I want to set up a permanent base with beautiful havelis. You may consider this your Hindustan for the time being. Imagine the mountains here as those of the ones you miss in Kashmir. And let the trees here remind you of chinar.'

Udaipuri did not know how to react to Aurangzeb's words. His obsession for jehad was beyond her comprehension.

❧ ❧

The campaign against the Marathas had not led to any results. On the contrary both sides had lost thousands of men. The region from the Krishna in the north to the Tungabhadra in the south was barren, the crops wilting in the hot sun and forests devoid of trees. People were deserting the villages and all one could see was poverty and famine leaving the ryots helpless.

But no one was willing to give up. Aurangzeb had enough supplies from the north while the Marathas were being supported by those from Madras and the firangis on the coastal belt. The Mughals continued their resolve to break into the Jinji Fort.

A disturbing piece of news landed at Aurangzeb's desk. Normally the news of the death of a few hundred soldiers would not shake him up and he would set the letter aside stating it was the will of Allah. But the news that Kambaksh had been secretly corresponding with Rajaram and that he had planned to visit him in the fort without informing Asad Khan and Zulfikar Khan was enough to spur Aurangzeb into action. He immediately ordered Rao Dalpat Bundela to keep a strict eye on Kambaksh. He then asked Asad Khan to intensify the attack on the fort.

But within a fortnight they received another jolt when Santaji from outside and Rajaram's men from inside retaliated and managed to loot their camp. While they missed capturing the Shahzada, they did not lose the opportunity to loot many elephants, jewellery and cannons.

Aurangzeb realized that there was no point in keeping the Shahzada there when he was being constantly watched over. He may as well order him to return to the cantonment. He issued orders to Asad Khan to escort the Shahzada to the cantonment.

Aurangzeb had established a new cantonment near Pandharpur and changed its name to Islampuri. He waited for the Shahzada to reach. When Aurangzeb learnt a fortnight later that they were within sighting distance of the camp, he ordered Asad Khan to stay back and asked the Shahzada to proceed alone.

Aurangzeb did not meet Kambaksh in his durbar but asked him to present himself in Zeenat's tent. The moment Kambaksh entered, he fell at Aurangzeb's feet and with tears in his eyes said, 'Abba Jaan! I will not leave your feet till you say that you have pardoned me!'

Aurangzeb was moved and patting his head with his trembling hands said, 'You have not committed a crime, Shahzada. What for shall I pardon you?'

Kambaskh stood up wiping his tears and said, 'Do you mean it Abba Jaan? I can't believe my ears when I hear you say that I have not erred. Why did you then ask Bundela to guard me? There was talk of me having joined hands with Rajaram.'

'Shahzada, we shall discuss those details later. I want to know why you were in correspondence with Rajaram. The letters have been sent by Asad Khan to me.'

'Abba Jaan, I made a mistake.'

'How can you commit such a blunder? You had been sent to capture the enemy. Instead, you start correspondence with him; isn't that strange?'

'Abba Jaan, I had gone there with all the intentions of carrying out my task but I soon realized that Asad Khan and Zulfikar Khan are in no mood to capture Rajaram!'

'Shahzada! Be careful when you speak so casually of one of my trusted commanders. Zulfikar Khan has performed many important tasks for the sultanate and Asad Khan's family has been with us for generations. Even at his advanced age, he is serving the throne.'

'I am aware of the facts and that is why I was hesitant to get it to your notice. I realized that Zulfikar Khan was hand in glove with Rajaram and had allowed his men to leave and enter the fort without getting captured by our forces. I confronted Khan when I came to know of it.'

'That is where you erred. You should have taken me into confidence before asking him.'

'I realized I made a mistake. Not only was I insulted but he did not mince words in insulting the throne as well.'

Kambaksh waited for Aurangzeb's reaction. He was overwhelmed with emotions, a mixture of fear, awe and anticipation all coming together as he stood facing the Shahenshah.

Aurangzeb had spent a lifetime noticing men and their behaviour. He was trying to ascertain the truth behind Kambaksh's words. His piercing gaze was difficult for Kambaksh to tolerate and he looked down at the carpet. Aurangzeb asked, 'Tell me exactly what Asad Khan said.'

'He insulted me by saying that I was born to a low-caste woman.' Kambaksh was in tears as he continued, 'Abba Jaan, he said the Badshah fell in love with a mere concubine who was available to anyone who wished to enjoy her beauty. Desperately wanting to prove my mettle, I attacked the fort, but unfortunately I did not get any support and had to suffer defeat, much to the merriment of Zulfikar Khan.'

Wordlessly, Aurangzeb left the tent asking Kambaksh to take rest.

The next day Aurangzeb called for Asad Khan and instructed him to continue the attack at Jinji. 'We have been trying to take over the fort for years now. I have realized where we went wrong, but this is not the time to point fingers. Continue your efforts. I shall decide the next course of action if we are not able to take the fort by monsoon.'

Aurangzeb, having despatched Asad Khan, imposed a hefty fine of eighty lakh rupiyas on him for the losses suffered under Kambaksh. He also issued orders to impound two of his palaces in Delhi till the fine was paid.

৵৹ৡৡ৵

Zeenat was looking for an opportune moment to chat with Aurangzeb. The month of Ramzan was about to end and the atmosphere in the camp was that of cheerful expectations. The festival of Eid was soon to arrive and news from the battle front too was encouraging. When Aurangzeb arrived in her tent after his siesta, Zeenat decided to broach the topic. She said, 'Abba Jaan, I am told you are weaving the cap you wear while reading your prayers with your own hands. Is that true?'

'You heard right, dear.'

'Why? You may as well order the daroga to get one for you.'

'That is not the point, dear. The Quran says that one has to earn one's bread.'

'But are you not doing so by ruling the sultanate? What more can a Badshah do?'

'That is my duty. I still have to earn my bread.'

'When people know you have woven a cap, anyone would be more than happy to oblige by buying it. How does it serve your purpose?'

'I have taken care of that. I have given instructions that the caps should be mixed with others sold in the shops. Do you think what I am doing is wrong?'

Zeenat smiled instead. Aurangzeb asked, 'Dear, I see you smile. Tell me, do I commit a mistake here?'

'Abba Jaan, you are a representative of Muhammad Paigambar himself. How can you ever be wrong?'

'I know you want to say something. Don't be sarcastic.'

'Abba Jaan, see the way you have treated Kambaksh despite knowing that he committed a grave crime. On the contrary you have penalized loyal Zulfikar Khan and Asad Khan.'

'I was expecting you to raise this issue but you must understand I have no other choice.'

'I am surprised when you say that, Abba Jaan. Muhammad Sultan, for a similar crime, had to suffer life imprisonment, while Shahzada Akbar was punished for a mere mention of a revolt and had to find refuge in a small village in Iran staying like a pariah. Muazzam's fate is well known to everyone with his children and zenankhana under your command. Kambaksh's crime was no different from others; yet he has been pardoned. People in the camp are gossiping about your biased treatment.'

Aurangzeb heard out Zeenat patiently and then, sighing deeply, said, 'I know what you are saying, Zeenat. People must be wondering why Kambaksh, being my youngest Shahzada, is being pardoned easily and how I am unable to say anything lest it upset Udaipuri begum.'

'Isn't that the way of the world, Abba Jaan?'

'The way of the world and the way the Badshah functions need not be the same.'

'Isn't the Badshah too a father, a brother or a son to someone? Would there then be differences in the way a Badshah and an ordinary man would react when it comes to these relationships?'

'He has to be different; else he cannot be a Badshah.'

'Abba Jaan, tell me how Kambaksh's crime is lesser than what Muhammad Sultan committed?'

'Muhammad Sultan committed a heinous crime. Imagine the situation then: there was a clamour for the throne at Delhi and Dara Shikoh was ready with his army to fight against me. We had managed to rout his troops, but at that time Muhammad Sultan joined forces with him. I was warned at the right time, else I would have lost my life. It is for that reason I could never pardon Muhammad Sultan. It was a question of who lives; and I had to make a choice.'

'Then you have answered my question.'

'I don't understand.'

'I might agree that your action was justified in the given circumstance. But later, when you had been firmly settled on your throne and Badshah Shah Jahan was dead, a mere mistake by Shahzada Akbar was enough to chase him out of the camp. Despite his sending repeated requests for mercy, you chose to ignore him. Why, Abba Jaan?'

'I agree I had no enemies and that there was no threat. Yet, I have not been able to pardon Akbar. But you must keep in mind that the only real challenge to the Mughal Empire has been from the Rajputs. Akbar had the audacity to declare himself the emperor sitting in a mosque in Rajputana. He had the backing of nearly fifty thousand troops while I had just a thousand and that too a mixture of slaves and khojas. Had Akbar shown courage, I would not have been alive today. Akbar sided with the Marathas and forced me to move to the Deccan to rout them. It is due to his actions that I am spending my time here. His crime is unpardonable.'

'Are you saying Muazzam too deserved similar treatment? You were not willing to pardon him.'

'There is a difference there. He was looking for some personal gain by joining hands with the enemy. Hence I have placed him under house arrest and not given him a harsher punishment.'

'What kind of a house arrest is it, Abba Jaan? He is not allowed to cut his hair, trim his nails or meet his begum. He is forced to eat whatever is served to him. Is that not being too harsh?'

'Muazzam is the eldest Shahzada and I had conferred the title of Shah Alam on him. If Allah wills he could succeed me to the throne. I know he does not have the courage or the will to revolt against me. I know he makes a farce of reading the Quran and indulges in all the luxuries of life. I hope this imprisonment will lead him to introspect. Once I see a change in him, I will allow him to lead a normal life.'

'I am not able to understand your lenient attitude towards Kambaksh despite knowing that he wanted to join the enemy ranks.'

'Well, I must confess I am not sure whether I would have actually taken action against him if I found out that he had sided with the enemy.'

'Are you saying he did not attempt to join the enemy? Don't you believe Asad Khan and Zulfikar Khan?'

'That is not the case, dear. I have my own ways of getting information. I don't believe Kambaksh when he said that Asad Khan had called him a concubine's son.'

'Then what is the reality?'

'You know Asad Khan is as old as I am and has never worked hard in his life. On the way to Jinji, the Shahzada decided to ride a horse. Seeing the Shahzada do so, Asad Khan too was forced to give up his palanquin and follow suit. Now, at his age, it was a difficult proposition to ride nearly eighty miles on horseback. The Shahzada was enjoying the trouble it was causing Asad Khan. Despite knowing his discomfort, Kambaksh refused to ride an elephant. No doubt Asad Khan was upset and waited for an opportunity to insult him. Kambaksh may not be well versed in politics but there are people willing to support him to put Asad Khan down. Now that I have sent Asad Khan back to Jinji, he will toil day and night to prove his loyalty.'

Zeenat touched her palm to her forhead and said, 'Abba Jaan, I ask you to pardon me if I have overstepped my authority.'

'What are you talking of?'

'I feel you are emotionally bonded to Kambaksh and unable to take a firm decision.'

'That may be true to some extent. But you have seen the way I have behaved with Shahu.'

'I am unable to follow you, Abba Jaan.'

'I had allowed Shiva to escape from Agra but when I captured Sambha, I had no option but to put him to death. Now his son Shahu is in our captivity but I have treated him as a family member. You would have seen that I behaved differently with all the three generations.'

'I do, but I don't understand your politics, Abba Jaan.'

'Remember, when you were in Aurangabad? Zebunissa and you had admired a portrait of Shiva.'

Avoiding his gaze Zeenat said, 'I do; now that you remind me.'

'I don't forget easily. I could have easily put Shiva away and despite knowing that he would escape I had turned a blind eye to it. But in case of Sambha, I had to behave differently. Else, he would have troubled me for the rest of my life.'

'Abba Jaan, was it necessary to put him through such torture?' Zeenat blurted out.

'I don't do things which are not necessary. Look at Shahu; I have sent out *firmans* in his name and seen the results they have generated. I treated each of the Shahzadas differently and, likewise, I am treating the Maratha kings differently too. Are you convinced now?'

'Yes, I am,' Zeenat said, looking at Aurangzeb. 'I will never understand your mind though, Abba Jaan. That I am convinced of.'

Aurangzeb did not react. Instead, he muttered, '*La ilahi illilah, Muhammad rasool lillilah …*'

❦

Brahmapuri wore a different look now with havelis built for the Badshah and his zenankhana as well as havelis for Shahu and his family. The amirs and other officials had their own permanent residences.

Zeenat, on a morning tour of the cantonment, decided to drop into Shahu's haveli. She sent word but by the time the maid had given the message, she was already at the doorstep, much to the embarrassment of Yesubai. She greeted her and requested Zeenat to take up a high seat.

Zeenat turned to Yesubai and asked, 'Bai, I hope things are fine here. You remember, Shivaji Raja's begum had made a request?'

'I do remember. Has the Badshah agreed?'

'You know my Abba Jaan's nature. It is surprising that he has allowed you to do your pooja and read your religious books. He was very upset when I put forth Shivaji Raja's begum's request. He did not speak to me for a couple of days.'

Yesubai was in tears and said, 'Begum Sahiba, I feel bad that you had to undergo such humiliation on our behalf.'

Patting her back affectionately Zeenat said, 'Don't take it so hard. It is not your fault. Your request is quite understandable, but you know Abba Jaan looks at everything from a political perspective. Everyone knows how much he liked Shivaji Raja. It would have been a different story altogether if Shivaji Raja were alive today.'

Yesubai said, 'One thing is for sure; you cannot understand how sad Rani Sahiba is staying here in captivity.'

'I can understand.'

'I have a way out. Will the Badshah release her if I were to fulfil a task for him? There is someone from the Badshah's family we have in captivity,' Yesubai said in a soft voice.

Zeenat stared at her and asked, 'Whom are you referring to?'

'Begum Sahiba, your brother's daughter is under arrest with the Rajputs.' Zeenat looked askance and Yesubai clarified, 'I am talking of Shahzada Akbar's daughter.'

'Oh! You are talking of Safiya.'

'Yes. Doesn't that worry the Badshah?'

'It surely does. I have seen tears in his eyes when he talks about them. It is a matter of shame for him that two of his grandchildren are being held by the Rajputs.'

'Would the Badshah release my mother-in-law, if we are able to get his grandchildren released?'

'How? They are with Durgadas.'

'You may remember that Durgadas and Shahzada Akbar were at one time our guests.'

'I am aware. That was the reason for Abba Jaan to march on to the Deccan. But now that Shahzada Akbar has left Hindustan and your husband is no more, how do you propose to get Durgadas to release the children?'

'It was many years back; I had sent a rakhi to Durgadas. He had come to meet me at Raigadh and had said, "If ever you need any help, however difficult the task may be, don't hesitate to ask." I said, "Would you be then willing to surrender to Aurangzeb?" He answered, "It is a brother's word to his sister." I know he would not deny my request to release the children. He may not believe the letter sent by the Badshah suspecting it to be forged. But, on the other hand, if the Badshah were to propose the release of Sakvar Bai, Durgadas would believe him. Begum Sahiba, if you feel my proposal will work you may present it to the Badshah.'

Zeenat was lost in thought for a while. She said, 'It is worth considering. I will have to stand guarantee!'

'Begum Sahiba considers me her daughter. Won't the mother do at least this much for her daughter?'

'I would love to do much more,' Zeenat said, putting her hand on Yesubai's shoulder and looking into her eyes for a long time. 'Unfortunately, fate has something else in store. I hope I can do something to redeem at least part of my sins. I feel I have an unknown bond with your mother-in-law! Let me see what I can achieve.'

Yesubai's face lit up with joy hearing Zeenat's words. She said, 'Can you send me one of the trusted Rajput sardars from the Badshah's camp? I would give him a letter signed by me as well as send an oral message for Durgadas. I am sure he would not dare to ignore my request once he sees the letter.'

'Sure. I will let Abba Jaan know of this tomorrow itself. If Allah wishes, things would turn out for good.'

Within a week a Brahmin called Ishwardas Nagar left with a letter from Yesubai towards Jodhpur. Yesubai had sent her trusted servant Jotyaji along with him.

᪥

The Subah of Ajmer was under Shujayat Khan. Ishwardas Nagar met Durgadas first and the moment Durgadas saw the letter he handed over Aurangzeb's granddaughter to Shujayat Khan, much to the satisfaction of Zeenat who was closely monitoring the situation.

Within a month Ishwardas Nagar presented himself in the cantonment at Brahmapuri and requested an audience. Aurangzeb decided to meet them in Zeenat's quarters. Ishwardas and the hundred-odd soldiers were asked to stay outside the Gulalbar while Safiya was escorted in.

Aurangzeb was restless. He was going to see his granddaughter after a gap of fifteen years. She was only a year old when her father Akbar had revolted against him. Aurangzeb was entranced the moment she stepped in; the girl had an ethereal beauty about her. Wearing a Mughal-style dress with a dupatta covering her head, she bent in an elaborate salute, her hand almost touching the floor. Looking at Zeenat, Aurangzeb said, 'Beti, I am sure you would not have recognized your niece.'

Safiya was seeing her grandfather for the first time. She had heard a lot about him in Rajputana, but it was difficult for her to imagine the old man with a flowing white beard as the Badshah and her grandfather. Hearing Aurangzeb speak she said, 'Hazrat Salamat, the daroga helped me recognize you.'

'It is not your fault, dear. Tell me, was your journey comfortable?'

'Yes. Ishwardas ensured that there was no trouble. Hazrat, you would not have recognized Durgadas too. He is such a gentleman!'

It was a comment that pricked Aurangzeb's ego. This was the same Durgadas who had helped Raja Jaswant Singh escape with his two queens. It was due to Durgadas that the Mughals had not been able to capture the Marwar region. He had been responsible for their defeat. He was the one who had made Akbar revolt against the Mughal throne. And now Aurangzeb's own granddaughter was praising Durgadas. He threw a knowing glance at Zeenat thinking, *See how the kafirs are able to change the minds of royals too!* He did not voice his thoughts; instead he said, 'Safiya, Shujayat Khan has been threatening to capture the territory of Marwar. That is why Durgadas has sent you back here.'

Surprised at the comment, Safiya said, 'I don't think that is true, Hazrat. Shujayat Khan has been trying for years, and Durgadas is quite capable of handling ten such Khans. In fact, Shujayat Khan is afraid of Durgadas these days. There is no question of his capturing Marwar.'

Aurangzeb closed his eyes in agony. *What a shame he had to hear these words from his own kin!* Opening his eyes, he asked her to come near him. Patting her back he said, 'Safiya dear, I don't blame you. After all, you have spent all your life amidst the kafirs. We will take care of you now. I am sure you know nothing of our religion. No doubt, you speak so highly of the kafirs.'

Zeenat sat admiring her niece. She was a spitting image of her mother. Her heart reached out to her at the thought that she had been an orphan for the past fifteen years. She got up and put her hand around her shoulders and lifting her chin gently said, 'Safiya dear, what Abba Jaan is saying is not wrong. I will teach you to read the Quran and the ways of life. Let bygones be bygones. We need not dwell over the past now.'

Safiya, removing Zeenat's hand gently, said, 'Phoofi Jaan, you are mistaken. I need not be taught to read the Quran.'

Aurangzeb was visibly disturbed. He said, his words tinged with sadness, 'We are influenced by our surroundings. I wish we could have saved Safiya from the influence of these kafirs, but Allah has something else in mind. But we have finally been able to rescue her! Safiya should take out all the useless thoughts from her mind now.'

'Ala Hazrat, I said I don't need to be taught as I know the Quran by heart.'

'What are you saying?' Aurangzeb blurted out, not able to believe his ears. 'Are you sure you have learnt the Quran? Who taught you in the midst of the kafirs?'

'Durgadas requested the help of an ustad who used to come from Ajmer to teach me the Quran. He taught me how to say my prayers, how to fast and read the kalmas. Not only did Durgadas ensure that I learnt it well, he would test me once a while to check my knowledge.'

'I can't believe it!'

'I can recite the Quran right away, if you permit me. For that matter, I can recite the Hadis, speak Arabic, Turkish and other languages!'

'I am astonished! Durgadas fought tooth and nail to destroy us. He managed to convince Akbar to revolt against me. Yet he taught my granddaughter the Quran. Something seems amiss.' He said, 'Safiya dear, didn't Durgadas try to convert you into a Hindu?'

'Hai Allah! Hazrat Salamat, how can you say that? A person like Durgadas can never think of doing this! My brother too is in his custody, you know!'

Aurangzeb asked impatiently, 'I hope he too has not been converted.'

'No, Hazrat. In fact, he has been taught a lot more than me, including horse riding, shooting, etc.'

Zeenat could not help admire her niece. She said, 'Abba Jaan, listening to all this convinces me that there are good people in this world.'

'I am unable to understand; Durgadas continued to have enmity with me. Buland Akhtar, Safiya's brother, continues to be in his custody. I feared that he would have been converted by now.'

Safiya could not help but chuckle. A little hurt at his granddaughter's impertinence, Aurangzeb asked, 'Dear, why do you laugh at me?'

'Hazrat, I wonder what makes you say these things about Durgadas.'

'What else shall I say?'

'He used to say that Hazrat had captured the Maratha queen and that she would be forced to be part of his zenankhana and his son would be converted to a Musalman.'

Aurangzeb sat for a long time without saying a word. Turning towards Zeenat he said, 'Zeenat, take care of Safiya. I will make arrangements to get Buland Akhtar released soon. He too will be under your care.'

Safiya said, 'Hazrat, I am really glad to see you. But I have a request; Ishwardas Nagar has taken a lot of trouble to get me here. He and Durgadas should be rewarded amply.'

'Sure! I was about to instruct my office to do so.'

'And not just Ishwardas and Durgadas; Yesubai too! We need to look into her request, 'Zeenat added, reminding her father of the promise made.

Aurangzeb barely heard Zeenat's words. Thoughts played havoc in his mind.

⋘⋙

The days were those of happiness. Aurangzeb's granddaughter had returned from Rajputana, after all. Aurangzeb's behaviour had changed for the better. Safiya was given a special place to stay in the Gulalbar with her own maids, khojas and servants. Ishwardas Nagar and Durgadas were given expensive gifts. Aurangzeb was keen to get his grandson released. Ishwardas returned to Marwar with Aurangzeb's message to Durgadas wherein he had agreed for a few terms and conditions.

One day Nagoji Mane of Mhaswad, along with Shahu Maharaj,

called upon Aurangzeb. Nagoji was earlier with the Mughals but had defected to support Rajaram. The *firman* issued in Shahu's name had worked, and Nagoji had come reading the same.

Accepting his salute, Aurangzeb said, looking at Shahu Raja, 'I did not realize your Ammi Jaan would turn out to be so smart. She managed to make me promise the release of Shiva's begum.'

Shahu Raja said, 'Hazrat Salamat, you are the protector of this earth and you know how to take care of all.'

'I am sure everyone is thinking of releasing you too in a similar manner, isn't it?' Aurangzeb asked.

'*Huzoor-e-Ala!* I am quite happy here under your care. In fact, I am really happy and I don't have any plans of leaving this place.'

Aurangzeb smiled and said, 'It seems you are getting used to the Mughal way of living. Now, if you don't mind, I would like to spend some private time with Nagoji Mane.'

Shahu Raja bent down in salaam and left. Turning towards Nagoji Mane, Aurangzeb said, his voice taking on an edge, 'It seems you have finally cared to remember us.'

Mane stood, looking down at the floor. He said, 'Jahanpanah, Parwar Digaar! I have made a huge mistake.'

'I hope you have got some sense now.'

'*Ji*, Huzoor.'

'Then listen carefully! I can pardon once but if the same crime is repeated, you know your fate.'

'Jahanpanah, I promise that not just I but my future generations will serve only the Mughals.'

'It seems you were swayed by the prospect of being called the Raja of Mhaswad, isn't it? But you did not realize then that you would never have been able to enjoy the same. The only one who can grant you any rights is the Badshah of Hindustan. Those promised by others would not even last a day. I hope you know that now.'

'*Ji*, Alampanah. The moment I received Shahu Raja's letter, I decided to return.' He added, after a pause, 'Though I was able to get a mere ten such sardars to come with me.'

'I can wait. The others will realize sooner than later. Mane, remember! I am not going to be swayed by your sweet talk.'

'If you have any doubt about my intentions, I am willing to leave my family in your cantonment. I am sure I will not fail in my duties.'

'I will consider that,' Aurangzeb said, caressing his beard. 'Mane, I know Rajaram will not survive the battery of assault from Hamiduddin Khan and Himmat Khan. But I cannot rest till he surrenders.'

'Huzoor, you may rest easy. Rajaram is not very happy with Santa, and neither are his troops.'

'I have a task for you.'

Mane was not expecting a task immediately after rejoining the camp. He asked, 'What task, Jahanpanah?'

'To capture Santa.'

Aurangzeb, sensing his hesitation said, 'Are you not ready for any task given by me?'

'It is a dangerous mission, Huzoor.'

'That is why I am asking you. Amrutrao Nimbalkar, your wife's brother, was killed by Santa. You must take revenge now. We will provide whatever support you need.'

They were both silent for a while. Aurangzeb knew that Mane would want to avenge his brother-in-law's death. He wanted to take advantage of his emotional state and said, 'Mane, remember! If you want the Manes to rule the Mhaswad region for generations together, you need to take this step. I must warn you though, of one thing.'

Nagoji Mane asked, 'What is it, Jahanpanah?'

'If you cannot catch Santa alive, get his head as a proof and take the papers regarding the jagir in exchange. If you are agreeable to this, I will ask the Wazir to make preparations right away.'

'I agree, Jahanpanah,' Mane said, his mind now focused on getting the jagir.

'Well done! I am sure you will be victorious. This is an opportune moment when Rajaram is not in favour of Santa. I will ask Hamiduddin Khan to get the Kazakh cavalry to support you. Get me good news as soon as possible.'

Nagoji Mane saluted and stepped out of the room, walking backwards.

⋙ ⋘

Durgadas was not one to be enamoured by the gifts sent by Aurangzeb. He replied to Aurangzeb's message with a counter-offer: 'If Aurangzeb is willing to acknowledge Maharaj Jaswant Singh's son Ajit Singh as ruler of Marwar, we are willing to release Buland Akhtar.'

The message opened old wounds. Aurangzeb had fought tooth and nail to annex the territory of Marwar and had spent enormous money to develop the territory. He had kept an eye on Rajputana despite being physically present in the Deccan. And now he was being asked for the same to be handed over to Ajit Singh!

It was a difficult choice; Aurangzeb had to either give up his favourite territory or forget getting his grandson back.

The choice, though seemingly difficult, finally went in favour of his grandson. Aurangzeb agreed to the conditions with a heavy heart. He insisted that Durgadas should personally accompany his grandson. Durgadas, on his part, was willing to take any risk to get the Marwar territory back into the Rajput fold. He was aware that Aurangzeb may even order his death after getting his grandson back but he decided to take the chance.

Durgadas, playing safe, sent a strongly worded message that he would escort Aurangzeb's grandson only after the complete handover of Marwar to the Rajputs. Aurangzeb wrote back saying he was willing to hand over the papers to Durgadas in his court and that it was Mughal protocol to do so. Durgadas agreed.

When the guard announced their arrival, Aurangzeb asked for his grandson to be sent in.

Buland Akhtar was escorted by the guard inside. He looked at his ageing grandfather and saluted. Durgadas was ushered in next. They asked that his sword, his small dagger and another knife be kept aside at which Durgadas, in a deliberately loud voice said, 'I am a Rajput and do not go anywhere without my weapons.'

The guard requested, 'This is the protocol followed in the Mughal court, sir.'

Durgadas replied, 'Let that be. I follow the Marwar protocol of the Rajputs. We don't even meet friends without the sword by our side. And here I am to meet Alamgir who has done nothing but fight with us,' and saying so, he unsheathed his sword.

Hearing the commotion outside, Aurangzeb agreed to allow Durgadas to come in fully armed. Durgadas, on entering the hall, stood looking into Aurangzeb's eyes.

It was a significant moment. The two of them, bitter enemies for the past twenty-odd years, were facing each other.

Asad Khan gently suggested, 'Please salute the Emperor.'

Durgadas obliged and then stood with his spine erect.

'Hazrat Salamat, I have handed over your grandson to you and request you to hand me the papers relinquishing your claim on Marwar.'

Aurangzeb curbed his desire to crush his sworn enemy, and said, keeping his voice normal, 'It is our good fortune that you are actually asking for our permission to take over the Marwar region. I have given the necessary instructions to the Wazir. You may collect the papers.'

Durgadas salaamed and took four steps back. Aurangzeb raised his hand asking him to stop and asked, his voice a bit low, 'Durgadas, I need to ask you something; hope you will answer honestly.'

'The Rajputs don't have a habit of lying, Jahanpanah; at least not in the presence of the royal throne.'

'My son Akbar ... he was brought up with a lot of affection. He was the one who received the maximum attention, yet you managed to turn him against me in a matter of months. What made him change his mind?'

Durgadas smiled for the first time. He said, 'Shahenshah, affection alone is not enough. You need to pour your heart out in love. Shahzada Akbar is a Musalman and not related to me, yet he was overwhelmed when he found that thousands of Rajputs were willing to die for him.'

'But I did love him with all my heart!'

'That is what you believed, Shahenshah! Had he experienced your love he would not have revolted against the throne. He believed in us and knew we were ready to lay down our lives for him. We were with him all the time; in jungles, eating and sharing whatever we found. We had to face a lot of hardship, but we were willing to undergo the trouble for his sake. Love prevailed.'

Aurangzeb heard him carefully and then, raising his voice for the benefit of those present said, 'Durgadas, I heard you. I know people do a lot for their own selfish reasons.'

Durgadas, hurt at the taunt, said, 'I think you misunderstand me, Shahenshah.'

'I don't think so. I wonder if you would have showered the same love had you not had the intention of getting Marwar back. It was not that you didn't have anyone to shower your love on. Anyway, Allah moves in mysterious ways and so do the men he creates. Durgadas, you may take leave now.'

Durgadas stepped out of the camp to be told that Shahu Raja was waiting for him.

Shahu Raja, along with Yesubai, received Durgadas with affection, hugging him tightly. Durgadas, with tears in his eyes, said, 'Raja, I never imagined even in my dreams that we would meet again.'

Seeing Yesubai, Durgadas said, 'Rani Sahiba, Durga Mata has finally showered her blessings. You should now focus all your energies on Shahu Raja.'

Yesubai could not hold back her tears. Emotions raged through her mind. Things had changed within a short period of time. When they were in Raigadh, Durgadas would wait for a chance to meet them. Now he would be an independent king at Marwar while they would continue to be prisoners under Aurangzeb. Trying to reign in her emotions she said, 'Durgadas, you have honoured the rakhi I tied to your wrist. I am really delighted. I wanted to express my gratitude hence I called you here.'

'This brother of yours will be happy to do whatever it takes to please his sister,' Durgadas said.

Yesubai wiped her tears and said, 'It's ironical, isn't it? I remember you had come with the Shahzada to ask for help to get Ajit Singh his right for Marwar. Now, it is my turn to ask you to help Shahu Raja.'

Durgadas sighed deeply, 'Don't be so despondent, Rani Sahiba. Everyone knows the valour of Chhatrapati Shivaji Maharaj. He is our hero. Had Sambhaji showed a little bit of faith on us, we would not have landed in this situation. But let bygones be bygones. Rani Sahiba, I may be far away physically, but I am always available when you want me. I will not fail in my promise.'

'Durgadas, it is so reassuring to hear such words in these dark times. I have nothing to offer but my tears.'

'You don't need to offer anything in return, Rani Sahiba. The Rajputs, unlike the Mughals, don't weigh everything in terms of loss and gain. We Rajputs love to sacrifice ourselves at the altar of love. Rani Sahiba, you are quite young and have a lot to look forward to. Let me tell you something which will cheer you.'

'You are like my older brother. I am eager to hear what you say.'

'Remember there is always a morning after every night, however dark it may be. I met the Badshah before coming here and notice that he is in a far weaker state of health than what I had seen in Delhi. I doubt he has many years to live. One does not need to be an astrologer to predict the turn of events after his death. I request you to spend the time in the service of the Lord while we wait for things to turn for the better.'

'Durgadas, I am afraid of one thing though; the Badshah is a devout Musalman and on top of it has a deep-rooted anger against my husband as well as Chhatrapati. I fear the day he decides to convert us. I don't fear this imprisonment but would rather embrace death than convert.'

Durgadas knew that the fear was not unfounded. After a while he said, 'Rani Sahiba, I understand Mughal politics a little and am sure that Alamgir Badshah will not resort to such things. Nevertheless, I suggest one thing.'

'Tell me, Durgadas.'

'The Badshah trusts only one person in the zenankhana: his daughter Zeenat. If things turn for the worse, take her help. I am sure she will not let you down.'

Durgadas and Yesubai spent a long time chatting. The call of the muezzin announced the hour for the evening prayers. Durgadas said his goodbyes and left.

჻ᴥ ᴥ჻

It had been two years since the camp had moved to Brahmapuri. The camp had turned into a small city, with havelis for the important officials. Aurangzeb walked down the streets observing the buildings around him accompanied by Hamiduddin Khan, who was astride a horse, while the Badshah was being taken around in a palanquin. They reached the banks of the river. Spotting a spire of a temple in the distance Aurangzeb remarked, 'I was told there was an ancient temple nearby. Is that a new one which I see over there?'

'Hazrat, we have not touched the temple as we were told it is an ancient one.'

Aurangzeb looked at the cluster of temples along the banks and said, 'Had I not given specific instructions that I don't want to see any temple in the vicinity of the camp?'

'But Huzoor, we have a lot of Maratha sardars. The locals too are Hindus and we did not want to hurt their sentiments. If you still insist, we ...'

Aurangzeb interrupted him mid-sentence, raising his hand in the air and said, 'It is good to know that you have learnt a few things. I am happy that you have learnt the art of tolerance.'

Hamiduddin Khan was not sure whether it was a taunt or genuine praise. He said, hesitating a little, 'I may please be pardoned if I erred.'

'No, Hamiduddin Khan. I agree with your decision. Shiva's begum had put forth a request to build a temple in the camp. Quite obviously, we did not agree to the request, but had I been aware of this temple, I may have been able to manage a few things differently.'

'I don't have the foresight which Huzoor is bestowed with,'

Hamiduddin Khan said. 'I am unable to follow your line of thought when you referred to this temple.'

'We have a lot of Marathas amongst us. Let them know that we have deliberately not razed this temple to the ground and that they are free to visit this and pay their respects, whenever they wish.'

They moved forward and stopped near Asad Khan's haveli where a few carts were being unloaded. Seeing the haveli Aurangzeb remarked, 'It is quite remarkable that our Wazir Asad Khan, despite his advancing age, is fighting the battle at Jinji with his son. It is time for my namaz now. Let us return.'

Returning to his palace, Aurangzeb did not move to his private quarters for his prayers. Instead, he went to the discussion chamber, where Bahramand Khan stood waiting with some papers.

'It seems you have some good news to share,' Aurangzeb said, observing Bahramand Khan's face.

'Hazrat Salamat, Allah has been merciful. Santa Ghorpade has been killed a few miles from here. He was shot down by his own men. Finally, the thorn has been removed.'

Aurangzeb, contrary to the expectations of those present, did not react with joy. Instead, he asked, 'Are you sure of the news? Have you verified it?'

Bahramand Khan was taken aback for a moment but said, 'There is no chance of any confusion. Nagoji Mane has carried his head back as proof.'

Aurangzeb did not react immediately. His fingers moved the beads in his rosary for a while. He said, 'There is no need for that. I believe what you said. I am not curious to see his dead body but ask Mane to present himself.'

Mane, waiting outside, was marched in. He said, 'Santaji was not an easy man to overcome. We had to work really hard. We managed to create a rift between Santaji Ghorpade and Dhanaji Jadhav. The moment the seeds of doubt were sown in their minds, they started arguing over every little thing. As expected, Rajaram started supporting Dhanaji and then it was easy for us to get Santaji.'

'How was Santa sitting quiet all this while?' Aurangzeb asked, curiously.

'Finding an opportune day, we tracked Santaji. He had less than two hundred of his own men accompanying him. He, in fact, sent a message one day expressing his desire to surrender.'

'Really? What did you do then?'

'Well, I was, for a moment, tempted to pardon him but then the thought of his having killed my brother-in-law in a brutal manner, trampling him below the feet of an elephant, crossed my mind. We refused his request. We finally tracked him down, camped near a lake. When he got down into the lake for a bath, our men attacked him and I was able to cut his head off in one clean stroke.'

'Well done! You have shown exemplary courage, no doubt. I am pleased,' Aurangzeb said. 'Let the world know that if someone thinks that he can get away by cutting off the ropes of our tents and playing with fire, he would have to pay with his beheaded body. Let his head hang outside the camp with a message to the world that anyone trying such mischief will be punished similarly.'

Mane stood there licking his lips at the prospect of his jagir.

৯৫ ৯৯

'Maasaheb, are you aware of what people are saying?' Shahu Raja asked, entering Yesubai's room in the afternoon. 'Santaji Ghorpade has been killed.'

'I know. The messenger Bhaktaji got the news a few moments back.'

Bhaktaji's white whiskers quivered as he tried to hold back his emotions. Shahu Raja said, 'Maasaheb, what will happen to us now?'

Yesubai pointed skywards saying, 'He is there to take care of us.'

'We were pinning our hopes on Santaji.'

'That is true, Shahu Raja,' Bhaktaji said. 'The news has been a bolt from the blue. The greed for a jagir led to his death. What a pity!'

'Bhaktaji, if Mane wanted the title so much, he could have asked us,' Yesubai commented.

'Once greed takes over, there is no wisdom left.'

Yesubai let out a deep sigh, saying, 'Now we have to leave everything in the hands of Tulja Bhawani.'

'Aaisaheb, we cannot sit here waiting for divine intervention. I have received a message from Pant.'

'What does he say?'

'I got the news through one of Hamiduddin Khan's men. We may be able to escape soon.'

Yesubai felt a little relieved. She said, 'I wonder how we will manage even if we were to escape. Had Santaji been alive, I would have felt hopeful.'

'But does it mean we are going to stay here for ever?' Shahu asked his mother.

'Who can answer that, Shahu Raja? We have to face our fate squarely. I am hopeful Durgadas will do something.'

'Maasaheb, I wonder if there is any hope for us. I doubt if Durgadas, sitting in Marwar, can do something.'

Yesubai was aware that their conversation could reach the Badshah. She said, 'Bhaktaji, you don't involve us in your discussions. Let all things not be discussed here.'

'Aaisaheb, I am aware of the situation. I will be careful.'

'Bhaktaji, I am worried that we have only Dhanaji Jadhav and a few people in our support now. I fear what fate Rajaram would suffer if Aurangzeb's men were to capture the fort.'

'Tulja Bhawani will never let that happen.'

'It is our emotions that make us believe that. But I dread to think if all the efforts put in by Chhatrapati would go waste.'

'Aaisaheb, you may not know that Shivaji Maharaj used to say that Bhawani Mata sometimes tests our devotion but will never fail us. Please rest assured; Zulfikar Khan will never be able to take Jinji.'

'But I know Aurangzeb has focused all his efforts there now. I have a plan ...'

'Tell me Rani Sahiba. But I wonder what we can do sitting here.'

'I want to deliver a message to Zulfikar Khan.'

'Zulfikar Khan? That is impossible! How can we reach him? And what is the message?'

'Tell Zulfikar that he may take Jinji and, if required, Thanjavur too; but let Rajaram be free. Let him escapte. If Rajaram is free, there is a hope for our Swaraj. But in his absence no sardar will be able to take the lead to continue the fight.'

'It is almost impossible to reach Zulfikar. But assuming one does; how do we know he won't betray us?'

'I am quite sure, Bhaktaji.'

'How will he allow Rajaram to escape unhurt?'

'I cannot tell all that right now but I am sure once he receives my message, he will find a way out. He had helped me earlier too.'

Bhaktaji was silent for a while. Yesubai, seeing his hesitation, said, 'Bhaktaji, if you are not sure, don't undertake the risky venture.'

Bhaktaji had tears in his eyes. He said, 'I am not worried about myself. What is there for me now? I can die any day. But I am worried about you, Maasaheb. Nevertheless, I will leave as soon as I find an opportune moment.'

Shahu Raja, sitting quietly for so long, said, 'What can Rajaram Raja do? Where will he manage to hide against the vast army of the Mughals?'

Yesubai patted his back affectionately, saying, 'A person born in the Shivaji Maharaj's household does not raise such doubts. The Badshah may be strong but who can compare with the might of Tulja Bhawani?'

The lamps flickered with a gust of a sudden wind, as if on cue, hearing Bhawani's name.

⚬✤⚬

It was the month of Ramzan and Aurangzeb, as per the tradition he had been following for many years, had moved to Solapur, where Shahzada Azam was stationed. The fort of Naldurg had a huge granary and was responsible for providing the necessary food supplies to the entire forces spread out from Junnar to Burhanpur.

The month of fasting was almost over and Aurangzeb spent all his time in prayer. The official work was at a standstill and he would not meet anyone unless it was unavoidable. He would partake of the barest of the meals and send the rest back. Weak and frail due to loss of energy, he continued his prayers, touching his forehead to the ground as he muttered the lines from the holy book.

It was past midnight, when Shamim walked in with a letter. He threw an irritated glance at her and continued to move the beads in his rosary. Indicating with his hand, Aurangzeb asked Shamim to open the letter in the light of the lamp. He quickly glanced at it and then, with a sigh he got up to follow her. There was a clamour amongst the guards and khojas outside, seeing the Badshah unexpectedly at that midnight hour, but Aurangzeb continued to ignore their salaams and moved towards Udaipuri's mahal with Shamim in the lead. Aurangzeb's steps faltered a little, his hands quivering with weakness, as he moved towards the zenankhana.

At the door, Shamim stood outside waiting for Aurangzeb to enter.

It was a disgusting sight! Udaipuri begum, drunk and almost unconscious, was sprawled on the bed. A quick glance around was enough for Aurangzeb to understand the situation and he shouted, 'Takhliya!' Everyone present moved away silently, leaving the two of them alone in the chamber.

Aurangzeb surveyed the room. As expected, empty bottles were piled up on the table while a tumbler lay on the floor the contents of which had left a stain on the carpet. The strong smell of alcohol was intolerable.

He had spent his entire life without touching a drop of alcohol. And he had been educating his ryots not to touch the vile liquid, issuing *firmans* against it. He had got tired of advising his amirs and other high-ranking officials not to partake of wine and such intoxicating substances. He knew that while they never openly confronted him, they would speak behind his back and continue to enjoy drinking. Realizing that his own officials and their wives indulged in such debaucheries, he had stopped telling the ryots not to drink alcohol. He was aware of the Kashmiri begum's habit but it shocked him to the

core that she had no respect for the pious month of Ramzan. To top it
all, she was not the young begum any more!

He glanced at Udaipuri as she lay sprawled on her bed, parts
of her body exposed. She was totally drunk. It was a sight that left
him shattered. He went to the bed and adjusting her dupatta on her
shoulders said, 'Begum, I am here now.'

She nodded in a semi-conscious state, clearly not being able
to recognize Aurangzeb. He repeated, as he shook her shoulders
vigorously, 'Udaipuri Begum, it is me! Please wake up.'

She managed to open her swollen and red eyes a little, but there
was no recognition in them. Aurangzeb said, 'Begum, I expected you
to show some restraint in this sacred month. But no! Here you are,
lying half-unconscious and drunk to the bone.'

Udaipuri, lost in her stupor, barely recognized Aurangeb's voice
and mumbled, 'Who said wine is sacred?'

'Begum, I am not talking of wine. I said you should not be drinking
wine in the sacred month.'

Udaipuri's muddled brain could hardly hear his words. She said, 'I
know wine is not sacred; nor am I.'

Aurangzeb realized Udaipuri was far too drunk to recognize him.
He shook her vigorously holding her at her shoulders and shouted,
'Begum, your behaviour puts me to shame! Here I am repeating
Allah's name throughout the day and – look at you – the only thing
coming out of your mouth is the foul smell of alcohol!'

Udaipuri's mind seemingly registered a few of Aurangzeb's words.
But when she spoke, Aurangzeb realized she had heard him all wrong.
She said, 'Oh, I see! It must be my khoja who talks of this smell of
alcohol.' And saying so, she slapped Aurangzeb's cheek coquettishly.

It was more than what Aurangzeb could tolerate. He got up angrily
when Udaipuri, holding the tumbler, demanded, 'Please fill it up for me.'

Then, seeing that the person in the room looked a little different
from her regular slave, she asked, 'Why is this old man here? I hate
old men. Youth is meant for fun and enjoyment.' Aurangzeb hurriedly
looked around and then realized that he had ordered the maids and

khojas out. He breathed a sigh of relief. It was an embarrassment he had to bear alone. Udaipuri, swaying on her bed, shouted, 'Sharaab! Sharaab!'

Aurangzeb ignored her and paced the room wondering how he should tackle the situation. In the meanwhile, Udaipuri had refilled her tumbler. Half of it spilt as she tried to gulp it down. She muttered, 'I am told the month of Ramzan is sacred. Is my love not sacred?'

'What a disgusting spectacle!' Aurangzeb shouted.

Udaipuri chuckled at his outburst and said, kissing the tumbler, 'You did not come when I wanted, I died a little …'

'What? What did you just say?' Aurangzeb asked.

Udaipuri was in her own world. She said, continuing her shayari:

'You did not come when I wanted, I died a little each day
The words remained silent, the night passed away.'

Aurangzeb grabbed the tumbler away, shouting, 'Begum, this is intolerable! It is my misfortune to see you in such a shabby state when you should have been devoting your time reading the Quran. What a sin!'

Udaipuri, still lost in her own world said, 'Who is this, sir?'

'It is me, Aurangzeb.'

'Oh! You mean my Ala Hazrat.'

'Finally you have recognized me!'

The taunt was lost on Udaipuri who said, 'Who does not recognize you, Ala Hazrat!'

'But my own begum did not do so.'

By then Udaipuri had come to her senses. Realizing her state, she hurriedly tried to adjust her dupatta on her shoulders and said, 'Please forgive me, Ala Hazrat.'

Aurangzeb, pained at the state of his favourite begum, said, 'I wonder who should ask for forgiveness! I am a sinner having to see such a thing in the month of prayers.'

Udaipuri, now fully recovered, walked up a little unsteadily and bowed her head saying, 'I am really sorry! I had sent you countless messages for the past two days. Finally, getting restless and feeling very sad, I resorted to drinking wine. I will never let this happen again.'

Aurangzeb gently took her to the bed and made her sit. She put her head on his shoulders while he rubbed her back affectionately. For a long time they sat silently. Aurangzeb prayed to Allah asking him to be punished in place of his begum. He knew she was too dear to him and prayed for her forgiveness.

After an hour or so, Udaipuri got and managed to look into Aurangzeb's eyes. She said, 'I sincerely apologize for the trouble I caused you.'

Aurangzeb's pain was evident across his creased forehead. He said, looking out of the window, 'Who am I to forgive you? Ask Allah for forgiveness.'

'I don't want to take his name when my lips are stained with wine.'

'A mere thought of Khuda is enough to get his pardon. By the way, you did not tell me why you were calling me for the past few days. And what was that you read out just now?'

Udaipuri looked down and blushed. 'I don't know what I mumbled in my drunken state. I hope I did not offend you.'

'It was not offensive; rather it pierced my heart and touched me somewhere. Why don't you repeat it? It went something like "You did not come when I wanted."'

Udaipuri said,

'You did not come when I wanted, I died a little each day
The words remained silent, the night passed away.'

'How true! The days passed by and the night too passed away. Begum, I too feel the same way. I had promised many things and I wonder whether I have enough time now to fulfil them.'

'What are you talking of?'

Aurangzeb let out a deep sigh. 'You won't understand and I don't want to elaborate. Suffice it to say you are not the only one making promises. It is just that we make different kinds of promises.'

Udaipuri was back to her senses by now. She said, a little

flirtatiously, 'May I dare to ask something if it would not offend Huzoor?'

'There is no question of you offending me,' Aurangzeb said. 'Ask what you have in mind. But make it quick; I have to go back to my reading.'

'Then leave it,' Udaipuri said, in mock anger.

'Now, please don't make a fuss about it. Tell me.'

'Well, the month of Ramzan is meant for giving alms; distributing largesse. I want you to release Shahzada Muazzam.'

Aurangzeb never expected Udaipuri to make such a request. He knew that she had no love lost for Shahzada Muazzam. In fact, he believed she was happy that he was in jail and away from danger. Her request took him by surprise. Seeing his lack of response, Udaipuri said, 'Won't you consider my request?'

'I did not expect you to take up his case. May I know the reason?'

'I will not get into the details but the fact is Shahzada Azam treats Kambaksh like dirt and behaves as if he is the future emperor. If Shahzada Muazzam is released, there will be pressure on Azam to behave properly.'

'I knew that my begum knows the art of love. I now know she knows the art of politics too!'

'There are no politics here. I am worried for Kambaksh.'

'Would the begum leave the habit of drinking wine if I were to agree to her request?'

Udaipuri knew Aurangzeb had touched a raw nerve. She had tears in her eyes as she said, 'I know you are taking advantage of my weakness. But, if you are going to agree to my request, I shall sacrifice that too.'

'Begum, I did not mean to hurt you. I have learnt that one cannot force anyone to follow the right path. I will release Muazzam soon. Let Allah decide their fate. I wish I don't have to see any more tragedies. You may not like it, but what I saw and experienced today would have to be redeemed by taking recourse to my prayers for days together. I hope you don't misbehave in front of the maids and the khojas. That is my only request to you.'

It was dawn when Aurangzeb left Udaipuri's quarters. Before leaving for his bath, he ordered Shamim to punish the maids and khojas. They had to bear punishment for having seen the begum in an inebrieated state.

⋰⋱

On the occasion of Eid, Aurangzeb announced the release of Muazzam and presented him with rich clothes. His sons were gifted fine Arabian steeds while his begum received exquisite jewellery. Muazzam was given the task of managing the subah of Kabul and asked to move there immediately.

The officials, who were enjoying their wine in the sacred month surreptitiously, were now emboldened to drink openly in the newly opened bars. Aurangzeb chose to ignore the mushrooming of the taverns and bars.

The camp was to move back to Brahmapuri from Solapur when Azam presented himself at the court and said, 'Hazrat, there is some good news. Rajaram has agreed to discuss terms for surrender and has sent his son with Ram Singh Hada to meet you. If you permit, I will present them to you.'

Aurangzeb was overjoyed to hear the news and said, 'Sure! What about Asad Khan and Zulfikar Khan? When will they take charge of the fort?'

Bahramand Khan replied, 'They are continuing their hold from outside. We expect them to penetrate soon. No doubt, Rajaram has pre-empted their move and sent his son for a discussion.'

'What are his terms?'

Azam said excitedly, 'What conditions can they put, Ala Hazrat? We have been after their life for the past ten years. They have no option but to come to us like a tame dog.'

'But if that be the case, my informant tells me that the fort of Jinji is well stocked and they have no fear of anything. On the other hand, had we not supported with our supplies from Naldurg, Zulfikar Khan would not have been able to manage the troops there.'

'That is true,' Shahzada Azam said. 'But our troops have managed to create a lot of problems for them. No doubt they want a truce.'

'What are their conditions?'

'They want Rajaram be allowed to leave Jinji scot-free.'

'What? We have been fighting the battle for years! Impossible! Shahzada, this is not acceptable to us. If we let Rajaram go away, he will once again instigate the Marathas against us. Tell Ram Singh that the terms are not acceptable. And ask Zulfikar to have Rajaram arrested as soon as possible and present him here. We have two of their family members here. He too can join them.'

'Jahanpanah,' Azam persisted. 'Rajaram has sent his son to meet you. Would you not give him an audience?'

'There is no need. I have no reason to give him the honour. I will see Rajaram only after he is under arrest. I am sure Khuda will get that opportunity soon.' Turning towards Bahramand Khan he asked, 'What is the status of the other forts?'

'Huzoor, our men are on the job.'

'How many forts have we taken under our control now?'

'Nearly all of them.'

'My information says that most of them are not.'

'Raigadh is under our control.'

'That is old news. What about Panhalgadh?'

'Unfortunately, we have not been able to take hold of it so far.'

'Oh, I see!' Aurangzeb turned to look at Muazzam's two sons who were in attendance. He said, 'Having released you, here's a chance to redeem your sins. I will consider you worthy of your release if you can get Panhalgadh for me.'

Muazzam's son Muizuddin bowed and said, 'Ala Hazrat, we will prove our loyalties soon. We will return only after we capture Panhalgadh.'

Aurangzeb turned to Bahramand Khan and said, 'Please give him all the necessary support for his campaign.' To Muizuddin, he said, 'Now carry on. I will give you other tasks as and when deemed fit.'

Aurangzeb noticed but chose to ignore the sharp glance Azam

threw at Muazzam's son. Quite clearly, Aurangzeb's ploy of giving them key responsibilities had irked Azam.

ഛൠ ൠഛ

After returning to Brahmapuri, Aurangzeb called for the royal astrologer Fazil Khan one day. Fazil Khan had been the royal astrologer since Shah Jahan's times and Aurangzeb had consulted him many a times to study his horoscope and predict certain events.

When Fazil Khan was ushered into the private chambers, Aurangzeb said, 'Fazil Khan, would you care to look at my horoscope?'

'Huzoor, I have done it many times before. Please command.'

'I want to know how long I will live.'

Fazil Khan studied the papers for a while, doing some calculations on his finger tips. He said, after a while, his face showing satisfaction, 'Hazrat Salamat, the horoscope is able to predict a man's future only upto the age of one hundred.'

'What about it?'

'Very clearly it tells me that you will live to be a hundred and more. But may I ask, why the sudden urge today to know your future?'

'I am told Bahadur Khan is on his deathbed. I wanted to know about my life ahead before meeting him.'

Fazil Khan left and Aurangzeb, soon after, accompanied by Mullah Haider and a few other mansabdars, left for Bahadur Khan's palace.

Bahadur Khan's munshi came running out to receive the Badshah and escorted him to Bahadur Khan's bedroom, where the once towering giant, now in his dying moments, seemed frail as a newborn child. He was past ninety years of age.

Bahadur Khan touched his right palm to his forehead seeing Aurangzeb enter the room. A special seating arrangement had been made for Aurangzeb. The munshi said, 'Ala Hazrat, Bahadur Khan made this special seat as a gift for you spending fifty lakh rupiyas. If you acknowledge the gift by sitting on it for a brief moment, Khan Sahab would feel honoured.'

Aurangzeb did not say a word but obliged for a few moments

before sitting down on the simple carpet near Bahadur Khan's bed. The hakeem, standing nearby, whispered, 'His health has taken a turn for the worse since this morning. I am not sure whether medicines will work any more. He has been waiting to meet you.'

At that moment a few khojas came in holding twenty trays filled with gems and jewellery. Bahadur Khan managed to say, 'Please accept this token of gratitude from this servant of yours.'

Aurangzeb touched the trays in acknowledgement. The khojas kept the trays on a side table and left.

The munshi whispered in Aurangzeb's ears, 'Khan Sahab has asked me to tell you that he wants to leave his entire estate including horses, elephants, jewellery and all his properties at your feet. If Huzoor raises his right hand in acknowledgement, Khan Sahab will know that you have acceded to his request.'

Seeing Aurangzeb raise his right hand, tears of gratitude flowed down Bahadur Khan's eyes. He nodded briefly and then closed his eyes. Seeing him open his eyes after a while, the munshi said, 'Khan Sahab would like to speak to Hazrat alone.'

Aurangzeb raised his hand dismissing those present and they all left closing the door gently behind them.

Getting up from the carpet, Aurangzeb came near the bed and held Bahadur Khan's hand in his. He was his milk brother and someone known to him since birth. Bahadur Khan held Aurangzeb's hand against his cheeks that were wet with tears. He said, 'Huzoor, I have very little time left in this world. I worked with all my sincerity for the throne and I hope that I have served well. But before reaching the other world I would like to apologize for all the sins I have committed. That is the reason I have called for you.'

Aurangzeb looked at Bahadur Khan's face. The receding colour on his face was an indication that he would live a few hours at the most. Squeezing his palm he said, 'As per our religion a man is supposed to confess all his crimes and get pardon for ...'

'That is why I called you, Hazrat. People consider you a representative of the Paigambar. If you pardon me I will be able to enter the gates of heaven. I am desperate to hear the words "I pardon you" so that I may leave in peace.'

Aurangzeb was in no mood to pardon so easily. He said, looking away from Bahadur Khan, 'You are my milk brother. The world knows how I have behaved with my own brothers but as far as you are concerned, I had nothing but affection.' He continued, 'The world may call me whatever it wishes but I too am a human being. My status is no better than Paigambar's shoe.'

'To me you are my Paigambar, Hazrat. I thus ask you to pardon me.'

'Bahadur Khan, every man sins. No one is free from them.'

'Hazrat, I have very little time left,' Bahadur Khan said, his voice sounding shallow. 'I see darkness now. I can hear strange sounds. Please speak the words so that I may leave this world.'

Aurangzeb got up and put his hand on Bahadur Khan's forehead. He said, avoiding his eyes, 'Bahadur Khan, I pardon you for all crimes except for one. I will never pardon you for that one crime of yours.'

Aurangzeb turned to see Bahadur Khan's eyes closed. He removed his hand with a jerk and without looking back turned and left the room.

As his palanquin moved towards his palace, the old incident continued to repeat itself. The more he tried to forget the more intense the memories came back. He could hear Nawab Bai's words. They were ringing loud in his ears and he put his fingers in his ears to shut out the noise. But it was in vain! Nawab Bai's voice continued to torment him for a long time.

It was dark by the time Shahenshah Aurangzeb reached his palace.

৵৹ৎ ৎ৹৵

Bahadur Khan's death was mourned for a month.

One day Yesubai and Shahu Raja visited Zeenat. Shahu Raja, after sitting for a while, excused himself but Zeenat asked Yesubai to stay back. Zeenat said, 'An interesting incident occurred a few days ago. I asked you to stay back to tell you about it.'

'I shall be honoured to hear it.'

'Now, come on! How often have I told you that you need not be so formal here!'

'I apologize, Begum Sahiba.'

'See what I mean! Anyway, let me tell you what happened. You must be aware that Kambaksh has been blessed with a baby boy.'

'Yes, I got the sweets with the good news. And I did send across a gift; whatever I could afford, to Shahzada Kambaksh.'

'Well, as per the Mughal tradition the Badshah is given the honour of naming the child. Even the top officials, whenever they have a child, get him to the Badshah. Kambaksh too did the same. But to his surprise Abba Jaan said, "You may name the child yourself." Kambaksh asked whether Abba Jaan was upset with him. You know what Abba Jaan said?' Zeenat asked, putting the bottle of perfume she was holding, on the side table. '"Kambaksh, don't worry, I will have the honour of naming *his* son." Now, knowing that Abba Jaan has turned eighty, that is *really* funny. It means he has to live upto a hundred to name Kambaksh's grandson.'

'Let him live to be a hundred and more,' Yesubai said. 'You mentioned that you wanted to ask me something. What is it about?'

'Oh, I nearly forgot. It was about Shahu Raja; he is of marriageable age now, isn't it?'

'That's right.'

'Why didn't you mention it ever?'

'What can I say? We are prisoners here.'

'Don't be so dejected. I am going to get him married.'

'Where am I going to find a girl for him, though?'

'Why not? There are so many Maratha sardars here who have daughters. You do the job of finding the right girl. I will take care of the rest. I know you are worried whether Abba Jaan would agree. Leave that to me. I will tell him he has to name Shahu Raja's grandchild too. That will make him happy!'

෴

Rustamji Jadhav's sister was found a suitable match for Shahu and the marriage was fixed soon. Zeenat managed to get approval to spend a lakh of rupiyas on the marriage. Yesubai was keen that the marriage was celebrated with the appropriate pomp and splendour, but there was the question of the trumpets causing a disturbance in Aurangzeb's prayers. Zeenat found a simple solution – they decided to conduct the marriage in the Mahadev temple at Brahmapuri. It was not only far away from Aurangzeb's palace, it also had a large ground in front of it, thus allowing the tents to be put up for the guests.

Aurangzeb, along with a few mansabdars, graced the occasion by attending the main dinner after the marriage.

Yesubai visited Zeenat after a few days and, on seeing the Badshah there, immediately pulled her pallu over her head. Aurangzeb asked, 'I hope the marriage celebrations went off as per your expectations?'

'When His Royal Highness has himself blessed the couple, it had to go off well. There is an important event pending, though.'

'Why don't you get that done then? If you need some more money, I will ask Shahzadi to take care of it.'

'No. It is not about money,' Yesubai said. 'I need His Highness's presence for the same.'

Zeenat, a little surprised, asked, 'What has Abba Jaan got to do with the Hindu traditions?'

'We have conducted the marriage with the blessings of the Shahenshah. I have to follow certain protocol of the royals too and hence, I would want the Shahenshah to name the newly-wed bride.'

'Oh, I see!' Turning to her father Zeenat said, 'Abba Jaan, Yesubai requests that you name the new bride.'

'Sure. Sure! It will be my pleasure,' Auranbzeb said, smiling. 'I am pleased to know that Shahu Raja and his mother are following some of our traditions. His father and grandfather had given me many sleepless nights but Shahu Raja is wise. I will surely name the bride, but I have a condition.'

Looking at Yesubai, Zeenat said, 'I am sure Yesubai will be willing to fulfil any of your wishes. After all, your wish is her command.'

'I would be happy to name her only if she gets her daughter-in-law to meet and greet me.'

Yesubai began by saying, 'But Your Highness …' but realized that Aurangzeb may not like what she intended to say and let that pass.

The old eyes had not lost their penetrating stare. Aurangzeb said, 'Bai, I am aware of the tradition that the newly-wed sits on the lap of the old person who christens her. He is supposed to feed her a piece of sweetmeat and then whisper her name into her ear, isn't it? We shall name the new bride in the presence of all the ladies.'

Yesubai rubbed her palms in embarrassment. She did not know how to put her thoughts across. She said, looking at Zeenat, 'Tell the Badshah that I would not want him to take any further trouble. He has been kind enough to bless the couple. If he tells us the name, we will go ahead and conduct the ceremony.'

Aurangzeb, listening intently to the conversation, said, 'It is no trouble for me. On the contrary, I will be pleased to do the honours. Let the world know that we treat our royal prisoner like a son. We do not differentiate. Zeenat, decide a suitable date and let me know.'

Yesubai said, licking her lips in nervousness, 'Your Highness, we have a slightly different protocol.'

'And what is that?'

'We conduct the ceremony in the presence of our goddess, Amba Bhawani.'

'That is fine. I will carry out the first part of telling her the name. You may then do your part of the ceremony. I don't mind.'

Yesubai had tried her best to avoid the situation but it seemed there was no getting away from it. She said, 'You have been too kind. We will carry out the function as desired.'

'I am pleased to hear that.'

Aurangzeb, fully aware of the torture Yesubai was going through, did not allow his face to reveal his inner thoughts. Yesubai, on the other hand, was barely able to conceal her embarrassment and the prospect of conducting the function against her wishes. She had been trapped!

Zeenat was blissfully unaware of the mind games being played in her room.

☙ ❧

The naming ceremony of Shahu's new bride took place in a hall specially decorated for the purpose. Aurangzeb made the couple sit on his lap and put a pinch of sugar in their mouths. The bride was named Ambika. Zeenat, Udaipuri and others presented Shahu with gifts while Aurangzeb gifted a gold coin as a token of his affection.

That evening when Aurangzeb visited Zeenat she commented, 'Abba Jaan, it seems Yesubai liked the name you have given to the new bride.'

Aurangzeb smiled saying, 'It is quite obvious; she is named after their goddess.'

'Abba Jaan, I overheard some rumours in the royal bazaar that the Marathas were quite worried about the whole ceremony. There had been a fear that you may in fact feed her a part of the betel nut you were chewing on; the way you do to your grandchildren. That would have been disastrous for the devout Hindus.'

Aurangzeb laughed out loud. His age showed on his face but the stare remained as piercing as ever. He said, 'What is wrong about that? Don't I do it to my grandchildren?'

'They were worried that this would be tantamount to them being converted. They were mortified.'

'What happened then?'

'I had to make Yesubai understand that you are like a grandfather to the new couple and that they should not make too much of it.'

'But what if I had actually put something in her mouth?'

'I knew you would not do so deliberately. In fact, I had given Yesubai my word. The whole clan was on tenterhooks till the ceremony was over. They heaved a sigh of relief only later. In fact, Yesubai thanked me profusely.'

For a long time Aurangzeb was silent. The gurgling waters of the Bheema, flowing near the camp, broke the silence. He said, 'Zeenat, you know I spent my youth here and now I am back here in my old age.'

'Yes, Abba Jaan. I am aware.'

'There is no one who knows these Marathas better than I do.'

'I don't get you, Abba Jaan.'

'I was sure Yesubai would be very hesitant to send her daughter-in-law to me for the ceremony. But I was keen to know whether she believed me. Having treated them as family I was curious to see whether I have been able to win their trust.'

'The ceremony did go well.'

'That is where you are mistaken, dear. I realize they were all smiles believing they had fooled me.'

'Fooled you, Abba Jaan? What are you saying?'

'You want to know? The one sitting on my lap was not Shahu's begum!'

'What? Who was she then?'

'She was his begum's maid.'

'Abba Jaan, how do you know this?'

'Zeenat, I have spent my life trying to read people's minds. Yesubai was trying to impress me calling me His Highness and such lofty names. But I have my spies everywhere. I had heard about Yesubai's plans to send her maid in place of her daughter-in-law. That way she would please me and yet save her daughter-in-law from the possibility of being fed something I was chewing on.'

'Abba Jaan, this is a figment of your imagination. I cannot believe it!'

Aurangzeb gazed out of the window for a while. The curtains blew in the wind and the noise of the khojas and the Tartar women guarding outside could be heard as they marched across. He said, 'Dear, I know you are hurt. But you would be more hurt when you realize how I must have felt on being told that there is no trust. I took care of them for so long, and I truly believed they considered me as an old affectionate grandfather. But all my efforts were in vain.'

Zeenat could not yet believe her father. She said, 'Abba Jaan, aren't you seeing this from your own point of view?'

'Why do you say that?'

'Yesubai's husband was tortured to death, his eyes gouged out, his limbs broken, and what not! Doesn't Yesubai know of all that? Why should it be surprising if she does not fully repose her trust in the person who was responsible for killing her husband and because of whom she was made a prisoner here?'

'I don't deny that I ordered the killing of Sambha. But that is what the job demands. Sambha, and his father before him, ruled the Maratha kingdom. They must have passed orders to kill men, making women widows. I am sure countless men would have had their limbs chopped off, and many others buried alive behind stone walls. Who is to keep a tab on all these so-called atrocities? Men by nature are selfish and make their own selfish deeds look noble when they present them to the world at large. I did many things in the name of Allah and I have no doubt I will be asked to justify myself when I meet Him in heaven. I firmly believe I have not done a single thing that would make me bow my head in shame. Yet, it surprises me people don't believe me.'

Zeenat was taken aback at the frankness with which her father had opened up his heart to her. She could see the pain on his face, yet she was not willing to accept his logic totally. She said, 'Please don't mind me being blunt. What you do may be justified, but the fact is that you don't trust anyone. Hence no one trusts you.'

Seeing a lack of reaction from Aurangzeb, Zeenat persisted, 'Abba Jaan, I hope you trust me at least?'

'What do you think, dear?'

'That is not relevant. What do you have to say?'

'Dear, when I look back at my entire life I feel a sense of emptiness. I realize I must have behaved in a manner not liked by many, but what hurts me most is that I have lost your trust too.'

'Abba Jaan, I am sorry to have hurt you. I didn't mean to.'

'No, dear. You need to know that Aurangzeb speaks his mind only to you and no one else. But I am not sure if you reciprocate the feelings.' Putting his rosary down he said, 'Zeenat, I come here knowing the pain I have caused you.'

'Abba Jaan, don't say that!'

'You heard me right, Zeenat. Only Allah knows the pain I carry in my heart for having destroyed my dear daughter's life.'

ംളെ ളം

Shahu Raja was presented with five palaces along with two precious gifts from the royal treasury: Shivaji's Bhawani sword and Afzal Khan's sword.

One night Hamiduddin Khan was presenting his report to Aurangzeb when he said, 'Huzoor, we had a lot of Maratha visitors in the camp during the Maratha Raja's wedding.'

Aurangzeb said, 'Had I not told you to ensure that all visitors are thoroughly checked? I hope that was being followed strictly.'

'Yes, Huzoor. I was told that you have granted permission to Shahu Raja to visit Tuljapur and Shingnapur?'

'That is correct. It is their family deity and they had requested me to visit the temples.'

'Huzoor, I am told that there is a plan for Shahu's escape.'

'Really? What precaution are you taking then?'

'We managed to catch two spies who blurted out the plan. We got the details of all the places Shahu was planning to stay at.'

'Who is involved in this?'

'We were unable to trace it back to Shahu Raja or to Yesubai. But there is no doubt there is someone quite senior behind this.'

'Do you have a name in mind?'

'Balaji Vishwanath is the name. He was the one who visited the camp under the guise of making arrangements and was seen many a time.'

Aurangzeb caressed his beard saying, 'It requires some courage to visit our camp and plan such a scheme right under our nose. But let us be careful; if we expose the plan right now, we will not be able to catch all the culprits.'

Aurangzeb thought for a while and then added, 'Tell Shahu Raja that he should accompany me to Solapur during the month of Ramzan. He can visit Tuljapur from there. We will make all the arrangements or we might even accompany him to Tuljapur.'

'I am sure this will put a spoke in their plans.'

'At times though I wonder if we can find a way to release Shahu Raja and pre-empt the insult to our prestige if he were to escape.'

'I don't think Rajaram is going to accept Shahu Raja so easily. He has been here since his childhood and Rajaram will be wary of him. We know how to create a rift between them and as long as they are at loggerheads, we can be at peace and can easily destroy both of them! But Ala Hazrat, how will Shahu Raja enter the fort when Zulfikar Khan and Asad Khan are camping there?'

'Zulfikar Khan has made that easy for us,' Aurangzeb said. 'Rajaram has escaped from the fort.'

'Oh I see! That is not good news. I don't think anyone is aware of this yet.'

'My spies got me the news in advance. Rajaram, I am told, is moving towards Vishalgadh. The question is how to stop him. I feel it is best that we release Shahu Raja. At the moment though, keep a strict eye on him. We will decide at the appropriate time.'

Hamiduddin Khan returned, lost in his thoughts. The turn of events had been beyond his comprehension.

ઓઉ ૭ુ૦

Aurangzeb spent nearly three months beginning with that of Ramzan at Solapur. He received a piece of good news he had been waiting for over many years; the fort of Jinji had finally been taken over. The Mughals had overcome strong resistance but had finally managed to capture one of the most important forts of the Maratha kingdom.

Unfortunately, the fort had been captured, but Rajaram had escaped long back. Zulfikar Khan had, on his own accord, not captured Rajaram's family.

When Zulfikar Khan requested for a meeting with Aurangzeb he was promptly denied, but then the persistent sardar came over to Brahmapuri. No one had the courage to stop the top military commander.

On his arrival, Bahramand Khan told Aurangzeb, 'Huzoor, despite your express instructions, Zulfikar Khan has come over and has requested a meeting. He has captured the fort after a lot of hard work and perseverance. I request Your Highness to grant him audience.'

Aurangzeb merely lifted his right hand in acknowledgement.

Zulfikar Khan swaggered in, heady after the recent victory, and saluted the Badshah as soon as he reached the throne. He had ignored the normal protocol of staying a few feet away from the Badshah when saluting and had inadvertently touched the pedestal of the throne with his feet.

Bahramand Khan, realizing the transgression, shouted, 'Khan Sahab, please maintain the decorum of the court. Hazrat Salamat has allowed you to meet, but you are not even aware of where your feet are leading you.'

Zulfikar Khan came to his senses and bowing in shame stepped back a few steps, while Aurangzeb watched the drama without speaking a word. He said, after a while, 'Please get a pair of reading glasses.'

Those present in the court knew that the Badshah was mighty upset. They were unable to understand the reason for the glasses being ordered. No one dared to speak.

Aurangzeb asked, looking at Zulfikar Khan, 'I am told you have shown great valour by capturing the fort.'

'It was possible only due to Huzoor's blessings,' Zulfikar Khan said, not daring to lift his head.

'No doubt it took seven years. I wonder how much more I have to live to see fifty such forts being captured at this rate. Can you do the arithmetic for me?'

Zulfikar Khan, realizing the taunt, looked up and pleaded, 'Huzoor, the fort was undoubtedly very difficult to capture, but I would like to assure you that we spared no effort.'

'You are right and deserve to be honoured in court. Khan Sahab, you are my aunt's son, but I wonder whether you were protecting

Mughal prestige or favouring the Marathas, when you allowed Rajaram's family to escape.'

'Huzoor, I feel I am being unduly questioned,' Zulfikar Khan pleaded.

'Then how do we explain Rajaram's escape from Raigadh first and from Jinji now? And on top of it, you allowed his family to go scot-free.'

'Hazrat Salamat, I have done whatever it takes and these hands have spared no effort in your service. I can assure you anyone else would have done exactly what I did.'

Aurangzeb's voice took on an edge when he said, 'Zulfikar Khan, you have shown me the strength your hands have when it took you seven years to do the job! Now I know the strength of your eyesight and it needs to be corrected. Please step forward.'

Zulfikar Khan heard the command and shivered to the core. He threw a desperate glance at Barhamand Khan for help, who said, 'Huzoor may consider pardoning Khan Sahab for once.'

'I am the one who should ask for pardon as I have erred in my judgement. Even Allah does not pardon such people. Zulfikar Khan, please step forward.'

Zulfikar Khan gingerly stepped forward keeping his head bent low. Aurangzeb, taking the pair of reading glasses, adjusted them on Zulfikar Khan's nose and said, 'You are my cousin and I need to take care of your health. I hope this will make you see better and also be able to differentiate between the floor and the throne.'

Zulfikar Khan's face turned red. He had been insulted in a packed courtroom. He stepped back a few steps repeatedly saluting, and stood in one corner, unable to face anyone present.

The commander, who had spent seven years of his life trying to capture the impregnable fort, had been reduced to a mere mortal in the Badshah's court.

◦◦◦

Aurangzeb's anger subsided after a month and he managed to honour some of the sardars who had fought valiantly to capture the Raigadh Fort. He knew he had to keep the mansabdars happy. Zulfikar Khan was sent on other duties.

It was his eighty-first birthday and he had issued strict instructions to not get any gifts for him. He spent the entire morning and afternoon reading the namaz in the zenankhana along with his begum and Shahzadi Zeenat.

Danishmand Khan came over to meet him that evening after the prayers. His presence was always welcomed by Aurangzeb. Danishmand Khan carried a book wrapped in a satin for the Badshah. Looking at the parcel Aurangzeb said, 'You know I have completed eighty years of my life now?'

'Allah is merciful, Ala Hazrat. I pray you live to see a hundred years and more.'

Aurangzeb smiled. 'What is your age, Khan Sahab?'

'I am just two years your junior, Ala Hazrat.'

'Oh, Allah seems to love you too,' he said, laughing out loudly.

After a while Danishmand Khan presented the book saying, 'I wanted to give you something different this time. It is a book written by the Englishmen.'

'What is the book about?'

'The book has stories written in the form of plays. And there are sonnets. One of them talks of your life.'

'What does it say?'

'The ballad goes on to talk of your life and how you, despite trying all your life, have not been able to get what you truly wanted.'

'That is so! I need to be born many times before I can reach my goals.'

'The writer then goes on further: he says you find life to be a trap. It is hope which keeps the man fooled into thinking that the next day will be better than the previous one. But truth eludes him and he lives on hoping to see the light at the end of the day. He takes up meaningless troubles, mindless pursuits and loses his happiness in the process. The desire to get his goal goads him to carry on and keeps challenging his fate. By the time he realizes the futility of all, he is too old and is left with nothing. It is time for him to leave the world.'

'*Waah!* It is excellent. It reflects a lot of what my mind thinks. Who is this poet? Which religion does he belong to?' Aurangzeb had closed his eyes and was contemplating what he had just heard. He continued, 'This poet has put across my deepest thoughts so well. How true it is! We continue to run after the mirage all our life.'

Danishmand Khan placed the book on the side table and said, 'Hazrat, despite all the knowledge man continues to be so since the time of Adam and Eve.'

Aurangzeb said, 'It is obviously the desire to experience the novelty of life that man continues to look forward to another day. Each new day is like a new begum and the urge to acquire newer things makes him continue his futile journey. Unfortunately, by the time he realizes it, he is almost dead.'

Danishmand Khan, the khoja, recalled his days since childhood as he listened to his master. He had never demanded anything from life, yet he had not realized the true meaning. Life, in the meanwhile, continued to move ahead at its own pace ... slowly.

৵ও৩৶

Within a matter of a week a piece of disturbing news reached Aurangzeb. Rajaram, after having escaped from Jinji, had established himself at Satara and had declared it as the new Maratha capital, thus creating a renewed sense of vigour amongst the troops.

Aurangzeb was preoccupied the whole day thinking of Rajaram. He finally called for a meeting of his key men and, without preamble, said, 'Rajaram has started a new campaign after declaring Satara as his capital. I am told his men have started plundering our territory from Karhad side.'

Asad Khan, standing nearby, said, 'Huzoor-e-Ala, I suggest we should return to Hindustan, now that the entire Deccan from Karnataka to Madras is under Mughal control. These Marathas are more of an irritant than a real threat.'

'I too would love to return, Asad Khan,' Aurangzeb said. 'But the Maratha strength lies in their forts. If the mansabdars here are willing to take charge of the forts, I will readily move the camp to Aurangabad.'

Asad Khan looked around expectantly but none of the mansabdars stepped forward to take the challenge. Aurangzeb said, 'You see, none of your men have the courage. You are getting old and quite obviously you want to return home. I did not expect a loyal soldier like you to make such a request. I thought you would fight till your last breath. I, on the other hand, am bound by my duty to Allah.'

'Huzoor, haven't we spent the last twenty years fighting here? We have spent enormous amount of money from the royal treasury, not to mention the loss of men, ammunition and other resources. We have won nothing in the last two decades. Should the troops not get some rest?'

'Do you think I am not getting old? But my duty does not allow me to sit back and relax. Allah will look after such souls who do not rest till the job is done.'

'Huzoor, we have experienced much trouble taking over the Jinji Fort. We will spend the rest of our lives trying to capture these forts.'

'I realize you and your men have lost hopes but I cannot. I am going to take charge and lead now. I have called for jehad and I cannot stop. Let the troops be informed that I will be leading them now onwards. I don't want to sit here in this camp any more. Charge! Charge now! The final charge!'

Orders were issued at rapid pace once the decision to march was made. Within a week, all the mansabdars were asked to move without taking their zenankhana with them. They were also told to pack light and carry only the bare essentials.

Leaving a small but efficient band of soldiers behind to guard the camp under the leadership of Asad Khan, Aurangzeb ordered Ruhullah Khan and Hamiduddin Khan to march towards Satara. On an auspicious day the Badshah himself marched out of the camp.

The evening before the march, he visited Zeenat to say his goodbyes.

'Abba Jaan, I am worried that you are taking on such a responsibility at your age,' Zeenat said.

'Dear, when Allah is there to take care, why should we bother?'

'That may be so but the Deccan is occupied by the Devil. There is famine one year and floods the next. Diseases are rampant and people are dying everywhere. There are not enough places to camp. Your begum and I will be worried sick.'

'I have left all the responsibility on to Allah. Now I will not rest till I die.'

'Abba Jaan, I would like to come along with you.'

'What? That is impossible! None of the mansabdars are taking their families along. I have asked them to forgo most of their things. How can I then ask you to accompany me?'

'Abba Jaan, how will we spend the days here while you roam the treacherous mountainous terrain?'

'I know I have never kept my zenankhana away from me; even during the difficult campaign against the Rajputs. But this time is different. I am going to personally supervise the capture of all the forts. The ladies cannot tolerate such hardships living in makeshift tents and sleeping in the wild.'

Zeenat was teary-eyed. The thought of her frail, bent father leading a difficult and prolonged march was impossible for her to imagine. She burst into tears, 'Abba Jaan, your words to me are as precious as those of the Quran's. But I am not going to listen to you. If my impudence would make you punish me and arrest me, so be it. But I am not going to let you go alone. When the trumpets announce your departure, my elephant will follow you.'

Aurangzeb tried his level best to reason with the Shahzadi but had to finally relent.

Aurangzeb's heart missed a beat imagining his favourite daughter negotiating through the treacherous ravines of the Deccan.

ॐ ॐ

The very fact that the Badshah was leading the charge created a renewed sense of vigour amongst the Mughal soldiers. The royal troops, along with their enormous cannon power, cavalry and foot soldiers marched through the Maratha territory with the intention of capturing their forts.

Within twenty days the troops reached Miraj and managed to capture the city without any resistance. The royal flag fluttered on the fort there and the town was rechristened 'Murtajabad'.

The army moved within two days and reached Karhad in a week to set up camp, with the Maratha fort at Vasantgadh looming a few miles ahead. Tarbiyat Khan, leading the charge of explosives, was asked to begin the attack.

That night Mullah Haider, the main kazi, came to meet Aurangzeb. 'Hazrat, the Musalmans from the town of Karhad want to seek an audience with you.'

Aurangzeb had just finished reading his namaz. He asked, 'If they are in need of some alms or donation of any kind, you may go ahead.'

'No, Huzoor. The Marathas razed their only mosque to the ground and they have no place even to offer their prayers now.'

Aurangzeb looked at some of the mullahs who had entered on cue from the kazi and asked, 'I wonder how you served under Shiva when his men were committing such atrocities?'

'Huzoor, Shiva Bhosale was not such. But his sardars did the mischief.'

'You may take some help from my men here. When I return after a month or two, let the mosque be ready. I would like to read my prayers in that mosque along with all of you.'

The men were dismissed and Aurangzeb went back to his prayers. Within no time, as per instructions given by Aurangzeb, the mosque was built. The bombardment on the fort continued as usual.

After watching the action for a week, Aurangzeb moved his camp to the banks of the River Krishna. The mighty army spread its cantonment along both the banks of the river making it look like a serpentine row of tents. The very sight was enough to make the

Marathas call for peace talks. Aurangzeb sent back a word that the men would be spared if they hand over everything and leave in peace.

Vasantgadh was handed over the very next day. Aurangzeb entered the fort seated on a palanquin. With quivering hands, he inaugurated a space for building a mosque before inspecting the enormous wealth looted at at the fort. The fort was rechristened Qili-e-fateh, to commemorate the first victory after a long time.

The very next day the troops were ordered to march on to Panhalgadh.

That night Aurangzeb spent the entire night reading his namaz at the mosque at Karhad thanking Allah for the victory. The tall minarets of the mosque relayed the call of the muezzin which was heard for miles around.

The next morning, Aurangzeb changed his plans and informed the troops to move towards Satara instead of Panhalgadh. Satara! The capital of the Marathas was under direct threat from the Mughals.

The first victory had been a jolt to the entire Deccan. It seemed that the true jehad had begun now.

oɔ૭ ૭ɔo

The march on to Satara was unexpected for the Marathas after the fall of Miraj, Karhad and Vasantgadh.

The march was halted at the banks of the River Urmodi in full flow during monsoons. They had to wait for nearly two months. The winters were about to begin but the waters of the Urmodi refused to recede.

Aurangzeb was being carried on a raised palanquin as he inspected the surging waters of the river. After a brief inspection, he instructed the troops to march forward. The elephants, camels and horses crossed the river with great difficulty while the bearers, holding Aurangzeb's palanquin, found themselves submerged up to their shoulders as they desperately tried to keep the palanquin out of the water's reach. Aurangzeb's manservant, following them with a spare horse, quickly got the horse into position and the eighty-two-year-old Badshah, jumped from the palanquin on to the horse. After a great struggle, the horse managed to cross the river much to the cheer and relief of the soldiers waiting at the other bank. The troops shouted a resounding 'Karamat! Karamat!' seeing their favourite leader safe.

The troops requested him to sit on the palanquin but Aurangzeb declined, preferring to continue on horseback and by nightfall they had reached within a mile of Satara. The advance party pitched their tents there waiting for further instructions.

Aurangzeb had no time for rest. He called for Bahrmand Khan and Hamiduddin Khan, engaged in surrounding the Satara Fort, for an urgent meeting. A map of the fort was drawn on paper for Aurangzeb to look at it while Azam, Tarbiyat Khan and others explained to the Badshah the configuration of the fort. Azam was given the charge from the western front while Tarbiyat Khan was to try and break open the Manglai darwaza on the east.

The Mughal troops, trying to gather fodder for the cavalry, scoured the territory for twenty miles around the fort while thousands of camels were put to duty for carrying loads of wood required to create ammunition stores. Hundreds of bullock carts were engaged in carrying sand. There was a buzz of activity all around.

The Maratha sardars were not ones to keep quiet. Subhanji, the fort keeper, and Prayagji Prabhu, the havildar, had an advantage as they were at a height and were able to precisely seek out targets from atop the fort. The Mughals, despite the losses, continued their relentless bombardment of the fort.

Azam reported with nearly three thousand men from the Konkan region, known for their ability to scale fort walls. They had been paid a princely sum equivalent to three years' pay for the job. They were accompanied by soldiers of the baheliya caste.

Tarbiyat Khan's men were busy creating a tunnel for weakening the walls of the fort while the bombardment continued to distract the Marathas.

Aurangzeb personally supervised the attack through the cannons, his vast experience a great help to the bombardiers. A cannonball from the fort landed a mere fifty feet from Azam's tent. Aurangzeb immediately ordered the cannonball to be sent to him for inspection. He lifted the ball to check its quality and then throwing it on the ground said, 'Shahzada, they are using cannonballs of far superior quality than ours. You need to produce such quality to make an impact.'

'Abba Jaan, the Marathas have used the services of the firangis.'

'You too engage them. You can withdraw from the royal treasury for this purpose.'

The shelling from the fort continued and a few cannonballs fell precariously close to where they were sitting. Azam requested, 'I urge you to observe the action standing a little further away. It would be disastrous if something were to happen to you.'

'How can I move away when the soldiers are willing to sacrifice their lives for me? They will lose their motivation if I am not in sight.'

A loud bang from the fort attracted everyone's attention. Azam looked in the direction nervously but Aurangzeb, mounting his horse, said, 'Now, don't you worry; this Alamgir Badshah was not born to be felled by some ordinary Marathas. Allah is worried that that the Paigambar himself has given me the responsibility to fulfil his task. He is behind me.'

'No doubt Allah is behind you. But Abba Jaan, we can speak at ease if you move a little away from the din of the shelling. I beseech you!'

Aurangzeb agreed, albeit reluctantly, to move away where they would continue their conversation. After a long time Azam saw his father in a light-hearted mood, recalling Azam's childhood. Despite the din and clamour of the battle, his voice was steady.

On return to the camp Aurangzeb found Hamiduddin Khan waiting for him and the moment he dismounted, he said, 'Hazrat Salamat, Allah is merciful!'

'What is the good news?' Aurangzeb surmised. 'Has the fort keeper surrendered?'

'Not yet, but I am certain he will do so soon enough. Zille Subhani, Rajaram had marched upon Khandesh to attack our forces there but fate has something else in store for him. He succumbed to an illness and is no more. It has been a big blow for the Marathas.'

Aurangzeb raised his hand upwards saying, 'Khuda seems eager to help his banda. It gives this old man a lot of hope. *Ya ilahi illillah!*'

Aurangzeb had raised his hopes a little too early. Despite two months of relentless attack the fort was yet to be conquered. The Marathas, finding the Mughal discipline lax, had found a way to collect water from spring nearby.

Aurangzeb instructed his men to guard the route and prevent the Marathas from collecting water. The work on the tunnel to blow part of the fort's walls had nearly been complete. Aurangzeb realized that unless he personally supervised the work, the men would relax. He toured the entire area each day and the moment the troops saw him come, they got busy.

Tarbiyat Khan informed Aurangzeb of their preparedness for the tunnel to be blown open using high density of explosives.

The Manglai darwaza was the target. The plan was to create a breach in the wall which would help the Mughal soldiers enter. The entire operation had been kept top secret. Aurangzeb, astride a horse, stood dangerously close to the fort watching the operation through a pair of binoculars. Seeing the Badshah inspecting the work, the Marathas had gathered on to the ramparts near the darwaza. The daroga, sensing danger, suggested, 'Huzoor, the enemy is dangerously close and I fear someone may take a potshot at you. I urge you to step back a little.'

Aurangzeb, continuing to observe through the binoculars, said, 'The true devotee of Islam never steps back and I don't think there is anyone out there who has the courage to take an aim at me.'

Aurangzeb raised his right hand; it was a signal for Tarbiyat Khan to light the fuse. The Marathas, standing at the fort, saw him raise his hand and shouted 'Har Har Mahadev'. No one was prepared for what happened next. With a loud booming noise a large part of the wooden tunnel created to penetrate the ground below the Manglai darwaza came apart and flew high in the air, landing on the Marathas standing on the ramparts. They were thrown high into the air and many were simply crushed due to the sheer weight of the wooden structure.

A slight smile of satisfaction crossed Aurangzeb's face. He looked at Azam saying, 'With the second explosion, we will create a breach in the wall. Please have the troops ready to march in.'

A group of men were ready to charge in when Aurangzeb raised his hand once again for Tarbiyat Khan to light the second fuse. Another loud explosion followed but, much to the surprise of the Mughals, the structure, flying high in the air, fell on to the soldiers waiting to enter. They were buried instantly. There was chaos everywhere. Aurangzeb, watching the goings-on, showed no sign of worry on his face. He instructed the Maratha sardar Dafle, standing nearby, 'There is a breach created. Dafle, your valour will be tested today; take charge with a few men and enter the fort. I am sure we will conquer it.'

Dafle, with a naked sword in his hand, charged towards the fort, shouting at his men, 'The Marathas are buried there under the weight of the explosion. Let us enter!' Much to his surprise the Mughal soldiers and the Maratha men ignored his command. The explosion had shaken them to the core and none had the courage to enter the fort. Aurangzeb had never encountered such a situation before.

While Prayagji Prabhu, the havildar, was dead inside the fort, thousands of Mughals outside had been buried alive. Allah had rendered justice in his own way.

No one was able to take advantage of the situation and chaos and confusion prevailed the whole day.

It was a disappointed Aurangzeb who entered his tent that evening. He could not sleep that night and continued reading his prayers till he noticed a huge glow outside. He was further disappointed knowing the cause.

The Marathas and the Rajputs, buried alive were now being consigned to flames at their funeral. It was impossible to extract each body and the troops had decided to go for a mass funeral using the very weight of the wooden planks under which they were buried, as fuel for their last rites! It was a mountain of fire that night.

The fire continued to burn for eight days and nights. Aurangzeb had no choice but to watch the flames sitting in his tent. He knew that many Musalmans too had been consigned to the flames but there was no time for religious debate on the last rites. The raging fire, in a symbolic sense, had burnt down the barriers of religion, caste, creed and any such human creations. Nor did anyone have the time to think of these issues in the face of death.

❧ ❧

The first one to rise from the rubble was Aurangzeb himself. He mounted his horse and reached the base of the fort. Most of the cannons on the Maratha side had been buried under the destruction and hence there was little fear of any shelling. The troops could not believe that their Badshah had dared to come so close to the fort for a personal inspection.

Aurangzeb, pointing his sword at the walls, said, 'It is my mistake; I should have lit the fuse. Allah would not let his true servant down. Anyway, I am going to write lines from the Quran on each of the cannonballs. Let the shelling then begin. I am sure the enemy would be forced to surrender soon.'

No one present had the courage to say anything and, seeing them silent, Aurangzeb asked, '*Kyon*, Hamiduddin Sahab, what do you say?'

'Huzoor, this servant of yours cannot say anything once you have spoken. We will follow your orders without any delay.'

'I am going to supervise the work along with you from now on. Let the troops know that Allah has personally put his robe on me and that no enemy can touch me. They will get the confidence only when they see me here.'

Hamiduddin Khan raised his hands shouting, 'Alamgir! Zinda Pir!'

All mansabdars followed suit, shouting, 'Alamgir! Zinda Pir!'

Aurangzeb returned to his tent and sent urgent summons asking Yesubai and Shahu Raja to proceed to Satara.

❧ ❧

The shelling began with renewed vigour with each of the cannonballs personally signed by the Badshah. Some of the cannons like Kadak Bijli, Murbat and Muluk were known to be lethal. The Marathas were worried that the water stored on the fort would soon get over.

One day Rama Pandit and Antaji Pandit arrived at Azam's tent for negotiations. The message was immediately conveyed to Aurangzeb who asked the trumpeters to announce the victory. Shouts of 'Alamgir! Zinda Pir!' rented the air. The fort of Satara had finally been captured.

A huge tent was set up near the fort walls to formally take over the fort. Shahu Raja stood next to the Badshah. It was a triumphant day for the Mughals. The capital of the Marathas was being taken over by the Mughals and the Badshah of Hindustan was present to personally take charge.

On cue, Subhanji, the Maratha fort keeper, was brought in. The chains, tying his wrists, went around his neck. The Badshah ordered his chains to be removed and then asked Subhanji, 'It seems you fought with a lot of valour; but eventually victory is ours!'

Subhanji saluted before replying, 'Jahanpanah, you have Allah's blessings. No one can fight against you.'

'Are you then ready to serve under us?'

'Ji, Huzoor. I shall hand over the fort as well as the fort at Parli, a few miles from here.'

'I am glad to hear that!' Aurangzeb said, looking at Bahramand Khan. 'Let the qiledar be given a mansab of two thousand men, and please honour him with the appropriate royal clothes, horses, elephants and our royal insignia. I also announce a cash award of twenty thousand rupiyas to him.'

Subhanji could not believe his ears. He saluted once more when Aurangzeb asked, 'I trust you would serve the Mughals with utmost loyalty.'

'Jahanpanah, I have another request.'

'What else do you want now?' Aurangzeb asked irritatedly. He glanced at Shahu Raja who continued to observe the carpet not daring to look up. He had not shown any interest in the discussion taking place.

'You had promised to hand over the territory of Parli too, once I hand over the fort. I request the Badshah to issue orders accordingly.'

Aurangzeb smiled. He said, 'Yes, of course! I will issue orders accordingly.'

Subhanji and a few other sardars were inducted into the Mughal hierarchy that day.

The next day Aurangzeb visited the fort sitting on his palanquin. Shahu Raja followed him on a horse. At the Manglai darwaza, Aurangzeb asked the palanquin bearers to stop. He said, looking at Shahu Raja, 'You see how your uncle tried to harass us but finally had to succumb to the Mughal might. You must now send letters to all the fort keepers to hand over their forts to us. There is nothing really left for the Marathas to rule now.'

Shahu Raja said, 'Your word is my command, but I would like to point out that the fort here was much easier to capture compared to the others. And the fort keepers there are quite an adamant lot. They would not agree to my summons.'

'Are you saying they would dare to disobey their own King? Aren't you their ruler now, after Rajaram's death?'

'That is correct, Huzoor. But most of them were on the side of my uncle. Now they have become greedy. If we capture Panhalgadh and Vishalgadh, we can get the rest easily.'

The sun setting down at the horizon had lit up the sky to a golden-red hue. Looking into the westerly direction Aurangzeb pointed to the fort at Parli saying, 'We shall take them soon. We managed to capture Raigadh, your grandfather's favourite fort. We then took over the fort at Jinji and now have captured Satara too. I am told the fort at Parli was the seat of Shiva's guru. Soon, the Mughal flag will be fluttering there. I wonder what makes your Maratha sardars fight relentlessly against us.'

Shahu Raja answered without batting an eyelid, 'Jahanpanah, I too do not understand. Fighting you is like trying to arrest the wind. I hope the Maratha sardars realize this soon.'

Stopping at a mosque near the darwaza, Aurangzeb asked, 'It looks like a very old mosque. I wonder who built this.'

Hamiduddin Khan replied, 'It was built during the time of the Bahmani sultan's reign.'

Aurangzeb got down from the palanquin and prayed in the mosque. He ordered the mosque to be given a fresh coat of paint. That evening he nominated Chhatrashal Rathore as the new fort keeper and the fort at Satara was rechristened as Azamtara.

 споС Эро

At the onset of monsoon, Aurangzeb ordered the camp to move.

Shahu Raja had suffered silently seeing the forts being taken over by the Mughals. He fell ill on the way and Aurangzeb decided to stop at the base of the Bhushangadh Fort, near the banks of the River Yeral for a month. The journey had taken a toll on Shahu Raja's health and despite the intervention of the royal hakeem, the fever did not subside for nearly a fortnight.

Aurangzeb visited him when he heard that his fever had subsided a little. Knowing that Shahu Raja placed his idols of worship in one corner of the tent, the khoja requested him to remove his sandals and produced a pair of silken slippers to put on. Aurangzeb entered the tent to find a pale shadow of the earlier Shahu. He asked, 'Raja, I thought it was an ordinary fever but you seem to be really ill. What is the matter?'

Bhaktaji and Banki Gaekwad, two of Shahu's trusted lieutenants, stepped forward and said, 'Huzoor, Shahu Raja is depressed that he is still being treated as a prisoner. He has stopped eating proper meals and lives on just some fruit.'

Looking at Shahu Raja, Aurangzeb asked, 'What is wrong with you? Haven't I told you many times that you should not consider yourself a prisoner? You stay in your own palace; you are welcome to stay in the Gulalbar too, if you wish.'

Shahu Raja said, wiping his forehead of the sweat, 'I am aware of the love and affection I get from the Badshah. I am grateful for it.'

Aurangzeb did not reply. Hamiduddin Khan said, 'Raja, you have not answered Badshah's question. Don't you know that Badshah and Shahzadi Zeenat treat you as a member of their own family? The Badshah is upset seeing your long face.'

'Raja, is it true that you consider yourself a royal prisoner?' Aurangzeb asked. 'I know what you want to say, Shahu Raja,' Aurangzeb continued. 'After your uncle's death, you were supposed to take over the kingdom but instead you see it being captured by the Mughals. You can tell me your thoughts; don't hesitate.'

Shahu Raja continued to look down at the floor. Aurangzeb realized he was not going to speak his mind and let out a deep sigh of exasperation. He said, getting up, 'I know what troubles the human mind the most. Trust your God. The garden may wither away in winter but the human mind believes and hopes for a spring which will bring back the greenery.'

Aurangzeb got up to leave when Shahu Raja rushed to touch his feet. Patting his back Aurangzeb said, 'You have answered my question. I am pleased.' Taking out a handkerchief from the pocket of his robe, he said, 'Take this as a token of my affection. It is a very sacred piece of cloth. I know you pray to your gods here in this tent. Keep it along with your other idols. I am sure your wishes will not go unfulfilled.'

Shahu Raja kept looking at the handkerchief for a long time after Aurangzeb's departure. The sudden clanging of bells announcing the aarti at the temple at Bhushangadh broke his reverie and he returned to his tent.

๛ ๛

The rains had subsided and Aurangzeb decided to move camp from Bhushangadh. The Marathas, having lost their capital, were now being led by Rajaram's wife, Tarabai.

Aurangzeb prayed one evening, as he sat alone in his tent: '*Parwar Digaar, you know the energy your follower has left now in his body. Yet I continue to work for you. I managed to somehow contain Shiva and then eliminated his son Sambha. Now I have removed Rajaram's threat too, but his wife has taken charge. I don't know if I can continue to fight one enemy after another'.* Realizing that he was putting forth excuses, Aurangzeb changed his words saying, *'I will never give up. I believe in your immense power and that you are behind me. I know you will not let me down.'*

Aurangzeb was now spending hours in prayers, asking and beseeching his Allah for strength.

He received the news that Dhanaji Jadhav had attacked the camp at Brahmapuri and taken many of the ladies and begums of the Mughal sardars as hostage. Aurangzeb despatched Zulfikar Khan in pursuit of Dhanaji Jadhav. On the other side, Tarabai had managed to intercept a contingent coming from Hindustan carrying wealth from the royal treasury. The Marathas had become active again much to the discomfort of the Badshah.

The royal retinue now halted on the banks of the River Man, near Khawapur. Zulfikar Khan ensured that the contingent from Hindustan could reach the camp. The troops were relieved to get fresh clothes, new horses, elephants and many such essential requirements. Within a short while there was a sense of renewed vigour amongst the troops.

The water flow in the River Man had reduced to a trickle in the hot summer. The troops had pitched their tents and camps along the dry sandy banks. The royal tent was a little further away. The camp was well guarded and there was no fear of a sudden and surprise attack by Tarabai or Dhanaji Jadhav. Most of the troops were engrossed in enjoying wine, dance and such frolic, having found a respite after a long time.

It was past midnight. The gong announcing the change of guards at midnight had been sounded some time back. The guard on duty near the river strained his ears on hearing a gurgling sound. He was unable to identify the sound though it seemed to be getting louder by the minute. Within a few minutes, there was chaos as huge amounts of water surged through the dry river bed, taking along with it the tents and camps.

There was no possibility of rain in this dry, almost barren

landscape, and the men were taken by complete surprise. The water level rose rapidly and within a few minutes, the Mughal troops were seen scrambling around, trying to save whatever they could lay their hands on before it got washed away in the flash floods. Aurangzeb had just finished his prayers and was about to lie down when he heard of the latest calamity.

He stepped out of his tent.

The clouds covered the moon, making it impossible to see anything around. Aurangzeb could not stand erect. His spine was bent with age, but the mind was sharp and alert as ever. He realized that there had been heavy rain upstream causing flash floods. Many men and animals had been washed away. People shouting 'Ya Allah! Ya Parwar Digaar! Tauba! Tauba!' could be heard all around.

Aurangzeb immediately despatched some men to help those in trouble and to recoup whatever could be salvaged before it got washed away. Limping his way back to the tent that morning, after having supervised the rescue operation the entire night, he commented to Hamiduddin Khan, 'I thought it was only the Marathas who were my enemy in the Deccan. But now nature too has decided to act against me.'

❦

Days and months were passing by, but the problems continued to mount. Aurangzeb, weak and bent with age, had not given up, his mind hell-bent on achieving what seemed impossible. His sheer willpower egged him on.

The entire Deccan was reeling from a famine for the second year in a row. Not a leaf was visible in the forests. The Marathas, on the other hand, continued their harassment, managing to loot many of the caravans coming from Hindustan and Bengal, causing further losses for the camp. Soldiers, not paid on time, added to the unrest. Senior leaders like Hamiduddin Khan were despatched in search of fodder for animals. The one-lakh-strong army along with five lakh other attendants was not a small population to manage.

The troops had become dispirited and were in no mood to work.

There were stray incidents of mansabadars being accosted in jungles by soldiers demanding their salaries due to them for months. Finally Aurangzeb relented by releasing a part of the zenankhana's treasury and giving a three-month advance salary to all the troops.

It would take months for the huge lumbering army to reach the fort and, by the time they set up camp and began their operations, the monsoon would begin, making the task impossible. The cycle continued endlessly giving no respite to the Mughals. It was an impossible battle which they were waging.

The Marathas continued their sudden attacks, causing immense angst amongst the troops and the ryots. The Marathas looted Gujarat once again. Aurangzeb heard of disturbances caused as far away as Kabul where Shahzada Muazzam was in charge but he continued his focus on capturing the forts at hand. He had left no stone unturned in his quest.

Mirza Raja Jaisingh's great-grandson and the Badshah's grandson Bedar Bakht had taken charge of capturing Vishalgadh, supported by Muhammad Aman Khan, Hamiduddin Khan, Ataullah Khan and Taribyat Khan. The Badshah himself supervised the entire operation camping a few miles from the fort.

Dhanaji Jadhav continued to harass the troops with surprise attacks every now and then. Yet, Aurangzeb's determination was unwavering.

Aurangzeb was desperate to capture the fort. Noticing that the Maratha snipers were hiding in the forest nearby, he asked a few of his men to search them down and kill them. To motivate his soldiers on the field, he sat with his purse, presenting a cash award of a thousand rupiyas to one and a few gold coins to another, while some other lucky soldier would get a pearl necklace, on the spot.

After attacking the fort for nearly a week, Aurangzeb decided to storm the gates with a few select soldiers. Bedar Bakht's action had already created a breach and victory seemed at hand. At that moment they got the news that the fort keeper had agreed to surrender. Aurangzeb asked the trumpeter to play the victory band instead of the signal for attack. Within a week of this, the Mughal flag was seen fluttering on the Vishalgadh Fort.

Aurangzeb allowed the fort keeper and his family to leave without arresting them. Reaching the fort with a lot of trouble, he managed to offer his prayers on its parapet. Hamiduddin Khan opened the Quran to search for an appropriate new name for the fort. The fort was renamed Sakkarlana.

The rains began that very night and continued relentlessly for more than a week. Aurangzeb had to make arrangements for a proper handover of the fort before moving on, but could not do so till the downpour stopped. The Mughal troops had reached Vishalgadh after negotiating narrow ravines in the mountains in the summers. Now they faced the daunting task of returning via the same route in the pouring monsoon. It was something the troops did not look forward to, but there was no sign of worry on Aurangzeb's face.

The huge lumbering army of foot soldiers, cannons, elephants, camels, horses and bullock carts trundled through the mountainous region while the rains continued to lash heavily. They stopped after covering a distance of thirty miles on the first day. The next day they were faced with a fast-moving mountain stream. On being told of the stream, Aurangzeb mounted a horse and marched ahead to have a look. He said, looking at Azam, 'It seems like an ordinary mountain stream. We can't stop at each obstruction.'

Looking at the dense clouds looming overhead, Asad Khan said worriedly, 'Hazrat, if the rains continue, it is going to be very difficult for us to cross this terrain.'

Dismissing Asad Khan's concern Aurangzeb said, 'We cannot give credence to such things. We are here to fulfil Allah's mission. We cannot stop.'

Shahzada Azam, drenched to the bone, said, 'May I suggest we stop till the rain abates a little and the water flow reduces?'

'No! We cannot! The water is not going to recede so soon even if the rain stops.' Aurangzeb's face was drenched despite his khojas desperately trying to hold a few umbrellas to protect the Badshah from the rain. He continued, 'I will wait here. Let the elephants move first. We will see how deep the stream is, and then others can follow.'

As soon as the elephants crossed the stream, Aurangzeb ordered his palanquin bearers to follow suit and soon, the entire contingent had crossed over.

But further trouble awaited them. The entire terrain was now slushy with mud, making the elephants and camels slip and stumble. The bullock carts got stuck in the deep mud and soon, many were left immovable. The soldiers had no energy left to push them beyond a point. They were drenched, wet, feverish, hungry, and soon, many began to fall ill. No one had time to look after the sick.

With a lot of difficulty and having lost a lot of their things en route, they finally managed to reach near Malkapur after a fortnight. Feeling firm ground beneath their feet was a welcome relief for the troops. Aurangzeb decided to halt for four days to give some respite to his tired bones. He had the power to order rest but had no hold over the rains that continued their incessant lashing.

The trumpets announced the next move after a gap of four days. They sounded flat and forlorn; even the trumpets seemed to have lost their zest. No one had the enthusiasm to move except Aurangzeb. They started moving, but soon they were stopped in their tracks by yet another fast-flowing stream. Realizing that it was not possible to cross, Aurangzeb announced another two-day halt and then somehow managed to cross over.

Strong winds, along with the rains, created havoc. They had already lost a lot of their equipment and luggage along the way, being forced to discard their belongings whenever they had got stuck. Now the gales added to the troubles and one night, the heavy winds blew away most of the tents. The royal tent, being held down by nearly ten khojas, managed to survive. The khojas had held on to the ropes throughout the night. While sleep was impossible, Aurangzeb had spent the entire night praying and reading the Quran.

The next morning, the nearly eighty-five-year-old Badshah stepped out of his tent to survey the damage. There was no need to say anything as the mass destruction the storm had created was plainly visible. Putting a trembling hand on Asad Khan's shoulders he said, 'Wazir, keep your hopes alive. This is Allah's way of testing our resolve. Such small hindrances are part of His grand design.'

'Hazrat,' the Wazir said. 'Do you call these small hindrances? It seems the end of the world is near.'

Aurangzeb smiled. 'Don't be so despondent. It hurts me to hear that. One has to bear these troubles to reach Allah. My ancestors, since the time of Timur Lane, have been tested by Allah. No one can find out what He wants. He is testing us by making us go through these difficulties.'

Asad Khan had no words to counter the Badshah's logic. He bowed and left.

Shahu Raja's tent was nearby. The tent was in tatters, but had managed to survive the storm. Shahu Raja stood in one corner, shivering in the cold. His men were packing his luggage and a horse was being readied. Seeing Aurangzeb, Shahu Raja bent in an elaborate salaam. Looking at his face Aurangzeb asked, 'I hope you are better now. Tell me; you are born in this region. You must be quite comfortable with the weather?'

The winds continued to lash making an eerie noise. Shahu Raja said, 'Jahanpanah, I may have been born here but I have spent all my life under your patronage. I am not used to these conditions.'

Bhaktaji, standing nearby, added, 'Huzoor, he has not eaten anything. I somehow managed to make some rice after a lot of trouble. None of the firewood was dry.'

'I understand. I shall send something from the royal kitchen. Shahu Raja, please don't torture your body. You must eat to remain fit.'

The camp got ready to move again. They trudged along through the mountainous terrain and finally, after a month and a half, covered a mere fourteen miles to reach Panhala. The sun god showered them with some warm sunshine for the first time and the troops were overjoyed. Aurangzeb announced a week of rest. The mere sight of a warm sun had energized the soldiers.

Aurangzeb eventually arrived at the camp near Pedgaon after two months of journey. The sardars were busy counting their losses and could not believe the amount of men and materials they had lost on the way.

The royal flag at Vishalgadh continued to flutter.

Danishmand Khan arrived at Bahadurgadh, where the cantonment was stationed. The troops got a month's rest before the royal *firman* was issued.

There were important forts to be captured, most notable amongst them being Torna, Sinhagadh and Rajgadh. Aurangzeb was not going to rest till they had been brought under the Mughal fold. The troops had barely recovered from their experience at Vishalgadh before they got news of the Badshah's plans to take Sinhagadh. Their morale took another blow.

Danishmand Khan and Asad Khan came over to meet Aurangzeb in his tent. Asad Khan, bent with age and troubled with arthritis, was barely able to walk.

Danishmand Khan began, 'Huzoor, the troops have barely recovered from the campaign at Vishalgadh.'

'I am aware. I was there with them and you don't have to remind me. But you must also know that we don't have too many years ahead of us. I cannot afford to have luxuries like resting for a long time. We need to move – now!'

'Huzoor, you have been on the move for years together. I have come here to request you to allow the troops to rest for a few more days.'

Shaking his head Aurangzeb said, 'No! Your suggestion is not at all acceptable. I was not born to rest but to take charge of my responsibilities and not stop till I fulfil them.'

'Huzoor, can you not reconsider,' Danishmand Khan persisted. 'I can understand your enmity with Shiva and then with his son Sambha. But are we not stretching it too far?'

'The jehad is not yet over!'

'I know that,' Danishmand Khan said. 'But I am privy to the gossip in Hindustan that you are chasing a gang of Marathas led by a mere woman. It is an insult for the Badshah of Hindustan.'

'What is there to be insulted about? I have made a vow to Hazrat Paigambar that I will eliminate the enemy completely. I am the one who has to face Him and I cannot stop till I complete my mission,' Aurangzeb shouted. He was out of breath and held his hand to his chest to recover.

Danishmand Khan and Asad Khan were surprised at Aurangzeb's persistence. His body had nearly given up but the zeal to win was as strong as ever. After a while Danishmand Khan said, 'Why don't you leave the task with your able sardars? We cannot afford to be made into a laughing stock.'

Aurangzeb was not one to give up. He said, 'Danishmand Khan, I am not fortunate to have such able sardars. If they could do what they were supposed to, there would have been no need for me to roam these treacherous mountains with an unsheathed sword in my hand. Now it is not the question of whether a woman or the terrain challenges me. The only thought is of victory. I have little time left and the jehad is still to be fulfilled.'

He continued, after a pause: 'You are not aware of the tricks my mansabdars are up to. They bribe the fort keepers and then celebrate the victory as if they have won the fort after a vigorous battle. I have to live with such deceit. I am forced to treat them with large sums as gifts. If Allah gives me a long enough life, I will teach them a lesson one day.'

Danishmand Khan was shocked hearing this. Aurangzeb's resolve was as strong as ever. Not only was he focused on getting the forts, he had plans of taking revenge on his men too! Asad Khan was worried that Aurangzeb's stubbornness was a huge drain on the royal treasury. They were now dependent on the money coming in from Bengal.

Aurangzeb read his mind and pre-empted him saying: 'Don't worry, Asad Khan. My treasury belongs to Allah and it never gets empty.'

'We lost a lot of men and resources in the effort to win Vishalgadh, Huzoor.'

'You are mistaken, Asad Khan. We are all His men. He will take care of us. I am not a Shahenshah, just a fakir who lives on a piece of bread given by Allah. I may be limping as my leg is broken but my resolve can never be broken. My faith in Him is immense.'

৵৹ ৹৵

The fort at Kondana was soon taken over and renamed Bakshida Baksh. Torna and Rajgadh too followed suit, but, by then, the monsoon began, and Aurangzeb was forced to retreat to Pune and wait.

Zeenat was worried that ever since her father had returned from Vishalgadh, he had been steadily weakening. He had stopped taking his dinner and even lunch was a frugal affair. He would spend most of his free time in the study of the Quran and prayers.

Zeenat came in one evening unannounced into Aurangzeb's room to find him reading a piece of paper. Coming close to him, she realized he was not reading but crying with his eyes closed. She exclaimed, 'Abba Jaan! What happened? Is it some bad news?'

'I don't want you to feel sad. Why do you want to know it?'

'Abba Jaan, I too am past sixty years of age now. I have suffered many a sorrow in my life. Another sad news will not make much difference and I will feel satisfied that I shared the grief with you. Let me see the paper.'

Aurangzeb handed over the paper with trembling hands. Zeenat glanced at the paper and putting her hand to her forehead exclaimed, '*Hai Allah!* What tragic news!' Seeing tears flow down her cheeks, Aurangzeb said, 'Did I not tell you it would hurt you? I wanted you to be spared of this trauma.'

'Abba Jaan, my dear sister Zebunissa has left us at such a young age. I never can imagine that,' she said while she sobbed. The news of her elder sister's death was difficult for Zeenat to accept. She asked, 'Abba Jaan, was it Khuda's will that she was to spend her last days in captivity?'

'Who can fight Khuda's will?'

'Abba Jaan, but you are the one who put her in jail, isn't it? And now I see you crying. Why?'

'Dear, you think I have no heart, don't you?'

'Abba Jaan, I cannot say that. You have bared your deepest thoughts to me over the last few years. But I am surprised that you put her in jail and now are crying over her death. I am unable to understand.'

'Dear, it was the Shahenshah who put her in jail and it is her father who is crying. Don't I love her?'

'But could you not have released her when Shahzada Akbar ran away from Hindustan?'

'Dear, what I could have done or should have done is all in the past. There is no point in discussing that. I always wonder whether Khuda will agree to my decisions. Do you think I loved Zebunissa any less? Since your mother died, I loved you both even more, but sometimes Zeb would behave in a manner that hurt me. She was responsible in instigating your brother against the throne, and I had no choice but to put her in captivity. You don't know this, but the day I announced the verdict, I could not sleep the entire night. I prayed to Allah begging for forgiveness. I asked Allah for the answer – whether what I did was right or not.'

'Abba Jaan,' Zeenat said, her tears continuing to flow. 'Why did you not release Zebunissa earlier?'

'As a Shahenshah it was impossible for me to do that. I could not ignore her crime, and the punishment she got sent the right message to all the mansabdars. Each night I would pray to Allah asking for his forgiveness. I wonder why Khuda makes one go through such torture. I used to fight and argue with my Khuda at night. Only later did I realize that it was all a game that Khuda makes us play. He is the puppeteer and we are mere puppets in his hands. He neither creates traps nor provides solutions for them. It is we who create our own traps and, having got trapped, we cry and feel bad, and ask Khuda to help us out.'

Aurangzeb stepped forward and with trembling fingers, wiped Zeenat's tears. Hugging her tightly he said, 'Dear, I can feel your pain but I urge you to trust in Allah. If He wipes your tears, you will get immense satisfaction.'

They both were silent for a while. Aurangzeb said, taking out a piece of paper from his bag, 'Dear, I wanted to speak to you about something else. Here, take a look.'

Zeenat was taken aback seeing the paper. She said, 'Abba Jaan, so you know of it?'

'Your father may be old and may have lost his energy; but he has not lost his ability to listen or read.'

'Abba Jaan, did I make a mistake?'

'Dear, how could you beg our enemies? They have been troubling us for decades and here are you – writing to them. Isn't it a matter of shame that the Shahenshah's daughter should write to the enemy begging her to give away her forts?'

'Abba Jaan, I have gone through a lot in life and am beyond shame and prestige now. I had written to Tarabai hoping that if she gives the forts to us, you would leave the Deccan and spend the rest of your life in peace. It is with that intention I wrote to her. Was I wrong?'

Zeenat looked into her father's eyes as she spoke. For a change, the Badshah was unable to meet her gaze. He said, trying to hide his emotions, 'Yes. This Shahenshah has never begged anyone. I did not give up even when nature challenged me. I cannot have the world laughing at me saying that Alamgir Badshah won the Deccan by begging to a woman. I have come here to win through jehad and not by any other means.'

'Abba Jaan, I know your resolve but your body has to support you.'

'If Allah wishes me to die, so be it. It is His will.'

Cupping his mouth with her palm, Zeenat said, 'Abba Jaan! Don't say that! The very thought makes me shiver. I never realized you would get offended at my request to the Maratha queen.'

Aurangzeb caressed her palm for a while and said, 'Dear, the sad part is no one is able to understand me well enough!'

It was the first time the father and daughter were having a real heart-to-heart conversation.

❧❧ ❧❧

It was the day of Muharram. Aurangzeb had announced a month of grieving over Zebunissa's death. He read the namaz each day at Sheikh Sallah's dargah. To make it convenient for him the khojas had pitched a temporary tent for him within the premises of the dargah itself.

After the month was over, Aurangzeb stepped out for a tour of the city. They stopped in front of a haveli and Hamiduddin Khan remarked, 'This is the haveli, Huzoor!'

'Whose is it?'

'Shiva Bhosale's.'

'Oh, I see!' He glanced at the Lal Mahal and continued his tour. He said, after a while, 'I did not know that he stayed in such an ordinary haveli.'

Hamiduddin Khan replied, 'They don't have the resources of the Badshah of Hindustan. They cannot match your prestige.'

Aurangzeb knew Hamiduddin Khan's ploy. He said, smiling, 'You are forgetting the fact that Shiva looted Surat twice and had collected enormous wealth. It is just that he has not used it for his own pleasures.'

'If he had spent the money in luxuries rather than build forts, we would have been spared all these troubles.'

Ignoring his comment, Aurangzeb asked, 'Isn't this the same haveli where my uncle Shaista Khan resided?'

'This is correct, Huzoor. Shiva had the audacity to enter the haveli personally and attack Khan Sahab.'

'You cannot be more foolish than to stay in a place that the enemy knows every inch. Quite obviously, you are inviting trouble for yourself.'

After touring the town for a while, Aurangzeb said, 'I was not aware that his town was so small. But he was obsessed with creating an empire for himself.'

Hamiduddin Khan muttered, 'How would he have the common sense to do that? He did not follow Islam.'

'I know what you mean, Khan Sahab. You must be wondering what kind of a fool I am to leave the luxuries of Lal Qila behind and roam around the Deccan for decades now. Who would spend his old age in such a condition, isn't it?'

'Hazrat Salamat, I don't think so; but no doubt, there are many amongst the troops who think that way.'

'I know you are hiding behind their words to express your own thoughts. I am happy that there is one person like me who does not think of luxuries. We need to move from here now. Let this town be called Muhiyabad from now on.'

ೞ ೞ

Nature decided to play havoc. After two years of unusually heavy rains, there were two years of drought leading to a complete scarcity of foodgrains. The fear of sudden attacks from the Marathas continued. Thanedars from various posts were sending letters of requests for resources. Money was running short. Aurangzeb had no time to answer all the requests.

The moment the Mughals moved on to a different place, the Marathas would find a way to take back their forts. The Mughals lost Torna and Rajgadh in this fashion, and Kondana too was likely to be taken back by them. All the good work done by Aurangzeb was being undone in a short period of time.

The town of Devapur was blessed with a natural beauty and had ample foodstock. But Aurangzeb had no time to enjoy it. He was frustrated that his body was unable to take the strain any more. The jehad, which he had called for while leaving Delhi nearly twenty-five years ago, was nowhere in sight of being fulfilled. All he could see was a hollow, uncertain future, which was disturbing.

One day, news spread that Aurangzeb was ill with fever. The royal hakeem was worried that his body would not be able to take the stress any more. People spent hours in mosques and dargahs praying for the Emperor's health. Zeenat spent all her time at her father's bedside. Aurangzeb would open his eyes once in a while and ask her to relax and not bother about his health, but she could not contain her emotions and sat sobbing at his bedside.

Finally, after nearly a week, the hakeem was able to see a ray of hope when the fever subsided. The trumpets announced his recovery and

Zeenat promptly called for the aulias and distributed alms amongst them. Hundreds of poor people were fed from the royal kitchen.

Zeenat asked him one day, 'Abba Jaan, would you listen to me for once? I believe we have done our task here. Let us move to a place where you can relax.'

Aurangzeb's face was pale from the long illness. His eyes had lost their intensity and his hands trembled continuously. His speech slurred; yet he said, 'No. I am told that the Marathas have taken back many of their forts.'

Zeenat, exasperated at his stubborn attitude said, 'Let the Marathas go to hell. Khuda will punish them. I beseech you for my sake, Udaipuri begum's sake, and for the sake of your Shahzadas to listen to me. Let us move towards Aurangabad and let Zulfikar Khan and others take care of the tasks here.'

'Dear, I have not finished the job given to me by my Allah yet.'

Zeenat was on the verge of tears. She put her forehead on his, saying, 'Abba Jaan, no one can fulfil his or her task here. Man's job is incomplete the moment he is born. Haven't the aulias tried hard? Yet, who can say that his life is fulfilled? Aren't you chasing a mirage? I am much too young to advise, but I wish you listen to me. Please leave your task for a few days and find some time to rest and recuperate.'

Aurangzeb patted her back and whispered, 'I know you have asked me to relax many a time in the past few years, but I cannot. My heart does not agree with me. I believe this illness too is a signal from Allah that the body may be tired but the mind is not. But I feel my resolve too is weakening now. If you so insist, let the world know that Ghazi Alamgir Badshah is now giving up his responsibility and turning his back to his duty to go and relax somewhere.'

Zeenat smiled through her tears.

ஒஒ ஒஒ

The long march from Devapur to Aurangabad began, but the twin effects of Aurangzeb's declining health and the fact that he had reluctantly agreed to return had a negative impact on the troops and their morale.

Twenty-five years had passed since the jehad had begun in the Deccan; many soldiers had in fact been born there. They had no clue of the luxuries offered in Hindustan, especially Delhi, and many knew only the nomadic life of tents and camps. Many felt demotivated that the entire efforts of the last twenty-five years had been laid to waste and that a helpless Aurangzeb was now returning, his task unfinished. The usual trumpets and drums, that announced the march of the cantonment, were silent as if it was a funeral procession.

After a gap of a fortnight, Aurangzeb recovered enough to sit in a palanquin. His body drooped and his head constantly touched his chest. He would once in a while take out his sword and try and wave it in the air, as if instigating his troops to not lose their hope on the jehad. He would clean his sword and check his arrows as if testing them to make sure they were ready for battle.

The mansabdars bowed their heads in shame seeing that their once strong Badshah still had the zeal to fight while they were silently returning without having completed their mission. They did not dare look into his eyes.

They had just crossed Bahadurgadh when they received a message that the Marathas were planning a surprise attack. Hamiduddin Khan was called and ordered to repluse the Marathas. The main contingent continued as before on the designated route.

Hamiduddin attacked the Maratha troops with lot of vigour but soon news reached Aurangzeb that he had been taken prisoner and that the Marathas were demanding a ranson of five lakh rupiyas to release him.

Aurangzeb slapped his forehead in frustration. Zeenat, sitting near him and reading the Quran, said, 'Abba Jaan, let it be! Don't get stressed and let the wazir handle the ransom.'

Aurangzeb nodded his head, and Zeenat, taking it as an acknowledgement, instructed the treasury head to release the amount.

By the time they reached Ahmednagar, it was evening. Aurangzeb was returning after a gap of more than two decades, but having gained nothing in the intervening period. Limping his way to his cot he said, 'Zeenat dear, I think the caravan has reached its destination. I can see the footprints of those who marched ahead but I don't think this body has the energy to follow them.'

Zeenat made him lie down and then, draping a shawl on him, silently walked out of the room, wiping her tears as she closed the door.

☙ ❧

It was Zeenat's belief that Aurangzeb should rest after reaching Ahmednagar as there was hardly any strength left in him. To add to the misery, the news reaching each day was not exactly encouraging.

Shahzada Azam's begum, Jahanzeb Banu, a favourite of Aurangzeb, had died in Gujarat. Zeenat tried her best to pacify Aurangzeb but he found the news extremely sorrowful and difficult to accept. Aurangzeb had loved Banu deeply. She was Dara's daughter and someone whom he adored.

He had barely recovered from the tragic news when he was told that Shahzada Akbar had died in Iran, adding to his agony. Hugging Zeenat he said, 'Dear, Allah can punish me with whatever He wants, but He should not make me hear of my children and grandchildren dying. I have spent my entire life in His duties. I never shirked my responsibilities and yet I am made to hear all these tragedies in my dying moments.'

Zeenat could not hold her tears and sobbed in her father's arms: 'Abba Jaan, look at the irony; Akbar was born a Shahzada but had to die in exile. Zebunissa and Akbar got nothing in return despite being born in royalty. On the contrary a poor man's son, born in an ordinary hut, enjoys better moments in life.'

Aurangzeb said, trying to pacify himself while consoling Zeenat, 'Whether one is born to a fakir or to a king is not in one's hands. It is one's fate. A long life can be a curse as one has to bear the vicissitudes of life and listen to the taunts and insults of others. I am now waiting for my last days.'

None of the amaldars had the courage to stop any tragic news from the Badshah. They were worried he would take offence if he were to hear it from some other source. They were in a fix; if they told him he would take it to heart, and if they didn't he would still do so!

Akbar's son Buland Akhtar too soon followed his father and died. He had been released after a lot of negotiations with the Rajputs and for which Aurangzeb had had to bear a lot of insults. The news of Buland Akhtar's death was a jolt to him and he lost whatever strength he had to continue living.

That night he had high fever and the royal hakeem had exhausted all his remedies. Zeenat and other ladies from the zenankhana gathered around his bed. The entire camp was drowned in worry. Aulias and the dargahs of fakirs gathered from all over and prayed at the dargahs of Hazrat Zainuddin, Hazrat Gesudaraz and Khawaza Nizamuddin. Each one prayed for the Badshah's recovery.

He recovered a little after a few days and was able to sit with some pillows propped against the wall. Shahzada Azam and Shahzada Kambaksh were the two shahzadas, of the three, present in the camp at that time. Kambaksh moved towards the royal tent with a thousand armed troops. The fact that he was marching on the tent with these soldiers spread like wildfire. Azam, on hearing the news, stood outside the tent with his naked sword drawn out. A skirmish erupted the moment they met each other outside the tent. Hearing the commotion, Aurangzeb tried raising his head and asked, 'Zeenat, can you tell me what is happening outside?'

Zeenat did not know how to answer his question. She did not have the courage to tell him that the two brothers were at each other's throats. Seeing her hesitate, Aurangzeb asked, 'Zeenat, what is it? There seems to be some commotion.'

Aurangzeb continued, 'Dear, I am waiting for Allah's final command. Don't lie to me at this stage. Tell me who wants to kill me and take charge of the throne?'

Zeenat replied, 'Abba Jaan, Shahzada Kambaksh was coming to meet you but Shahzada Azam misunderstood his move and challenged him. They have reconciled now; please don't worry.'

Zeenat helped Aurangzeb lie down. He had got up to move towards the door but luckily Zeenat intercepted him. Even the smallest effort left him breathless. He said, 'Tell the hakeem that his medicines seem to be working. Ask Asad Khan to gift him a thousand coins tomorrow.'

He muttered lying down, 'Allah is merciful. He is the one who presides over the last day of the judgement. He is the one who shows the path.'

Seeing him recover, Zeenat instructed Asad Khan to stop all the official work and gave strict instructions that they should not get any disturbing news to him. She guarded the room zealously not allowing anyone to enter without her permission.

One day, seeing him relax, Zeenat said, 'You had asked the other day regarding the commotion outside the tent. It was Shahzada Kambaksh and Azam fighting over their rights to occupy the throne after your death. It is shameful to know that they were fighting on this issue when you are lying here in such a state.'

'There is nothing shameful about it, dear. The old order changeth, yielding place to new. It is Allah's diktat. The earth too is eagerly waiting to take me in now.'

'Abba Jaan!' Zeenat cried. 'Don't say so. Take my life if you want, but don't talk of going.'

Aurangzeb said, 'It is not in anyone's hands, dear. I am thinking of Kambaksh and Azam. What is your advice?'

'You should resolve their fights while you are still the Badshah.'

'They are not willing to compromise. Muazzam may be far away but he is the eldest. His sons are themselves greying in age.'

'Abba Jaan, you need to find a way out. I have spent all my life in the zenankhana and have no experience in such matters.'

'Let me tell you what I think,' Aurangzeb said, his words slow and measured. 'Kambaksh should be given the territory of Hyderabad while Azam should manage the subah of Gujarat. The rest of the Hindustan should be ruled by the eldest son Muazzam.'

Zeenat could not stop her tears. 'Abba Jaan, your thoughts are quite logical but would these three brothers agree?'

'Why do you doubt?'

'They will want to take each others' territories. They would not be contented with what you give.'

'I am going to hand over the territory of Hyderabad tomorrow itself.'

Aurangzeb called for Kambaksh the very next day. Kambaksh fell at his feet and started sobbing. Aurangzeb said, 'Shahzada, you are grown up now. Stop crying!'

'Abba Jaan, I cannot see you in this condition. I don't know what to do.'

'Hold yourself. Come, sit next to me and listen to what I have to say.'

'Abba Jaan, you need to take rest. I will come later.'

Aurangzeb patted his head with his trembling palms and with tears in his eyes said, 'Kambaksh, dear, my dear son … I want you to know that I walked the path as shown by Khuda. I told the same to others too but none followed me. I want you to listen to me just this once. I want you to know that you are not on your own after I die. I am leaving the subah of Hyderabad for you. If you feel happy and do your job properly you will have nothing to complain. My journey is about to end but yours is yet to begin. Don't allow things to go wrong. Take charge of the subah and leave for Hyderabad right away.'

Kambaksh could not stop sobbing, and putting his head on Aurangzeb's bed, he said, 'Abba Jaan, I don't want any position. I want to be in your service here.'

Aurangzeb patted his back and said, 'Don't be foolish. Now, I want to see you leave for Hyderabad, tomorrow at the same time. And don't leave silently. Let the trumpets and bugles inform the camp that you have left and let the world know that the Badshah has taken care of you.'

For a long time, Aurangzeb caressed his favourite son's palms holding them in his trembling hands.

Hearing the trumpets Aurangzeb was relieved and asked, 'Zeenat, is that the announcement for Shahzada's departure?'

Zeenat said, coming close to his face, 'Yes, Abba Jaan. He has followed your orders.'

At that moment Kambaksh entered the room and putting his head on the floor sobbed uncontrollably. Aurangzeb called out to him loudly, 'My son!' Tears rolled down Aurangzeb's cheeks as the father and son hugged each other. Kambaksh was about to leave when Aurangzeb raised his hand calling him back. He whispered in his ears, 'I hope you will take care of Udaipuri begum. I am leaving her in your care. Don't allow her to come with me. Dear, I have to take leave now. Take care of yourself.'

⋘ ⋙

It was four days later that Shahzada Azam was despatched likewise to Gujarat. After Azam's departure, Hamiduddin Khan came in with Fazil Khan and met Aurangzeb. He wanted four thousand rupiyas to conduct a ritual for the emperor's health. Aurangzeb said, 'I will sanction the money, though I don't believe in all this mumbo-jumbo.'

Even the effort to speak a few words was enough to put Aurangzeb out of breath. Hamiduddin Khan and Fazil Khan, unable to see their beloved emperor suffer, cried silently. Aurangzeb called for Hamiduddin Khan and said, 'You have followed my orders sincerely. I want you to follow one more time … my last order.'

Hamiduddin Khan blinked back his tears and said, 'Please command me.'

'I had reserved a place for my coffin in the Sheikh Zainuddin's dargah at Khuldabad. If I have been a true follower of Allah, He will call me on Friday. If that happens, don't delay in taking my body to the dargah for burial.'

'Hamiduddin Khan could not stop the tears and said, his voice hoarse, 'Zille Subhani, you have been a true follower. I am sure Allah will show some miracles and give you a hundred years to live.'

Aurangzeb was silent. He raised his hand to dismiss them. They retreated silently.

Another two days had passed. On Thursday night Aurangzeb felt a little better and called Zeenat to sit near him. Zeenat had not moved out of his tent and had spent all her time at her father's feet praying continuously. She was reading from the Quran: '*There is only one Allah and He is omnipresent and infinite. He does not give bith to anyone nor is He born to any. There is no one like Him …*'

Seeing Aurangzeb stir in his bed she asked, 'Abba Jaan, Allah seems to have heard my prayers. You seem better today.'

Aurangzeb was silent and had his eyes half-open. His voice was feeble. With his fingers he signalled her to come closer, and keeping his hand on her head said, 'Dear, my time is nearly over. You are the only one born to me who has been with me till the end. I am eagerly waiting for Allah's summons now. I ask you to pardon me. Unless you pardon me the doors of heaven won't open for me.'

Zeenat placed her head on Aurangzeb's head and sobbed uncontrollably. 'Abba Jaan! Abba Jaan! You haven't done anything which needs me to pardon. Don't torture your heart unnecessarily.'

'It is not unnecessarily, dear. When I was young and capable, I too felt that there was no need for pardon. Now I understand! It is true that it may not have any meaning and I wish I had understood the meaning at the right time. It is too late now!'

'Abba Jaan! Abba Jaan!' Zeenat cried, not knowing what else to say.

Aurangzeb's words came in haltingly. 'Dear, who knows what the purpose of my birth was and why I spent so many years doing what I did. Khuda was generous enough to give me a lovely childhood and an energetic and fulfilling youth. Now all that is mere dust! A lovely blessed life has been wasted!'

He stopped for a moment, out of breath with the effort. Zeenat wiped the forehead off its sweat and draped him in a shawl. Patting his shoulders gently she said, 'Abba Jaan, the world looks at you with a lot of hopes. They would be shattered if they were to hear your words.'

Aurangzeb's breathing was laboured now. A few hours passed by. The khoja came in to reduce the lamps. The entire camp was steeped in silence. Asad Khan had ensured that there was no movement around Aurangzeb's tent. Seeing her father asleep, Zeenat opened the pages of her Quran and started reading from it, her back resting against his bed, 'He is always happy, He is infinite ...'

It was past midnight. Zeenat looked up from her reading when she noticed some movement on the bed.

In a hollow voice, Aurangzeb asked, 'Dear, what day is it?'

'Abba Jaan, it is Jumma.'

'Oh! Allah's day. I need to offer my prayers then.'

'Abba Jaan, you have no energy left to get up. You may do so lying down. You have been reading your prayers your entire life.'

'Who knows?' Aurangzeb said, his words coming out haltingly. 'I had been blessed with such a precious life but I chose to waste it. He was so close to me yet I could not see Him. Now all I can see is darkness ahead.'

Zeenat could not bear his sad comments. She said, 'Abba Jaan, you have given to countless people; won't you give me something?'

Aurangzeb struggled to open his eyes. Putting his hand on her head he said, 'Dear, what else does your father have to give, except his blessings? I had nothing when I came and I am going to leave empty-handed. Now I have to face Him and bear His punishment for all the crimes I have committed here. I don't know why memories are flooding my mind. I want to see Bedar Bakht once. I have bid farewell to Kambaksh but I feel like hugging him.'

He stopped suddenly. His vision was getting hazy and he started mumbling lines from the Quran.

Zeenat got up and looked out of the window. She heard him utter, 'La ilahi illillah.'

Dawn was breaking on the horizon. Aurangzeb's soft uttering of the words from the Quran could be heard in the silence of the morning. The rays of the first light spread in the room and reached the bedside. It was much later that Zeenat realized the silence in the room. The words had stopped. She rushed to the bed and touched his forehead. A scream erupted from the tent:

'*Ya Allah! Ya Khuda!*'

The death of Aurangzeb set in motion the beginning of the end of the Mughal might. He died without naming anyone as the successor. Much against his last wishes, the sons immediately took to fighting amongst each other as soon as Aurangzeb died. Muhammad Azam declared himself the Emperor but was soon defeated by Muazzam. Kambaksh was the Governor in Deccan while Azam was ruling Gujarat. Azam and his son were killed by Muazzam and he crowned himself the Emperor taking on the title of Bahadur Shah in June 1707, at the age of sixty-three. Kambaksh died in a battle in 1708.

P.S.

Insights
Interviews
& More...

N.S. Inamdar (1923–2002)

The printed word had captured my imagination at a very young age. It had almost taken over my life and I revelled in it. I must have been around ten years of age. I had put forth a request to my mother to buy me a book and she was at her wits' end in finding a way to convey this to my father. He had just returned from his office, hung his cap and coat on the peg near the door and had put his legs up on the table, waiting for the usual evening cup of tea.

My mother finally blurted out, 'Listen, our son has a request.'

'Yes!' My father said, wiping his luxuriant moustache, as he sipped his tea. 'What do you want, beta?'

'I want a book.'

'A book? What for?'

'To read!' I said. He smiled. Much to my mother's surprise, he said, 'Well, if he wants one he should get one!'

Thus began my love affair with the written word. I would borrow the books from the library and read them eagerly. I discovered a virtual gold mine in the public library in the town. I was possessed, like a man from a famine hit region who sees a feast being laid out for him. I simply devoured the books…

The author writes of his foray into formal writing:

It was a few years since Independence. My job ensured I did not have to worry about my daily needs. I got transferred to Pune and wrote to the editor, Mr Sathe, of *Swarajya* magazine. My letters were comments on their columns. He must have been impressed with my writing because he called me over for a cup of tea. He said, 'If you decide to write something, we would be happy to publish it.' This was music to my ears. I wrote a lot over the next three or four years. I remember my short stories or articles getting published in various magazines, sometimes four or five in the same month. Mystery stories, as a genre, were becoming popular and I wrote a large number of such short stories for *Swarajya*. It was the anniversary of the 1857 uprising. I thought of writing a story based on that period. We decided to serialize the story and it ran for well over fifty episodes. I had thought of writing a novel based on actual events but that did not materialize despite my efforts. I then decided to create a story of my own. There had been a murder of a Brahmin named Gangadhar Shastri Patwardhan during the Peshwa period. No one had been able to find out why he was killed and who had committed the crime.

A plot had begun to form in my mind now … The more I researched, the more the story evolved as a complex plot. I had to research the period around 1857 and the history of the then Maratha rulers. I studied in detail about the East India Company and its workings to get a feel of the time. Having completed the novel, it was an arduous task to find the publisher. The top publishers in Pune did not bother to entertain me.

It was then that someone suggested Continental Prakashan. My experience was wonderful; they treated me well and my novel got published.

N.S. Inamdar's very first novel *Jhep* got him the state award. He writes: I received the very first letter of appreciation from someone as well known as G.N. Dandekar. I knew that if he had liked my novel, it would surely be well received. And it did! *Jhep* got many accolades and I was introduced in several functions and social circles as 'the author of *Jhep*'.

N.S. Inamdar writes of his second novel *Zunj*, based on Yeshwantrao Holkar: I thought he was a true hero of whom little was known to the common man. He had defeated General Wellesley, the British soldier who had routed Napoleon! Unlike *Jhep*, for which I hardly needed to travel, this novel required me to travel to Indore, Bhopal, Gwalior, Maheshwar, Mandu fort and many such palaces and forts.

When I put forth my problem to Anantrao Kulkarni, the publisher of Continental, he solved it in a jiffy! He said, 'Look, I am getting my new car in a few weeks. You just apply for leave. We will travel all over for a month and ensure you get your research done.'

N.S. Inamdar's relationship with Continental Prakshan's Kulkarni, who published all his novels, was unique. For a publisher to spend a month travelling with his author, helping him in his research and providing all the support required is something remarkable and rarely seen.

Inamdar, in his autobiography published by Sun Publications in 1992, talks of the way he used to dictate into a tape-recorder for his novels. *Rau* was the first novel where he used this technique.
I thought of recording my lines on a tape-recorder. That way I would be able to complete my work much faster. I visited a factory in Pune which was making these machines for Aakashvani. Unlike the cassettes of today, those days we had spools which were quite large and

cumbersome to lug around; it is not easy for a writer to talk to himself as he dictates to the recording machine! I had my favourite relaxing chair in which I would sit back and keep talking into the instrument!

The author writes of his thoughts which triggered the writing of his novel *Rajashree* on Shivaji:

I used to feel extremely dejected at times while going through the tons of material available on Aurangzeb. The Mughal court during those times used to record all matters of the court, down to the appointment of the lowliest of the clerks. Sir Jadunath Sarkar's comprehensive research on Aurangzeb has used many of such records preserved in our National Archives and other places. The Italian traveller Manucci has recorded, in great details, all the events in Aurangzeb's life right from his struggle to capture the throne till his death and beyond. Unfortunately we do not have any records of how Shivaji Maharaj and Sambhaji escaped from Agra, the route they took to reach Pune, and the problems they faced while returning. We have to depend on hearsay. It pains me to know that we have no such records to refer to...

There was enough and more written on Shivaji Maharaj. Men like Babasaheb Purandare had made it their lifetime pursuit to sing paeans for him, telling and retelling his story to millions. Ranjit Desai's *Shriman Yogi* was literally the last word on Shivaji. There were movies and television serials on many events of his life. Yet, there were many episodes which had left me clueless: for example, why would Sambhaji, his own son, defect and join the Mughals? It was a question which needed to be answered. After his coronation, Shivaji went through a lot of turmoil in his personal life. Unfortunately, our elders and historians seem to have focused on Shivaji's victories and conquests and have not thrown much light on the latter part of his life. It seemed almost deliberate. A historian Kurandakar had written about the lack of clarity on whether Shivaji's body was formally cremated as per religious rites or just consigned to flames. It led me to wonder why he would be treated so after death. There had been some unconfirmed historical accounts about a case of attempted poisoning by one of Shivaji's generals. Another story spoke of Shivaji's senapati refusing to salute him during his coronation ceremony. Bheeshma's vow had been Bheeshma's undoing. So was Shivaji's, who had proclaimed that 'no one should claim a hereditary right over any appointment'.

In my novel *Rajashree*, I have given the author's note at the end. I wanted the reader to form his own opinion and not get influenced by mine. After the publication of the novel, I happened to meet a retired Army officer who recounted his days in Lahore, many years before India became independent. His commandant, a Major General then, on seeing a portrait of Shivaji in his room exclaimed, 'Isn't that Shivaji the Great?' The young officer, who had just been commissioned, was surprised that the General knew about Shivaji. The General continued, 'Who would not know him? His guerrilla tactics are a subject of study in military academies the world over.' The senior officer was General Ayub Khan, who later became Pakistan's president. 'Those were the days when Partition had not separated us,' the officer said.

I have been writing for more than forty years … I had reached the pinnacle of my career in my government job, giving my family the financial stability and securing pride in my job for myself. I knew money doesn't last for ever. I realized that the footprints on the sands of time would soon disappear but I was confident that my work, if not for ever, would at least remain for a significant period of time. I wrote many novels but the special seven, which made me a household name and whom I lovingly imagine as my seven daughters, would be a matter of pride for my future generations.

Nagnath S. Inamdar (1923-2002) was a prolific writer of historical fiction. Over a span of fifty years, he wrote sixteen historical novels. Some of the most popular ones, apart from *Shahenshah*, are *Rau*, *Mantravegla* and *Jhep*. N.S. Inamdar's forte was getting the historical characters to life. Shahenshah is probably the only novel in modern India on Aurangzeb.

Jhep was the first novel written by N.S. Inamdar and is the story of Trambakji Dengle, a messenger in the court of Bajirao II, and his efforts to save the Maratha Empire from the British. *Zunj* is a story of the Maratha sardar Yashwantrao Holkar of Indore. In *Rau*, the author brings forth the trials and tribulations of Bajirao Peshwa I, as he decides to give the status of a wife to a Musalman dancer. He was opposed by one and all, including his mother, brother, wife and son. The tragic love story was made into a popular Marathi television series by the same name. More recently, it captured the nation's imagination with the launch of the movie by Sanjay Leela Bhansali, based on the author's original novel. The author portrays the love affair of Bajirao Peshwa and Mastani with remarkable sensitivity. Talking of *Shahenshah*, in his three volume autobiography, N.S. Inamdar writes:

> I had heard of a novel on Aurangzeb by a Hindi author Acharya Chatursen Shastri but

472

that seemed to focus on him as a Shahzada and not as a Shahenshah. During my travels in to the interiors of Maharashtra, I wondered how the Mughal Emperor could spend twenty-five years of his life in tents, camps, and living a life of hardship along with thousands of soldiers. Some of them were, in fact, born in the Deccan and had never seen the splendour and riches of the capital city of Delhi. The officials, despite being eager to go back to their life of luxury, had no option but to follow Aurangzeb's call of jihad against the Marathas. It triggered in me a sense of curiosity to explore the subject further.

During his travels the author would visit places of historical interest apart from spending time on deep study of manuscripts and other reference materials. He writes:

I had heard of Aurangzeb's destruction of temples but a visit to Siddeshwar temple near Mangalwedha on the banks of the Bheema was an eye opener. The priest, whose family had been managing the temple for generations, informed me that he had heard from his forefathers that not only did Aurangzeb leave the temple intact but, much to their surprise, ordered an annual donation for its upkeep. The practise continued much beyond his death. It was, till Independence, followed by the Nizam of Hyderabad and now, after Independence, the annual donation comes from the collector's office from Solapur. It was quite a different picture of Aurangzeb than what I had in my mind!

During his research, the author met a teacher in Miraj who showed him some old manuscripts wherein the Mughal Emperor had penned love sonnets. Unlike the popular belief that Aurangzeb hated poetry or music, the author was confronted with proof which was quite different!
'I had studied Sir Jadunath Sarkar's comprehensive study on Aurangzeb and remembered his extensive description of how he had treated with love and kindness Shivaji's grandson, Shahu and his mother. I was now ready to write on Aurangzeb, having gathered enough material from my research.' Thus began the author's quest to write about Aurangzeb.

N.S. Inamdar became popular with his very first novel *Jhep*. He had been a regular writer for a magazine called *Swaraj* and had also written two novellas but the first full-length novel made him a household name so much so that the protagonist, caught in the end by the British, became a subject of fascination and people were keen to know what had happened to him. 'I was asked the question all the time: what happened to him? Such was the curiosity of the readers that I wrote a separate article describing what happened to the protagonist after he was caught, in the popular Marathi magazine *Kirloskar*. The readers thanked me for my gesture,' the author writes in his autobiography.

Accolades and awards followed the publication of *Jhep*. In fact, the author describes in detail the kind of troubles he underwent to find a suitable publisher. After being rejected by the top publishers of that time and being accepted with love by Continental Prakashan, N.S. Inamdar published all his books through them. He writes of a lesson learnt in integrity when, as a child, he was asked by his teacher Davre to run an errand for him at the post office 'I returned with some change, a little more than what was expected,' writes the author. 'When Davre sir asked me how I got more change, I said it was to your benefit, thinking he would be happy. Instead, he put his hand on my shoulder and told me gently that what I did was not right and that I should return the extra money to the post master. I was stunned; instead of berating me he had gently chided me. It was a lesson I had learnt for life. Much later, when I had become famous, whenever I met Darve sir I would touch his feet. He never understood why I would give him such respect but I knew the value of what he had taught me!'

'In school we had one Khanderao Khirsagar as a history teacher. He would regale us with such interesting tales that we would never want the class to end! The fascination it created in me about history was to last a lifetime,' writes the author.

Reading was something N.S. Inamdar picked up as a habit since childhood. He remembers asking his father for a book when he was only ten years old. His father was quite amused by the request but he fulfilled the same. N.S. Inamdar would spend hours in the local library as a young boy, devouring one book after another, as he lost himself in the world of fiction, history, and everything else.

An interesting fact about the author was that he did not write many of his novels with pen on paper but dictated them into a Dictaphone!

It was a task that not many were able to carry out: the task of copying on paper what he had dictated into his recording machine. The author writes how he had to get a tape recording machine specially ordered. 'Those days the recording machines were quite bulky, unlike the tape recorders of today,' writes the author. 'I had to lug around the huge recording machine wherever I went. But recording allowed me to put my thoughts on tape faster than what I would if I were to write it down. Of course, my poor assistant had to spend hours and hours, sometimes rewinding multiple times to get the correct word!'

Having translated a few chapters of *Shahenshah*, I spoke to Mr Arole, the author's son-in-law and the copyright holder, for permission to translate the novel. Not only did he ask me to send the sample chapters but he also read my translation of Ranjit Desai's *Raja Ravi Varma* and compared the same with the original before giving me an appointment. I asked Mr Arole why novels like *Rau* and *Shahenshah*, while having been translated into Hindi, had not been translated into English. 'Frankly, many people approached me but I found their work transliteration. When I read your novel I never felt that it was translated from the Marathi. It felt like a lovely English novel,' he said, referring to my translation of *Raja Ravi Varma*. I had now got his go-ahead for *Shahenshah* and I dived into it the very next day! Unfortunately, as the author was no more, I was not able to get his perspective of what he thought of his characters, except for some glimpses from his autobiography. There were many questions which came to my mind after reading *Shahenshah* but I had to rely on various historical accounts, especially the five-volume work by Sir Jadunath Sarkar for a better understanding of Aurangzeb. But finally, as a translator, I was loyal to the original and did not try to put my own views into it.

N.S. Inamdar writes about the style used for *Shahenshah*:

Aurangzeb was deeply in love with a Hindu maid when he was ruling over the Deccan as a subedar. I had to ensure that the language used reflected the romantic dialogues they would have exchanged. I had to struggle with the choice of using contemporary language as against the one he would have used in those times. Aurangzeb's mother tongue was Turkish while the language of the court was Arabic or Persian.

There were Rajputs in the court who spoke a different language. I wanted the readers to feel they were living in the era in which the events took place without, at the same time, making it difficult for them to understand the words.

I found N.S. Inamdar's style easy to read and to translate. Despite a highly researched work, he has stayed away from technical jargon using a minimum of Persian titles prevalent at that point in time making it easy for the reader and not get distracted from the narrative.

A Brief Commentary on Aurangzeb

In one episode in *Shahenshah*, N.S. Inamdar shows how Aurangzeb was a victim of his father's distrust since childhood. Shah Jahan, earlier Prince Khurram, had himself rebelled against his father, and had gone so far as to commit oblique fratricide. The author portrays the lament the young prince has because of his father's doubt. The distrust, mainly from Shah Jahan, finally reaches sadistic proportions thus sowing the seed for revenge for Aurangzeb. In a particular episode on 28 May 1633, not mentioned in the novel in detail but taken from history records, Aurangzeb, then just short of fifteen years of age, showed exemplary valour by defending himself against a charging elephant. He was praised by Shah Jahan but Aurangzeb, in his characteristic style said, when he was also reproached for his brash behaviour, 'If the fight had ended fatally for me, it would have been no matter for shame. Death drops curtains even on emperors. The shame lay in what my brothers did!' It was a taunt targeted at Dara, who had not come to Aurangzeb's rescue. As Waldemar Hansen writes in *The Peacock Throne: The Drama of Mughal India*, 'the reverse side of the braggadocio; hidden envy and rankling feelings of inferiority were already expressing themselves with the sanctimonious self-righteousness which was to become Aurangzeb's virtual trademark of expression.'

One of the most hotly debated topics in Mughal history is about the supposed incestuous relationship between Shah Jahan and his daughter Jahanara. N.S. Inamdar handles the issue delicately as he puts his views through Aurangzeb where he laments that his father Shah Jahan should be reading namaz five times a day rather than indulging in immoral acts. His advisor wisely tells him that some questions are best left unanswered.

Shahenshah is the story of Aurangzeb who died at the age of eighty-nine, ruling as an emperor for fifty years. The first forty years of Aurangzeb were spent as a Shahzada, the next twenty-three years ruling the empiror in Delhi while the last and third phase of his life, for twenty-six years, was spent fighting for jehad in the south.

Aurangzeb's reign from 1658 to 1707 covers nearly the entire second half of the 17th Century and created the largest Empire till the British took over the Indian subcontinent. His empire was larger than that of Ashoka, the Guptas or any other Indian empire before. Except for the Marathas, whom he was never able to conquer completely, Aurangzeb did not really have any large enemies threatening to take over his empire. Unable to accept the way Shivaji and his son Sambhaji escaped from Agra, he finally found his revenge when he captured Sambhaji and tortured him to death. Sambhaji, refusing to accept Islam and the conditions put forth by the Mughal Emperor, was tortured mercilessly. It remains one of the cruellest acts of Aurangzeb.

Such was Aurangzeb's desire for revenge that he spent the last twenty-six years of his life in tents and cantonments fighting the Marathas in the Deccan, leading to a drain on the treasury and the morale of his soldiers. While he finally managed to capture Sambhaji, and took the young Shahu under his fold, very few could see the signs of the decline of the Mughal Empire which were to follow. Despite realizing the tragic plot unfolding itself, Aurangzeb, in his single minded and adamant pursuit, got on to a horse at the age of eighty-two to conduct the war himself for six long years till he finally succumbed to death at Ahmadnagar, which he calls the 'journey's end,' the '*khatum-us-safar*'. Napoleon is said to have remarked, 'It was the Spanish ulcer that ruined me.' So was the case with Aurangzeb – it was the Deccan ulcer which ruined the Mughal empire.

I was a little surprised that N.S. Inamdar refers to the torture of Sambhaji in a very oblique manner and does not describe it in detail. Perhaps he did not want to lose focus on the main narrative.

In his outstanding book *A Short History of Aurangzib*, Jadunath Sarkar writes: 'The life of Aurangzib was one long tragedy – a story of man battling in vain against an invisible but inexorable Fate. A tale of how the strongest of human endeavour was baffled by the forces of the age. A strenuous reign of fifty years ends in colossal failure. And yet this king was one of the greatest rulers of Asia in intelligence, character and enterprise. This tragedy in history was developed with all the regularity of a perfect drama.'

Aurangzeb is regarded by most as a tyrant, a zealot, and someone who killed his brothers to take over the Empire. Everyone has read of the way he threw his father Shah Jahan into Agra Fort where he remained under house arrest till his death. Most people reading Mughal history do not know that Aurangzeb's act was just one of the long list of atrocities committed by each of the Mughal Emperors since Akbar.

In *India: A History*, the brilliant historian John Keay writes about how Prince Salim, who would later be called Jahangir, attempted to seize Agra during Akbar's absence and went on to proclaim himself the Emperor in 1602. Akbar sent his senior commander Abul Fazl to make the rebellious prince understand his folly but was coolly murdered by Salim. Many people in the court preferred to install Prince Khusrau, Salim's eldest son as the next Emperor but Salim, after becoming the Emperor Jahangir, captured Khusrau who had fled to Lahore. Jahangir ordered his son to be blinded for having shown the audacity to rebel against his father! To continue quoting the book, John Keay writes, 'Sovereignty does not regards the relation of father and son,' explained Jahangir in his enlightening but decidedly naïve memoir. 'A king, it is said, should deem no man his relation.' It becomes evident to any student of history that the distrust between father and sons and between siblings would be found with recurring regularity in the entire Mughal dynasty. The enemy within was much more powerful and revengeful than the enemy outside! Jahangir is credited to have quoted a Persian verse: The wolf's whelp would grow up a wolf, even though reared by man himself. It is not surprising that this turned out to be apt. In 1622, Prince Khurram, Jahangir's son, on whom he had bestowed the title of Shah Jahan, managed to dispose his elder brother (the blind Khusrau) and rebelled against his father. The whelp was indeed worth of the wolf! While the father and son managed to bury their differences, Shah Jahan, the moment he ascended the throne ensured that he killed his one remaining brother and many sundry cousins lest anyone try and usurp his position.

Shah Jahan's four sons rebelled against him and it was Aurangzeb who managed to win. Shaista Khan asks Aurangzeb, 'You have a choice: either kill or get killed. What do you want to do?' It was thus not unreasonable that Aurangzeb, having proclaimed himself Emperor, threw his father into house arrest at Agra Fort. He was following the Mughal tradition and may have justified his act on the grounds that he was merely treating his father Shah Jahan as he (Shah Jahan) had treated Jahangir and Jahangir had treated Akbar! It becomes evident that to label Aurangzeb alone as a murderer would be incorrect, when generations before him had committed similar acts of brutality.

At the core of it, *Shahenshah* is a story of a tragic human being. Despite achieving all the greatness which could crown Aurangzeb as the single biggest ruler of Hindustan, he died a heart-broken man. He was an Emperor who had no vices, was extremely intelligent and worked hard like no one did. He did not hesitate to pick up his sword and lead the army at the age of eighty-two! His attention to public affairs was remarkable. He worked harder than the lowliest clerk in the Empire. His disciplined life was an example which few could follow.

The paradox of Aurangzeb's long reign was that it left an Empire in tatters. The study of the Mughal Empire under Aurangzeb is of great interest to a student of Indian history. Coming to any simple conclusions about the Mughal Emperor would be at best naive.

I enjoyed translating the novel immensely. The quality of the manuscript was greatly enhanced by the magic wand of my editor and I hope the readers enjoy it.

October 1618: Birth of Aurangzeb

February 1628: Shah Jahan becomes Emperor

May 1633: Aurangzeb fights an elephant

May 1637: Aurangzeb marries Dilras Banu

February 1638: Zebunissa born

December 1639: Muhammad Sultan born

October 1643: Muazzam born

June 1658: Shah Jahan imprisoned in Agra fort

May 1658: Aurangzeb officially begins his reign

January 1666: Death of Shah Jahan

August 1666: Shivaji's escape from Agra

February 1667: Kambaksh born

March 1672: Satnami rebellion

December 1675: Guru Tegh Bahadur beheaded

January 1681: Prince Akbar crowns himself Emperor

1695: Akbar's daughter restored to Aurangzeb by Durgadas

February 1707: Death of Aurangzeb